Four Countries – One Life

Lydia Cutler

Print ISBN: 978-1-54397-571-0

eBook ISBN: 978-1-54397-572-7

Fiction—Jewish life in USSR—Jewish emigrations from USSR—Israel—family relations—American dream

Cover design by Gene Cutler

Edit by Debra Ginsberg

Proofread by Sharon Upham

Printed in the United States of America.

info@fourcountiesonelife.com

To Mama, Papa, and Osik

Don't you worry about me
I am truly fine, I think

PROLOGUE

Kiev, USSR

1950

My hiding spot is a tiny crawl space in our family back room. The room is crammed with my bed and my brother Josef's cot, our parents' sewing machine and a bookcase, but as I'm a skinny four-year-old, I am able to squeeze in.

"I don't hear them. I don't hear them," I whisper to my old gray cat, Vasilisa. I'm wearing my new red ruffled dress, my long brown curls hang listlessly; my big chestnut eyes silently beg to escape.

"See, I closed my ears real tight." The cat understands; she coils into a ball on my lap and purrs.

There is no door between the two rooms, just the heavy yellow curtain in the doorway.

"Out of my life! Out!" my father, David Goldbloom, bellows at my fourteen-year-old brother, "didn't I tell you one more complaint from your teacher and you are out on your behind? Did you think it was a joke?"

Our mama Gita stands by Josef. "David, stop that. He is a stubborn boy, but where would he go?"

I jump up from my corner. Vasilisa falls and meows loudly. I stumble out from behind the yellow curtain and run toward my brother. Mama's hands are trying to shield her son, touching his shoulders, his arms, his face. Tears tumble down her reddened cheeks.

"You … don't you dare! I knew it! Because you baby him, he is trouble. That good-for-nothing…"

Papa rolls his fingers into fists. He grabs a heavy fork from our dining table. Red fury replaces the white in his dark eyes. His short gray hair is plastered on his sweaty scalp.

"You are not my son!" he roars.

Mama, her arms outstretched, hurls her body against Josef. She is a second too late.

"Aaaaaa!" Josef's shriek tears at my heart. There is blood on his face, neck, and shirt.

"Please, don't die, please," I sob. No one pays attention to me. I collapse on the floor in front of Josef.

CHAPTER 1

New York, USA
George Washington Hotel, Manhattan
Ocean Ave, Brooklyn

1975-1976

"Wait here on the side, away from the arriving passengers," an immi-gration official ordered us some hours ago. We moved closer to the wall and watched as the travelers who were American citizens and the tourists waving passports of different colors cleared through customs. Our Russian-speaking group of twenty-two had to come on the same Sabena flight #17 as those people, but we, as the new immigrants to the United States of America, would enter last.

"Lilli, how are you holding up?" a woman from our Russian-speaking group asked. They all felt sorry for me. Being six months pregnant wasn't an illness, as my husband, Sergey, liked to point out, but it created a fat belly that needed propping up and legs that more often than not wanted to fold under me.

"At least we're off the plane and on the ground," another woman volunteered to comfort me. "We're actually in America."

A stateless, poor, non-English speaking herd, that's what we were. Should I feel happy that we'd arrived in America?

The baby inside me started to kick. I took my coat off and made a seat for myself on the floor. I wanted to remove my boots too, but they had no zippers and my big belly prevented me from bending and pulling them off.

The five or six youngsters in our group, all approximately our son Gil's age, were running in circles in the middle of the emptied terminal. The children of immigrants were used to waiting ,and learned to entertain themselves. Unfortunately their games ended when the uniformed guard admonished them and ordered them to be still.

Four-year-old Gil appeared at my side. "Mama, my feet hurt, and I'm hot. When will they let us into America?"

Sorry for my little son, I suggested, "Take off your coat and sweater, fold them on the floor next to me and sit on top of them. See how I did. The rest of the questions I can't help you with. Maybe ask your father."

"How's the weather out there on the streets of New York?" someone asked. "I heard September could be really warm here."

I didn't turn around to see what idiot spoke. Really, like any of us knew the answer.

"If I had an American HIAS representative in front of me, I'd let him have it," my husband, Sergey Kaplan, declared. "They call themselves 'Hebrew Immigrants Aid Society.' They call this help? Before handing us visas, American consulate people checked and rechecked us a million times. Each one of us has more papers proving our legitimacy and the right to come through those gates than the lot that passed in front of us."

"Papa, what if they won't let us in?" Gil said, worried.

"My son, you better believe they'll let us in. And you know what else? One day we are going to travel all over the world and come back waving our American passports, not a worry on our minds."

I looked at my child's anxious little face. What did he understand? This was a fourth country and a fourth language for him. We moved him along with our four suitcases and last-minute bundles. Sergey's parents fed him tales of the wonderful life awaiting him in America. I knew nothing of life in America. I didn't have their blind trust in golden streets.

Eventually a woman waving a paper American flag led our group outside to wait for a bus. We boarded and rode through the warm, milky evening fog. Exhausted, most of us dozed off.

Suddenly: "Broadway! We just crossed Broadway," someone reported with great excitement, reading from a street sign at the intersection's light. We all came alive.

One of our friends summarized the group's reaction: "All those old movies where everyone wanted to act and sing and dance on Broadway, at last we are here."

"So let's sing and dance," I quipped. The ones who heard me laughed.

"We are going to stop in a moment," the HIAS representative announced. "Make sure you don't leave anything on the bus. Settle into your rooms, please, and go to sleep. In the morning, read the information packets you were given. Good luck to all of you."

A string of brightly-painted, barely-dressed, high-heeled women leisurely pranced in front of the hotel. "Fresh meat is here. Boys, come to mama. We've been waiting for you," they called loudly and seductively. The words were in English, though no one needed the language to grasp the women's intentions. Our men forgot their tiredness. They used a mixture of languages and gestures.

“Girls, wish we could, but we don’t have the money, and you wouldn’t like us for free. We could barter with you for … some old clothes.” One pulled out his pocket’s lining to prove its emptiness. It was hilarious. We all cackled.

Another guy added to our giggles, saying: “Someone in America wants us already.”

Upstairs in the room, Gil fell asleep on a cot, too tired to even check his surroundings but Sergey and I were too restless to follow his example.

“Let’s go and walk Broadway, where we saw the sign,” I suggested to Sergey. “It should be bright there with all the lights and the advertisements, like in a movie. Let’s ask your parents to watch Gil. He is dead to the world anyway.”

We walked and walked, making sure the signs on the corner posts still said “Broadway,” but there were no bright lights around, no crowds of people, only dark, dusty storefronts, a few homeless persons, and piles of garbage.

The next morning, we checked the instructions given to us by the HIAS people. Their organization had arranged our flight to the United States and loaned us the money for the plane tickets and the hotel. From that point on NYANA, the New York Association for New Americans, would be our contact with the outside world. The NYANA offices were located on Union Square.

We left our hotel, checking the map at every crosswalk. Now we saw Manhattan in the daylight. We had heard about the skyscrapers, seen them in postcards. Soulless, stuck-up monsters who don’t give a damn about the ant-creatures in their pit? Or proud giants shielding humans, providing them with space to work? Would they accept us gawking newcomers?

The tense crowd on the street overwhelmed us. Everyone seemed to be rushing somewhere. No one looked left or right, just ahead. And the faces! The clothes! None alike. Were they all Americans? Many carried little brown paper bags. A lady in a business suit stopped and pulled a cup of coffee out of her bag. That's what those bags held—store-bought breakfasts. Back in Kiev nobody would believe that. Before going to work, we breakfasted at home and brought homemade sandwiches or even jars with soup or salad for lunch.

"Lilli, look, the trash is all over the sidewalks. Does anyone pick it up? Look at that man. He took a cigarette out of the packet and dumped the empty packet right under his feet." My Sergey stopped and stared at the man.

"What are you looking at?" the man snarled. Not even understanding his words, I held on tighter to Gil's hand and walked faster.

The little grassy park in front of the NYANA building seemed a nice change from the concrete sidewalks.

"Squirrels? Are those fast, running things squirrels?" We looked at each other and smiled. We'd never seen gray ones. Russian squirrels were reddish and bushier. "That's amazing. In the middle of a big dirty city. In Kiev they would be hunted down for food or recreation long ago."

"Check out those drunks sleeping on the grass. Now, here is a familiar sight," Sergey observed.

"Yes, but could you believe the squirrels play on top of the sleeping people? I wish I had a camera. The rat-sized animals overtake adult-sized persons." I felt disgusted and pulled Gil closer. He didn't protest once, seemingly overwhelmed by the novelty of it all.

"Lilli, we are living in New York from this day forward. You'll have your chance for picture taking, if it continues to amuse you."

On the NAYANA floor of the building, a young woman came out to greet us. Short and round, Barbara didn't look like our imagined American official. In a mismatched peasant skirt and long-sleeved, button-up shirt, she seemed like a hippie who had discovered the necessity to make a living wage. Her Russian was a mixture of Ukrainian, Polish, and English.

"My family came to New York from Poland when I was in fourth grade," Barbara explained while we were walking to her cubicle. "You are at the start of a rough road. I'll try to ease it for you."

"First of all, the bad news: Lilli is not getting language classes. Only the head of a household does. Anyway, between Gil and the baby she is expecting, she is not going to work in the near future."

"But I need the language to move around, shop, live," I spoke in English, using my limited elementary-school vocabulary, soon switching back to Russian. "You didn't see how humiliated I felt in the morning when I took HIAS check to a bank window at the hotel."

"What happened?"

"I showed them the check and asked, 'Give me money.' One clerk spoke with the other and said something to me. Both looked perplexed, and the people in line were whispering. I didn't know what to do. We didn't eat since the airplane and couldn't go buy food with that check."

"I'm sorry. This check is payable to Sergey, not you. He needed to say, 'Cash this check' and show something with his photo and name on it. Lilli, you'll pick it up. There are people who live here all their life and speak their native language only, but you, you are eager to learn. Trust me when I tell you, Lilli, you'll speak English soon."

Gil questioned us every morning: "Are we going to walk to one of those icky old buildings with the millions of chairs and people again? And then sit and sit and wait and wait?"

"Yes, we are. Remember what we explained to you. There are important offices in all the buildings where we go and wait for our name to be called. In one of them, they gave us the little booklet with pages they call 'food stamps,' so we could buy stuff to eat. In the other, we received the white card so we could go to a doctor when we need him. Actually today, we'll have to find the hospital called Beth Israel. There a doctor will check Mama's stomach to see if everything is okay with the baby," I explained.

Daily, we journeyed through Manhattan's streets on foot. "Please, where is this?" I would ask a person who seemed not as harried as the next, pointing at the address written on a scrap of paper. Most continued walking; some stopped and tried to explain where the nearest train was. We preferred to walk. It was free and less confusing. After a while, the city seemed easier to navigate. However, in my sixth month of the pregnancy, I had to rest often during our long city walks.

I washed my only maternity dress often, hanging it to dry over the hotel's tub. Some mornings it remained damp when I put it on, and I let it dry under the warm September sun.

"Guys, did you start buying household stuff for when you find an apartment?" The fountains of helpful information came from those sitting patiently in NYANA's waiting chairs. We learned the secrets of cheap shopping. On Manhattan's 14th. Street, we bought pots, dishes, sheets, and even a small TV, hoping it would help us to learn the language, from tables outside of stores.

> *Dear Papa,* I wrote in my weekly communication, never letting on about the pregnancy, because I didn't want to worry him,
>
> *I designated the chairs in NYANA where all Russian-speaking immigrants sit as my letter writing place. They're uncomfortable to sleep in, and the Russian language I know already. When we are in those other offices, I try to understand every word spoken around me. Would you believe that last time I bent my ear to the neighboring conversation, only to realize*

after thirty minutes ... the women spoke Spanish! Don't you laugh. It's my life, and I'm not even smiling.

There is a lot of pessimism in NYANA's waiting room. Right this minute, a man next to Sergey waves his hand left and right, dismissing Sergey's hopes for any engineering job, even an entry level position. His advice is to rent a cab and drive it until something better comes along.

It's true, there are thousands of Americans without jobs, but Sergey is willing to work for half the salary, and his hands-on experience is extensive. Well, we are being called to our advisor. Would you give my regards to Josef?

Later in the day we took a subway train to the Sheepshead Bay section of Brooklyn to look at apartments to rent. Agitated by the bad news earlier, Sergey started his speech right away: "Lilli, I want you to know I'm not going to drive a cab or load boxes in a supermarket. I am an engineer-mechanic. I know everything there's to know about metal and machines. Even if I start at the bottom, in time I would advance."

"I agree. Just remember, you have to study English as much as possible at all hours. Could you repeat what you just told me but in English? Of course not. How would anyone trust you with a respectable job?"

After I spoke, I glanced at my husband's face. *Why can't I watch my stupid mouth?*

"That's it," he said. "You already squashed my hopes. I shouldn't share my ambitions with you—you always stick them in the mud." Sergey forced the sentences out in one breath and moved away to the opposite train bench. He wouldn't talk to me until the late evening or even longer.

As if by the command of an invisible music conductor, the noise in my head began. It was my own symphony—the sound of cloth being ripped. Soon the headache would follow.

Still not speaking, we picked up two applications in the price range NYANA was allotting us for the one-bedroom apartments in the neighboring buildings on Ocean Avenue—one for us and the second for Sergey's parents. We hardly cared how those apartments looked. But we needed to leave the hotel and start living.

We moved in with our four suitcases, bundles, bags, a folding kitchen table for which we paid more than we intended, and three hopefully fixable chairs rescued from a garbage heap.

Barbara from NYANA referred us to *Chassidim*, the ultra-orthodox Jews in Borough Park who distributed beds for the Jewish needy. On the day of our move, two black-coated, black-hatted, bearded men appeared at our door, hauling three mattresses.

"Hello," I greeted them, opening the door. The men didn't respond and turned their faces away from me. Oh, of course, I thought, it was the way I was dressed, in shorts, a scanty blouse, and barefoot. They wouldn't care that I sweltered in any other clothes, or that the baby kicked me day and night. I knew Jewish orthodox women dressed modestly. Long sleeves, long skirts, even their hair was covered by wigs or hats. I hid in the kitchen.

The men placed the mattresses on the floor and started explaining something to Sergey. They spoke Yiddish, the language spoken by our elders when the children weren't supposed to know what was going on. In the Soviet Union Jews were not accepted as equal to Russians and mostly tried to hide being Jewish. On the whole, that language remained incomprehensible to us but for a word here and there. So, when these men spoke Yiddish we caught the familiar word *fiselah*—little feet. From the men's gestures Sergey understood *fiselah* for the mattresses' wooden frames would arrive later, and he would have to attach them himself.

Lowering my swollen body to the mattress on the floor was a nightly chore. Tying Gil's shoelaces became a huge production. Every day brought new difficulties for my pregnant self.

"Sergey, would you get me a soup pot from that bottom cupboard..."

"Don't you want me to study?" he muttered, sitting on the wobbly chair, desperately trying to understand a *New York Times* article. "If it's not one thing, it's another. What's with you and this pregnancy? You didn't ask me for any pots when you were pregnant with Gil."

"My papa fetched pots when I was carrying Gil. Actually, my papa cooked for us most of the time. I was bedridden for seven out of the nine months. Or you forgot that?"

"Now I know why I couldn't eat those dinners."

Knowing how little furniture we had, our building's super suggested we buy a sofa from him for forty dollars.

"Lilli, I saw this sofa on the pile ready for a sanitation truck. He is making an easy forty dollars on us," Sergey reported after going downstairs to see it.

"I'm sure he didn't buy it from a store. My body is aching. I need some comfort. Let's hope it doesn't smell."

It did smell. Of urine. I bought a fabric remnant for a cover. Still, ugh! I had to turn my nose away from that sofa whenever I sat on it.

On the last evening of 1975, we listened to Gil sneezing and coughing, hoping it was a simple cold and not worse. But when he didn't ask us to read a book to him before he went to sleep on his mattress, we knew our child was sick.

Sergey and his parents were watching TV in the living room. If not for them, I would have undressed to my skin. Nine months and one week pregnant, I was hot, itchy, and achy all over. I sat on the smelly sofa, then stood up and sat on the chair, and then stood up again and paced the length of the apartment's hall a few times.

"Lilli," said Sergey's mother, "your bare feet stepped in water somewhere and now the whole floor needs thorough cleaning. Why don't you wear slippers?"

"I can't wear slippers. My feet are swollen. I've told you so many times already. Anyway, I'm the one who washes my floor, and I'll do it when I think it's necessary."

Sergey stared at me with murder in his eyes. I'd told his mother off! Suddenly I realized where the wetness on the floor came from.

"Baby! My water broke! The baby is coming!"

I moved quickly, putting my clothes on and checking on sleeping Gil.

Sergey's mother wouldn't keep quiet. "You can't go to the hospital with filthy feet." Not even Sergey paid any attention. The two of us ran all the way to the Sheepshead Bay subway station.

"Lilli, there's a cab. Let's hail it. The train could take too long."

"Can you tell us how much it's going to cost to go to Beth Israel Hospital in Manhattan?" I asked the unshaven driver with a cup of coffee in his hands.

"I don't know." The cabby was in no mood for idle chat—he was spending New Year's Eve in his car. "Whatever meter tells, plus the holiday rate, plus what the goodness of your heart tells you," he clarified, if we correctly understood his accented English.

Pedestrians didn't venture onto the street—too cold and too late. The roads were cleared of snow. Cars were rushing their owners to holiday tables.

"Sergey, do you have enough money to pay him?" I asked, glancing at the fast rolling meter.

"Please give me some credit. Of course I brought the money."

There was nothing else to worry about … only the pain of labor, my life, and the baby's. What was I thinking? I was a moron! I almost died four years ago, and here I was in a taxi going to give birth, again. And Papa wasn't here to watch over me and help.

***

Gil had been a breech-baby. Back in Russia I'd floated in and out of consciousness for many hours. The pain never subsided. The memories flooded me.

"Please, kill me!" I'd begged the nurses at the time. "Please, I cannot take it. Something is splitting me into pieces! Where is the doctor? Any doctor, please!"

I tore the nightshirt the hospital had provided and threw their bedding on the floor. My legs, making scissored movements, were high in the air.

"She is possessed, this Jew," I heard.

When medical residents appeared in the room, they all glanced at whatever was or wasn't between my legs. Finally, one of them checked his watch and said, "Twenty hours already. Maybe we should inform her doctor."

I felt a needle in my buttock. Then something tore inside of me. Then … nothing. No, something was happening to me, in me. I lost any sense of reality, not knowing what was a dream or what was a fact. Pain, pain. It seemed to get easier at times. Or maybe I lost any feelings in that torn body. Pain, pain. It didn't go anywhere.

"Don't worry about her being ripped," the doctor's familiar voice said, the voice of my doctor in the Soviet free-for-all hospital, the one Papa had paid privately to take good care of me. It had been a teaching hospital. She was explaining to the students who surrounded me.

"It will heal eventually, like on a dog." Her students didn't laugh. It wasn't funny.

I couldn't staunch the flow of the cruel Russian voices in my head.

"This Jewish bitch didn't let us sleep all night. Screaming, carrying on. You would think she is the only one giving birth." That was the first I heard after regaining consciousness. The nurses complained to each other, deciding, "Let her stay in the corridor. There's no bed available in any of the post-delivery rooms anyway."

Why didn't I describe Gil's delivery to Sergey? It was too humiliating. I wanted to bury and never unearth it. Though I told all of it to Papa. He was the one to take care of me.

***

The taxi brought us to the entrance of the Beth Israel Hospital. Sergey reached into his pocket and counted money. I knew he had no idea what the right tip should be.

"He'll let you know if it isn't enough," I whispered, seeing his hesitation.

"If I start asking him, I won't have any money left," my husband said angrily. Yet, after the driver gave him an irate look, he pulled out a few more singles.

We walked inside the hospital and an orderly brought me a wheelchair at once.

"Honey, sit here in this chair," she said and pointed to it.

"I could walk," I said, surprised.

"Now you're with us and we take care of you," an older woman, probably a nurse, explained with a smile. "Don't worry about a thing."

I didn't understand most of their words. I understood the kindness. They took me to the large bathroom, helped to remove my clothes, even folded them neatly. I felt taken care of.

One of the nurse's assistants explained they would wash me inside a large plastic bag, since it was too risky at this point to get me into the tub and then out of it. Did I understand them correctly? Were they saying something about garbage bag? In fact, they brought out a huge, black plastic bag, helped me inside it, soaped me, and poured water to wash off the suds. While two of them worked around me, a third nurse held the bag. Goodbye, my filthy feet.

In the room, Sergey paced back and forth, checking everything in it. He even examined the softness of the mattress and opened the drawers by the bed.

"They let me wait for you here," he explained. "Your room has a shower and a phone. Could you believe it? What do you think I should do? When is the last train to Brooklyn? If I miss it, where would I stay all night?"

"My contractions are still far apart. It could be a long time. Go home. I'll call you when it's all over."

I wanted to hold on to every experience of this American labor. I would relate them all to Papa in my next letter. It was only fair. Four years ago I'd deluged him with every minuscule detail of the suffering I went through. I was looking for sympathy and knew he would provide it. I didn't think about the misery I brought him with my tales.

Won't he be surprised with the news of a second grandchild! First he will worry, making sure I was okay. Then he'll be glad and joyful. Hopefully he was on speaking terms with Josef, so my brother would know he was an uncle for the second time—not that he cared.

The doctor, whom I knew from the outpatient clinic, checked on me a few times. When the contractions began to come one after the other, and I started to shriek, I was wheeled into the delivery room. I heard, "Relax" and, "Push" repeated again and again, understanding their meaning at once. Then a few fast incisions of a doctor's scalpel and my American child was born, announcing himself with a lusty cry.

"Guess who you got here?" asked the older, black nurse who had been with me since my arrival.

These people around me weren't aware that every touch, every word, every look rescued me from the past. Maybe they brought me the luck I needed so much. Of course they did, they brought me my lucky charm—my brand new son. I knew it was a son. I'd known that from the beginning of my pregnancy.

"A crocodile?" I whispered hoarsely. The delivery room personnel burst into giggles. Even the serious doctor laughed.

"Very good," someone acknowledged. "Now, guess the sex of this beast."

"A boy crocodile, of course. I like them that way," I continued, slowly choosing words.

"You won. Now, take a look."

Gil? The face peeping from the white blanket was familiar and loved. It was Gil all over again with a perfect oval face, clear pink skin, and dark hair.

No, there was a difference. Gil's intense stare made me fidget nervously. This new baby—I couldn't believe it—he cried, then stopped crying for a split-second, and his eyes twinkled. Then he was wailing again as loud as his tiny lungs could cope with.

My son was born a happy person.

I slept. My dreams brought me back to the morning after my first child was born in that Russian hospital. I had smiled in my dream, the morning nurse told me later.

"Are you asleep?" she asked. The words were in English—I was in New York, in the United States of America. "I'm asking because you said, 'Mandarin.' I didn't know if you were dreaming or were asking me to fetch you some mandarins."

I didn't want to open my eyes, concentrating on that special citrusy smell.

"Dream."

I tried to go back to that pungent smell. It didn't work. I opened my eyes and surveyed my private room. The night before, Sergey noticed a telephone on the night table and a shower behind the door. I was many seas away from the Russian post-delivery room with fifteen women bleeding into their diapers, no shower, and nurses marching in and out selecting whose bed to clean and whose to ignore.

Let them go to hell. I wanted to remember that aroma again.

Mandarins…

***

The Russian nurses wheeled me out from the delivery room and left me in the corridor. I tried to adjust my aching limbs on that narrow gurney, and after a few tries my left arm found a more comfortable position. But then a passing nurse's aide bumped against that gurney, causing a fresh jolt of pain to ricochet through my tortured body.

A smell reached my nostrils—unexpected, pleasant, and spicy. Slowly, as not to disturb that scent, I turned my head. A spot of orange brightened my dingy pillow. A bag of mandarins nestled next to my face. There was a note inside.

"Be well. We are all rooting for you. Regards from the family. Love, Papa."

It was too early for the time when the hospital accepted packages for the patients. Papa must have found someone to slip a few rubles to.

My papa; large, almost entirely bald, sloppily dressed in the same kind of clothes throughout the year. When I was a child, listening to my relatives talk about our likeness, I hoped I didn't look like him at all. My dear, dear papa. I'd call him as soon as I get home. For now, I'd better call Sergey. He didn't know how to find information and didn't know we had a brand-new son.

"Hi, Sergey. Are you ready for the results of my efforts?"

"Of course. Tell me."

"We have a boy, an absolute copy of Gil. Beautiful baby, but you ready for this? He opened his eyes for a second and looked at me laughingly."

"Great. It's great. But newborns can't see and have expressions."

Joyfully, he repeated the announcement to his parents waiting in the room.

"How is Gil? Any better? Maybe you should take him to a doctor?" I prodded, knowing Sergey was unlikely to do it by himself.

"Gil is better, a little. He's asking about you. I explained about the new baby but it didn't make an impression. He misses you. Lilli, when could I come and see you?"

"Come any time and see both of us. It's not a Soviet hospital. They actually encourage visitors in here."

Three days later, we took a taxi again. We were three people now—two hugely smiling adults and the third, a bundled package in my arms.

At home I couldn't wait to hug and kiss Gil, who hadn't gotten much better, and as a nursing mother I didn't dare get close to him.

I blew him kisses from the hall, saw his chalky face against the mattress on the floor—still without its *fiselah*—and hated myself. I had wanted a second child and my first one was paying dearly for it already.

Gil had the flu. After I returned home, Sergey did take him to the doctor, whose office was on the first floor of our building. The doctor listened to his chest, peered into his throat, ears, and nose, and prescribed medicine. That same day, Sergey caught whatever Gil had, and his temperature jumped to 103° overnight.

I prepared meals in the kitchen and took care of the baby in the living room. My mother-in-law came to help, but it created too much commotion, and the moment Sergey's fever came down I refused her help.

Three more days passed. Our baby was six days old.

How did I look now that I was not pregnant? I touched my hair—I hadn't washed it since the hospital. Did I brush my teeth, at least? Everything hurt so much. It was a mistake having a second child. At least Gil had me to himself for the first four years. This new baby … had I imagined the happiness I felt in the hospital? Why do I keep calling him baby when we named him Ben? Such a perfect Hebrew name; we both agreed at once that should be his name.

The baby started to scream. He was loud. He didn't beg, he demanded.

I couldn't move. I sat stonily on the wobbly, wooden chair. Sergey was out looking for a job. He would need dinner and rest. He had lost weight.

I needed sleep. My breasts were leaking milk—that's why the baby was screaming—he was hungry. I forgot to call Papa. My head was splitting. I didn't even hear the usual tearing noise preceding it. My head…

"Open up! Are you deaf? There are other people in the building. Where did you live before—in the woods? Open up!"

I bolted from the chair. Someone was banging at the door and shouting. Benny's wails were hoarse. How long had I been daydreaming?

At the door stood a woman dressed in a housecoat, disheveled, hands busy rubbing a wad of tissue against her runny nose, probably sick with the same flu that had knocked out Gil and Sergey.

"I'm sorry, please excuse me. My baby…" I forgot the needed words of explanation. I didn't want the door to stay open, letting in the drafts, and didn't want to invite her in because she was sick. I was still searching for words when she unleashed her perfect English vocabulary.

"Oh, foreigners, of course. I should have known. America is too generous. They are coming in droves and don't know the first thing about behaving in a civilized world."

I listened. I didn't shut the door on her and her resentment. I agreed with that woman. We were foreigners here as much as we had been in other places. By now I should have gotten used to that fact.

CHAPTER 2

Kiev, USSR

1951 – 1954

"Lilli, where are you? Lilli Goldbloom, you are the only four-year-old who could disappear in her own home."

We were fourteen people in our four-room apartment and we were all related to each other. The Goldbloom family had many aunts and uncles and cousins. If they didn't live here, they came to visit every Sunday. I liked to sit in some unobserved corner and listen to the adults talk.

These four rooms on the third floor of a four-story building were given first to the two Goldbloom families: my parents—David and Gita with Josef and me, and also Papa's sister Mira, her husband Sam, and their two children—my cousins Ada and Misha. We all moved into what I learned later was originally a three-room place.

It was after World War II ended and surviving Kiev citizens returned home. Following the Nazi's bombings, most buildings, especially in that part of the city, were in shambles. The rebuilding and reconstruction was done by the teams of captured German soldiers who were brought to work day and night. Still, it wasn't fast enough for the citizens coming back after the horrors of the gruesome war. At the very least, people needed a roof above their heads. Our families were unimaginably lucky to get that apartment at Pushkin Street in the best part of Kiev, in its very center.

Pushkin Street was the greatest street to live on. It belonged to a central Kiev district that carried Lenin's name and was one short block away from the main city street with its crowds and parades. One short street down we had a famous drama theater. Only half a block to the right stood an opera house. All city museums were located a ten or fifteen-minute walk away.

Enormous chestnut trees grew on both sides of the street. When sidewalks sizzled from summer heat, the trees shaded us. Even as a little girl, I liked to stand, head bent backwards, admiring the fluffy white flowers. In fall, a prickly army of chestnuts bombarded the pavement. Sometimes I got hit by a fallen chestnut but didn't mind. They were my friends, those chocolate-colored fruits that shone between green shells.

Soon after, Aunt Vera and her husband Leon arrived to live with us. Aunt Vera was my papa's and Aunt Mira's sister. Old mother Goldbloom lived with Aunt Vera and Uncle Leon. Somehow the inside walls were moved, creating one more room. Ada and Misha moved in with their parents in the biggest room, freeing a smaller pass-through one for the newcomers. My cousin Sveta, Aunt Vera's daughter, was born after they came to live with us.

So then we were three families. Tight living. All the rooms were small. One kitchen for the three wives and the grandmother, bathroom with a tub, and a separate tiny toilet. We still were lucky because so many Kiev citizens existed in much worse conditions.

After we all settled in, Uncle Sam said, "My parents are old and they are my family. They need a place to live."

My papa used to say, "Families have to stick together." Of course he was thinking of Goldblooms. But then he didn't have much choice but to agree to his brother-in-law Sam's family to move in.

There was only one unoccupied place in the apartment that would fit a double bed and the sewing machine and that was the washroom. The bathtub was carried out of the apartment, its pipes cut and stuffed with rags so water wouldn't drip. The bathroom sink remained. Uncle Sam's parents moved in with us. They washed up and did their laundry in that sink. When they ate, they set up a heavy board on top of the sink, turning it into a table.

That's how the Goldblooms lost the use of the bathroom.

On many occasions, my papa said that he took a lot of nonsense from his brother-in-law, Sam, but there was one point where his patience snapped and evaporated. That was when Sam announced, "I'm responsible for getting this Pushkin apartment for all of you. Thanks to my high rank after the war we were given this plum location."

David Goldbloom, my papa, exploded: "Your importance ends when you step out of your room. You're not big anything when you stand in our communal corridor. You wouldn't even live in Kiev after the war if it wasn't for my connections in Moscow. Your rank was of no use. Only the generals were on the list."

He sounded as if he wanted to strike his sister's husband. Instead, he turned around and walked into our room, locked the door, and even threw the key under the couch.

After we lost our communal washroom, everyone in the apartment walked to a public bathhouse for their weekly showers. Not me. I was adamant—I wasn't going to undress and be naked in a place where there were many other people, women or not. "No!" I repeated until Mama got a zinc basin from someone and rested it on two stools in the communal kitchen to wash me. "Don't come in!" I yelled every few minutes when a relative tried to enter.

"I'm a woman. You don't have to be shy with me," my Aunt Vera said, and Mama let her in. Resentfully, I crossed my arms in front of my chest and sat rigid until she left. Of course my mama didn't sympathize with me. She was sick so often, going to all those doctors. While I waited there for her, I saw those doctors looking at her without her clothes on and probing her from all sides.

That's probably why Mama wasn't shy and also when she washed the floors in our communal corridor, she stood on her knees and pushed the ends of her skirt inside her bloomers. I pointed out, "Mama, everyone can see your underwear." She just shrugged and said, "Let them look somewhere else. I don't have time for nonsense."

I loved my mama very, very much, even though I often hid when she called me to accompany her to all those trips to a hospital for treatments or tests. I preferred to stay in the room where the bathtub previously stood, in the middle of the old couple's withered, shaky bed which had traveled with them from one end of the country to the other. I liked to have an adventure, closing my eyes, I imagined it was a boat.

I didn't want Mama to know how often I stayed in that room. Didn't want to upset her, knew she feared the clinging, wet-cement odor from that bathroom would seep into my lungs. I hated that smell too; it made me cough. But if two people slept there and stayed there all day long, how dangerous could it be?

One Sunday at my usual post in the corner, I listened to our relatives' favorite topic. Once again it was about one Goldbloom sister moving in and the other Goldbloom sister relocating her children into the back room, when someone said, "There was no other choice, Mama Goldbloom wouldn't live with Gita. Mira did what she had to do."

They were talking about my mom… I didn't understand the reference. What did all of it have to do with my mom? We all lived in the same apartment, our doors were not even two steps from each other. The adults were strange.

I asked Mama what the aunts meant and she said, "The Goldblooms like only Goldblooms. I'm not one of them. Sometimes I try harder, but most often I ignore them. You're a Goldbloom, so you they like. Don't worry."

"Mama, I love you. If they don't like you, I hate them," I cried.

"Nonsense. Life doesn't work that way. You just live it with whoever you meet through the course of it. Feelings don't count."

"Jew girl," the big boy yelled at me in the yard where we played. I went home to cry.

"What's wrong now?" my mama asked. I didn't answer. She wouldn't understand. "Stop the wailing and go wash your face," she ordered sharply. Mama was always busy with taking care of the family.

"Vasilisa, we are Jewish," I whispered into my cat's ear. She seemed to be the only one who didn't react to this word. Maybe she knew already; everyone else did.

I checked myself in the mirror, trying to see some strangeness there, a real, earthshaking difference from people other than my relatives. Not pretty, I thought. Not a big surprise here—my aunts said I resembled Papa, and he was a man and old at that, with a bald head fringed with gray hair. I looked and looked, but my face, framed by dark, brown curls the color of our chestnuts when they fell down, with its huge round eyes and lips pink and wide, was just ordinary.

The stone courtyard where the neighborhood children spent their time was a square by-product of the four buildings facing each other. Old ladies gossiped on its benches. Clotheslines stretched from one building to the other, displaying patched, starched sheets and frayed long-johns and undershirts.

A few Jewish families lived among Russians and Ukrainians in the four buildings. Children of all ages played together, but often the bigger boys called the Jewish kids "dirty kikes" and "chicken shit" and tripped us. It hurt to fall on the asphalt. My knees bled and my dress got dirty. My cousin Sveta would cry and run to our grandmother to complain.

Grandmother Goldbloom, wearing an ankle length, colorless skirt and head-kerchief, sat on the bench with other old ladies arguing about whose grandchild was the smartest. She doled out candy to the biggest boys so they wouldn't be nasty to us. They ate her candy, laughed, and called us names.

With whom could I talk about not wanting to be Jewish? Maybe there was a way out of it, but it couldn't be easy, I thought, or everyone would do it. My relatives talked about being Jews as if it was normal. My aunts even told me to marry a Jew as my mama chuckled, because at five I was too young to get a husband. But she didn't argue with them.

Still, why did they lower their voices when mentioning anything Jewish, the way I did when whispering it to my Vasilisa? If it was good, you yelled it out aloud. If something was bad you kept it quiet.

In our yard, the subject of being Jewish was also brought up when we divided into teams to play games. We played war between Russians and Germans, hide and seek, ball games, and tear-the-human-chain. My cousin Misha was strong, and other boys wanted him on their team, so mostly he wasn't called "dirty Jew" and other names.

When we were too tired to play, we sat around and discussed different tenants from our buildings. We knew the history of every family. When the older ones died, the younger stayed and got married, and their babies were born. A few Russians and Ukrainians married Jews. Their children pretended not to be Jewish, and some were lucky—they didn't look Jewish at all.

During those talks in the yard I tried to shrink, terrified of being pointed out. When they said, "Let them go to their Israel," I had no idea where Israel was or why we had to go there.

Or when someone said, "That Jew is like all of those over-smart chicken-shits that hid from the Nazis in Siberia during the war." It couldn't be true? My father's legs got frostbitten in the snow when he defended the city of Leningrad. Mama wrapped them in woolen shawls every night to warm them up.

I discussed it all with Vasilisa who was my personal cat. Other relatives would play with her, but she knew she was mine. Once she ran away, and Mama and I went looking until we found her. Then, some time later, in our corridor she gave birth to five ugly, naked kittens. Always underfoot, the kittens used to pee in everyone's galoshes. Mama wanted to drown them in the River Dnepr, which she told me everyone else did. But I cried, and she agreed I could give them away to the neighbors. I walked around with each newborn kitten in my arms and begged neighbors to adopt it. Then only Vasilisa remained in the house.

"You know," I said to her, "when Papa was fighting the Germans, he and the whole bunch of them, Soviet soldiers lay in the snow for the longest time and got awfully cold. Don't you like snow, Vasilisa? It's very beautiful, fluffy and sparkling. But if you and I stayed in it for a long time, we'd be cold too."

I wasn't that silly, of course. I knew my cat couldn't answer me. Nevertheless, after I voiced my confusion, I breathed a little easier.

The boys told of newspaper stories about Jews doing mean things, like stealing and lying to the rest of the Soviet people. My relatives weren't like that. I didn't know anyone who was like that.

Why couldn't I be born to parents who weren't Jewish? At least Mama didn't look like a Jew, because of her fair hair and light eyes. And Josef looked like Mama—wide grayish-blue eyes, silvery-blond hair. He was gorgeous, our Josef.

If I could only talk to Josef … but he was ten years older than me and never home. He loved me more than anyone in the world, and I'd die for him. I knew that for sure.

Josef was the eldest of our brood of five cousins in our Pushkin Street apartment. He was the strongest, the quickest, and the loudest of us all. He was the one blamed when anything was broken, or when fights were initiated or even considered.

"Josef, get away from Lilli's carriage with those dirty hands of yours." I knew I'd heard that when I was tiny. Mama said I couldn't possibly remember that. So how come I remember his sunny, smiling face above my pram? I couldn't be mistaken about his face that made me feel so safe.

***

Soviet children started school at age seven. I couldn't wait until my seventh birthday, because it came in November and the school year started on September the first. I longed to become a student. Mama spoke with the school's administration and assured them I could handle the work.

Because we lived on Pushkin Street—on account of Papa's connections or my uncle's rank—we belonged to a most prestigious school district. The children of actors, politicians, and painters studied there from first to tenth grade. There were still plenty of ordinary people like us around the area whose children went to the same school. Not that we mattered; we couldn't provide free concerts and interesting trips and important visitors.

Schoolgirls wore brown uniform dresses with white pinafores for the holidays, and black ones for every day. My outfit was the prettiest. My mama designed and stitched it; she was a genius with the needle. The bows that perched top and bottom on my brown braids were Mama's most intricate handiwork.

School became a chore very quickly. I couldn't draw the straight line or write neat letters and numbers. I cried often, and my tears made a mess on the pages of my notebooks, which made me cry even harder. Coming home, I threw my book bag on the floor and screamed and screamed.

But one day, the ambulance took my mama to the hospital. It was because her heart didn't beat properly, my aunts explained. When she returned home a few days later, and I came from school and started screaming like most days, complaining about my difficulties learning, my mom slapped me on my behind.

"Stop carrying on! You wanted to go to school. You'll learn. Not a big deal. Josef drew a straight line and wrote beautiful letters. You'll learn as well."

Because our apartment was communal and we spoke loudly, my cousins knew of my troubles and boasted that for them school was easy. Ada was six years my senior and Misha two. I envied their accomplishments.

***

In our classroom of thirty-seven, five kids were Jewish.

"How come you don't look Jewish and your last name isn't Jewish but you're Jewish anyway?" asked one classmate, turning to Boris, one of those five.

The tallest boy in class, Boris didn't know where to rest his panicky eyes. He skimmed the faces of his pals but found no sympathy. As soon as I heard the question, my backside started sliding down my seat and my eyes discovered an interesting spot on top of my black desk.

"I'm not Jewish," Boris answered almost inaudibly.

"Speak up so we can all hear your lies," another bully chimed in laughingly. More of our classmates joined in on the mockery; guffaws became general. By then, the only part of my body visible above the top of my desk was my head.

The bell called the next lesson to start and our teacher walked in.

"What is going on here?" she inquired, looking from one to the other.

The boy who started the tumult spoke. "Why does Boris say he isn't Jewish? It's a lie!"

The teacher transferred her attention to Boris, who stood by his desk, staring at the blackboard. My heart dived. What would happen now? Would they punish him for lying?

The boy didn't look so tall anymore; he seemed to shrivel. His checkered shirt, starched and ironed at home, hung messily out of his uniform blue pants.

"Boris," she called gently, "why don't you tell us what nationality you are? It's okay whatever it is. You're with friends." Her quiet voice boomed in the soundless room.

"I'm Ukrainian," Boris whispered.

"Boris, I'm waiting for the truth. I taught you to speak the truth," she insisted. She didn't sound gentle anymore.

What if she asks all of us? Would I have to admit being Jewish?

Boris stood there. He'd probably convinced himself he was Ukrainian when he was three or four years old. For him to say something else was a lie. I saw a dark stain spreading on his pants. The laughing whisper touched every desk—"The Jew wet himself."

I tried to be sick the next day, but Mama sent me to school anyway.

***

At age fourteen, my darling Josef was in trouble more than ever. His marks were never good, though he read voraciously and remembered every date in World History. He liked to recite poems and the names of birds and animals instead of listening as our mama begged him to do his homework. The principal asked her to come meet him many times and she did, but that was a secret from Papa.

"Papa would kill Josef. Don't you go blabber it to him," she ordered me. "Don't open your big mouth. You always want to help, and instead you spoil things. Be quiet."

"Now I know better, Mama. I was three and a half when I asked Papa not to beat Josef for skipping school, because I thought Papa knew about it already." I was upset and wanted to cry, but forced my tears back.

This time Mama had to tell Papa everything, because the school expelled Josef for good. What would he do without school? What would our papa do to him? Would it bring a new illness to Mama?

I wanted to cheer everyone up and changed from my household things into my new street dress. It was red with ruffles. Mama had also made a little matching pocket for my hankies, which she'd attached to the long strap I wore across my belly.

It didn't help. No one looked at me. Mama yelled at Josef and pummeled his chest and arms with her hands. He let her do it. Then she sat by the table, crying into her hands. I started to cry, too. We all waited for Papa to come home.

First Mama served us our dinner. We were quiet and ate in silence. I didn't like most of the food. That's why I was "skin and bones," everyone said. This time I ate every bit on my plate. My papa was tired. When he asked how everything was that day at home, the time came to tell him what happened to Josef. I was so scared that I ran into our back room to hide.

It was a very small room, built when the third Goldbloom family moved in. My bed and Josef's cot, a bookshelf and our parents' sewing machine stood there. I had a secret place behind all that furniture, close to the wall. Vasilisa climbed onto my lap at once—she always knew where to find me.

"I don't hear them, I don't hear them," I repeated in a whisper. I even closed my eyes, squeezing them with all my might. I knew the yellow curtain in the doorway would never muffle the sounds of my papa's rage.

"Out of my life, out!" he shrieked. "Didn't I tell you one more complaint from your teacher and you're out on your behind?! Did you think it was a joke?"

I heard Mama's tearful loud voice: "David, stop that! He is a stubborn boy, but where would he go?"

I jumped up from my corner. Vasilisa fell and meowed loudly. I stumbled out from behind the yellow curtain and ran toward my brother. Mama's hands tried to shield her son, touching his shoulders, his arms, his face. Tears tumbled down her reddened cheeks.

"You … don't you dare!" Papa yelled, "I knew it! Because you baby him… he is trouble. That good-for- nothing…" Papa rolled his fingers into fists. He grabbed a heavy fork from our dining table. Red fury replaced the white in his dark eyes. His short gray hair got plastered on his sweaty scalp. "You are not my son!" he roared, flinging the fork at Josef.

Mama, her arms outstretched, hurled her body against Josef. She was a second too late.

Not a sound for a few moments after that. Suddenly: "Aaaaaaa—"

There was blood on my brother's face, neck, and his shirt. Did Papa kill Josef? I didn't see or hear anything after that.

When I opened my eyes, I was lying on the floor. What was I doing there? What was happening inside of my head? I heard a strange sound on the inside of it, like when Mama took apart her old blouse to make a new one for me. Someone was tearing a piece of fabric in my head. "Mama…"

"Lilli, I don't have time for you now." Mama was shaking me. Was I asleep? The red drops on the floor reminded me of what happened.

"Josef? Is he okay? Papa?" I asked.

"Your papa couldn't find any more hurtful words, so he flung a fork at his son. The fork is a heavy and sharp utensil. It sliced Josef's earlobe. He'll live."

I followed Mama out the apartment to the outside staircase where Josef sat on the steps. His face was clean from blood, the smudges of iodine on his ear covering the rip. On Josef's back I noticed an old knapsack Mama sewed out of the potato sack a while ago. I peeked inside. A bar of soap, clean underwear, a candle, dry bread, and a few rubles—all things a person needed to go on the road. They were sending my only brother away!

I didn't think I had any tears left—I was wrong. I hugged and hugged him, wetting his shirt.

"Don't you worry, little sister, I'm not going anywhere. That's the 'pretend going away.' I'll slip inside later. Mama will let me in."

The next week Josef's life changed. Papa found a job for him at the fishing rod factory. Josef's old school rushed the records to a night school so he could continue there for a couple more years. The night school held a reputation for accepting troublesome youngsters and teaching them good behavior. Maybe Josef would learn not to get into messes. He wasn't bad, he just had difficulties with the adult rules.

He didn't have to go far for his job, merely to a dim, broken-down structure behind one of the neighboring buildings. In the mornings, I walked my brother to the wall connecting our back yard to the next one. He kissed me, climbed up the short wall and into a broken factory window, disappearing for the rest of the day.

"Let him see what it means to earn a buck," proclaimed our papa. "Maybe he'll feel differently about life and the father who breaks his back to feed and clothe him. And between work and night-school, he won't have time for folly."

Josef didn't mind. He was bored with his schoolwork anyway.

Now I saw my beloved brother less and worried about him more. I wanted to help him and I needed his help for me. I was only a little girl...

CHAPTER 3

Kiev, USSR

1955-1960

I turned seven and just finished my first grade when seventeen-year-old Josef graduated from his night high school. His marks barely made it, though the family breathed a sigh of relief. Mama had just returned from the hospital, where doctors treated her for something that sounded to me like spasms in her brain.

"Mama, are you going to be normal if there is something wrong with your brain?" I wanted to know.

"Try not to drive me crazy and I'll be fine." Still, I tried to watch her for any signs of craziness.

She and I accompanied Josef to a diploma presentation event. Our mama dressed in her navy suit and white silk blouse and I in my very adult red crepe-de-chine dress.

"Josef Goldbloom," the high school principal called, and instead of handing the official paper into Josef's outstretched hands, he walked down the steps and bestowed the son's diploma to his mother. The man knew who was responsible for Josef's nearly perfect attendance.

***

Soviet military service, which was compulsory for the young men who didn't go to college, was the only organization waiting with open arms for the boy with the last name Goldbloom, poor academic performance, and wild ways. Not even David agreed to risk Josef's survival with the army.

The Jewish quota in Kiev universities was miserly. Josef's only chance remained with a college in a small faraway town where not too many local graduates looked upon higher education.

One afternoon our father David burst into the apartment delivering exciting news—as per his point of view.

"One of my acquaintances heard that the university in Kamenetz-Podolsk is opening a new mechanical department in their agricultural university. Not many people know about it. We better go there at once," he yelled out.

Mama stopped ironing. "Agricultural? To live with the cows and the girls who milk them? He isn't going. Over my dead body!" She propped the heavy cast iron against a stand and planted both hands on her hips. "It's too far. What is he going to eat?"

I turned away from my parents and their squabble. Papa just wanted to get rid of Josef. Mama screamed and protested but she wouldn't change anything. How dare they send my only brother away! Maybe they would reconsider? I didn't budge from the room, hoping.

Mama still raved against such development, but nevertheless brought out Josef's pants, needing patching. All was decided. "David, help me to take down your old army trunk from the attic and bring home a few boxes I could use to pack cookies in."

I found my cat Vasilisa and carried her into the back room to cry. Josef was there leafing through his favorite books, choosing which to take along. Why should I cry, if even he didn't care? Let him leave. At least I would have the room all to myself.

Maybe he was sad too but didn't show it to me?

Would he find someone there to stand by him like Mama and I did, to hug and kiss him when he was angry at the whole world?

"Vasilisa, we would be all alone with you," I admitted quietly to my cat, hugging her. "They are ready to let him go and he is ready to leave."

Train tickets in their hands, Papa with Josef, hauling a collapsed trunk tied by a rope, left for Kamenetz-Podolsk in a western part of Ukraine. A week later, Josef became an agricultural college student.

The mechanical department never materialized. But the school of animal husbandry chronically experienced a shortage of students. Its dean liked our worldly and presentable Josef. Also, Papa found out that the roof of the dean's house had a leak. Together, Papa and Josef fixed this roof and the dean liked Josef even more. I heard nothing of Josef taking any entering exams which was obligatory to all. Papa returned home.

At the end of summer, following a hospital stay after a terrifying soar in her blood pressure, Mama cut my twiggy braids and finished sewing my new brown school dress. On September 1st I started second grade, and Mama took in a few sewing orders—Josef needed our help with food money.

I was really mad at her now. Since Josef left, I'd hoped she'd have some free time to teach me things she taught Josef when he was my age. Like bicycling—I could borrow someone's bike—or rowing a boat in the river—it was still warm for that. Or maybe to dance? I'd like that.

"Lilli, I'm sorry, but the times have changed. I'm not young anymore. I can't run following you on that bike and I'm too heavy to stay in a small boat. And dance? Come on, Lilli. Hey, don't we have fun sewing your dresses?" She was right about that.

Every afternoon I rushed home from school, skipping stairs and not stopping anywhere, hoping to find mail from my brother. His letters sounded exuberant. It was evident he didn't need us.

"The teachers are great," Josef wrote. "My marks are good because I read many books about animals and plants. I always loved this stuff. And anatomy is easy. Guys next to me complain it's difficult to remember, but you know my memory—information gets in and stays in."

***

"Gita!" Papa shouted on entering the apartment. He sounded outraged. I became scared. Maybe I did something wrong?

"Do I have to listen to a total stranger going on about my wife's beautiful new dress of the latest style?"

I'd hoped he stopped noticing what Mama wore. She loved fashionable clothes, which she made from her customers' leftovers. He couldn't stand when anyone noticed her because of those clothes. He was mean.

The heated squabble accompanied my parents from the kitchen to our room. Mama, wearing a housedress and a pinafore on top of it, carried a dishtowel, drying her hands, her mouth opening furtively in defense of herself. My papa was not listening—he wasn't through with his arguments yet.

If only I could have been deaf for the horrid words that followed. I left my pencil and lined school paper at the dining table where I was writing the same letters again and again. I ran to my corner in the small room behind a yellow curtain, Vasilisa at my heels.

"I'm tired. Could you get that?" Papa wanted to make his point clear—the bang of his fist on our table echoed around. I heard my pencil falling on the floor. He continued, "I expect a dinner and a quiet evening at home. Agitation I get elsewhere."

Mama wouldn't listen anymore. She wasn't scared like I was.

"Am I to understand that one of the neighboring gossips met you? Did she say I was with a man or going to meet one? Why are you so angry? I sewed a new dress and wore it to cheer myself up. That's all I did."

"Gita, are you stupid or naïve? I didn't ask her about a man, but it was implied. Nobody wears a new dress to go to buy milk. And if I know you, a man was waiting around the corner."

Why was he always carrying on about a man? I never saw her with any man. Mama liked to wear beautiful dresses. She always told me to dress nicely and cheerfully and my mood would magically pick up. Papa was silly. How had the two of them ended up together?

I was five, maybe, when Mama told me for the first time, "Lilli, if a person doesn't follow current fashion—he's stale, limited, and a bore." Did her mother teach her that?

Then … did I fall asleep hearing my parents quarrel? Not a sound came from the big room. I climbed out of my hiding spot, waking up Vasilisa, and peeked through the curtain—no one was there. It meant Papa had left the apartment and would sleep at one of his siblings'. Mama cooked in the kitchen—the dinner had to be ready, no matter what.

After Josef's leaving, Papa folded his cot and pushed it into the attic with the rest of old household stuff. It freed a floor space in the back room where my bed, a bookcase, and my parents' old Singer machine remained. Papa brought in a cardboard box with cobbler-shoemaking tools. Then he pulled out the bottom of our wardrobe.

I stood there flabbergasted—not knowing that bottom came out. Inside the hidden space, leathers of different sizes and colors were stored. He took a few out, closed and locked the wardrobe.

Then Papa moved a chair closer to the sewing machine. The factory manufacturing leather goods in my room was born.

"Lilli, whatever is going on in this room is no one's business. Got it? If you want to invite someone over, ask my permission beforehand," Mama ordered. "Keep your big mouth shut if you don't want us all to be arrested."

Of course I understood. I was not a little child—I was eight. I heard whispers of people being taken away in the middle of the night. They, too, tried to earn money working at home, illegally. I didn't like my papa doing forbidden things. We were Soviets and we couldn't do the things the capitalists did in their countries. But we didn't have the money to buy new furniture or a refrigerator. I didn't know how to help my family.

I tried not falling asleep because my dreams were scary. The KGB agents were after me, while I was determined not to give away any secrets.

"Lilli Goldbloom, tell us the color of the latest pair of boots your father made?" they demanded. "You, Lilli, aren't as smart as we are. And you're not as strong as we are. You would break under torture."

"Mama, why is it our papa doesn't have a normal paying job like other fathers?" I asked. She had returned from the hospital after doctors removed some cancerous nodules from her arm and they ordered her to rest it. In that rare idle moment, I sat on the sofa next to her, and Mama let me in on my papa's story.

He went to college part-time, working full-time because his older brothers were married and his mother and two younger sisters needed help.

Then he was promoted to a managerial position and stopped going to school—seemed like a waste of time.

"He wasn't a manager for long. They dropped him for someone non-Jewish. Or maybe educated. Or better connected. The reason didn't really matter. But for your papa it became the matter of pride—to prove himself. Your papa is a born organizer. He loves being the boss and he's good at that. But he didn't predict, though he should've, the top people being replaced all the time. He would come up with the idea for some new leather manufacturing shop, be it gloves, sandals, belts, etc. then discuss it with one of his old influential friends, who would promise support. David would run all over town, find a place for it, get machinery, hire workers, even produce samples, and then … once again, someone above that old friend changed his mind regarding the necessity of such product."

I knew all that. I picked up some of the relatives' discussions and my parents' arguments. I overheard Mama saying to Papa, "So now that you've finished the hard part and the factory is running, they installed their figurehead above you—again. Why are you surprised? So you won't be a boss in this place, sit down and work. Whatever you earn, it's better than nothing."

I didn't tell Mama I knew most of what she told me. Adults don't realize the children have ears to listen to the things they were interested in knowing. As we were talking, I leaned into her warmth, happy to stay like that forever.

She continued with her explanation: "He never listens and doesn't learn from his experiences. He is too proud and stubborn to change. That's why we exist on the pittance he earns while he organizes, and then, Lilli, he comes home and manufactures pocketbooks, boots, gloves, belts and whatever else people need, so we could put away in case of an emergency. There is always an emergency: private doctors' bills, our furniture is shabby, your future college, your future wedding."

Many evenings, one of my parents would return home looking fatter around the middle. The leather swatches were wrapped around their bodies under their clothes. That's how the raw material was smuggled into the apartment. The clandestine distributors came and went, taking the ready goods with them, usually late at night.

"Vasilisa…" Terrified, I whispered into my cat's ear. "Should I sleep all dressed? That skinny man wearing a cap just walked out with a roll of belts. What if the militia were to catch him and come back here to our third floor, arresting Papa. They'd look everywhere, searching for more leather stuff—probably inside my bed too, and here I'm wearing only my nightshirt." I resolved to ask Mama to sew some pajamas for me.

Relatives who visited our Pushkin home left with a small bundled package of leather remnants to be dumped somewhere far away. We couldn't use the dumpsters in our yard—the KGB snitches checked the garbage of suspected individuals. What if we were on the list?

***

Josef sent us his latest photograph. His face shone through the bright blue-gray eyes. I didn't tire of staring at the perfection that was my brother. Mama swore he looked better than most movie stars. The women in the grocery lines all over our neighborhood agreed with her.

I often accompanied Mama to wait in line for sugar or flour, because they sold it "into your hands." Each pair of hands, even very young, received an allotted quantity of whatever we waited for.

Mama carried the photo in her purse. She got a new purse to fit the eight-by-ten cardboard frame with the picture.

"A handsome boy," the women would repeat, passing Josef's photograph from one to the other. "Is he married?" one asked, and all of them bent their ears to listen to Mama's reply.

"No, of course not. He's too young for that," she answered. Her eyes glowed and hands sheltered the dear face back into the bag. Her darling son deserved the best.

Before Josef's first school break, I helped Mama clean the apartment. She liked everything spotless. Usually the most thorough cleanings were reserved for the May 1st Labor Day and the November 7th Independence Day celebrations. Josef's visit was far more important. Mama polished the floors, dusted inside all the cabinets, shined silverware, also cooked and baked and fried enormous amounts of his favorite foods.

In school, girls from our class tried out for a show "Ballet of the Dolls." The teacher said I didn't have coordination for the dance. Every girl from the second grade was chosen but me. I didn't know how to fix my coordination. I didn't say anything to my mama because she was busy with the preparations for Josef's visit.

My brother came home. He smelled differently, from perfume or cigarettes, or perhaps some other people's smells. He wore a green trendy coat a size too small—maybe borrowed to make an impression. Yet he hugged us like our old Josef. Then he slept for a long while, making up for a lack of sleep in his noisy dorm. Then he ate a lot of foods Mama prepared.

"Lilli, what is the matter?" he asked.

Mama was right—it wasn't easy for me to keep secrets. I tried not to blabber, but it all just spilled out. About the show and the teacher and the gauzy outfits everyone but me, on account of my poor coordination, was going to wear in a dance.

His face got red with splotches of white, like the time when a neighbor complained about some prank Josef had nothing to do with.

"Don't you worry, my little sister, you're going to dance and wear a ballerina costume," he said, and looked at Mama. "Is her ballerina dress ready?" he asked.

The next morning, Josef dressed with a green tie he unpacked from his bag and that tight green coat and went to the school to talk to my teacher. I imagined that she simply looked at our handsome Josef the way he smiled and agreed. And I felt important—my older brother who was studying to be an animal doctor, and only here for a short visit … yet took time to help me out.

For the show I wore a light blue dress with many layers of gauze under its skirt. I held my arms bent at the elbows and my legs straight. My family sat in the first row. Mama wore a new silk dress she sewed for the occasion. Josef looked splendid in a starched white shirt under the green tie. Even Papa agreed to a haircut and a gabardine suit. My darling brother clapped the loudest. My eyes were at him all the time. He was the reason for this perfect day.

Zoya was my best friend at school. Her hazel eyes behind heavy glasses were always calm. Her chubby cheeks wouldn't dissolve, no matter how much dieting.

"How come you are so skinny?" she asked, approaching me in class.

I didn't know the answer. Mama tried to fatten me up, but I wouldn't eat most of the foods. They didn't taste good, like that disgusting *farina kasha*, which sometimes I agreed to eat, but only with the bits of herring in it.

Zoya liked to read as much as I did, and we exchanged and discussed books. She was an A+ student in all subjects but gym. "I'm too fat to wear gym shorts, I'd rather not," she admitted to me.

First we lived on the same Pushkin Street, with only a narrow road in between, which we crossed back and forth many times a day, visiting each other. Then her parents were able to exchange their apartment for a better one a few streets away. I thought my Mama would be glad she didn't have to hide Papa's leathers and things whenever Zoya knocked at the door time and time again. Even Mama could do nothing with the horrid smell of that stinking glue he used. He needed that resin glue for his work, and my head felt forever stuffed from it. Thankfully, Zoya never questioned that sharp odor. I got used to it, but my head didn't.

When the American film *The Twelfth Night* was shown for strictly adult audiences, Zoya and I were both seven and in the first grade. Someone's older sister went to see it and the whisper in school promised a lot of kisses and awesome clothes and beautiful American actresses. The two of us decided to go and try to get in. The line for the tickets snaked for a few blocks. We approached a young woman who smiled a lot at nothing in particular. She smiled at us, too, and didn't mind taking our money to buy us tickets.

A teacher from our school sat in the next row and recognized us. The next day the principal's office called our parents in and we all stood there quietly while the principal himself lectured us on proper behavior. We were ordered to pay our parents back the money we spent on tickets. Zoya's parents told her to choose books she was willing to part with for the money. I had to wait until my birthday's gift-money.

It was the first time for my papa in the principal's office. Unshaved and sweaty, coming straight from work, wearing a striped shirt with a frayed collar under his work jacket, and wrinkled pants, he stood by the door, away from the rest of us. The pockets of his jacket and pants were protruding from multitudes of objects stuffed in them. I felt ashamed.

"Lilli," reproached my mama when we came home, "since Josef left, I didn't expect any more calls from any principal's office. You're a good girl. Please spare me the aggravation."

Mama was always in and out of surgeries and tests and treatments. I promised to myself to not upset her and try to be a help whenever I could.

As our school years were rolling on, Zoya and I remained best friends, even though there were things I'd not talk to her about.

Every winter, Zoya and I liked to play on the hill in the schoolyard. Snow was my favorite thing in the whole universe. Snow was safe. The cleanest clean. It protected everything it covered and then it waited for warm spring to disappear.

I believed the snowflakes were soft and gentle, descending slowly so as not to break anything in their way. And when they all were down like a fluffy, sparkly cover in between naked trees, our imagination transformed it into our private faraway world. We laughed and laughed, rolling down and down through the white feathery blanket, not noticing the empty tree branches which scratched our faces and grabbed bits of our coats.

Zoya giggled. "You're going to roll down and break into little pieces."

"That's why I suffer you around. You're going to fetch my mama to pick me up and fix me back together," I retorted.

Yes, Mama Gita could fix anything, my broken body included, but would she open the door to someone while Papa was working inside the back room? I didn't want to play anymore.

Zoya noticed a change in my mood. "Hey, Lilli, when you get silent, I think you're sick. Let's try to return you to health. Let's go to your house and ask aunt Gita to give you an enema. Ha ha. Anyway, I wanted to show her a picture of a skirt to die for. She could make one for each of us. From the different fabrics, of course."

To go to our house? Now? Did I mention to Mama that maybe I'll come with Zoya? I didn't remember.

"I bet my mama would like you much better if you take me to your house first and explain this last chemistry formula. Honestly, I tried to listen when the teacher explained but it's all Chinese to me. Please…"

I started every class trying to concentrate. If I understood the concept of a lesson at once, I'd remember it. However, most often my thoughts were going around and around about Mama being sick more often, and Papa stitching the leathers with this stinky glue of his and saying we didn't have the money for anything frivolous—everything I wanted. When the bell rang at the end of a class, not a single word from the forty-five minutes lingered in my head.

We walked to Zoya's. I relaxed and we were laughing again, trying to mix and divide our mothers' good qualities into one perfect woman.

Zoya sighed. "Lilli, your mother is the greatest. I envy you so. She took my ugliest dress and changed it in front of my eyes. She just added a few vertical tucks and shortened it. I can't believe it's the very same dress. You're lucky to have her for a mom."

Was she crazy? A housewife wasn't as respectable or valuable as a woman who worked outside of her home.

"You're the lucky one." I didn't know where to start listing all the advantages Zoya had. She wasn't Jewish. Should I mention it?

"Zoya, your mother is an important person. People need an appointment to talk to her. She sits in a big office in the Ministry of Education and everyone around obeys her. Even our director, the bitch-lady, is all ears when your mom talks. Who wouldn't envy you?"

Zoya's grandmother was home, as usual. Wrinkle-faced, beaded bleached eyes of a peasant, wearing a long skirt and dark head kerchief, she hadn't changed since arriving from the village twenty years ago. She opened the door and glanced at me with an obvious scoff, before mumbling her toothless hello.

Zoya went into her bedroom, anxious to change into the new outfit that she claimed made her look slim. I walked into the living room to check their bookcase for new tomes.

The voices from the bedroom were hushed but the words of the elderly lady distinct:

"You brought that Jew again. Are there not enough good girls in that school of yours?"

What if some of that venom not only dripped inside of Zoya's ears, but stayed there? Even one poisonous drop of it? Zoya lived with that old witch in a two-bedroom apartment. How could we remain friends? I ran out the door and into the street.

At home I didn't cry. I was thirteen—not four years old anymore. The numerous words of hatred I heard in school and on the street and in the yard were stored in the darkness of my dread. My personal storage with no sliver of light, never seen by others. I always figured if I didn't give a voice to any of it, the words would evaporate in time. The scene in Zoya's home shook me. I described it to my mama.

"So what did you expect? We know them for how many years? You were in their house only half-a-million times and she in ours even more. Get over it. I'll tell you another story. You're so hard-headed, you're in need of an additional lesson."

I sat on the sofa bed and lowered my head, thinking I should lock my ears deaf like I did when I was a child. No, I had to listen.

Mama spoke, leaving aside a pattern she was preparing for a customer. "You know how your papa likes to be a big-man-around-town and forces his help down everyone's throats. It often creates sticky situations no one needs. Anyway, he heard that a son of an old acquaintance of his wanted to get a job at the institute where Zoya's father is a professor.

"The family isn't Jewish, and the young man would get that job anyway if he was half-good. But no, your papa suggested his help. He called Zoya's father and the mister professor said his 'no' before he learned any facts. From one to the other, everyone at the institute knew the story.

“Zoya’s father assumed the job seeker was Jewish. He couldn’t imagine we kept non-Jewish company. Later, that man applied and was hired, all by himself.

“Lilli, I told you and I told you, and beat it into your behind when you were small: don’t look for fairness. There is none where we’re concerned. Stick to your own people when it’s possible, to avoid hurt.”

I was five when my aunts told me, “Lilli, you should marry a Jewish man.” That’s what they meant—to be with your own kind of people to avoid hurt. Were they right?

The next day at school I didn’t approach Zoya. She, too, didn’t know what to say. As the days went by, we missed each other too much and soon moved away from the bitter incident, stepped over, and buried it.

“Zoya, didn’t you want to show some picture to my mama? You could stop over tomorrow,” I suggested.

“And later, we could walk over to my house. My mama was able to get a new magazine with the excerpts from some foreign bestseller. You could borrow it if you want.”

I didn’t see her grandmother; she stayed out of sight. The pollution was there, though, hidden and forbidden to come out.

CHAPTER 4

Kiev, USSR

1961-1965

Hooray, he did it! He graduated! My Josef showed to all that he was the best. I always knew it. His university diploma read: "Scientific Specialist in Animal Husbandry." With our hearts beating nervously, we at home waited for his assignment. University graduates were sent wherever specialists in their field were needed. They could send him so far away from us so that we would hardly ever see him.

"Mama, I'm going to be in charge of the whole damn herd of cows and horses and sheep." Josef's voice on the phone sounded exuberant. "Can you believe that? And not so far from you, four hours away by train."

Our mama wept with delight. She didn't have to say, "I told you so" to our papa and the rest of the Goldblooms. Her beautiful son had worked hard to earn his university diploma and big-time managerial position.

At the usual queue to buy a chicken or milk, here came again the old Josef photograph. Bursting with pride, Mama showed it to a few women nearby.

"My son," she announced, "is very important. He's responsible for raising all the farm animals in all of the rural area around Chernigov." She lowered her head, hiding her smile, and added, "Never did I imagine giving birth to a cow-and horse-worker." Mama was reserved in her bragging.

Papa didn't think much of Josef's achievements. Listening to our exuberance, he raised his arms widely and shrugged—not for a moment did he believe his son would do anything worthwhile with his life. He didn't plan to change his opinion.

Josef wrote vibrant letters in his huge slanting handwriting, describing animals' illnesses and late-night emergencies and a comfortless yet adventurous life on the farm.

"The local big guys drink vodka all day long and not even stop by the animals," wrote my brother in one of his letters. "Not one of them has an education above middle school. They live here all their lives and work at doing nothing. They wouldn't know what to do about improving cows' milk production, even if cows themselves spelled it out using their piss."

"He is heading for trouble," my papa concluded after he read the message. "They will eat him alive. He forgets that he is all wrong: young, educated, and Jewish."

Once or twice, Josef mentioned the strain of being the only Jew in this deep rural area. He felt eyes watching him at all times, expecting him to slip and prove himself inadequate. He ignored the whispers, but one night a bullet flew through his window, charging into his chair. To complain was senseless. Josef started packing a rifle nightly. Our papa proved to be right.

One night, the area bureaucrats went on a drinking spree, contaminating the animals' feed with some poisonous chemicals. Josef never told us if he was able to save the herd.

And then there was no mail. "Did we get the letter?" I asked every day, coming home from school. "He's preoccupied with the problems," we explained to each other. Mama was ready to jump off the third-floor window, when a thick envelope, containing many pages, arrived announcing Josef's impending marriage to a woman we'd never met:

> *"We went to the same university and saw each other at the parties and school functions, dating other people. Natasha graduated a year earlier and since works here in town as a civil engineer. I came to buy some supplies we needed at the farm, and here she was.*
>
> *"Mama, I hope you would give her a chance. Although she's not Jewish, Natasha is so many things you admire. Don't rush to judge her, that's all I ask."*

A few lines were directed to me: *"My little sister,"* he wrote, *"Natasha is a great girl. She knows fashion in her sleep. You could discuss styles and/or boys all you want, just wait and see."*

At the end, my brother added, "Both of us are city dwellers; neither counted on life without a culture or indoor plumbing for long."

They decided to live in Kiev.

A few weeks following the letter, the couple arrived to share our crowded space. We never learned if the rifle became handy.

Josef's old cot came down from the attic and into our parents' room. That's where I settled. Josef and Natasha used my old single bed behind the yellow curtain.

I was fifteen and it was blissful to have my brother back. I invited everyone to meet my sophisticated, lovely sister-in-law.

My parents' disputes moved through the corridor into my aunts' rooms.

"Don't expect me to be thrilled!" our father bellowed. "All my life I'm being called a dirty kike. Now he hands my Goldbloom name to one of them, the name callers, and expects to get away with it? No! I'm not going to be a part of it."

"David, I'm upset as much as you are. But let's be realistic. There were no Jewish girls in the area. He is a man. He needs someone to share his life. And Natasha seems like a nice girl. She'll help him to settle down."

Our mama was prepared to accept a woman who shared her love for Josef. She bought groceries and went on a cooking spree—let everyone know—we were celebrating the new union. "This is my new daughter," she announced to all the relatives.

Soon the relatives were used to seeing Natasha at all family functions. Their verdict reached my ears: "She is fine, considering…" No one expected Josef to comply with conventions anyway, and Natasha, with her brown curls, pug nose, and small joyful eyes, was a sweet girl, so the hubbub regarding Josef's marriage settled down.

The newlyweds kissed a lot and giggled. All our relatives in the apartment knew when Josef took a shower—we were back to using our washroom after the old couple died—because Natasha stood guard at the door.

"You, dearest husband, would splash some water on and leave," she exclaimed laughingly, holding her both hands on his hips.

Josef couldn't find a job, any job. No place would hire a person without stamped permission to live in a city. The recent newspapers' articles criticized ungrateful young people who, after acquiring free Soviet education, left the state-assigned jobs. The authors shamed graduates, listing mostly Jewish names. They weren't so much interested in others.

That was our reality. Those were the rules. Josef left his job after two and half years. First, they wouldn't admit you to a college in your town, then they send you to work somewhere you don't want to live for a minimum three years, and oops—you lost the privilege to return.

Josef forfeited rules. He became an outlaw, legally not able to work or even live in an important city like Kiev. If only he would work his full term—he had a slim chance to be allowed to come back. Slim only, because Kiev didn't need a specialist in animal husbandry.

"Stop berating me!" Josef circled the old Pushkin apartment, never lowering his voice, addressing all who heard him. "I don't give a damn about the rules. Did you want me to be murdered? I couldn't take another day in that shit! All I want to do is to live where I was born and where all my crummy relatives live. Is that a crime? Is it my fault that we all are branded with a fucking permission stamp? We fence cows and horses so they won't wander. The humans we let board trains and buses, then order them to stay put."

I wanted to cry out to him: "Yes, my darling Josef, you committed a crime against yourself the moment you forgot about this stamp in yours and mine and every other Soviet passport stating a place where you belong. At this moment you belong at the farm with the cows and the horses and the mean people who don't like you. I love you and wish it wasn't so."

Since Josef's reappearance at our apartment, our parents were arguing all the time.

Mama nagged Papa: "You have enough important connections to help Josef stay in the city. What do you want him to do—forever be intimidated by those drunks who hated his guts? To live forever on the farm, a gun under his pillow?"

Her questions didn't require answers. Papa couldn't help, even if he wished to.

Our father didn't hide his contempt. "Whose fault is it that he didn't want to study in high school? Did I force him to get married and quit his job and return here? He lives with the consequences of his irresponsibility."

Soon, Josef and Natasha moved out from our Pushkin apartment and rented from some family a windowless storage space converted into a room. Non-Jewish Natasha easily found a job with a large Building and Development firm, even though she didn't have a stamp in her passport. Civil engineers were in demand. Josef proceeded to meet people about employment, buying them vodka, getting himself drunk and losing hope. No befitting job would keep a specialist and a Jew without a proper stamp allowing him to live in a city.

I remembered Mama's tears when Papa took Josef away to school. I remembered her whimpering and repeating, "I lost him forever." Mama wasn't overly dramatic—she knew the odds.

For a year, my brother knocked at every door of every relative and acquaintance who maybe had a needed connection in the needed office responsible for getting a needed permission to stay in Kiev legally. In desperation, my brother and his wife moved an hour or so train-ride away to a town with no paved sidewalks or roads. There they shared Natasha's parents' decrepit house where three of her siblings already lived.

"We didn't have to beg anyone for that permission," Josef explained to us later. "The official came, sat at the table. We brought out vodka and drank it till the man produced a stamp and stamped my papers. Now I'm authorized to live in that stinking hole. Hooray for vodka!"

Probably, I was the only joyful person after that miserable year of everyone crying and screaming, because I had my brother close enough to take a train every Sunday and to visit him and Natasha, walking a long way from the train station through the market's dirt roads, staying close to people's fences so passing cars wouldn't splash me with mud. Natasha and I perused the new fashion magazines and gave each other advice on what to wear. Josef kissed me on arrival and climbed back onto the roof where he was building a second story addition to the house. He wanted to have a separate entrance and a separate kitchen and bathroom as well. He lived for too many years in our communal apartment with the relatives. At least our relatives didn't get plastered on vodka and call him, "The *Yid* who stole my daughter."

After trying to find any job with animals or around animals or about animals, that had any connection to the field he was trained in, Josef gave up and went to work as a laborer in the die-maker shop at a radio-factory.

One afternoon, I was the only one at home on Pushkin Street when Josef walked in.

"I learned anatomy and physics and pharmacology. I know all there is to know about getting eggs from a half-dead chicken. Little sister, tell me why did I need all this knowledge? I wasted my life."

My brother wore dark blue work-clothes, his hands were black with grunge, and his blond hair was greasy. He'd changed from a witty, smiley youngster with a wild streak into an angry, depressed man of twenty-five.

I didn't have my Vasilisa anymore to comfort me. I wept for my darling brother's life. I didn't expect anything better for my own.

***

Mama became gravely ill and we forgot to worry about Josef's affairs. She was fifty-four when the word "cancer" was whispered into our papa's ear. She needed a mastectomy.

Usually Mama treated her sicknesses like a nuisance, not tragedy. Once, she took me for a visit to her brother's home. There were a bunch of her old girlfriends and I learned that in her youth my mama was a champion bicyclist. Even then she had pains in her stomach.

Milky-faced Aunt Rose described those old times: "Gita tied a heating pad to her midriff and won the race. The public went wild. They cheered her bravery and stoicism."

"What happened after?" I wanted to know.

"After? She married David, and David's family—your Goldbloom's lot—forbid her racing, her shorts, her friends, her life... 'David doesn't want me to dress fashionably to attract men,' she explained. What men? Does he know his wife? Gita is a saint, and with all the work she does during the day ... well, her dresses are all she has left. Sorry, Lilli, for my outburst, but I waited many years to say it."

The conversation upset me. Not that I didn't hear the screaming and the carrying on at home. It always distressed me to no end. I wanted to know what my role was in my mama's sad life. Did I, too, unwillingly add to her burden? Did I overwork her with the demands for my new outfits? She enjoyed creating them as much as I did. But did the additional work make her sicker?

What about the laundry and the ironing and the shopping for food and cooking? Did she have to do all of that? She worked all day long every day, and we all depended on her. Yes, I didn't ask her to polish the apartment's parquet floor or starch silly white doilies to cover threadbare furniture. She wanted to preserve the dignity of our living.

There was a wide window-sill in our room where Mama took care of the beautifully growing aloe plants. Once a year she transplanted its sprouts to small pots and the two of us went to the open vegetable market to sell those. I was seven, I remember being seven during one of those trips on the tram with the carefully packed boxes containing aloe plants for sale when I promised not to say anything about that to any of our relatives. Mama didn't want them to guess that Papa David didn't make enough money. It was entirely his fault. It was all his fault. I couldn't look at my father without distaste.

The cancer ward became as known to our family as our own home. David-the-organizer found a reputable doctor. "Doctor, could you save my wife, please?" He paid the doctor money under the table. He brought candy and cakes for other doctors and nurses. He was an experienced negotiator. Josef and I surrendered our hopes into our father's hands.

Mama befriended the entire hospital's staff and patients. She recognized their children and grandchildren. She shared with all of them the tales of her smart, gorgeous, and kind son. The famous story about Josef bringing home a potato sack filled with branches of a buckthorn bush was told from room to room.

Those bushes grew on the deep rocky cliffs on the outskirts of Kamenetz-Podolsk in the western part of Ukraine where he went to school. He heard that its bright red berries would help cure our mama's eczema. Two of his friends tied Josef to a rope and lowered him down the cliff. Then, Josef made a long train ride, and appeared at our house. His unshaved face scratched from the prickly branches, making Mama forget about eczema and every other worry.

Now, Josef rushed into Mama's hospital after work, bringing satisfied smiles to the nurses and other patients. Natasha stopped by at lunchtime, taking a bus from her office to see our mama.

I came early mornings, before school, first stopping at the fresh produce market for a farmer cheese, then yelling "Mama" outside her hospital's window, saying, "Sorry" to twenty other mothers hopefully peering out their windows. I waved to them all, blew kisses to my own mama, and went to find a familiar nurse.

"Please, please, I know it's too early, but she likes that cheese for breakfast."

And off to school I went. Sometimes Zoya waited for me at the entrance. "How is Aunt Gita?" She cared, but I didn't plan to discuss the sickness that didn't feel like ever going away.

The night before the surgery, I found my mama in tears.

"Mama, what is it? Are you in pain?"

"Look at that young woman in the corner," she murmured. "She's twenty-six and never been married. Probably never been with a man."

Mama stopped and checked the expression on my face. She never discussed sex with me. I hardly knew what to say and waited for her to continue.

"She is up for the same surgery. What man would find her attractive after she loses a breast?"

My dearest mama was worrying about someone else while waiting for her own mastectomy. Would I ever be as brave and kind?

Chemotherapy treatments followed the surgery. I accompanied Mama to the hospital and waited in chairs with other patients and their families. The patients-in-treatment were changing often. The ones we greeted on Mondays didn't always return on Tuesdays. A cancer community was a short-lived one.

My mama didn't plan to die. She didn't make any arrangements for death. She never told me what to cook and how to clean and everything else I needed to know.

That hope for Mama's recovery didn't linger by my side when I came to school. During classes, I imagined her dead and me continuing with schooling like I was a regular schoolgirl. But I couldn't be. Motherless, I needed to be at home. Why did I need school anyway? Josef ended up with a diploma he couldn't use. He became obsessed with building his own house. I noticed some gray hairs in his blond mane. He suffered for Mama. Natasha did too. The two women had become fast friends—they both thought the sun woke up at the same instant their beloved Josef did.

I believed so too, only I still expected him to protect me from life's complications. I still was his "Little Sister."

Sitting in school at my desk I heard some flip-flops on the inside of my head. What was my teacher saying? Zoya would explain it to me later. No, but I didn't have time to go to Zoya. I wasn't even interested in any of it.

Mama's treatments finished. She ordered a faux-breast made out of heavy flaxseed, which she inserted into her bra for appearance sake. When fully clothed she looked unchanged. Invisible to all, the deep cuts on her chest throbbed relentlessly. She went back to scrubbing and cooking and sewing. David went back to yelling at her, finding fault if not with *her* way of dressing, then with *mine*. I couldn't stand him. I stopped calling him Papa.

"Gita, you're bringing up a streetwalker," he fumed. Not in front of me, though. I walked out of my aunts' rooms and in the corridor overheard his proclamations. "Her skirt hardly covers her private parts. I can't think of any excuse for that."

"Lilli looks splendid. She has legs for the short skirts, and why shouldn't she wear them when everyone else does?" Mama answered him while washing the floor in the kitchen. She told David off, so hopefully he wouldn't bother me with that short skirt issue. He didn't understand me at all.

Mama was the one who taught me to dress stylishly. "Don't let your clothes to be boring. The seasons change—fashions change, fashions change—standards change, standards change—tastes change. Yet make sure anything you wear looks good on you. Otherwise it's not worth it."

***

My last year in high school arrived unnoticed. Now, besides the regular class assignments and impending high-school exams in all subjects, the college entrance exams loomed ahead of me. Every afternoon I came home announcing, "I can't do this anymore! What kind of life this is? What is a person supposed to do with all this work? I refuse! I absolutely refuse! Let them toss me out! I hate everyone!" Then I picked up my books and settled down to study.

My head … what was inside of it, an orchestra of drunken sailors? No, just a lot of seamstresses opening seams in the old clothes that someone left inside. I hardly could sleep, but when I did … a girl looking like me tiredly doggy paddling against the current. Did she swim long enough to anchor somewhere or did she drown? Sleep, sleep … don't wake up, find out about that girl. I was the one who was tired and knew only one swimming style—the doggy one.

I didn't want to go to college. I didn't want to study anymore. Enough schooling! But what else was there?

"Every good kid goes to college, only the halfwits, morons, and misfits don't," my mama said. Our entire society agreed with her. The teachers talked of college as the only choice. Zoya's mother asked, "Lilli, where are you going to apply?"

"Zoya, tell her to leave me alone. Can't you explain to your own mother that your friend is dumb and isn't going to college?"

"Lilli, you're only saying that because of Aunt Gita. She's going to be all healthy before the exams. Don't make any stupid decisions now."

What did she know? Where would I apply? Where would they accept me, a Jewess with average grades? David said it was too dangerous to let a girl go away to school. In his opinion I would be raped the moment I got off the train.

Following the advice of a neighbor, Mama rubbed a fish-oil salve into her chest where her breast used to be. "Gita, your scars will disappear entirely," a woman assured her. My headaches became fiercer as our home was infiltrated by that new fishy smell.

Was I the only one in the apartment suffocating between this and the odor coming from David's resin-glue?

His home factory never slept. Our family needed money for private doctor visits, money for the upcoming "rainy days," money for "Lilli's future," whatever it turned out to be.

Mama seemed sicker. She would stop her cleaning and sit there on the floor in the kitchen or on a stool in the corridor. The weakness attacked her any odd time. She couldn't raise her head or arm. Her belly grew huge. Again, the doctors probed and checked her and consulted with each other.

"In all probability, the cancer metastasized into her other organs," they told David. "Only surgery can provide a sure answer."

"Mama," we told her, "don't worry, you don't have cancer anymore. The mastectomy got rid of the breast cancer entirely. The doctors are sure it didn't spread. Your stomach has bothered you all your life. If it was cancer—you would be dead years ago."

"Your colon's infected," the doctors lied so as not to worry her. "We'll go in, remove part of it. It's a common enough procedure. Don't fret."

Mama waited for that next surgery. She hoped to get better. We waited for that next surgery. Why did *we* wait for it?

My high-school exams were coming closer. The regular classes were finished. I sat at our dining table surrounded by schoolbooks, holding my head with my hands all day long.

"Aaaaaaaa…" I started to say and forgot to stop. Releasing this sound unplugged some block inside of my breathing pipe. It felt more helpful than the studying and worrying.

"Aaaaaaa…" I continued screaming. I saw Mama advancing towards the sound. She could hardly stand or walk, though she cooked dinner in the kitchen.

"Lilli, don't you do that," she ordered. I kept screaming. The walls of the small apartment were opening up. The heavy furniture was becoming smaller. My head felt lighter.

I saw my aunts Mira and Vera running from their rooms towards me. Why were they home from work?

"Lilli, you frighten us," begged my aunts.

I saw them all, but they couldn't force me to stop. I would continue with this screaming forever.

My aunts brought me to the district clinic. They thought they could help me. How? I stopped with my hysteria and slumped in a chair in a waiting room, oblivious to my surroundings. Their private conversation with a doctor, who knew the extended family for many years, didn't take long.

> *"As per opinion of the medical committee of the above clinic, please be advised that it is imperative for Lilli Goldbloom to be freed from taking final exams. If the above recommendations are not taken in consideration, the school would be solely responsible for the potential grave consequences."*

The letter allowed me to not go through rigorous exhaustive exams. I took the letter to school and went home. Zoya's unvoiced question didn't matter. Nothing mattered.

CHAPTER 5

Kiev, USSR

1965 - 1966

Mama's last surgery happened three months before my graduation from high school. We knew the doctors suspected her cancer had metastasized and were pretending it wasn't so for her sake. The surgery was needed to make clear how far it had gone.

On the morning before, the doctor came out and said to David: "Your wife is remarkable. She entertained the room of pre-surgical patients all evening, telling stories of her many surgeries and swift recoveries."

When the doctor came out the next time, it was soon after.

"I'm sorry," he said. "We only opened and closed her up. There was nothing we could do. The cancer has spread to every major organ."

Josef and I leaned on each other, holding hands. David's face twitched, his legs crumbled underneath him. But when he reached his hands towards us, we moved further away. We didn't want to share his grief or let him share ours. He sank into a chair and sobbed.

Now he was upset? Who cared? Where was he all those years when Mama took in sewing orders and worked deep into the nights because he was on one of his organizing jaunts? Did he stop his jealous outbursts whenever she spoke with a man or put on a beautiful dress? She cried a river-full after every mean scene of his. If it was true that cancer starts from nerves' exhaustion, our mama was its primary candidate.

He always accused Mama of flirting with men. What about Josef finding him with that woman in our apartment when Mama and I were away? They were watching television together, or so he said. Like we believed that's all they were doing.

When Mama woke after the surgery, the word "cancer" wasn't uttered. She was told a piece of her colon was removed and there was a long recuperation period ahead of her.

***

"Lilli, walk with me for a couple of blocks," suggested David. Usually, if he needed me for anything at all, I pleaded being busy with studying for a college entrance exams. But at the present we had a dying Mom in the house and his request could concern her. Wordlessly, I walked behind him.

He walked and I followed. We stopped a few blocks away from our house, where a sunny street gave way to a dark passageway behind some buildings. David couldn't abide the wide and bright streets. He felt safe when surrounded by walls instead of mulling people. I didn't move and didn't speak, didn't look at him.

He spoke tiredly: "Lilli, what are we going to do about your college? What would happen if you applied to one out of town and were accepted? Mama needs help and who knows how long she has."

I just lost it. "Since when did you agree I could apply to an out-of-town school?" I was so mad with him that for a few seconds I didn't continue. Just raised my arms high in the air, probably asking someone invisible above to get involved and to set things right. "You were terrified to let me go away and don't pretend otherwise. After all the arguments you had with Mama when I went even on the overnight backpacking trips with my class. Mama said, 'Let's trust her, she is a good girl.' You were mumbling something about women being weak and helpless. Remember?"

He raised his shoulders, hiding his head turtle-like, but didn't speak. I continued, "I'm not going anyplace, because Mama is sick, not because you said so."

With every word I got angrier. Who did he think I was—a heartless imbecile?

"Maybe you would remind me about the Jewish quota in Kiev universities, which is the smallest of all of them, and I wasn't the best student on the face of the Earth?"

I should've stopped right there but didn't.

"The issue of college is closed. Rejoice!"

My head started to ache. The narrow asphalt strip where we stood was behind some office buildings and a few restaurants where the stink of waste piles inside and around the open garbage containers permeated the air. My head reacted to the stench with more throbbing. I stood there for a while longer, looking at my father.

This shrinking old man wearing outdated loose clothing loved me. It didn't change. Mama's sickness wasn't his fault. Their marital relations were none of my business. He had been rushing home to do chores he didn't know existed before; he didn't complain about sleepless nights. He had discovered gentle, patient words that softened the look in Mama's questioning eyes. "You'll be fine," he kept reassuring her.

"I'll be fine. We'll be fine, Papa." I turned around and walked away.

It wasn't like I had a yearning for some profession or preferred one work to the other.

Since I was a little girl I'd resented the scores of limitations around our lives. In the incapability to change my situation, I rebelled against my parents for their practical approach to life.

"Lilli, don't start daydreaming now," Mama said in between new outfit fittings. "You don't have some obvious talent or skill. Economics are always good for a girl. Teaching is still a priority with most, but you lack patience. For engineering you need strong math abilities."

I detested these lists of my deficiencies. Every time, I stormed out the door, shouting, "You got stuck in the last century," or "I'll surprise you all," or "There is no way I'll spend my days behind a desk."

Silly girl.

One of my cousins had an acquaintance at the local Economics College, which meant Papa would slip an agreed upon sum of money into that person's pocket in exchange for passing marks. It didn't guarantee acceptance, it only provided a chance.

"Can't hurt to try," offered my parents. Didn't make any difference to me.

The money exchanged hands. I received my passing marks on the college entrance exams but wasn't accepted by the admittance committee. "Goldbloom" was too long of a name not to get noticed.

***

My papa's brother held an important position in the Ministry of Building and Development. He arranged a position in one of their offices.

The first time I walked in, I overheard, "One relative more, one less … doesn't make a noticeable change."

A large room was filled to capacity by other valued peoples' nieces and daughters and cousins. The only male in this room made a shushing sound to whoever had spoken and walked over to me.

"I'm Grigory. Don't mind the local gossips. We're like one big family here." The guy was tall and rod-like straight. I bet he worked hard on his stance, trying not to bend to all those females. Grigory proceeded with his explanations, and I turned my attention to the matter at hand.

"Here, this is an adding machine. You set your fingers on the buttons. Feel the number five here. It's marked by a small bump. Now touch all the rest of the buttons around number five. That five is like a starting point. Try to add the numbers on the page, do it slow, touching that little bump on the number five."

Grigory left a few meaningless pages on the desk in front of me. I stared not at the papers but at the desk. This was my coffin from that day on—a scratched wooden coffin for generations of faceless relations before and after me.

Towards the end of my first day, Grigory stopped by me again. "Good. You picked it up fast. Here, add this column and this one. Always check yourself, looking for alternative ways of checking. Remember: numbers can play dirty jokes, but they don't lie."

He praised me? He had praised me. My fingers got the movement right. I couldn't believe it. After years of trying, even Mama had stopped nagging me to hold a sewing needle correctly.

Grigory stopped once more. "I have to tell you, Lilli, we don't have enough work for you. Your uncle wanted you here, so try not to die from boredom."

"*Boredom*" sounded wonderful.

Every morning I took a trolley, walked into the office, moved my chair slightly away from the desk, sat down, and moved it back into its place. I was ready for my workday.

I added, subtracted, or multiplied numbers. That was all. Sometimes the sheets of paper with rows of numbers were typed, sometimes written by a hand in a hurry. In these cases, there was some adventure in deciphering. Checked my results more than once—the earlier approval carried responsibilities.

The first month passed. Grigory stopped by me at the end of the day.

"Lilli, you passed probation. You are good—fast and accurate, but there's still not much to do for you here. We could use you in one of the branches. Tomorrow, you start there."

What did I care? The new office was in the garage for the trucks belonging to the ministry. Now I took a bus instead of a trolley. It was winter by then, and the bus took a long time to overcome the layers of snow that covered the streets. If I was late on my first day, they could fire me—no … my uncle wouldn't let them.

"Hello, my name is Lilli. I was transferred from the main office."

"Oh, hi. I'm Lilli too. How funny is that? Why would they transfer you? There's no work for the two of us in this swamp. Did you have much difficulty finding us? Sometimes I think they move the place nightly. For the entire twelve months I've worked here, I've searched for it."

Her breathless monologue was funny, if only I could laugh, but I couldn't.

Lilli Ivanova, doll-like, dressed in all the colors of the rainbow, mismatched pieces of clothing with missing buttons, constantly looking for lost items, and laughing non-stop.

"It was bad enough during summertime with mud up to my ankles and trees spreading their branches in all directions with their dense leaves camouflaging the building. And now you can see trucks standing any which way around the parking lot and mountains of snow everywhere in between. If it snows during the night, the trucks are lost under it. The drivers come in the morning and first thing—they curse the snow, then they dig. This is the working garage; they need to get to those vehicles. Maybe one day I could stay home and say, 'I'm too short and couldn't find the building behind the obstructions.'"

So they didn't need another girl in that or the previous place. They paid my salary, and I brought it all to Mama. Please, Mama, enjoy your daughter, the bread-winner.

Six days a week I came to this peculiar location. The desk was different, the chair was different, the movements of my fingers adding and multiplying rows of numbers were the same. My fingers moved monotonously and precisely. The faster and surer they moved, the easier it was not to think. I turned into a machine.

I didn't question what the numbers meant. Living in the Soviet country, I was used to secrecy. Codes were adopted commonly and only one or two higher-positioned people knew them. I guessed the numbers were related to the work hours of the truck drivers, to their loads and the distances they had to deliver them.

Our room was cut off from the management office. The drivers came to punch their timecards when changing shifts; they were loud, happy to interact with other people instead of sitting in the silence of their trucks. The most noise came from the yard when trucks were arriving and leaving. I appreciated the noise, the noise prevented anyone from listening to our ongoing conversation. I loved talking to my namesake.

"You, Lilli Ivanova, are even better than my cat Vasilisa who died a few years ago. You don't sleep when I talk to you." For the first time in my life I shared even my misgivings of being Jewish. Her carefree personality accepted all of it with ease, humor, and kindness.

Nights at home were draining. Mama couldn't sleep, moaning, shuddering from pain. We called emergency ambulances. Their doctors injected more and more doses of morphine. During the day, Papa and Mama's older sister, Besya, took turns at her side. I didn't ask how the days went. Being there at night explained it all. I couldn't imagine how a person endured such pain around the clock.

Often I fell asleep in the office, my head flat on the desk, while my friend did all the work. Or I talked. Lilli Ivanova didn't interfere in my long speeches. She understood the urgency to release the words that were tearing at my insides.

"Since I was a little kid, it always was hard to study, to remember things. I studied and studied for hours, the entire evenings. Mornings came and I didn't remember. My brain seemed empty. Now Mama keeps saying she is sorry I didn't go to the out-of-town college because of her being sick. I always knew I didn't want to go to college. Never wanted to go to college. It's like I did something for her to get sick. Maybe wished for it."

Lilli Ivanova jumped up from her chair furiously. Our room was the size of a desk and a chair on each side of it. She bent so her face came close to my face, her eyes almost touching my eyes.

"Lilli, listen to yourself," she cried out. "You were a child, then a teenager. What did you do? Went to school, did your homework, went out with your girlfriends…"

I couldn't pay attention to her. I needed to expose the dread throttling me.

"Lilli Ivanova, listen to me, please. Don't jump, don't say anything, please listen…

"I was fifteen at the time. We had some relatives at the house. Younger women were venting on and on about the difficulties of getting fashionable clothes. Then I boasted, 'My mama makes any outfit I want at any time.' All of a sudden that man, he is my cousin by marriage, said I was killing her. He told me one day I would kill my mama. 'You are killing her with your demands. She is a sick woman, your mother is.' I thought he was a jerk for saying it. What if he was right? He said it three years ago." Lilli Ivanova closed my mouth forcefully with her hand.

"You wanted clothes? Your mother wanted to give you those clothes. The cousin you are talking about is a moron. We all have morons in our families. You are half dead now with all the hours you stay awake."

"Now? Who cares now? Let me continue; that's not all. I need to tell you all that I think now day and night.

"I got mostly good marks. But what was the price? I spent all my after-school time with the schoolbooks. And then Zoya had to tutor me on top of it. I lost patience. I lost concentration. I didn't remember from one day to the next. All the years I lived with a fear someone would realize there was a zero in place of knowledge in my brain. I would do anything not to go to college. And now my mama is dying and I'm free from college. Do you understand what I am saying?"

I couldn't go on. I slumped in my chair, my teary cheek on the desk, hands trembling.

"Hey, new Lilli, the phone call is for you." The manager's voice coming from the main office startled me. We didn't have a phone inside our room. I couldn't give the main room's number to anyone because I didn't know it.

Papa had called. They wanted me home at once.

I grabbed my things and ran, holding my woolen plaid coat, my fur-lined boots that I exchanged for heels while in the office, and a pocketbook. I ran to the bus stop through the snow piled on the streets.

Suddenly my body was still moving ahead while my left foot stayed behind in the sidewalk crack, the only spot not covered by the white blanket of snow.

"Ah…!" I cried out. My hands freed themselves from the items they carried, trying to hold on to … the air.

"Okay, I got you, stop waving your hands."

Someone's strong arms pulled me back and up. I couldn't stand. I sat on the sidewalk, sobbing, holding on to the person who'd just saved my leg from breaking.

"You could let go of me," he suggested. "If the place you were rushing to is in the close vicinity, I'll take you. Just stop gripping my arms," the man appealed. "Especially if you still need the things floating around the street."

I let go of the man's arms. He stepped away and returned with my coat and boots and pocketbook. I tried explaining:

"My mama is dying. She's dying right now. Maybe she did already. I got a call. My father called."

"You can't save her. I take it you're not a doctor … just that you're too young to be one," the man said, smiling.

Was he flirting with me? Who cared? I had to get home. Maybe she hadn't died yet.

"We talked and talked with her. And then she could n't talk anymore; too tired…"

I couldn't hold my tears. Also I couldn't stand on my left foot. The man bent down and tried to massage my swollen ankle. I wanted to go.

"There's a taxi," I said and waved for the cab to stop. "Please, help me to walk to it."

Only inside the car did I realize that I hadn't thanked the man. I didn't even look at him and wouldn't recognize him on the street. How romantic it all would have been on any other given day: the nonchalant, tall, and handsome—I imagined—man saving me from a certain death. I didn't believe in fate, but all was possible.

Our apartment door was slightly ajar. I limped inside. My papa and Mama's sister, Besya, were standing at the side of Mama's sofa bed.

Mama's face was murky white, her eyes in and out of focus. There were a few pillows behind her back as she half sat, stretching her arms towards her sister. I didn't know if she tried to get more comfortable or wanted to hold on and not to let go. She looked right through me. Did she know any of us?

Joseph walked in and took her hands in his.

"Mama, Mama, I'm here."

Big and loud, he broke the stillness of the death, but not the progression of it. Our mother closed her eyes and stopped fighting—she had heard the signal she waited for.

People came separately and in groups. The flowers spilled onto the stairway.

Where did they go to get flowers in all the snow?

I didn't know my mother met and interacted with so many people. They were from the hospitals and the neighboring buildings, some from her younger years, like from jobs and clubs and schools. The words of thanks, the quiet cries, the loud shrieks. I noticed my own friends huddling in the corner, protesting their own loss. Zoya didn't have any tears left. Her eyes looked hollow. They all loved my mother.

"Lilli, come upstairs with me, lie down for a while," the neighbor from the floor above suggested. She led me upstairs and to the bed, pulling heavy blankets over me. I slept.

The relatives woke me to get ready for the funeral. "Lilli, dress up, it's time to go."

In our apartment I stood in front of the old imposing redwood wardrobe with all the family's clothes. As a little child, I watched Mama's customers trying their outfits on in front of its mirror. I wondered if they noticed how beautiful it was, or only stared at themselves, their expressions changing to awe. They'd walked in as drab housewives and left as beautiful princesses. My mama gave birth to princesses!

The mirror! It was covered with a sheet according to the death customs. Mama explained it to me when I was six and her own mother, my grandmother Zelda, died. According to Jewish customs persons should not be vain when someone close had died. At least that explanation was given to a little me.

Did I have any dark clothes? I looked at the bright colors of my outfits, all made by my mother—every little detail to perfection: reds and yellows and more reds. My mama didn't think of this occasion. She thought of everything but that. That was all her fault!

I wanted to throw things around to show her my disappointment, but she wasn't around to see it.

I put on my only dark dress, a brown school one.

Someone reminded me, "The cold is bitter outside, and it'll be colder at the cemetery. And don't forget the high boots, the snow is deep."

The aunts blanketed me into heavy shawls, crisscrossing my back and chest with them. My snow boots were new and fashionable. Mama waited in a queue for hours to buy them. I was ready.

At the cemetery a snowy lot opened in front of the crowd that came for my mama. On one side there was a freshly dug hole with dirt around it.

I noticed new snowflakes on top of the dirt and at the bottom of the hole. Snow didn't stop falling. It was not as light and gentle as I used to think. It was bothersome.

I held on to Josef's trembling hand and shut my eyes. Natasha held on to his other hand.

***

The days went by. David cried. Joseph and I sat and held each other; we still blamed our father for Mama's death. Not rational at all. Natasha cooked, and we ate. Natasha cleaned too. She knew that Mama would appreciate the neatness. She loved her so very much.

A week later, Josef and Natasha went back to their house. I took a bus to the office above the trucking garage. Lilli Ivanova wasn't there.

"Is Lilli Ivanova sick?" I asked the woman in the other room.

"They transferred her out," the woman explained. "Didn't you see her at your mother's funeral?"

I didn't have a clue. I didn't see, or maybe forgot. Now I was alone, there, here. I sat down and sobbed.

At lunch, I walked to the would-be romantic spot where a stranger had saved me. I looked at the wide crack in the sidewalk. Maybe I'd wait here and when he appeared I'd ask him to marry me. It made sense. Though first I'd make sure he was handsome and dressed well.

I checked that place for the next five lunch hours.

"Oh, hi. Remember me?"

The man recognized me. He was real and I couldn't believe my eyes—he was an adult and not bald or fat or short. The usual Russian fur hat, a longish coat of deep blue, imported leather boots—he was all fashion.

“I didn’t thank you the other day. So, here, thank you very much,” I said. Usually I didn’t know how to make small talk. Yet with that man I felt comfortable, maybe because he wasn’t a complete stranger.

“Do you work around here?” I asked.

“Not really, just attending to some business from time to time. How is your mother?”

The word “death” got stuck inside my throat.

“I’m sorry,” he said, “I understand. Do you have time? Let’s walk for a while.”

We walked, not talking, to the bus stop.

“I’m sorry about your mother,” he said again. “Do you take a bus?” he asked when we approached the bus sign.

“I do,” I replied, forgetting that it was my lunch hour.

A bus arrived, and I stepped up. The man took his glove off and shook my hand. The wedding ring on his finger shone.

He was handsome and dressed well. There still wouldn’t be any wedding bells in my near future.

CHAPTER 6

Kiev, USSR

1966 - 1970

"Lilli, take a day off of work tomorrow and meet me at my factory's gates in the morning, at nine," Josef said on the phone in his usual "it's-been-decided" voice.

We met in front of the radio factory where he worked as a toolmaker.

"Here's a pass to get in. You do realize that this is a military institution?" he asked. Of course I knew. Every factory in the USSR was secretly manufacturing something for the army in one capacity or another.

We walked into a large courtyard surrounded by buildings. Each of them exhaled a different level of noise. The thick brick walls were painted dark green a long while ago. Broken windows carried layers of aged dust. The rows of trees, their leaves covered with filth, in the middle of that square made me think of Martian organisms.

Glad to be away from my lonely adding machine on top of the trucking garage, I dressed in a summery outfit of open-toed shoes and a short ivory-colored frock. I clutched my large bright tote to avoid touching any grime, including my brother in a laborer's uniform.

Josef interrupted my unpleasant discoveries of the real world of factories.

"I spoke about you with the head of the computer department that provides record-keeping services for the whole place. Today their supervisor will interview you and maybe hire you after that."

"Why did the head of the computer department talk to you, just another guy from a tool-room? Why does he contemplate hiring me? And I won't even ask why I need it."

"That's some fine opinion coming from my little sister. Was I ever "just another" guy? The man owes me a favor and it's perfect time to collect on it. You need it because I decided you need a change. Even if the office you work in belongs to the Ministry of Building and Development, it's still a cubicle above the garage, and you're all alone there. Isolation is good only when you plan on going mad. Are you clear on all topics?"

"Welcome to the world of grownups," I muttered to myself. "Different relatives shuffle you from place to place and you feel lucky to have those relatives."

Louder I asked, "I'm curious, did you supply a lover for that computer place boss? Or did you discover who his lover was or what?"

"I do have plenty of dirt on him," Josef laughed proudly, "but all you have to do is pass the test, whatever it is."

We walked into a carbon copy of the room I entered on my first working day a year ago: big, windowless, desks, girls, chairs, adding machines.

The supervisor was a short woman in her middle thirties, a pockmarked face, a row of gold teeth, and poorly applied makeup. She smiled her greetings while making eyes at Josef-the-hunk and suggested I add a few rows of numbers for the test.

I stared at that amusingly ugly person who giggled girlishly, then followed the buzz of many young women who wanted to watch me testing for the job.

Here we go again, another group of cousins and daughters.

Before I touched the buttons, I glanced over at Josef closing his eyes. He was afraid I was not up for the task and he'd be humiliated.

I let my experienced fingers do their bidding. I wasn't worried—that was one chore I performed effortlessly. After I finished the adding, a few applauded. I asked for more columns to add—just to show off.

"I never saw any girl's hand fly so fast, you don't even see the movement," whispered one of the women standing behind me. They checked my totals. It wasn't necessary. I didn't make mistakes.

Josef and I walked out after the test. He seemed mute.

"What's with you?" I insisted. "You brought me here because you'd hoped I could do the work. You didn't think I would be a louse, did you?"

"I don't really know. You're my little sister. I don't expect you to do or to know things. I wanted to help. I didn't think beyond that. You were marvelous. I'm stunned."

"Thanks for nothing. Don't you worry, I don't know things and cannot do things. The adding machine is the only fluke. My hand learned the motion for some inexplicable reason."

The computer center hired me. The pay was for the piecework. On each page there was a total count of numbers to add, or multiply. Valentina, the supervisor, calculated the cost of each page. There were exceptionally busy days, and the girls made nice earnings during those times.

I wasn't interested in money. David provided my necessities. I was hungry for people. Soon I stopped flying my hand, sat by one of the girls, and talked. I shared stories of my previous job: the coincidence of working in a small room with another Lilli, and of her disappearance from my life. I joked about the time when a handsome, though married man, saved me from almost breaking my leg on the snowy sidewalk. The stories were many. I was watchful of people's reactions. I wanted them to like me.

I met Josef during many a lunchtime and some other times. It was great to turn around and see his dear face nearby or even at a distance.

My brother brought me up on the ongoing bickering at home with his father-in-law. For years Josef laughed off the man's drunken proclamations and fist waving. At the present he'd reached his limit and pushed the old man around a few times with his fists.

We discussed David, pleased that he was still distressed about our mama's death.

"Is it possible he's truthfully remorseful for mistreating her?" I asked, and complained, "He gets on my nerves. Just sits there in the darkness and cries. What am I supposed to do—cry next to him? I do my crying far away from him."

"My little sister, nothing will bring our mama back. David loves you, even if he never showed me some of that love."

It was true—David doted on me. He cooked his infamous dinners: big pots of soup with potatoes, onions, carrots, pasta, and usually a few kinds of cold cuts, for the two of us. He hung our clothes up and dusted furniture. I figured his sisters washed the bathroom, kitchen, and the corridor in the apartment. Let them do it—Mama bent her back for all of them for more years than I knew.

I stayed out as much as possible. Even strolling under pouring rain was preferable to the suffocating closeness of many people in our apartment. Coming home late, I ate standing in the kitchen and went to my bed in the back room, not even turning on the light. Tried to sleep, rarely succeeding. David—I continued calling him that—didn't interfere with my living—if anyone could call it that. Truth be known, I didn't think of David.

I didn't think, period.

***

One day, David appealed to me: "Lilli, the two of us were invited to the wedding of the Shapiros' daughter. You were friendly with her as little girls when all of us adults came together. I didn't give them any promises on your account, but it would be nice if you could go."

Why not go and dance my legs off? I thought, agreeing, surprising even myself.

The music played loud and people danced, having fun.

Mama would dance, too. She liked to have fun whenever she could. But … she was dead, and here I was enjoying the party, and here was David … watching me, wishing I'd hook up with one of the eligible men and make his life easier.

An hour into the wedding, I walked out with the married friend of the groom. I wasn't looking for a date, just an excuse to leave.

Outside the wedding hall I said my goodbyes to that married man. Maybe he counted on something more than taking me out the door. I didn't want to be mean to someone's wife.

During the day at the computer center, we often stepped up to the roof for a smoke. One morning, as we sat there puffing and gossiping, one of the girls, who stayed behind in the office, rushed up yelling that Valentina's husband was roughing her up. We ran downstairs and surrounded the warring couple.

"Don't you touch me, you brute!" Valentina shouted indignantly, her face and arms bleeding from the powerful punches. "I won't feed you for the next week and won't love you even longer."

The tall burly man proceeded to pummel his tiny wife. Both behaved unemotionally: one of them giving and the second accepting the punishment. He defended his manly honor and she her womanly needs.

When the husband, who worked in a different wing of the same building, left without speaking, Valentina wiped the blood, checked the bruises covering her face in the hand-mirror, and chuckled, showing the proud gold of her teeth. "I will still get my loving from Fyodor."

Fyodor was Valentina's lover for the last five or so years. It was common knowledge between us girls in the computer center that she didn't wear any underpants year-round, not wanting to waste any valuable time when he called on her.

We dispersed, returning to work at our desks, with nothing interesting anymore to observe.

Welcome to the world of grownups—it stinks like swamp.

Josef stopped coming over to see me. I didn't glimpse his dear face in the dining hall of our factory or passing by anywhere else on its territory. His life became fully invested in building a floor above his in-laws' house. He worked through the lunch-hour to make himself some needed tools. At the end of the workday he rushed to catch an earlier train to his suburb and start work before dark.

Some months later, Josef surprised me when all of a sudden he entered our adding machine room.

"Little sister, you're going to a night college," he stated, kissing me. "David agreed too—you need to continue your education."

My face didn't show any reaction. I wasn't jumping up and down from happiness, and didn't want to upset Josef by blurting, "Go to hell," or something similar. He continued, "The factory opened the two-and-a-half-year junior college for its workers. I already shared a bottle of vodka with the principal and you are in."

The walls of my old hateful school surrounded me, closing in and choking.

My patience couldn't take another word. I hit Josef in the face with my fists. Josef easily grabbed my hands with one of his and forced me into the corner, behind some metal storage cabinets.

I shouted, "Dream on! I'm not going to school, no way. Don't do me any favors! Speak the truth— David bought you that vodka. You were looking for an excuse to get legitimately drunk. You didn't much care with whom to drink it. HA! The first time you drink vodka on my behalf with a manager of this place and threaten to expose his love life, I get a job in this dump and start taking two buses every morning instead of one. At least at my last place they paid me if I worked or not—now my pay has all but vanished, not that I care. The second time you decide to drink more vodka and here I am a student. Think again."

Josef's face spread in an ear-to-ear grin; my hostility was evaporating. I knew I'd do whatever Josef proposed. Though I dismissed David as easily as yesterday's rainwater. I lost the fighting spirit against the two men who wished me well.

***

The factory's college was open weeknights so workers could finish their dayshifts.

"If you could believe it, I'm the best student in the class," I boasted to my coworkers. "Most are older laborers from manufacturing shops. They don't remember any of the subjects from high school, or maybe they didn't ever attend school. You know the type: from small towns and villages originally, married early, have big families to support. A diploma would add some money to their paycheck, so they sign up, come, sit there, and try not to fall asleep."

I observed my mostly male classmates wearing all those dark unfashionable clothes: wide pants, sizable, never-washed jackets or the coats that seemed to hide the total person underneath it. I felt slightly superior, but also envious, because they were on the road to betterment, but the reason for my being there was anyone's guess.

One day, when one of the teachers didn't show up, a bottle of homemade vodka appeared from under all the clothes on one of the men. I became one of them and we partied. The group stayed together. If weather permitted, we remained outside, drinking from the bottle. In rain or cold, some diner or cafeteria unwittingly provided glasses and chairs.

After one or two drinks, I retched, feeling like I left my insides splashed on that building wall or bathroom stall. The experienced guys recommended me to graduate down to a cheap wine, buying a bottle especially for me. They shared jokes and pitfalls: nosy mothers-in-law, wives who didn't want to meet their wifely duties, or shortages of toilet paper in stores. I laughed hysterically, feeling accepted and comfortable, ready to stay wherever we were drinking later and later.

I still had a lot of friends, although some of them stopped inviting me to their homes. Others did but watched me closely to see when the time was right to pack me out of there before I started embarrassing them.

Everyone from my circle of acquaintances was dating, falling in love, even getting married.

I was pathetically bored.

One winter day, a new girl came to work at the office, and soon she asked me to help her with her wedding. She said that she liked how I dressed. Actually, she did say it, but I volunteered my help. She lived with her married sister, shy and lonely, a real live waif. Went out with a boy, another pitiful waif. He proposed, and now she needed a dress and food and guests. I went on a helping spree. So much fun!

We invited a couple of girls from our office. The bride asked groom's male cousin to bring a few men for the company. He obliged. I didn't see faces; I worked on perfecting the wedding. What a joke of a wedding: ten, maybe fifteen guests.

Suddenly, I saw this guy in the room—he looked like a painting or a sculpture, and I wasn't drunk as to misjudge his looks, not having any time to eat or drink the entire day.

He stood there, with his hands inside his pockets, and looked at me with a slight smile on his face. Was he mocking me, sneering? Why would he stare at me? Was I that funny looking? I ran for the bottle of vodka. Fast, fast. Without any food in my stomach, I got drunk in a matter of minutes. I remember dancing barefoot on the table, tasting food with my toes. Reaching for food with my toes and trying to bring it to my mouth—screeching: "Feed me. I'm hungry."

Now I was drunk beyond drunk and needed to throw up. Run out the door even without my coat and without my shoes. It was cold winter. Snow as high as a tall human. I fell and tried to stand up and throw up. Threw up. And then I felt hands all over me. I felt hands on my body, but I felt snow too. The hands felt good, warm, much better than wet snow on my bare skin.

"Oh no!" "Get off me!" "No, no!" And then I stopped. I understood what had happened.

The piercing pain brought on more retching. I puked up the food consumed at the last moment, which didn't have any time to go farther inside of my stomach.

CHAPTER 7

Kiev, USSR

1970

When Natasha asked if I'd come to work for the institute where she worked, I agreed at once. If they'd take me, I'd obtain a new life, new friends, new skills, and interests. I'd try my best to start anew.

Natasha asserted her point of view: "There are educated men and women where I work, in contrast to the crude factory workers."

She meant I would have better prospects for finding a suitable husband. Finding a husband would definitely save a lot of headaches for David. I wasn't an easy daughter to have at home.

The management agreed to hire me because my sister-in-law knew someone in the higher up office. The people working in this place wore business suits and fashionable dresses instead of dirty uniforms. I didn't notice any centuries-old dust stored in the corners.

In my new office there were stacks of pages with engineering calculations on everyone's desks. Natasha explained that their civil engineers were building roads and bridges and some other stuff—military for sure, even if they called themselves "civil." They traveled to the construction sites and measured distances and developed projects.

Our department's assignment was to check the hand-posted numbers against references in the specialized manuals. The fast on-site entries often carried serious mistakes that could sabotage the entire structures.

"Why couldn't your engineers check each number before they scribble it in?" I asked Natasha.

She laughed. "Do you want to change a system which works for everyone? The way everyone looks at it — they found a sure way to employ more people. It's double work, even triple, because after *your* girls check it there's someone in charge of the project who makes sure *you* don't sleep at your desk."

Why wouldn't I sleep at my desk or go for a walk or talk to a live person if the papers from my desk went to another desk for rechecking? Luckily, I landed another mindless job.

My days at the new place started about the same like in the old one. I walked into the crowded room, said extended hellos to my co-workers, listened to their last night's happenings, went to the bathroom, came back to my desk, and for fifteen or twenty minutes checked a page or two.

Then I stood up again and took stairs up to the next floor, where Natasha and her girlfriends greeted me and shared someone's daily donation of home cooking, before going downstairs to work again.

It was an easy life, no reason to complain.

***

That particular Tuesday at the end of May of 1970, I woke up and dressed to go to work, but at the door altered my intentions, reversed my steps, and got out my old two-piece red bathing suit.

"I'm sick. I've the flu," I called into the office on the way to the beach. "I'll go to the doctor and bring you a note from her."

A wish to be by myself in a large uninhibited space without walls enclosing on me. A beach seemed perfect.

May arrived unusually warm, yet still not a month for swimming or tanning. The only people I passed on the way to an enclave of white sand were a loud group of card players.

The sand felt kindly warm to the touch. I relaxed and thought of nothing. It felt blissful and quite wonderful to lie on the sand, slowly sifting my lazy fingers through those tiny particles.

Unexpectedly, the blue of the sky started to darken and the waves were getting higher. In a moment, the sand would cool off too. Nature dictated conditions. Pooh at the people. We could observe or close our eyes—it didn't care.

Wasn't I part of that nature? I'll stay here and see what happens. My life would be wonderful. I laughed out loud.

"What's so funny?"

A man in his late twenties stood next to me. I'd heard him talking to the guys from his card-playing group before. Being of slight build and medium height, he seemed like a young boy, yet he was in charge.

"Humans are nothing when it comes to nature. Don't you agree?" At twenty-three, I had learned to ignore the one-liners used by guys. Why didn't I disregard this one?

"Oh, we change it plenty. Unfortunately, not for the best. Did you forget Michurin, our renowned botanist? He said, 'We shouldn't wait for nature to hand us its gifts—we have to take it by force."

Wide smile, an ocean of freckles, windblown sandy hair, vivid green eyes. "*Don't be afraid,*" the green lights said, greeting me, welcoming me, calming me.

We stared at each other. I didn't mind his stare. My brilliant red two-piece swimming suit didn't hide my body. I didn't want to hide it. I looked great.

At any other time, I'd come up with some clever remark and establish my territory. I didn't do it. I felt comfortable staring at the man and letting him stare at me.

He was too skinny, too short, too many freckles. His worn-out, old-fashioned trunks were dreadful.

"I'm Sergey."

"I'm Lilli."

"May I sit with you?"

"Wouldn't your friends object?"

"They aren't my friends, exactly. They are my subordinates. I'm their *Komsomolsky* leader. We're having an important 'political' meeting right now. As I see it, a game of cards is it. It helps your brain to develop more than any political discussion."

Sergey had a manner of speaking with authority. A leader gave speeches in front of many people and he was used to them listening and paying attention.

I went to many *Komsomolsky* gatherings at school and work. They were boring, but I didn't mind, remembering how proud it felt at age fourteen to be accepted as part of that Communist Union of Youth.

The man standing in front of me belonged to the selected cast of leaders. He just introduced himself and already trusted me with his openness. In the Soviet country, no one spoke like that in front of a total stranger. Though times changed and bold words didn't lock you up, it could cost you a job or put a question mark on a hidden list in someone's drawer. I was unnerved by this man's frankness.

“Sergey!” someone from the group called over. My new acquaintance stood up slowly and unwillingly.

“May I see you, Lilli? I would like that very much,” Sergey said, almost whispering. Suddenly he realized that his swimming trunks covered only the small bottom part of him and he tried to shield the rest with both arms. A grown man on the beach flapping his arms around his naked chest—it presented one comical picture. But it was heartwarmingly comical—he was shy with me.

“Yes,” I said, hiding a smile. “I’d like to see you.”

“Later today? I have to go back to the plant with my men. After that, if you have time … I’d like that very much.”

We met that same evening. I changed six outfits before deciding on the short cotton dress with its purples and yellows. Sergey wore a business suit and a tie. The tie, lighter gray with stripes, matched the darker gray of his suit. His shirt was white and his shoes were black. He handed me a small bouquet of delicate violets; his strong, callused hand touched mine gently.

We walked slowly. The park, not five blocks from my Pushkin Street, seemed an appropriate first date destination. I looked around for an outsider’s opinion of us walking hand in hand. What would I say, seeing a girl in a bright little dress next to a guy in a somber business outfit? They were poles apart, surely.

The park could’ve been empty for all the attention we received. Some lovebirds on the benches locked in passionate kisses; mothers watched children playing before their bedtime; elders discussed some prehistoric events while playing chess.

I arched my neck towards the sky, and up there caught sight of the tall, ancient poplars swinging their tops. I imagined they approved of us, promptly sharing their opinions with each other.

We were too excited to sit. Walking and talking, Sergey kept turning to look at me.

"The guys, you saw on the beach, work with me at the plant that fixes household appliances. I'm an engineer-designer. My work often consists of coming up with a 'miracle cure' for some oldest refrigerator or TV set that stopped working. I don't have to explain to you, Lilli, that most people don't have enough money or connections to buy a new one."

"But your hands..." I mentioned the calluses I felt on the palm of his hand, " aren't the hands of a designer."

"You noticed? I worked as a blacksmith's helper since I was thirteen. Don't look so forlorn. It happened a long time ago. I'm not doing it anymore."

I had never met a y thirteen-year-old child who worked in a blacksmith shop. I imagined an airless place with an open fire and an iron block and a young boy with a huge, heavy hammer beating at metal lying there. Even my Josef was older when David forced him to start working.

We spoke of books and new plays, his work and my mama's death. We both were slaves to soccer and went to a stadium as often as we could.

I walked by this man's side, not getting bored or self-conscious. He gave me a feeling that everything I said was important and clever and funny.

"My shoelace is untied," Sergey declared, like it was a fact of national magnitude. I almost laughed at the absurdity of his tone but checked his face and shushed.

He took my hand.

"Lilli, I feel like I've known you forever. I'm not good at this one-on-one deal. I'm much better at the big audiences. I could talk nothings until my public is tired and sleepy and I still would be on my feet. Do you know what I'm saying?"

He wasn't a fashion savvy. Who wore a white shirt with a tie to walk in the park? But it wasn't the clothes that were essential. His every word was earnest. I felt special being with him.

"Lilli, please come to our family dinner this Sunday. Would you? You'd like my mom. I have the greatest mom. Please?"

Through the end of the week, to the astonishment of the entire office, I stayed at my desk, actually doing the work I was getting paid for.

We met Wednesday and Thursday and Friday. Sergey waited on the steps of the office building when I came out. I looked into a mirror before leaving my office and liked myself, not wishing to change a thing.

One of my co-workers stopped by me to share her opinion: "Lilli, your date is funny. Yesterday, as I was leaving the building, he declared that he was waiting for Lilli Goldbloom, asking if I knew you. He'd been joking non-stop till you appeared. Then he became deaf and mute in a second. This is love."

I knew that too.

On Saturday, we met early and rented a little rowboat on the River Dnepr. That was our first silent date since we met on Tuesday. The quietness wasn't oppressive; it didn't surprise or embarrass us. It explained things better than words ever could.

"See you tomorrow," we both said.

"I'm Lilli." I shook the hands propelled at me on the threshold of Sergey's home and smiled in response to smiles offered to me.

"We're Sergey's parents, the Kaplans." The two middle-aged people kissed me. They seemed very nice. The mother was short, plump, and blond. The father tall, though stooped, wearing glasses. Sergey told me that he was injured during the war and since didn't see from one eye.

“Look around before we sit down to dinner,” they told me, pointing at the oriental rugs and the imported furniture. Their apartment was furnished with the best. I perceived the pride—these were items you didn’t just walk into a store and ask to be delivered. You needed important connections with all kinds of people to secure such furniture and dishes and curtains and lamps, even the apartment itself. And the woman of the house was the one who could get anything she wished. It was that simple. Sergey told me she worked at a shoe store. If you need shoes, you call her and get those. But where do *you* work? - at a stadium. So when the woman’s son needs the tickets for a soccer game — here you come. And so on and on and on…

We sat to eat—Sergey and I on one side of the table, his father and mother on the opposite.

At first they toasted my health. “You, Lilli, are a beautiful girl. We’re thrilled to have you at our son’s side.”

Wow! My head was spinning—it was pleasant to make an impression. I warmed up to compliments, relaxed, sat more comfortably in their mahogany dining chair, preparing to answer the usual inquiries about my family, job, education, but the topic of conversation turned sharply to the woman of the house, Sergey’s perfect mother.

I nodded my head in agreement, listening to the continuous praises. “You prepared absolutely perfect soup,” and “Only you could roast such tender beef,” and “You look exceptionally lovely today.” It got tedious and I stopped agreeing.

How come she doesn’t stop them? Doesn’t it embarrass her? Probably because I don’t have my own mother, I tend to notice things like that.

She brought new courses, cleared dirty dishes, and in between listened to all the acclaim, a satisfied smile appeared on her pouty lips. She didn't ask for any help from her men and they didn't volunteer. She refused my help as well. She preferred being glorified.

I'd ask Sergey about it later. On second thought, I'd better not. He had advised me that his mother was the best.

I felt evaluated yet not criticized by Sergey's parents, glad to glimpse Sergey's delighted smile throughout our visit. The Kaplans accepted me. I didn't realize that the course of my life depended on that visit.

As soon as we were outside, Sergey spoke, "Lilli, I don't think we should wait. Let's do it. What do you think?"

A summer night seemed like an agreeable background for amusing riddles or wishful understandings or pleasant invitations. We met only a week ago. Was that his proposal? I never heard one before, so I wasn't a good judge.

"I don't know," I murmured. "That's big."

Could I ask someone for advice? David would be thrilled—a Jewish man with an engineering degree from a well-to-do family. But do I want to get married?

Josef? Lately, he didn't call at all. We communicated through Natasha. A few times I took a train to their house and he was on the roof fixing some leaks and didn't come down. Was I guilty of some unnamed misdeed? I needed him.

I took another day off work and went to see my brother at home.

"Josef, it feels right. He loves me. I think we could be happy together."

"What do you understand? You think because he is some kind of leader it will be better? Those activists know how to lie and cheat so people will believe whatever shit they tell. They are the worse swine."

Josef didn't trust the men in the leadership positions. Josef didn't trust the men who wanted to marry his little sister. Josef didn't trust men. But that was Josef's problem.

My girlfriends? Would they see behind Sergey's drab clothes or small build? Zoya, where were you? I didn't have the nerve to summon my childhood friend after the years of running away.

Mama, why did you leave me? You always had an opinion ready for Josef. Typically, before I needed it, you went ahead and died.

A few sleepless nights later I took a city trolley to the cemetery where my mama was buried, hoping that this meaningful place would provide the answer.

Mama, what did you think about David when you met him? You told me he was the most charming man you ever knew. Did you think so at first? How did you know he was the one for you? But who cares anyway? He was cruel and mean and heartless to you. What advice could you possibly give me?

I stared at the delicate pink granite Josef carved and inscribed by hand using gold dust. When creating this exquisite, one of a kind monument, he splashed his anger at the entire world in addition to spelling love to our mama.

I turned around. Sergey stood a few steps away. I had told him I'd be here. He'd arrived unnoticed and waited. Nothing pretentious about that man. That is the way I am, take it or leave said his green eyes, looking questioningly from the framework of boyish freckles—all of it had already found its place in my heart.

I spoke so he could hear: "I'm going to be really fat in a few years. All my family is fat. It's in the genes. My mama had health problems since she was a young woman or even earlier. Various ones. There's a lot of sickness in the family. So my genes are definitely defective. Otherwise, if you still want me…"

I didn't finish my speech—Sergey's kiss didn't let me. He got his answer and he was happy, as was everyone else who wished us well.

***

To my delight, Sergey's parents weren't suggesting we move in with them. And I asked my father if we could live with him. He was thrilled. Installed a sliding door in between rooms and moved into the small back room, closer to his work corner with its sewing machine, freeing the first, bigger one for us, the newlyweds. The expression on his face was that of perpetual, joyful bewilderment, like he had to pinch himself daily, not believing his good luck—his only daughter married well—his work was done. Now he could die anytime, without regrets.

Actually, I preferred for my papa to live a very long life.

CHAPTER 8

Kiev, USSR

1970-1972

We didn't know I was pregnant. It was Sunday a few months after Sergey and I were married. We had planned to visit Sergey's parents when I started cramping and then bleeding profusely.

I tried to explain to Sergey what was happening: "It's not like a period at all. I feel like I have a broken faucet in between my legs. Maybe we should go to an emergency room."

The hospital was near by. The two of us ran all the way there and waited. The aching in my belly developed into breath-stopping pain. The blood soaked through my clothes. I sat, paced, half-sat and half-laid in turns until being called in.

"How far along are you?" the doctor on duty asked.

"I'm not pregnant," I answered, but started to wonder when I'd had my last period.

"Well, you're having a miscarriage," she insisted after checking me. "Any previous pregnancies?"

"None." I answered probably too quickly, but I believed it.

They registered me, found a bed, and told me to wait when the labor-like contractions started. "We'll induce it in a worst-case scenario."

Why so? I didn't understand. In a threadbare hospital gown, my face made-up for our Sunday outing and now smeared from too much crying and rubbing, I stayed in bed and whimpered and then hollered through the ever-increasing pain. After a couple of hours, seeing bloody globs coming out of me, I crawled to the nurses' station and begged for a doctor to check me again. Then I was operated on. A dead fetus was scraped out of my uterus.

Was it my fault? After all, I was pregnant once before even if I declined remembering it. The doctor concluded there was no permanent damage, but she could've been mistaken.

A few days after the miscarriage, in our Pushkin Street apartment, sitting next to me on our opened sofa bed, Sergey chose to switch the topic of conversation from the painful subject to one he hoped would improve my mood. He leaned closer and spoke in a whisper, aware that a few of my relatives who lived in our communal apartment were possibly right outside of our door.

"The moment you're better," my husband confided, "we're going to apply for emigration to Israel. The process has started, though not many people are aware that the door out is ajar. Secretly, I've been listening to the *Voice of America* radio station. The Soviets signed a deal with the Americans. In exchange for American grain, they are letting some Jews go. A number of Jewish families applied for permission and there are more every day." He explained slowly so I wouldn't misunderstand the importance of his words.

The whisper didn't mute the excitement in his voice. Only then, Sergey glanced at me. I knew what he saw—the face of a drowning woman near death. He cursed loudly and dashed to our joined photo album to separate his childhood photographs from mine. The breakup of our young marriage was the single solution to my husband's plight.

"Are you leaving me?" I needed to amass strength to ask the question. After all, I'd just lost the baby and was not prepared for losing a husband too.

"Do you think it was easy for my parents to agree to this step? They're applying along with many other smart, intelligent people. You prefer to stay blindfolded and ignorant—too bad. For my family it's a done deal—take it or leave it." Sergey shouted his last words, neighbors be damned.

I was not his family? The Kaplans had obviously planned to emigrate before Sergey and I met. A decision of such importance couldn't be last minute. And now Sergey was going to go to Israel with his parents. Without me. But he'd just asked me to go with them…

"Don't you understand that nothing will ever change for us in this damned land?" He forgot to whisper but caught himself. "The working people are going to lead miserable lives forever. The party leaders will enjoy their comforts forever. The Jews will be despised forever. Are you that naïve or that stupid to not see it? We have a chance to get out from under their thumb. We should grab it!"

Only one part of my body hurt from the surgery. But the pain inflicted by Sergey went up and down and across through every cell of me.

"Sergey, I see now we didn't really know each other. Deciding to get married, we acted on impulse. I don't blame you alone. I was there too. I believed we had the same values. How could you reconcile yourself being a leader of the Komsomol organization with wanting to leave our motherland? After all, the young workers there at your plant trust you."

"They do, they trust me with their lives. We all know how dangerous it's even to whisper about thinking of leaving this country. And nevertheless, a few actually came to me with questions, wishing to get out of this hellhole we call our home. I never lied to them or to you. Remember our first meeting, me playing cards with the guys at the beach? We discussed our lives, which to most seemed like a dead end.

"I mentioned to you that the game was more important than the Komsomol meeting. It was not a joke. I believed you understood and agreed with me."

"How can we leave the Soviet Union? They told us to go live in Israel since I was a little girl, and I cried because what was Israel? My home is here, where my papa's father was killed in a Cossack's pogrom and my mama's father froze to death on a sidewalk in Siberia during the war. To leave this land?"

"What about my parents? Didn't they suffer enough? Enough, believe me. 'Enough' is the key word. There will never be an end to our misery if we stay. Don't you see it?"

I couldn't see *his* truth; my *own* overwhelmed me.

I was four and five and six, walking by my papa's side with a delegation from one of his enterprises in a May 1st parade. I waved a little red flag and yelled out: "Communism throughout the world! All workers unite against the capitalist oppression!"

We learned about our heroes who overthrew bloodsucking *Tzars* and gave power to the workers. They built the brand-new country and defended it from the Nazis so the next generations would live in a perfect society where all its citizens were equal. I was part of this history.

As a young schoolgirl believing in the importance of saving natural resources, I'd spent many days collecting recyclable paper and metal late into the night. Pulling an old bed frame from the dump through city blocks, climbing from floor to floor in the department store asking for used wrapping paper, that was my personal good deed on behalf of my motherland—anything to assure the win of the great ideals.

But what if the ideals were fiction? What if our heroes died for nothing?

Was it possible that our entire huge country breathed, spoke, worked, and defended a myth? Was it better to admit that for over fifty years we all lived a lie?

Should I listen to my husband instead of my conscience?

For many days after, sitting closely and whispering—the walls had ears too—we tried to discuss our future. Again and again our debates ended in him packing his books or clothes or photographs, though not leaving. The first few times I replaced it all in its proper places, then stopped and ignored the mess. Our room appropriated a look of constant packing.

Mama's sister, my aunt Besya, came for a visit one day when all of Sergey's possessions covered the chairs, and sofa, and part of the floor. He left that morning after not finding any more things of his to remove from shelves and hangers.

"Lilli, darling, what happened?" she asked bewildered.

"He's going to leave me one of these days, and I can't tell you the reason."

I didn't think my aunt would run to the KGB with the information, but I couldn't pronounce the appalling words. She hugged me, and I cried, sitting by Mama's older sister all evening.

"Where is David?" Aunt Besya wanted to know.

"Papa is trying his best not to get involved. The moment Sergey and I start to argue, he leaves for one of his siblings'. He wants me to agree with everything Sergey says. A divorced daughter is worse than a spinster daughter."

"Lilli, Gita did whatever David wanted, even though she was one of the spunkiest girls I ever met. At first she always used to argue. Me, I never even tried. I followed your uncle's wishes and never complained. I've had a good life. That's how it is. Some women get divorced when it becomes intolerable. If you can live with whatever he wants from you—do it. That's my advice."

Would Mama agree with her sister on that?

Soon after my miscarriage, I became pregnant again. Gil was born in November of 1971. Pale oval face, long dark curls, ten fingers and ten toes; a pair of enormous chestnut eyes stared with intensity into mine. Newborn Gil, named in memory of my beloved mother, was too perfect to continue the lineage of helplessness. Our baby deserved the best of everything and he had a brave, clever father who was willing to give it to him.

I looked at my own birth certificate. Mother's name—Gita Gorsky, Jewish. Father's name—David Goldbloom, Jewish. I took out my passport with the sickle and hammer on its cover, the internal document all Soviet citizens coming into their adulthood proudly received at age sixteen. Lilli Goldbloom—Jewish. We were Jews.

And because we were Jews the State of Israel wanted us. It all came together, at last.

More and more Jewish families were granted permissions to leave for Israel. Sergey met with a group of mostly young, courageous Jews who secretly studied Hebrew and Jewish history. They were anxious to arrive there and be productive at once. Some extra vocal Jewish men and women were proclaimed a "danger to the Soviet security" and imprisoned for any number of fabricated reasons. Their names became symbols of martyrdom in our tight community.

Sergey's new acquaintances used many ardent words. A few times I came to listen and couldn't avoid their truth. I'd lived that truth for all of my twenty-four years, not recognizing it.

The general population knew nothing. The workers still went to their factories in order to win the ongoing competition with capitalist America. The *kolhozniks* were planting a grain acquired from America, which at times yielded a harvest in Soviet soil. It wasn't the first and it wouldn't be the last time for the superpowers' economic negotiations and it didn't impact most people's lives. But at this particular time — we, the Jews will be the winners. We, the Jews, not all of us who wanted, but some of us were able to leave the morass of our birth.

After we submitted our applications for emigration, Sergey was fired, promptly. No organization would risk harboring "a Zionist sympathizer," "an enemy of the Soviet people." I stayed home with my infant, not bringing in any income. My retired father bought groceries and paid for all our necessities.

The cost of saying goodbye to the country of our birth was staggering. The government found a sure way to milk its Jews if they desired to leave. They charged fees for every transaction, including refusal of Soviet citizenship. Apparently, we never valued it high enough.

I emptied the old china cabinet from Mama's good dishes and a few odd crystal pieces and took them to a second-hand store that accepted items on commission. My fancy dresses, winter clothes, and tomes of Russian classics disappeared the same way.

In the spring of 1972 we were packing in secret. After standing an hour in queue, Sergey and I bought four imported suitcases. They looked like oversized, flat yellow boxes. To walk home we had to be careful of gossiping neighbors—anyone would wonder why we needed those, so we used separate routes. The suitcases were for essentials, like Gil's diapers and our summer clothes and some towels and bedding. The rest of the well-used, assorted household items accumulated by my mama throughout her married life and gifted to us by Papa, would follow in the large wooden crates.

I didn't know how much longer my papa would be able to subsidize us, and I wasn't ready to empty his pockets. In desperation, Sergey found a man who'd started a business of lending money to departing Jews at exorbitant interest rates. The man collected fingerprints from his borrowers, making sure his investment was secure.

The awaited permissions hadn't come yet, and we didn't have any guarantees they would.

I nursed, changed, and bathed our baby. From constant laundering by hand and ironing—an infant's delicate skin required it—the diapers, which had previously served as our bedding, turned into a grayish-yellowish mess taking over the dining table, chairs, sofa and every other surface in our room.

I didn't venture outside, leaving the business of taking Gil out to my papa. My papa … he was always there, helping. In these months we spent a lot of time together and he told me stories I never knew. With sorrow he admitted that his sister Vera and her husband Leon had wanted to leave the Soviet Union after the war when for the short period of time it became possible, but he along with her other brothers forbade her. They meant to save her from the unknown.

He never forgave himself. "You, Lilli, go and live anywhere but here. Look at Gil. Did you ever see a baby more beautiful?"

"Papa, why won't you come with us?"

"Here is a hard and cruel life, but I'm used to it. I know how to go around and get whatever I need. Every little win is an event. Why would I want an easy life?" he chuckled, making it into a big joke.

I knew he wouldn't go. I knew it from the very beginning.

***

Something was wrong with our infant son. He nursed hungrily, releasing a greenish liquid stool after each meal and in between. His bawling stopped for only short minutes and only while in our arms. We assumed that was a regular for colic, though a young pediatrician in our local clinic offered a more serious diagnosis: "I suspect dysentery. It requires hospitalization."

To chance my baby's life in one of those infection-spreading, overcrowded hospital rooms was out of the question. One of Papa's friends recommended we take Gil for a second opinion to a retired pediatrician who happened to be his trusted friend, and a Jewess as well.

"Since you are in a constant state of tension, your milk reflects it," the doctor explained. "Everything you feel, your baby does too."

Then, listening to our revelations about waiting for permissions to leave the Soviet country and go to live in Israel, she smiled cheerily. "Well, because you are going to a different climate, I don't advise starting him on any regular food until you get there," she advised. "The moment you step on our God's land and feed him the perfect food of Israel, he'll be healthy. I hope you'll remember me then. Thanks for trusting me." She waved away the money for the visit.

Our clothing needed patching and cleaning, missing buttons affixed and broken zippers replaced. The old pots and silverware had to be shined before they could be packed. No use to start a new life with old worn stuff. I was chronically tired, my hands dry and red from all the washing; my back cramped from the bending. What if we wouldn't be permitted to emigrate?

I heard the rustle in my head. Sometimes, turning my head left or right—there it was—a quiet swish inside of it. When Gil fell asleep and I dared to settle on the sofa to doze, I easily heard its whispery nagging.

That sound reminded me of fabric tearing when Mama used to open up the seams of an old dress to recycle it for something new. The threads held strong; at times the material broke while the thread remained intact.

Mama, are you sending me a signal? You know my new life would be a good one, like the new dresses you used to fashion from the old ones.

The Soviet TV station brought news of the Zionist traitors who throughout their lives bled dry the Soviet state before abandoning it. The anticipated emigration of our family was the biggest secret yet. I didn't talk to any of my friends—I didn't even know if I still had any. With whom could I discuss our leaving? Who would listen to me and not run away in fright for their own lives? No one I knew.

Sergey's father came up with an idea for us to get a dog of a good breed in case we had any problems with making ends meet in our new life.

"I'm sure they could use a clever kind to watch their farms and factories. We'll bring a male puppy and find the same breed female and mate them. No expenses whatsoever, and then we sell puppies," he declared.

Sergey bought a Great Dane puppy and named him Alan. We were provided two lists: one of the dog's impressive pedigree and the second a mandatory list of foods to feed the dog: milk and fresh farmer cheese, beef and sea fish.

I read that second list in a state of astonishment. "Sergey, isn't it enough that Papa buys food for the two of us? I'm ashamed to meet his eyes already."

"Is there anything that doesn't require a long confrontation with you? David doesn't complain, yet you do at every step of the way. How much food does a puppy consume anyway?" I understood my husband's state of mind; he was the one responsible for his family's well-being and there were too many problems to overcome.

My papa didn't like dogs. Alan felt it and hid under the table the moment Papa walked into the apartment.

"Papa, please emigrate with us," I tried again. "I need you there even more than I do here."

"You have a husband now. Actually, I didn't think I would ever say it to my daughter but you have enough sense of your own. I trust you."

In July of 1972, the permission for the entire Kaplan family to leave the Soviet Union was granted. We were given two weeks to clear out.

The rustle in my head raised its voice to a scream. What kind of person am I—abandoning my father? Josef in all probability wouldn't be any part of our dad's life. They never saw eye-to-eye. Actually, where was Josef? With all the preparations and taking care of my baby, I didn't see much of my brother. He came to us once or twice, his face molded into grimace. I couldn't think of Josef's feelings and moods, I had to deal with those of my husband.

***

The day of the departure was a scorcher. I prepared a short cotton dress with tiny pink flowers; it seemed comfortable for a long, hot trip. I clung on to Gil—hoping the feel of that tiny body which depended on me for everything would fortify my strength. We sold his stroller along with all other sellable possession and I couldn't put him down even for a second. The eight-month-old infant tried to wriggle out of my clutches, and I held on.

The separate room we were brought to at the airport had no windows. The only furniture was a long wooden table set in the middle of it. The inspectors were going through the items in our four suitcases. Everything was spread out for observation and discussion. Alan was tied to the table's leg. He didn't mind staying in one place—the heat got to him too.

There were still hours before our plane left—plenty of time for sneering officials to intimidate us. In the overheated, airless room, my husband didn't wipe off his sweat anymore. He did the main work of opening and closing, showing and pointing, displaying and explaining. As part of the essential items to carry with us, he included his technical books, and each was leafed through and looked at in length. Our underwear and the socks and the toys were touched and turned and checked.

My head didn't stop buzzing, my heart didn't stop yanking. I stood by Sergey hugging cranky Gil yet tighter; we both were sweating rivulets.

Oh, Gil, hold Mama closer. Please save your mama.

"My baby's hungry. I have to nurse him." My announcement called for a conference among the officials and permission was given for me to step into the bathroom.

In the bathroom I realized that I wore a dress without a front opening. A small dirty room with only a sink and a toilet for its furniture didn't provide any surface to set my son down. I couldn't undress. I couldn't nurse him. Idiot me. I gave him a bottle with water and he emptied it at once.

The costume jewelry I dropped in between other things attracted our searchers. The two pairs of inexpensive silver earrings, not listed as valuables in the custom declaration, were fished out.

"Take it, just take it." At the moment I didn't care about the ornaments and nevertheless had to listen to a lecture on integrity.

"What would happen if everyone just picked up something silver or something gold and left with it?" The officers of the Soviet customs explained to me patiently that mines belonged to all Soviet people jointly.

This torture, too, came to an end. With a small group of other Kiev Jews we were allowed to proceed towards the plane. A baby, a dog—who tried to pull Sergey away from the plane—a bag with diapers and water bottles, a briefcase with documents, were all the things we needed to exit the old life.

Head, oh my head, shut up your sounds, I can't deal with them!

The heat was blistering. The corridor, formed out of border soldiers with their dogs, opened up to let us, the rebels, through and immediately closed behind us.

My tired brain certified the barking dogs wearing the green soldiers' uniforms. I couldn't separate one from the other. Gil felt heavier; I gripped him tighter. Step, step, another one, step…

Don't think—walk. Don't stop—walk.

Then I turned around and saw my father for the last time. Would Josef take care of him? Who would love me?

CHAPTER 8

Nazareth, Israel

1972

The sense of belonging at last,

of being in a proper setting,

seemed to soothe her troubled spirit -

for once she was not fighting the world,

but was a part of it.

Moss Hart "Act One"

It was summer of 1972. Sergey and I with almost eight-month-old Gil, and also Sergey's parents, landed in Israel. I didn't expect much of anything. What was Israel? The country of freaks no one wanted? The country of geniuses that looked down on everyone—and it didn't matter, because they were hated anyway?

Most of our household belongings, in huge wooden crates, went from Kiev to Italy and further on to Israel by sea. We were told they would arrive in a few months. Our hand luggage consisted of four yellow suitcases, mostly Gil's diapers, coarse squares of cut white sheets, some bedding, including pillows and blankets, a few summer clothes, a couple toys and books, toiletries—not much really. Our imported suitcases couldn't expand; they were hard and flat.

On arrival at the Lod airport in Tel Aviv, the heads of the households were asked to fill out some forms. The rest of us, mostly women and children, waited. It was hot and stuffy inside the terminal. A few overworked fans didn't help much. Holding Gil in my arms, I stood guard at the luggage area, waiting for a pet carrier with Alan.

Our terrified Alan, his head down, tail down, and legs shaky, was delivered to me. Soon my husband returned with the assignment. Our family would go through the absorption process in a center for the newcomers in Nazareth.

My in-laws proceeded to a town called Kiryat Tivon. Both places were in the northern part of Israel, an hour or so away from each other.

A slim girl of about nineteen, in a soldier's uniform, led me clutching Gil in my arms, and Sergey, holding Alan our Great Dane on his leash, out from the terminal. Hot! I'd hoped to find relief from the airport's sweltering heat. Forget it. Never before had I stood directly under the blazing sun. The girl pointed to a car with a driver waiting. It was even hotter inside of that car. I sat Gil down by me in the back seat. If only I could get rid of my dress that had sweat-glued to my body and get washed...

First we were riding through the city streets when I noticed a few stores—at least, they seemed like stores, yet they had cars inside of their windows. Cars on display? How did cars get inside the windows, and why did they have to be displayed if everyone knew what cars looked like? Back in Kiev in order to buy a car, even if you were able to scrape enough money for one, you needed to sign up on some list and wait and wait, maybe for a few years, for your turn to come.

"Did you notice, it's not as hot anymore? We're going north," Sergey said, patting pitiful, loudly-panting Alan.

Enchanted with the scenery, I didn't notice the weather any longer. Since we had left the city, the green hills lolled as far as the eye could see, rocks in between the trees, and red flowers in between the rocks. It seemed too perfect to be real. Was I on a movie set where the landscape had been built per the director's orders?

Exhausted Gil slept leaning on my left shoulder. I moved him to my right side, and the view on the left of the road opened up.

Blue sea—clear blue, not a speckle of any interfering color—stretching into a sky of the very same color.

"Sergey, it's awesome." I had to share the wonderment that came over me. "Did someone arrange it? Was it here before, like in the previous century?"

"You know Jews, they come up with things. I am sure we'll learn the history of every tree and rock pretty soon." Sergey, too, looked from side to side, as excited as I was.

An overwhelming number of Soviet Jews were highly educated professionals: engineers, doctors, scientists, and other professions. When the mass immigration from the Soviet Union started, the absorption centers were built to teach them the language and the ways of the new country before they could start their productive lives.

We arrived at the Nazareth *Mercas Klita (*absorption center.) Our yellow suitcases were unloaded on the paved plaza. People surrounded us. The Russian language greeted us from everywhere.

"Hello. How are you? What city are you from?"

"You'll like it here, you and your baby," encouraged a young, tall, bespectacled woman on my left.

A loud whiny voice rose up behind me: "What's to like? Everything is in Hebrew. All my life I listened to my parents speaking Yiddish and thought it was Jewish. Now I come here and Yiddish isn't good enough—learn Hebrew. I'm not a child to fit my ass in the classroom chair."

How many opinions did we have to listen to before we even entered our apartment?

Inside the apartment I undressed, then undressed Gil, and proceeded to nurse him. I still fed him my breast milk because he'd had problems with his stomach since birth, and to continue with the breast milk seemed the best solution. Though, more and more I was worried that my milk didn't provide enough nourishment to my child; he still wasn't able to sit by himself. I didn't know whom to ask.

"Sergey, it would make sense if you could please walk Alan before anything else. I'll unpack after I finish with Gil. We all need some clean clothes to change into. See if there's food available to bring in here. If not, I'm ready to starve. I'm not moving another step."

It was nice there, really and truly. Never before had I lived in an apartment where the living room, bedroom, kitchen, and even a bathroom with shower, belonged to one family only— my family. In the bedroom there was a double bed for us and a crib for Gil. The drawers for our clothes stood there as well. The living room had a sofa and an armchair. The corner place served as a dining area with the table and chairs. Our kitchen owned everything needed for cooking.

In the morning, before we went to breakfast, I nursed my eight-month-old child, thinking once again that it was time to wean him.

After breakfast I carried Gil to the nursery while Sergey walked to the office to ask some organizational questions. The offices along with the Hebrew school and the dining hall were located in the administrative building. The nursery school and kindergarten were closer, on the way between the apartments and Hebrew school.

In the bright and airy nursery room, Gil started to holler the moment I lowered him into a playpen. What was I supposed to do now?

A nursery worker dressed in a pair of tight jeans and a cheerful yellow t-shirt walked over to us, said something in Hebrew, took Gil out of my arms and placed him back into the playpen. There he immediately fell on his back, next to another baby boy, screaming wildly.

Still speaking, the girl turned me towards the exit, waving goodbye. Her smile, showing small white teeth, didn't disappear through the whole experience.

I stood outside, by the nursery's window, and listened to Gil wailing. My tears, tied to the sound of Gil's cry, emerged at once, but I knew better than to return.

Sergey waited at the entrance to the classroom. I wanted to explain my teary face but didn't get a chance. He had news of his own.

"Lilli, they suggested we call a *kibbutz* that will take care of Alan while we're living at the center. I agreed because it would be tough for us to keep him here."

Back in Kiev I had begged Sergey to reconsider buying a dog. So what if his father thought it was a clever idea? My papa David had kept us in groceries for months since Sergey lost his job. The special diet for the Great Dane puppy cost a small fortune.

I still smelled the puppy's pee on my fingers. A third-floor communal apartment wasn't suited for housebreaking a dog. I wiped his puddles and hung smelly rags outside our window on the nail by the flower-box.

I didn't want to part with Alan. He, too, was our baby and knew only us as his parents. I stared at my husband. We were almost the same height. My eyes were almost level with his. I wordlessly agreed.

The kibbutz sounded like the right idea. I should've said so to Sergey.

***

Inside the classroom we all were students of Hebrew. We were of different ages. We came from different countries. We spoke different languages. We were called "*Olim Hodashim*," which meant "new people who came up." Israel, as God's country, was up there high, and now we joined others who lived here already.

"*Shulchan*," our petite teacher, Irit, pronounced clearly, pointing to a table. We learned the Hebrew word for a table. The eighteen-year-old soldier tucked her yellow hay-like strands of hair flying in all directions into a rubber band.

"She couldn't be Jewish with those clear-sky eyes, tinkling laugh, dancing walk," the Russian whisper traveled lightning-like through the class.

"With that tiny nose sticking up?" added some other doubtful person.

"KGB transported her from a Siberian *kolkhoz* to spy on us." That wisdom brought on loud laughter amid those who understood the Russian language.

To those who didn't, the joke was explained later on, outside the classroom. One word of Yiddish or two of English, maybe some elementary-school French or Spanish, allowed us all, Jews previously thrown all over the planet, to be at home together.

That's how we all learned. It didn't matter if outside of the class the name of the object was "table" in English or *stol* in Russian, now it became *shulchan* for all of us in the class. Every learned word was precious. Every new sound meant freedom of expressing what was on one's mind while being understood by all others.

I felt at ease. I carried the tension within me and it vanished. I realized that for close to twenty-five years living in the Soviet Union, I'd held my breath in, always thinking what if someone insulted Jews, should I leave or explain that I was "a good Jew?" If I dyed my hair blond, would I look less Jewish?

Here I was a human and that was it. That was my new tag—representative of a human race. Heady stuff!

"My dear children, the waves of hatred are upon us. The government presented a bunch of famous 'token' Jews on TV who described their 'perfect' life in the Soviet land. The very next day the newspaper articles were urging the bandits on: 'Why are we so lenient towards the parasites whom we generously gave refuge?' Thank God you are not here!"

That was the latest letter from my papa.

Many nights the same dream woke me up: the crowd of my relatives and other Kiev Jews huddled at the center of the enormous square, surrounded by the chain and the border soldiers and the militiamen, I with Sergey and Gil stood on the outside of that gathering.

I heard shouts: "Lilli, get us out. Lilli, don't you want us to survive?"

Why did I feel guilty? They could leave there, like we and many others did. They were afraid of the unknown. I was not responsible for their lives. Why did it feel like I was?

Sometimes, walking through the absorption center grounds, I passed an angry group of Russian Jews and heard, "What do those Israelis think, they outsmarted us? Others tried through the centuries and lost. They want us here so our boys will fight their wars. We didn't bring our children here to be meat for the Arab tanks."

It pained me greatly. It horrified me. Who were "they" and who were "we?" Weren't we, too, Israelis now? If the war were to start, all our children would fight to protect our common land.

While we, the Soviet Jews, lived our lives in the various cities of the big Soviet state, laboring in its every industry, discovering new chemicals and opening new chapters in physics and mathematics, defending that place in the wars, singing its patriotic songs and waving its red flags, we never were accepted as equals by those around us.

But this tiny country in the desert had proclaimed all of us, the Jews, their citizens since the day it was established. Its people were dying, fighting with the numerous enemies so we'd have this place to come to.

The Soviet society of takers, not givers, brought up those emotionally deprived people I overheard, to my sorrow, during my walks through the absorption center. For the first time in their lives they had stopped being someone's bastards and became dearest children. But they didn't see it; they didn't feel it in their bones.

Who asked us to come? We were running from hell. Yes, the hell became cozy, a habit. We warmed it up with our own body heat. So what? Often enough, we were reminded of being guests in that stinking inferno, not welcomed ones at that.

By immigrating, we had done something drastic, daring, and difficult, and we did it against all odds and against all forces. We moved to the place where we belonged.

Were those people just scared? Is that why they whimpered and moaned and wailed? In the fifty-five years of Soviet involvement in the souls of those people, they forgot to think for themselves. Why bother when some bureaucrat in some office did it for them and even for free. Maybe it was too late for them—they couldn't appreciate the freedom. They had no idea how to handle it.

Luckily, I had too many things to occupy my days to listen to them all.

One day our neighbor, Oleg, approached us in the dining hall: "Listen, Kaplans, we plan to go on an outing later tonight. Are you coming?"

Sergey and I exchanged a sorry look. "Sorry, we wish we could. Maybe the next time," I answered.

At nine months, Gil still wouldn't walk. He wasn't interested in learning; used to being carried in his parents' arms. It limited our movements, because he was a heavy bundle to bring on the long hikes. And we didn't own a stroller for him. Sold it along with my mama's china, most of our clothes, Gil's carriage and crib, books—everything that found itself a buyer. It was an expensive enterprise to leave the Soviet Union.

"Walk, baby. Walk to Mama," I would beseech Gil, who stood motionless, gazing at me with his intense brown eyes, dimpled arm holding a chair or a table's leg.

Then, "*lo*," his voice adamant—the Hebrew word coming from the mouth of my baby! He himself decided what he would or wouldn't do. The curly-haired head turned from side to side, underscoring his "no."

The plaza in front of the administrative building became a village meeting hall. After dinner, people stood there in groups talking animatedly. Just days, weeks, months in the new country and they were hotly discussing its politics, traditions, and sports news with the understanding of countrymen.

I loved to watch my husband at those improvised meetings. He had a gift of engaging people. They listened to his opinions, respected his knowledge. *He's mine*, I wanted to yell.

One afternoon, we had just finished dinner and were standing outside; I beside Sergey, who held Gil. A large group of friends joined us. Sergey started his usual world history lecture, while I turned my back to him, speaking to my girlfriends.

"Could you believe," I admitted to them, "in Kiev I was the most fashionable of all my friends. I'm an absolute hick now. Before we left there, some well-wisher wrote to us: 'Bring cotton dresses, because it's very hot in Israel.' I sold all my modern clothes and brought only a few shirtwaists along. I didn't think about how heavy Russian cotton fabric was and how long it took to dry it after the wash. Now, I'm sick just looking at the same few dresses day in and day out."

Suddenly, behind me a hair-raising sound—the shriek of a child, my child. I spun around but didn't see my Gil. What I did see didn't make any sense: everyone standing mime-like, bent under different odd angles, their arms stretched in front of them. There were maybe fifteen or more of them. Inside the strange group, like a hero on the stage, was Sergey in half-turn. His face was dark red and the veins on his neck were swollen.

Then another scream, that of multiple voices at once. And then a loud sigh of relief from all of them, at once, again.

I didn't move, because I was afraid. Where was Gil? I wished to shut my eyes and not look, because I was afraid.

Only then, I saw him in his father's arms and he was crying, but laughing at the same time, because everyone around him was laughing. Their laugh was hysterical. People who went through trauma needed release—they laughed.

Sergey told me what happened. He forgot some paper on the table in the dining room and wanted to go back to retrieve it. Believing I was still beside him, he half turned and stretched out his arms holding Gil, saying, "Take him, I'll be back in a second." But I wasn't there, didn't hear him, didn't see his outstretched arms holding our baby. At the same moment as he let go of Gil, he realized he didn't see me taking him, and he tried to reach him back, grabbing the only part he found—the leg. It turned the little boy upside down—the small, brown-curly head was an inch away from the concrete.

It was the next moment when I heard the shriek and the unexplainable picture. Many arms were propelled to grab that precious head and held on to the small feet and the arms and the body.

We were wondering later if there really were so many people in that bunch, or if it only looked like that?

"We were taught that there was no God, but I wonder now," I mused that night, after our little son was sleeping in his crib.

And Sergey answered, "There're a lot of good people around. Maybe they do God's work?"

To buy a stroller, we needed money. Fellow Soviet emigrants were suggesting that Russian linens sell well at the market in the Arab part of the town. We waited for our baggage to arrive, hoping there were some things there we could sell. Then maybe to buy, if not a stroller, at least a pair of shoes, so we could teach Gil to walk on the pavement.

Except, the next day after the plaza incident, a young woman from Argentina, whose son played with Gil at the nursery school, brought two pairs of baby shoes to the class and handed them to me. She noticed Gil never wore any shoes and guessed he had none.

***

The July heat was warm but not oppressive. The red flowers in between rocks were unexpected. The sky was the lightest blue all day and the darkest when night came with legions of reachable stars.

There were more great people than bores around and I loved to listen to them, to share laughs and hopes with them. I felt that the people around us, our family included, were rapidly undergoing metamorphosis to accommodate the place where we lived.

"I don't care if Israelis mispronounce my name," said a sixteen-year-old girl, who at her young age had already had plenty of chances to pay a heavy price for being Jewish in the USSR. "My name is Jewish. I am Jewish. They are Jewish. No one is trying to insult me."

I loved her opinion.

I cried listening to the old man, who was a Red commissar in the revolution of 1917 and a war hero in 1942. He grieved: "How could I explain to someone who didn't live where we lived how belittling it was to stand in line for a loaf of bread, only to be told after an hour wait that they were out of it?"

I imagined my papa standing in the long line to get a loaf of bread. He wasn't upset if they were out. Why bother being upset on account of a regular occurrence? That was why my papa didn't come to Israel with us, but rather stayed in the familiar swamp. He knew how to survive in it.

***

"Guys, check this…" I burst into the dining hall holding a newspaper printed in Russian, impatient to share the best news with all who sat there. "Two mothers from different parts of the country gave birth to triplets. The same day! From only two births we have six Israelis. Hooray!" I felt like those mothers were my sisters. I wanted to go and visit them. I felt love for their babies.

That news was on top of my next weekly letter. I couldn't wait to share my joy with Papa:

> *"Dearest Papa, why do I feel exhilarated on account of those babies? I feel I am part of those happy families. You could say: 'Mazal Tov!' to me. I accept congratulations on behalf of the parents."*

I didn't know if all my letters were delivered through the iron-fisted Soviet censorship, but if they were, my papa used them well, reading and rereading to all who weren't afraid to listen. Was Josef among them?

The letter I soon received from Papa David answered my silent question. And that answer was worse than I ever imagined:

"Dear children, I read Lilli's letters in which she sounded happy and worry- free. I hope her seemingly positive words were true and not her tries to calm my nerves. The relatives and the good acquaintances I let read those letters were thinking maybe there was someone else there in charge of her correspondence. Not me, dear Lilli. I believe your letters are as truthful as you wish your life to be, even if for now you are struggling. Lilli, you keep asking of Josef ... I didn't want to upset you, but ... I'll rather you learn it from me. Your brother was fired. Right after you left here. They called him in and confronted: 'Your sister is a traitor to our motherland.' They told him they knew, of course, of your plans to emigrate but expected him to come clean and publicly denounce you. He didn't. Don't worry. These are not the old times when they sent you to the gulag camps for something like that. Those who fired him, told him, on the sly, they envy you and surprised he didn't follow you as yet. Still, they had to do it. Josef is mad at you, even after I explained you didn't list him as a relative in any documents. Like it makes any difference. They know what each one of us does and who is related to whom and what we eat for breakfast. Josef still steams, but he found another job. They won't starve."

***

The year was 1972—the year of the Munich Olympics.

We were glued to the news. Our Hebrew class discussed this event in all possible details, in Hebrew of course. Little Irit, our soldier-teacher, explained that the athletes who went to the Games were using their own money to train. They were trying hard to be ready, but they couldn't compete with the state-sponsored sportsmen like the Russian athletes.

One of our former Soviet citizens, a heavy-built, middle-aged man, raised his hand. We knew his story, but others and Irit didn't. His words dropped like stones: "I was a champion wrestler in my younger years," he started. "My achievements were impressive for everyone in this sport, yet I've never been allowed to fight outside of the country. Every time my Jewish name appeared on a contenders list, it was crossed out by someone above.

"One day they suggested I quit—I was too old. They threw me a going-away party and presented me with a watch. Even allowed me to stay at the club to be a supply manager. I thanked them and accepted. My family needed my salary to live on.

"You are saying the Israeli boys don't have the money. Don't you worry. Since the Russians started to come—the boys will have plenty of the best trainers in the world."

We all knew similar stories. They were filed inside of our minds like something to cope with, like everything else we couldn't change.

I wrote in one of my letters:

Papa, keep your fingers crossed for the sons of Israel. For me, they are winners already. They went ahead to announce to the entire people's community that they were Jewish, and are competing as equals to the rest of them. It's not the first time for Israel, except for me it's a first.

The early morning of September 5, 1972.

"The Palestinian gunmen broke into the Olympic village where the Israeli sportsmen slept. Our boys are dead," the announcer said, sobbing. "The best of the best, the strongest of the strongest. Our pride and hope, our present and future. Could we ever trust anyone to save us? Should we ever trust anyone to protect us?"

We witnessed the heartbreaking history from inside the involved nation. The Games continued. The world went on ignoring the Jews as usual. Nobody cared—we wanted to scream. To scream at whom, if no one listened?

It became motionless in our land. Our family was in mourning. The small family lost eleven sons. When the caskets were lowered from the plane and put on the cars and driven to the cities, the silence endured. The silence of the people who knew tragedy well, yet vowed as before: "Never again."

We, the younger generation of the *Olim Chodashim*, weren't yet battle-hardened Israelis, or like the older Soviets who went through the big war. We didn't know how to go on after a tragedy of such proportion. Reluctant to continue our studies or any other daily activities, we huddled in the plaza listening to a radio.

Sergey itched to get involved, so he wrote an open letter to the *Knesset,* daring them to threaten the world with grave consequences. The entire absorption center signed it. I thought my husband felt some slight relief by saying his piece.

Our small children didn't understand why their adults wouldn't play and laugh. Then days passed and ongoing life called for our attention, and then we started to smile, slowly learning to go along. Like in any other Israeli family, after the mourning period, life in our Kaplan family continued. Hebrew became a personal friend, friends became close relatives. Who were those people to me?

Through the years in the Soviet Union, I made friends easily, even though with my closest Russian and Ukrainian friends there existed an invisible barrier. Most of them were too prejudiced or maybe too timid to step over. And I wouldn't dare.

I crossed that barrier when I left them all in the land where I was born and remained a stranger. Now I had obtained a whole new set of *my* people—a whole country of them.

Maybe there was a God, even though I never believed in his existence, and he wanted us to be here at home, in His land.

CHAPTER 10

Nazareth, Israel

1972-1973

"Today two more guys got rejected when applying for engineering positions," Sergey declared when he walked into the dining hall after I was inside already, and even before reaching our table. The panic in his voice was obvious. He scraped his chair away from the table, sat down, then moved it back with the same bang. My husband was upset and purposely started conversations with hordes of people inside eating. At the moment, everyone around ceased their movements to listen.

"What are you so upset about? Even if a few guys didn't get that great job at their first try. They will get it on a second. And *you* will get a job. I know you will. You didn't even start looking yet. So we stay a little longer here and your Hebrew will improve…"

"You don't know what you're talking about." He stomped out, not finishing his meal.

Later at the plaza, my girlfriends wanted me to understand Sergey's point of view.

"You didn't want to come to Israel. He insisted and now feels responsible," they said in one voice, explaining what they thought were Sergey's thoughts. "He is worried he won't be able to provide for you and Gil."

"We've been married for two years. Did he ever try to communicate any of his intentions to me before he presented them as decisions? Here is the problem in our family the way I see it: we both understand Sergey's difficulties. Only one of us is aware of mine."

I found Sergey in our apartment with all the blinds pulled down, keeping out the blistering sun.

"Do you realize how small Israel is and how few mechanical engineers its manufacturing plants can employ?" His voice was tense, expectant of my negative reaction. "Loads of people, mostly from the USSR, are coming daily. From our own circle of friends, sixty-five percent or more are engineers. Isn't it true?"

I stood by the door, my hands clasped behind my back, waiting for the punchline.

Sergey continued, "It could take months for me to find more or less passable work. You don't have a profession and, anyway, Gil is too young to be left full-time at a daycare. How long do you think the *Mercas Klita* will keep us living here, accumulating debts?"

"Any suggestions?" I asked, knowing there were.

"I've decided to sign up with ZIM, the shipping company. I heard they hire engineers to work as the mechanics on their cargo ships."

His words knocked me down. I sat on the nearest chair.

"When did you decide this? Why not try to find a normal job first? How could you leave the baby and me here without any money? Who gave you this 'brilliant' idea? Does that person know you have a wife and son?

By the way, does this same person realize that you're terrified of water and can't swim?"

"What difference does it make? If the ship is down, everyone will drown anyway. You always think the worst! Mom's neighbors' son works on the cargo ship and makes good money. He buys great clothes for all the family from whatever European cities they go to. It's much cheaper over there."

"Your mother? I should have guessed. She still tells you what to do. She possesses you like her furniture or china. What does she know about working on a ship besides the fact that they buy clothes in Europe? I can't believe this worthless fact will decide our future and leave me and Gil alone."

The fight was lost before it started. Now anything I said would be an affront to his mother. I could never contradict anything this woman said. She'd start listing all the unfairness life ever dished out in her direction and out of overwhelming pity her son would do whatever she asked of him.

Sergey started his seaman duty, and Gil and I stayed on.

***

Papa, if my previous letter sounded slightly moody, please ignore it. Our staying in the absorption center is a good thing. Our meals and rent are paid for (it's all going on our bill to be paid in the future,) and I don't have to worry about the money situation for a bit longer.

The Israeli autumn appeared unnoticeably. The clouds took over the clean blueness of the sky, filling it up with ceaseless rain.

Neither my baby nor I owned any warm clothes, so mostly we stayed inside. Most of the old occupants left *Mercas Klita,* moving to different parts of the country, following their jobs or families. To make new friends seemed bothersome and pointless. I felt like an overgrown third grader left over in second grade. *Ulpan* didn't provide the follow-up level of Hebrew classes and I didn't feel like repeating the beginner one.

I played with Gil and composed letters to Papa David, not knowing which ones would reach him and which would be opened and discarded by the government screeners.

Papa, how are you? Do you take care of yourself? I still hope one day you'll change your mind and join us here. You'd not be lonely and dependent on me, like you fear; there're plenty of men your age who work and are involved in life and get married. I'd like to prove I could be a much better daughter to you. Is it selfish of me to wish you close by?

If you ever talk to Josef, don't rush into any judgments of him. That's what you mostly do. Then the arguments start. You need each other.

They say sensitive children easily pick up on their parents' misery. Gil refused to leave my side. He wouldn't stay at the nursery, refusing to eat there. Once again, he declined to walk, and I carried him, heavy at one year, seating him on my hip, the way Israeli mothers did.

Early one morning, my child woke me from a heavy dream: "Mommy, mommy, my tummy hurts. Fix it," he cried.

But I was in my dream running away from my mother-in-law. And though she was the foe in many of my dreams, this dream was the strangest yet.

I dreamed I was a fighter in the Russian underground during the war with the Germans. Sergey's mother found out about my involvement and swore to interfere. I heard her voice clearly proclaiming, "Not on my life," and "Over my dead body."

It was a life-or-death situation. First I tried to convince her to let me be and as a last resort was speeding away. I watched my own legs moving like they were someone else's and begged them to move faster.

Hearing Gil's cry, I felt disoriented and shouted: "Mama, I'm coming. I'll help you."

My reaction had nothing to do with either the dream or reality. It skipped back through the period of seven years into the many nights when my mama cried, trying not to surrender to pain.

Out of my bed, with my eyes open, I spotted the smooth stone Israeli floor and the standard *Mercas Klita's* furniture.

Now I was the mother and my baby needed me.

Gil felt hot; sweat soaked his pajamas, gluing it tightly to his slight body. The sheets smelled of urine. I pressed him to my chest, kissing his burning face, hoping to calm us both. I needed medication for his fever. I should find someone who had children and knew what to do. Last time I tried to give him pills, he vomited them out.

Listening to Gil's constant whimpering, I washed up and dressed, then distracted him by parting with my beloved straw bag, which he proceeded to take apart straw by straw.

I knocked at every door in our building but no one answered. Were the people having breakfast in the dining hall or still sleeping?

I needed help now.

The outside was rainy and gloomy.

Trying to get back to Gil as soon as I could, I ran all the way to the administrative building. At the entrance to the building I tripped on the slippery step and started to cry.

I sat on the wet step for a few seconds to collect my strength, when a man walked out from the building and stopped by me.

"Lilli, what happened?"

His name was Leo and he was fairly new at the *Mercas Klita*. Sergey had spoken with him a few times and reported back that the man was a doctor and lots of fun. I didn't appreciate his perfectly groomed looks and the slow, visibly-admiring-his-own-words manner of speaking. Leo arrived in Israel with his wife, their little boy, and his elderly parents, who usually watched both the wife and the child while Leo pranced around paying attention to pretty women.

"Leo, hopefully, you can help me." I explained what had happened and the doctor responded immediately by returning home to get his doctor's bag. I ran back to Gil.

Leo was kind and professional. "It's just a flu. I have medications. I don't travel without all the stuff I need for my own kid. I'll give him some now, and later I'll stop by again. Don't worry, Lilli." He patted my hand.

I was disappointed in myself for my previous negative feelings towards Leo. In a much better state of mind, I went out again and brought a breakfast from the dining hall for Gil and me.

It was close to ten at night when I locked up the door and switched off the lights. After spending all day with my sick child, I felt grubby. After undressing and leaving my clothes in the bedroom, I walked to the bathroom, turned on the water in the tub. I was so tired. The warm water felt relaxing. I closed my eyes and drifted slowly to sleep in the tub.

Suddenly I was aware of someone inside the apartment. I didn't dream up the softest, almost whispery steps coming from the living room. *Who was there?* The answer came before I voiced the question.

"It's only me, don't be alarmed." The Russian words reached me through my terror, not pacifying it at all.

The dread was rising in my throat. I didn't scream. In the next room my exhausted child slept fitfully after a day of fever and pain.

Stepping out from the tub, I grabbed the only cover I could find in the bathroom—the towel. To get to my clothes, I'd have to cross the living room.

Leo was sitting in the chair by the dining table. His lazy smile and fingers opening the buttons of his shirt one by one illustrated his intentions.

"I knew you'd be waiting." His eyes gloated over my wet body under the bath towel, the eyes of a predator salivating on seeing his food ready for consumption. "But my family … it takes time to settle them all for the night," he explained as languidly as he usually spoke about everything else.

My clenched dead-person's fingers held tight onto the towel. It wasn't big enough to cover most of my soapy, dripping body.

"Leave at once," I hushed, as serenely as I could under the circumstance. "Leave before I scream."

"Why scream if not in ecstasy? You haven't had a man in your bed for a month now. You need me. Don't forget, I am a doctor." His words were drenched in desire. I realized that so was my body. I detested the man, but my body didn't know that. It ached with its own need, like some primal independent organism inside of me.

Help me, please, somebody, I begged voicelessly, collecting sensibilities around my wetness.

My next words I spoke audibly: "If I decide to use a man to help my needing body, at least it will be someone I like." I spoke just above a whisper. Just a step away from me, the man in the chair stopped smiling and unbuttoning and leaned closer to hear.

I continued: "Or are we talking rape?"

On the outside, I was getting bolder.

On the inside, the images, forcibly hidden for many years, never talked about, never admitted to myself, were shaking my soul. The whitest meanest snow of my life deepened under my feet. I was back in Russia flat on my back, pristine cover under me, and someone unknown and heavy on top of me.

The sleepy sob of my child brought me back.

Thankfully, the man could see only the outside. He stood up. A rapist he wasn't. He was big and burly and at this moment very much dejected. The bulge in his pants was still there—I hadn't missed the extension since the very beginning of our encounter—except the bulge of his ego had evaporated. He became all business and worry.

"I guess I misunderstood you, Lilli. Sorry for that. Will you tell Sergey or my wife?"

"I don't know. Right now, I don't know. By the way, how did you get inside the apartment?"

Leo pointed at the key lying on the dining table. "I took it earlier when giving the pill to your little boy."

"A doctor administering to the sick … the joke is on me—I felt such relief when meeting you today. Leave at once."

Why would I tell his wife? Sergey should know, because it made me sick when he admired the "good" doctor. No, he wouldn't believe I didn't encourage the man. A few times I repeated the rumors about "the good doctor" being a real sleaze, he shrugged and muttered something like, "Women and their devotion to gossips."

***

Sergey loved his job on the ship. He liked to explain to whoever was at the plaza: "Machines are machines. It doesn't matter if they are inside the ship or the machine shop. I know machines and the crew respects my expertise."

On his return after a month, my husband, holding little Gil, once again presided in the center of a small crowd in front of the administrative building. If before he supplied his opinions of history and politics, now he relived adventures from the foreign ports. For citizens who, until recently, lived the lock-and-key existence of the Soviet Union, it sounded fairytale-like.

Did the sea get stormy, Sergey's listeners wondered.

"Nobody enjoys having his stomach inside out. And I'm no different from the rest of the guys," Sergey responded with a prideful smile.

I wrote to my father:

Papa, it's so great to listen to Sergey's pride in himself. I was wrong not wanting him to take this job.

I continued sharing our life news with my father, who hungered for it. I didn't have any news of mine to share. Like before, I watched Sergey from the sidelines, but the bitterness wouldn't leave. I didn't begrudge my husband his joy but wanted to have some of my own.

Sergey's shipmates knew the stores in the ports where the ZIM ships made their stops. They taught him to bargain in Italian and French. With his small beginner's salary, he bought us some warm sweaters and coats.

The new clothes, though badly needed, didn't bring much enjoyment to me. We could've bought all of it in Israel, too, if he'd found a job on land.

"Papa, what am I to do?" I started my letter after Sergey left again. Then stopped and tore the page.

Our family occupied the apartment in the *Mercas Klita* the longest. I guessed that each time our case came up, social workers remembered that the head of the Kaplan household wasn't available to move his family out.

My husband was at sea. I was on land.

My mind made up, I walked into the main office with its typical Israeli hubbub and said, “If there is an apartment available, we would like to move out. Hopefully in Haifa, because the port is in Haifa and the ZIM offices are there too.”

There was an apartment. A temporary one. Its owners were living and working in Europe, renting it out for the time being. I didn’t care to look at it.

“I’m sure it’s perfect. At Sergey’s next leave, we’ll move. Thanks for everything.”

CHAPTER 11

Romema
Haifa, Israel

1973

The crates with our Kiev household items were delivered from the port in Haifa to the high-rise building in the Romema neighborhood on the day Sergey's ship returned from England. Standing on the sidewalk, I held little Gil and watched over our worldly possessions while Sergey borrowed some tools and forced the tops of the boxes off.

What were we thinking when we'd packed? Why did I need Mama's chipped china or the fragile German balls we used to decorate evergreens for the New Year celebrations? I noticed my tennis racket. I never learned to play tennis when I was a young girl. Did I imagine having the time or money to learn it here, now?

Thankfully we left the furniture for Papa. He wouldn't have objected if we packed the entire apartment in those boxes.

I took Gil upstairs and left him inside his crib. Sergey needed my help in bringing everything up to the apartment.

"*Shalom*," a man said at the entrance to our building. He was tall, broad-shouldered, wore glasses, and pronounced the Hebrew greeting with an unmistakable Russian accent. "I'm Simon. Let me help," he continued in Russian, picking up the end of the sewing cabinet, easing Sergey's load.

"My mom used to have the exact same machine, but we didn't bring it over," Simon said.

"How come? Did your mom stay back in the Soviet Union?" I asked.

"No way—my mama was the one to force our whole family to leave there at the first chance. Though she knew she was dying, knew the cancer wouldn't allow her even one tiny step on this land, it didn't matter. 'They don't deserve my dead Jewish body,' she said. 'I'm going home to Israel to die.'"

I'm going home to Israel. *I'm going home to Israel.* It sounded like the mantra worth remembering forever.

"Simon, stop in later for a cup of coffee. Please, bring your family to meet us?" I asked.

Simon and his wife Sonia knocked at our door that same evening.

Sonia was the picture of perfection—slim, waist-long reddish hair, wide hazel eyes. She walked in holding a sleeping infant girl, named Mira, wrapped in a lace coverlet.

Little Mira was born just days before they boarded the plane bringing them out of Soviet Latvia. That's how they arrived—carrying their dying mother on a stretcher and their newborn daughter in their arms.

That evening, Sergey and I discovered two kind-hearted, like-minded people we didn't ever want to part with. We settled Gil and Mira to sleep and thanked our lucky stars—those babies would grow up Israelis and not unwanted Jews in the hateful land.

Sergey entertained us with his travel stories, many of which I heard for the first time.

"Where is your ship going for its next tour?" Simon asked.

"Actually, I quit my seamen job." Sergey's admission was so sudden that at first I thought he was joking. I stared at my husband, not knowing whether to laugh or to applaud or to get upset that he hadn't mentioned his news when we were alone. What were we going to do for money?

I came up with a plan of taking in alternations when Sonia asked if I could slim up a few things she wore while pregnant with Mira.

"Sure I can. Actually, I'm good at fixing up old clothes," I boasted, and the idea was born. Why not earn some money by doing it?

In a matter of days, I wrote and distributed leaflets advertising my services throughout our Romema neighborhood. The women were quick to check me out. Though couldn't charge "real" money for some old dress to be let out or taken in.

I liked how Israeli women dressed. Mostly halters and jeans. Or t-shirts and short-short skirts. It accommodated weather and was fun to look at. They were so beautiful and full of life.

I worked cautiously, longer and longer hours, trying to compensate for my inexperience. The women, sensing my timidity, flagrantly haggled down the lowest of prices.

Once, Felix, the neighbor across the hall, overheard the bargaining going on in our doorway.

"*Geveret*," he cut in through the barrage of words. "Lilli just started out. If you like the work, pay, and if you don't, take this elevator down and don't come back."

To my astonishment, the woman paid the asking price and returned the next day with more clothes needing alterations.

Two months passed with me laboring in our enclosed balcony at my sewing machine, and it still didn't look like my business would pay off. Gil stayed at home with me. Seeing that my work wouldn't provide any worthwhile income, I decided to look for a job outside of the house, checking the ads for retail or factory work. Inevitably, when I tried to get my child to stay with a babysitter in one of the neighboring playgroups, he cried and remained by the door waiting for me.

My husband got into an argument with a ship captain and decided that he had to look into jobs on the land. Luckily, pretty fast he found a job as an engineer-designer in a metal production shop.

"I'm worried about that loan-shark person from whom we were stupid enough to borrow money from back in Kiev. I can't forget he took your fingerprints and threatened to find you anywhere if you're not going to pay him back. He is a scary guy. With you working now, let's start repaying him, at once," I suggested.

"Lilli, grow up! Back then we couldn't figure out any other way to pay for the plane tickets and those crates to be shipped and to the authorities for allowing us not to be Soviet citizens anymore. The man is a crook, charging us a fortune in interest. We'll repay his money of course. But now I need a car to get to work every morning. I work, but I waste time on commuting, it takes two buses and they are never on time. It wastes my time and energy."

"A car? Sergey, have you gone mad? Since when did a car become a primary necessity? First you pay your debts, and later you think of your life conveniences."

Sergey continued like he didn't hear or see my astonishment: "I heard Ilya from downstairs is selling his Audi. It's in a great shape, almost new. Maybe we could arrange some kind of payments."

"I can't believe you'd even consider another loan. Anyway, Ilya's family is leaving for America. He wants the money now."

We'd heard of more and more of our former compatriots using Israel as a convenient bridge leading to other countries. They, who were persecuted throughout their life for that quirk of nature of being born to Jewish parents, were proceeding further in search of better destinies.

Let them leave to try to become someone else in some other country. I had arrived.

The car became the wall between Sergey and me. I cried, he broke things. Sergey complained to Simon and I—to Sonia. The arguments ceased when Sergey's boss learned of the dilemma.

"Don't you worry," he dismissed any misgivings. "You're good for the money. I won a lottery when I hired you." The man co-signed the entire loan and Sergey bought the lemony yellow Audi.

If we went somewhere in the car, I couldn't stop obsessing.

"The people like us. They accept and believe us. Suddenly, you arrive in your expensive car. I can't explain to all that we, indeed, didn't have any money, and the bank lent you the entire amount because that boss of yours trusts you. Who would believe such a story? The neighbors will think we are loaded, pretending to be poor."

I was six again, begging my yard-mates to believe that my family, though Jewish, wasn't rich. I would say to those other kids, "You remember that my mama borrowed from your mama three rubles last week, and couldn't even return them the next day as promised? And she makes all my dresses herself. That's why I have a lot of clothes."

Sergey was fuming listening to my reasoning. "I don't plan to do any explaining. I plan to enjoy the car. There's something very wrong with the way you think."

Reluctantly, I gave up, still telling the car story to all who would listen.

***

October 6, 1973 Israelis observed *Yom Kippur*, the Day of Atonement. The day when God checked our personal deeds for the year, would decide our fate. It was our second *Yom Kippur* in the land where history began. During the first one we followed the proceedings with the hesitant interest of the newcomers. This year, it felt slightly less surreal to be here.

We decided to spend it together with our best friends. Festively dressed, mostly in white as was prescribed for this day, we walked to a synagogue and listened to the prayers, overwhelmed by emotion. On the way, we stopped and said to our neighbors and others we met: *Hatima Tova,* with meant we wished to all of them to be deserving God's good signature for the new year.

I looked at us all, the damned people from many countries. Tired, almost wiped out, persecuted for centuries, our people built their own corner. They stopped asking anyone's permission to exist. They didn't apologize for their own way of praying to the God they gave birth to.

We came here to live: to work, to give birth, to love, to laugh, even to cry, whatever happened. I thought of Simon's mother who came here to die.

It was our own very old place with our own very old language, our own very old traditions.

At the end of services, we needed a moment to calm ourselves. I noticed many others around with burning eyes and hesitant steps.

Because of the *Yom Kippur* no one had to go to work. It was the day of rest and contemplation.

The sudden signal of danger, never heard by us before, the sharp, non-stop sound of alert interrupted that rest. Gil woke up, adding his own wails.

"What is it? Oh, my God, what does this siren mean? It can't be good!"

Only in old war movies had I heard a similar sound. It called forth the bloody battlegrounds and screamed of the cattle cars carting Jews to their death.

"Radio, turn the radio on!" Sergey yelled. We listened with horror of the Egyptians and the Syrians attacking Israeli borders at the same time. The holiest day in the Jewish calendar became also the bloodiest.

From the sixteenth-floor balcony we watched the men from all neighboring buildings running to the buses already waiting for them at the schoolyard across from us. They changed into their uniforms, lugging machine-guns, but also their boots. Most men still wore the white sneakers customary at *Yom Kippur*. They all were Israelis who observed the Day of Atonement.

They were running to their gathering points after receiving the radio-signals that a war had started. They had many live rehearsals, as did their fathers and grandfathers before them, as would their sons after. There was no disorder or confusion. It reminded me of a scripted filming after a fifth or sixth take.

"Where should I go?" My Sergey wasn't a soldier, yet, in our new home. He desired to defend it like he'd never wanted anything before. In the minutes since the war had been announced, he was sickened by inaction, by the helplessness. He ran across the way to our neighbor Felix.

"Felix," he started to beg, but saw words weren't needed—the veteran of the previous wars, who used a prosthetic since losing a leg in the Six-Day War, was hopping on his only foot, uniformed and ready.

Our neighbor didn't hesitate: "Come on, drive the car. We'll go where they know me. We could be helpful."

I emptied Sergey's old briefcase of the documents we stored there, those we used to immigrate; we didn't need them anymore—we had arrived at last. I packed a change of underwear, a sandwich, and some other items Sergey might use. The bloody scenes of many World War II movies played in my head. I was scared, but just a bit. After all, I was an Israeli.

Late at night, the two men returned. The commanding officer in the battalion in which Felix had served previously had smiled sadly: "Guys, if we have to grab the likes of you, one without a leg and the second without the language, we're in a worse shape than we are. Go home and go to work. Someone has to when so many of us are at the front fighting."

The reports were horrible: nine countries were united against our one. We learned that eighty thousand Egyptians attacked five hundred of our boys along the Suez Canal. The one hundred and eighty Israeli tanks faced fourteen-hundred of the Syrian ones on the Golan Heights.

Jews were dying, and the world behaved as usual: the Soviets were supplying the Arabs with additional arms. The United Nations, headed by Kurt Waldheim, waited to see which way the wind would blow. Only the United States started their airlift of help, and not at once either.

The families around Israel were losing their sons and fathers. At home in Israel we walked the streets with little transistors held tightly to our ears. The flowers, as usual, sold at the flower stalls. The sight of them helped me to understand the people coping with the realities of constant war. The jokes like the one about the egg shortage—all eggs are on the Golan, if you need them—reminded me that we were alive. I wanted to be like them, to know what to do at every moment. I listened eagerly to my neighbors. I'd remember all that for the next war.

The first few bloody and brutal days of fighting turned around and Israeli's forces were able to repel the Arab armies at last. After the Israeli army freed its own territory from the enemies, they went ahead, deep into Egypt and Syria, when the United States State Department issued a warning and ordered a cease-fire. The Jews weren't supposed to go into the Arab land.

We at home lived through alerts, running downstairs to the shelter. Our children were subdued at times, crying at others.

One day, after a siren sounded, I was the first back on our floor. I heard a phone ringing inside the neighbor Ruthie's apartment. Was it right to walk in uninvited? But we were at war and Ruthie's husband was a soldier. What if it was some news about him? Hesitantly, I pushed open the unlocked door, lowered Gil to the floor, and picked up the receiver.

A man on the other end spoke in rapid Hebrew and I caught but a few words before he hung up. I stood there, crying when Ruthie returned, and tried to give her the message I didn't understand.

"Just tell me if he's alive?" Ruthie kept asking, and I repeated the words I understood, again not making much sense. Then, we both were crying, but kissing too, because the war was on and the guys were dying and my Hebrew was poor and I was sorry.

I knew that Papa, back in Kiev, was going crazy with not knowing how we were doing during the war. Soviet news filtered and adjusted any faraway happenings according to their needs and dislikes, and Israel got the bad rap regardless of all.

I needed to get to a post office and send him a telegram. Leaving Gil with Sonia, I ran as fast as I ever did.

The siren went off when I was halfway to the post office. I fell to the ground. How would Sonia take Mira and Gil and their toys and blankets and water and cookies down all those steps and into a shelter?

My telegram seemed silly—using English letters I'd spelled Russian words, trying to console my father, saying we all were fine, and Sergey was working—which meant he was not a soldier at the front.

***

Sergey worked long hours where he, the *Ole Hodash*—newcomer—from Russia, was suddenly in charge of the work being done. The old owner and the Arab workers were the only ones left in the shop on the floor during the longest eighteen days of war.

I was getting used to living with a war going on and it saddened me but proved the point—there were wars in Israel, and nevertheless the life went on.

2,688 Israelis were killed in the war of Yom Kippur.

CHAPTER 12

Kiryat Shprinzak
Haifa, Israel

1974-1975

We'd just moved from the temporary apartment and were starting anew again. The apartments in Kiryat Shprinzak were populated primarily by the young couples and *Olim Hodashim* and managed by Amidar, which was government subsidy. I still hadn't had a chance to look for a job outside of the house, though I planned to do so at once, since Gil had started a nursery school. Sergey's salary increased slowly but steadily and would grow more with the growth of the company. I was happy that we were able to repay the loan to the man who lent us the money back in Kiev.

And then Sergey parents announced they didn't want to live in Israel anymore. That wasn't sudden. We heard whispers and complaints before but did not take those seriously. America was a shining star with the promise of immediate riches. Rumors were spreading about someone who went to America and became a millionaire.

Sergey's parents were entitled to their views as much as we were to ours. We didn't care about any rumors. We were enjoying our young family and our life. If his parents wanted to leave Israel and go to America—they were welcome to go there. My Papa David stayed back in Russia, didn't he?

Every weekend we brought Gill to their house, they found another reason why we all had to go. First Sergey was reasonable, saying he loved his job, his friends, his life, and this strange, worrisome country. He didn't care about the many others who left for America and found riches there upon arrival. Then he started to shout in desperation.

I didn't say much when the Kaplans debated. He was their son and his words carried more weight. After the words ran out, Sergey slammed the door and we left hastily, carrying Gil. In the car on the way home I hugged them both and told them how much I loved my men. I assured Sergey that he'd covered all the bases and his reasoning was truthful, intelligent, and convincing. He spoke for both of us.

I asked Sergey if he minded visiting his parents by himself, since loud screaming debates were upsetting to Gil. "Mom…" our child popped in with his opinion, "I love my grandma and grandpa. I love you and Dad too."

One thing I knew about dynamics in the Kaplan family—his mother always won. Why couldn't I find the right words to make my own feelings count? But Sergey knew all the reasons and said all the right words. He himself had used them when arguing with his parents.

The anticipation of a disaster surrounded me. *If only I could stop time.*

One day, when Sergey was at work, I took a bus to Kiriat Tivon and brought Gil along to soften the tone of the discussion, even remembering to wear a skirt instead of my favorite pair of bell-bottom jeans. "You don't look like a wife and a mother," my mother-in-law objected whenever seeing me in my preferred get-up.

"You love your son," I begged them. "He's happy here in Israel. We just started living. Give us a few years and we'll prove to you that our home is here."

"And who are you to talk? You didn't bring one non-chipped plate to this marriage. I couldn't believe that your fool of a father didn't buy you a decent set of dishes when you were packing. Saving for his whores, I bet." Her words had been waiting for a long time. Now they started jumping out, hitting hard at every reachable spot in me.

I felt sick. I wanted to protect myself and my father and my child, who listened standing next to me. I forgot why I came. All I wanted was to stop the old woman from spitting venom.

I took a bus home, not saying a word about the trip or conversation to Sergey.

Was there anything left to say?

Then the day came when I knew without question that my worries were well founded. Sergey repeated his mom's words, if not with conviction, at least with understanding.

"Mom's doctor said her heart is weak and the long, hot summers don't do her any good. She would benefit from a cooler climate," Sergey mentioned on the way home from his parents. "Remember, when we newly arrived she worked double shifts at the factory, standing all day at the machine that spit out ballpoint pens? After that her health was never the same."

The older Kaplans were successfully yanking Sergey to their side.

Of course, his parents were old and his mother's heart was weak and their small pension was barely enough to live on, but they weren't starving, were they?

My father's written advice was explicit, "Follow your husband, Lilli. He's the head of your household, and I agree with his decision. You'd have more choices in America."

My mother-in-law's threat was real: "You're not staying in Israel since we are leaving it. Your child needs you. But don't be surprised if you wake up one morning and he's gone. We aren't leaving without Gil. He's our only grandchild. He's our family. He's one of the many reasons we are getting away from here. He's too sensitive to live through another war. I could still hear his crying for weeks after the last one."

Could they really kidnap my baby?

Sergey always gave in to his parents. Why did I expect anything different now? Even though this particular situation had been forced on him, with time he spoke his own words, using his own logic to convince me they were right:

"Living in the Soviet Union, we didn't know what to expect elsewhere. Israel was the only country we were able to immigrate to. It's a great place. You, Lilli, won't ever hear me say otherwise. But it's tiny. The Israelis work and defend themselves from one war after the other all the time, so the prospects aren't what I would like us to have. In America, there are opportunities of bigger proportions. I'd like to try them."

He was logical, and still I didn't want to go anywhere else. I wanted to stay here, home.

"We are leaving and I'm not repeating myself again! Enough! If you prefer to pretend otherwise, be my guest!"

It was 2:00 AM. on a sticky September night. I ran out of our new apartment barefoot wearing a skimpy gauze nightdress. I ran for the three long blocks uphill and then sat on the ground near the water station.

Sitting on that hill in the middle of the night, I suddenly realized that my sheer nightdress didn't leave anything to the imagination. Why did I fight him so vigorously? It was true that I could be happy in Israel but was not as yet entirely. My world of anxieties, uncertainties, and fears didn't translate into Hebrew—it spoke my own language. It settled in for the duration.

I walked back. The small stones were cutting into my shoeless toes. I walked up the three flights of steps in total darkness and with my fingertips pushed open the unlocked door.

"Sergey," I whispered coming into our bedroom. The covered by sheet, unbending silhouette didn't stir, the illusion of sleep preserved.

"Sergey," I called once more. "Okay, we'll leave here. We'll go to Brussels and from there apply for entry to America like Svetlana did, the daughter of your old coworker. Just for the record—now we're leaving home, our first real home. I know you agree with me."

***

Sergey woke up every morning and went to work, like nothing out of the ordinary was decided between us. I woke up every morning and wanted to become invisible, so neighbors wouldn't see my shameful face.

"I couldn't withstand the pressure. I'm spineless," I wanted to admit to all of them. "Yes, my husband has a great job. Yes, we live in a beautiful city. No, we're not afraid of the wars." What else could they possibly ask me?

The thought of leaving Israel, the country that had fought for its right to exist since declaring its independence, was treachery in my mind. And treachery in the minds of those who would stay on and continue the fight.

But hide I couldn't. Instead, I took Gil to his new nursery school. They were nice to me, asking if I'd found a job yet, and if I needed I could pay them partially or postpone the payments till later. That's how my days started—with lying to the people who wanted to make my life easier.

I took a bus to Sonia and Simon's apartment to cry.

"Sit here while I feed Mira," Sonia said. "You can cry while you wait," she added. I cried bitterly and no makeup could cover my swollen face. When she was done with her chores, Sonia sat by me and cried too—she didn't want us to leave. We didn't talk. What was there to talk about?

***

Then I didn't have time for tears anymore. We could fly to Europe as tourists but wait there for a visa to the United States, as refugees. My work of severing ties with our possessions and accumulated friendships, of telling half-truths and lies started. The first lying trip was to Amidar, the government subsidized agency that rented inexpensive dwellings to Israelis. Less than a year ago they'd handed us the key to our new apartment.

In the young state of Israel, the shortage of affordable housing was stark. Some families had to wait for years, while for the *Olim Hodashim,* the new arrivals, housing was available on a priority basis. While there were always people waiting to rent an apartment, there were those who left for an easier, less-conflicting life someplace else. They left quietly and privately, buying plane tickets to go overseas and not returning. Their apartments stood locked, empty, and not paid for.

The needy country decided to get reimbursed for those. Now, when applying for a travel passport, citizens were obligated to prepay their rent for six or even twelve months. The harsh treatment was provoked by the harsh reality.

I pushed the door with the sign *"Amidar"* on it.

"*Shalom*. I have to talk to someone about a release from the rent prepayment." My voice squeaked from tension. I wiped my sweaty palms on my denims and checked to see if my bellybutton was covered between the low-cut pants and high cut t-shirt. I looked and felt like an Israeli.

"And what do we owe you, *Geveret*?"

The man who asked the question was in his early thirties. One of his blue eyes was in some way not identical to its partner. Both his eyes were the brightest blue I had ever seen, yet they differed in deepness or maybe perception.

One was a fake, I realized with a jolt and shuddered. Another war, another hurt, and here I came with my lies. I turned around, deciding to drop the matter. The image of Sergey's face appeared in the doorway. "I knew you wouldn't do it," it mouthed.

I walked back inside the room and sat across from the guy.

"I know you don't owe me anything. But would you personally refuse an all-paid-for-trip to Europe if it presented itself by the way of rich relatives?" I asked without a smile, my hands clutching each other on my lap, knuckles white.

"I wouldn't, no way. But I'm not that lucky. Never been. See my eye?"

He pointed at the beautiful fake I spotted before. He smiled and the good eye smiled with him.

I'm not going to do this. If Sergey wants to—let him do it.

"So, what is the story? My not being lucky means nothing to you. At least, I was born here while you had to run away from the Communist 'heaven.' Am I right or what?" The guy seemed to be bored and talkative.

He continued, "Here I am sitting and doing nothing and the *Ola Hodasha* comes in and tells me she got lucky and not in our common people's way. I sincerely hope you get lucky in that way too…" The jokes were pouring out. "You want to tell me you don't have the money to put down for the apartment while you'll be away. And you want to ask me to stamp my permission to let you leave without that payment?"

I couldn't believe my ears—he was doing all the work of explaining. My pounding heart needed help to stay inside my chest.

"I get petitioners like that all day long. And I turn them around and tell them to look for the money or stay put. I don't believe them. They aren't going to return. So why should the poor country lose money on a bad deal? They're the bad deal, if they have to be held by the money strings. But what is the choice of this poor country? I'll tell you—their children, the next generation of Israelis. That's why we have to overlook the nastiness."

He seemed to contemplate that idea for a while; in the next second the blue of his eye flowered again.

"I trust you. You like Israel. Don't ask me how I know it. I see a lot while sitting in this broken chair. Do you think they could at least buy me a new chair for all the money I save them? Anyway, today I can perform my good deed and let the Jewish family originally from the Soviet Union see the world. I will do it and let my bosses kick my backside and yell their share. Don't forget to come see me on your return."

The man opened a desk drawer and rubber-stamped my papers.

I walked slowly. I counted the stairs on the way from the building and later counted the number of steps to the bus stop. The counting helped me not to feel, not to have emotions, not to suffer. I was walking out on my conscience and needed to know how far behind I was leaving it.

I counted minutes on the bus and the steps to our house. In the back of my mind I knew Gil anxiously waited to be picked up from his school, but I couldn't see any more Israelis wishing me well.

***

I stood motionlessly inside our apartment. The events of this day pulled up an old memory, the one I'd tried not to think of since I was eleven.

I was at my favorite summer camp. We had a new counselor whom no one took seriously, often playing the mean jokes on him. That particular morning, I started down the stairs and I saw him standing in my way, his legs and arms spread widely. I had to halt.

He smiled slowly: "I overheard your last name—Goldbloom. Is it Jewish?"

He knew it was. His question wasn't one of curiosity. It was to make a point—"I could bite," it said.

The man had chosen me, Lilli Goldbloom, to pay back for everyone's dislike of him. His arms and legs were immovable. I couldn't run away.

"No, it's German," I whispered, hardly moving my lips.

His smile spread from ear to ear. "Germans wouldn't be very happy to have you as a compatriot." The smiling mouth stretched into a grimace, the laugh became loudly hysterical.

With all my strength, using one quick movement, I forced his body aside to the wall and ran. I ran further and further away from him, never managing to get away from myself.

I, who inhaled war movies and books of German atrocities since I knew how to watch and read, had chosen to be German. Why? The man was only preventing me from passing him, not putting words into my mouth.

At age eleven, I lied to a Russian anti-Semite in order to get away from the tag of my birthright. At that age I was already exhausted of being Jewish. Even despised "German" sounded a notch better than "Jewish."

At age twenty-seven, I lied in order to leave the place which had accepted me because I was Jewish. I lied to a Jewish man who lost his beautiful blue eye while defending all of us from becoming extinct. And then I'd move away and watch his son defending my son in yet another war.

CHAPTER 13

Brussels, Belgium

1974-1975

On December 24, 1974, after living in Israel for two and a half years, we flew from Tel Aviv to Brussels. The fervor of crowds at the airport, the multitudes of luggage-carriers, the paths in all directions subdued even our three-year-old Gil's "Why?" and "Where?" and "How long?"

"They all speak gibberish. I don't know what they're saying," he admitted.

There would be enough time to explain to him that French wasn't gibberish, and he'd better learn the next language.

"Sergey, what does Svetlana look like?" I asked as we were standing in the middle of the terminal looking for the twenty-three-year-old girl who'd promised to meet us.

"Lilli, I worked with her mother back in Kiev, before we and they immigrated to Israel. She was a child when I saw her once. How do I know how she looks now? She'll know us if she sees us."

"I'm afraid to ask—how would she recognize us? We're here for an hour already. She didn't find us or she didn't show up. Do we have the address of that hotel where everyone stays?"

"I've it written down. When we spoke on the phone she pronounced it slowly, and I spelled it in Russian so I'll know how to say it. Don't worry."

I was worried. Not that much about the girl or hotel or address. Gil's forehead felt hot. He asked Sergey to hold him. We went outside, deciding to get a taxi. It drizzled, and Sergey took off his jacket to cover Gil.

At last we were first in a taxi line. An old wiry driver loaded our four yellow suitcases inside the trunk. Sergey unfastened the inside pocket of his jacket and took out a folded piece of paper; he read the address. The cabby looked at him and examined Gil and me. Then he laughed: "Russki?" Not waiting for an answer, he drove off.

While Sergey paid the driver and unloaded our four yellow suitcases, I stood in front of the hotel holding my sick sleeping child, surveying the building that had lost its original color before the beginning of this century.

The smells of borscht, fried onion and garlic cooking, the children's cries, the cacophony of many voices met us in the vestibule. Inside, a pretense to be grand remained—the chandeliers and curved balusters, chintz sofas and a huge fireplace.

Somehow, in the last year, the hotel had become housing for the former Soviet Jews on their way from Israel to other parts of the world. Everyone in that hotel spoke Russian.

The first thing we unpacked was a thermometer. Gil's fever passed 102°. I, probably, should've checked my temperature too, because the furniture around the room seemed to swim. I asked Sergey to go downstairs to see if we could get any help. He came back with an aspirin and mentioned someone with chicken soup. If needed, a doctor could be found, but the guys told him the evening of December 24th was the wrong time to bother anyone.

That was the first day of our ten-month stay in Brussels.

"Mom, lay down with me," Gil whispered. I didn't wait for another invitation. Did I fall into a dream world at once? Was it my dream or that of my sick child? I swam in a river; the water was hot yet my body was cold. Someone said it's the chicken soup, and I replied: "No, no, it's the water, but please heat it more, because I'll freeze to death."

Someone handed me a drink of water.

"Good morning. Feeling any better?"

A woman, who sat on the chair by the bed, seemed vaguely familiar: smiling, round face, reddish tangled hair all over her shoulders, very pregnant stomach and a rod-like posture.

"Yesterday I brought you chicken soup. You were out of it completely."

"Was it yesterday? I'm sorry. Thank you. I thought you belonged in my dream. What's your name?"

"I'm Raya Kaminetzky. Your Sergey knew my Peotr from someplace before. They recognized each other when you arrived. Do you need anything else?"

"I don't even know. Do they feed you here with some breakfast?"

"They do feed you, though you'll have to pay for it."

"Is there any other choice?"

Sergey had to find the missing Svetlana. He had communicated with her through her mother, and the younger woman insisted we come to Brussels before New Year's if we were serious about getting visas to the USA. Was there a valid reason for her rushing us? Did she have any connections that could help us to get to the United States?

He mentioned Svetlana at the hotel and got ironic smiles in response.

"Guys, don't smile please. You obviously know Svetlana better than I do. I don't really count on her help. I just would like to talk to her, that's all. Is there a volunteer who knows where to find her?"

I stayed in the room with Gil. Both were over the twenty-four-hour bug or whatever had made us sick the day before, but we were drained. Snuggled and warm under the blanket, we hugged and leafed through his favorite books we'd brought along.

Sergey returned, beaten by the facts and the gossip he heard. We went to eat breakfast.

"Yes, Lilli, I found Svetlana, drunk since the day before, passed out naked on the sofa … her underwear drying on the chair, mumbling something about waiting for her clothes to dry before she could meet us at the airport. That was after I repeated my name for the tenth time.

"Okay, Lilli, let me say what is what. We don't need Svetlana. When she wrote to us, she repeated the rumors floating around the Russian community. They expected January closings of the foundations that were helping to resettle Jewish refugees from the Soviet Union. We're still in December, so there's a hope, though a slim one.

"I learned that there're two such foundations here in Brussels. They're the Tolstoy Foundation and the Catholic one. They provided living expenses and were the link to the different consulates, including the American. They arranged interviews for the entering visas."

Sergey spoke fast but toneless, not touching the food on his plate.

I picked up on the past tense he used.

"They did? What about today? What about us?"

"I told you nobody knows. Don't interrogate me." I noticed him tightening the belt of his jeans. My husband was a unique individual who lost weight after missing a meal.

"As a matter of fact, today, the 25th of December, is some kind of a religious holiday. What do we know of religious holidays? Communist Party said—there is no God, and if you are going to celebrate him—prison. Apparently, here they celebrate him. And today everything is closed. Tomorrow I'll start making rounds, and we'll know more or less where we stand."

I had better sit down and write a letter to Papa, I decided. He was worried sick about us. But there was no news to share, none whatsoever. I could entertain him with stories of us being sick for a day, of chicken soup appearing from thin air, or maybe about Svetlana's underwear on the chair drying. Would he laugh?

That was our second day without a home.

A Catholic agency listed us on their roster of resettling Soviet refugees. That was good news. Also, we were able to sign up Sergey's parents, who had stayed back in Israel for the time being.

The same day we found a slightly less expensive hotel. The money we'd hoarded after selling our appliances and furniture in Israel was dwindling fast.

We continued looking for an apartment, treading the city streets daily, looking for "To Let" signs on the windows and doors. Our labors paid off—one room furnished in a variety of forest-green colors, with a kitchenette stuffed with pots and dishes, became available. Its weekly rent was yet cheaper than the second hotel's.

I reached for our suitcases, stored under the hotel-beds and repacked them once again, not forgetting the hotel-sheets and the towels from the bathroom. I had never stolen before. Did I become a thief? What crime was worse—treason or thievery? Because, in my opinion, our leaving Israel was treason.

***

My first job in Brussels was only for one night.

After I registered with the Jewish Family Services, the same evening they sent over a tall, heavyset woman to fetch me. Wordlessly she kept checking her watch and frowning. Understanding that time was of the essence and believing we didn't have a language in common, I grabbed a short, lined windbreaker without changing the clothes I'd worn all day and followed her down the stairs.

I didn't know where she was taking me or what the job entailed. In the car on the way wherever we were rushing, the agency woman tried a variety of languages, not getting very far with me until she used a Hebrew word. There I was on familiar ground, and we communicated with no difficulties.

They had a client—a lonely bedridden woman dying from cancer. She needed a sitter around the clock. Her regular one had taken an emergency day off. The sick woman's children were living in Israel and for years had begged her to come live with them. For whatever reasons, she'd chosen loneliness.

How would I talk to her? What language did she speak? What if we didn't have one in common? Would I lose my first paying job? I didn't ask.

We walked into the dark, medicinal-smelling apartment. I saw the sick, the kitchen, the medication, and the key to lock the door when I left in the morning.

The woman slept and we didn't have to converse.

My chair stood by the sickbed. The woman moaned. I tried to slightly shift her body, remembering my mama during her last weeks searching for a more comfortable way to position her back and legs and head. I couldn't budge the woman— she was too heavy.

She asked for a bedpan. I found it and forced it under her massive buttocks. She asked for a drink. The juice stood on the table and, slightly raising the upper half of her body, I helped her to drink it with a straw. I obliged the woman's wishes, but what language did she use? I understood her desires clearly. What were the words?

I sat on that polished wooden chair in the darkened bedroom and coerced my memory to reproduce the words I'd just heard and obeyed. Then it came to me—a few Ukrainian, a few Yiddish ones. And maybe death carried its own international dialect familiar to all?

A pale hand from the sickbed waved me out of the room.

Kind woman— she knew the chair was hard. Or maybe she just wanted to be alone.

In the small living room, furniture stood tightly packed. The darkness prevented me from being too nosy. Was it a small piano in the corner or a large box or maybe one of those sideboards with fine dishes inside of it?

I moved to a sofa. It was covered against the dust, like everything else in this room, by the dark cotton fabric. The smell or touch of living didn't interfere.

The appropriate atmosphere for thoughts of loneliness and death.

Who was at fault for that woman not being close with her children? From the mixture of her languages, she came from the Ukrainian "*shtetl*" where Jews were forced to live before the revolution. Had that woman ever lived with her adult children? Did they have a falling out? Was it important enough? Couldn't she or they let it go? Was it worth it for her to die alone?

Could a fate of a lonely bed and a speechless sitter befall me too? Sergey and I, we married so fast, without first knowing each other. He wasn't a demonstrative person, not an easy man to live with; half of the time I didn't even know what he was thinking about. But he was honest and honorable…

The sound of fabric shredding inside of my head was already ongoing for a while … though my head didn't bother me yet … strange…

The blinds in the apartment were down. I tried to stay awake, shaking my head, dripping cold water on my wrists, walking the length of the room cautiously, in case there were loose floorboards.

A loud moan sounded from the bedroom and I rushed back.

"What?" I asked in Russian, forgetting she probably didn't know it. Not getting any answer, I stayed in the bedroom, learning to turn her from side to side. It became easier with practice.

At some point, back in the living room on that sagging sofa, I fell asleep. The woman said something, waking me up. I jumped up and rushed in. A bleak light trickled in through the blinds.

From her sickbed, the old woman pointed at the drawer in her nightstand. I opened it and saw the exact amount of money I had been promised for the night. Spending the night with a person on one of her last days paid well. She pointed at the money and then at the door. The agency lady, too, had told me to lock up and go home in the morning.

Was it the morning? I did see some light through the living room window. The dying woman wanted me to leave. Maybe she needed a rest from a stranger watching her? And she did point at that drawer with the money.

It was cold outside, drizzling and foggy. The short jacket I grabbed when leaving my apartment didn't warm me up—I shivered.

The street seemed empty and eerily quiet for the weekday morning hours. I checked my watch. I never looked at it in the darkness of the apartment. Three o'clock in the morning! I left the sick woman all alone. What was I thinking? I looked around. I was in the center of the square where numerous streetlights provided light. That was the light I saw through the window. I decided I'd better return to the apartment.

What building did I come out from? I didn't go too far. A few steps away I glimpsed a door with intricate old writing above it—that was the one I remembered walking into.

Suddenly a forceful grip assaulted my left arm. An unexpected presence paralyzed me for an instant. I saw a man's hand gripping me. A strong smell of liquor fouled the air.

What was he saying? Damn, damn him and damn everyone who speaks French!

"Go away, go away, go!" I shrieked and pushed his hand off me, running along that square, screeching "Idiot!" and a variety of Russian curses at the top of my lungs. My voice turned raspy from all the screaming. I hoped someone would hear me.

My heartbeat sounded deafening in my ears, covering all other sounds. At first the man tried to keep up. Still running, I turned and saw that he had stopped, looking bewildered. Completely out of breath, I had to stop too.

Hey, there were people on the street.

What an imbecile I was!

If I weren't so panicky, I would laugh at my stupidity. The ladies of the night—the shortest of the short dresses, the boobs hanging on the outside, the bright painted faces and hair—the working girls. And their customers here and there.

That's why the French moron approached me. I certainly looked the part in my tiny skirt and the worn high white boots. Coming from sweltry Israel, I still wore all my skirts recklessly short. The boots were a relic from Russia from the time I followed the fashions. On arriving in Brussels, I noticed the Belgian women wearing mid-calf-length skirts. Unfortunately, changing styles was not on my current agenda.

A taxi stopped and a passenger got out. I rushed in, almost colliding with him. Inside, closing the cab's door, I pronounced the name of the street we lived on. I tried to say it clearly, though my voice didn't master the French pronunciation. A red-faced, fat cabby waited for a few minutes, saying who knew what. His words became louder and the looks into the back of the car angrier. Until he stepped out of the car, opened my door and, grabbing my arm, pulled me out.

I couldn't run anymore. I stood there crying. The next cabby had more patience in his older years.

"Anglais a little? Good! Very good! No cry."

I dried my eyes with the sleeve of my jacket. He smiled and even applauded one or two claps. Then, he gave me a scrap of paper and pencil, improvising a writing movement. I wrote my address. Along the way, his broad shape turning in my direction for emphasis, the man lectured me on right and wrong places to spend one's nights. At least I imagined that was what he was saying.

At our house I paid the man, but he didn't leave and waited while I buzzed Sergey. My confused, grumpy husband, dressed in a denim jacket and his underwear, came down to unlock the door.

"What are you doing here?" he questioned, and listened to my teary tale. The driver still didn't leave. He listened to our conversation, hanging from the car's window, nodding his head agreeably. One could believe the man understood Russian.

"You took the money and left a sick woman alone? Do you have any brain? And why is this character still waiting? Okay, take his cab and go back."

Sergey walked over to the smiling driver, saying, "And you better bring her there in one piece. Here, I'm reading your plate number. No monkey-business of any kind." He spoke in Russian to the nicest of all cabbies in Brussels, who definitely didn't plan to drive me back to where he picked me up.

I went back. Sergey was right. He usually was. Did I hate or love him at that moment? Probably half of each. Who else would care more about a woman he never met than his own wife? But I married him and not another man. Still, it would be nice, for once, to be on his list of priorities.

The sick woman in the apartment slept. After checking on her, I stayed on the familiar sofa till her regular helper walked in.

***

Sergey, Gil, and I walked all over Brussels. Not simply to view the sights of that old beautiful city, which was regarded a capital of Europe, but to find cheaper groceries or to stumble on "*Travail*" or any other "Help Wanted" posted on a tree or building. My papa sent us a pocket French-Russian dictionary, so we recognized some words.

When we passed by the queen's residence and explained to Gil the reasons the guards were posted there, he was amused that the country actually had a queen.

"I would like to meet her. Could you ask the soldiers, please?" He looked so angelic, wearing the bright orange sweater that accentuated his pale face and dark eyes. He looked so earnest, believing that his wish was obtainable.

I declined outright. "No, Gil, it's not possible."

"You'll have to grow up and do something helpful and brave for this country for her to meet you," explained his more patient father.

The night after we stood by the queen's residence, our baby didn't fall asleep for a long time. I watched him turn from side to side and then smile in his dream. Maybe his wishes came true and he met the Belgium queen Beatrice, even if it was only in a dream.

One day we stopped at the plaza near the train station and I recognized the place of my recent escapade.

Sergey smiled. "Here is a red light district. The guys showed it to me when we were looking for jobs. So that's where you stopped to make some money at night."

I didn't laugh at his joke. I remembered the horror of being alone in a weird place with no means to ask for help. As it happened, the street our apartment was on belonged to the prostitution trade as well.

"Lilli, you wouldn't believe," Sergey burst home aflame. "The girl wore the tiniest white mink and her Jaguar had twelve cylinders. I didn't know where to look first." My husband seemed proud of himself, while I had no idea what he was so excited about.

"Sergey, who? What? What's this all about?"

"Now I understand about those spectacular cars on our block. One of the girls from the car propositioned me. Probably it's an exceptionally slow night for them."

"How would you know she propositioned? Maybe she asked you the time?"

"A man knows when a woman suggests sex. But it's not the point. Her Jaguar had twelve cylinders! I couldn't believe it."

My husband ... the car took prerogative. Nevertheless, he noticed the girl.

There were a number of luxury cars parked on both sides of the street on any given night. Their owners, the young women, wearing evening attire, came out to stretch their bored shapely legs. The men walked over and often presented flowers to the girls before accompanying them into the cars and driving away.

We didn't have the money to go out. We didn't own a TV or even a radio. After Gil was asleep on his cot, we stepped out onto the apartment's little balcony and enjoyed the show. A nightly ritual of watching beautiful prostitutes and their patrons became our entertainment.

Even more fun was observing the other, obviously cheaper kind of girls. They were always the same ones, and soon we realized the reason. One night a new woman stopped at our block to advertise her trade and the regular one beat her to a bloody mess. The incident was over before a hurried pimp arrived. His ward was back to her little fun dance in the middle of the street, directly under our windows. Long yellow hair, red or purple leather mini skirt, five-inch heels—the girl danced to her own rhythm, enticing the men who drove by, entertaining herself and us, her thankful audience.

Sergey found a job building a villa for a Polish aristocrat. Those were still around, real and fake royals of Eastern European origin. Once a week, a young duke or whoever he was, picked up his crew and drove them to a building site.

All of his laborers came to Belgium on temporary tourist visas and didn't have proper permits in order to work. They worked fifteen hours a day, slept in a barn, and ate some porridge with bread. Saturday evenings, our tired guys returned home for the one day of rest. They washed and ate and slept, cursed the duke, yet hoped the work would linger on. It did, for three rainy, muddy months.

Raya and Peotr Kaminetzky, the very first friends we made in Brussels, received their long-awaited visas to Canada. Raya promised to take me over to the apartment where she worked as a maid for the last five months. I brought Gil to the "Russian" hotel and left him there to play with other kids. The two of us women walked over to a tram stop.

"Raya, are you sure that man would hire me? What if he doesn't like me?" I was afraid someone would snatch the job from me and wanted to rush my slow-walking nine-months-pregnant friend.

"You better stop running. If I fall, you'd be the one to deliver my baby. I predicted it would be airborne, though with you running faster than any plane, I think we're looking at a Belgium citizenship."

"How can you joke in your situation?"

"Why not?" Raya asked me. "You'll be amazed at how much we're able to bear. All of us are. I won't be shocked to learn that you'll be leaving this place pregnant as well."

"All is possible. But you're actually due any minute now. Aren't you fearful?"

"Would it help if I carried on and complained? The baby will be born in Brussels, or in the air, or at the airport on the other side of the ocean. It doesn't matter.

"It'll be a happy child, regardless. He or she will have a birth certificate without a hammer and sickle, without a line stating 'Mother is Jewish, Father is Jewish,' like a beware sign. Agree?"

***

"Hello, Alexey Nikolaevitch," we both said in Russian to the tall fragile man who opened the door. He didn't answer, but looked pointedly at my midriff.

"You're not pregnant, I hope?" The man didn't waste any time. At age ninety, who would?

"I'm not pregnant, but did Raya not perform her duties because of her condition?"

I forgot to worry about getting the job. The man started to laugh. His laugh was too hearty for his feeble state, and in the next moment he was choking and coughing. His shockingly full head of snowy hair bobbled up and down. The two of us helped him to the armchair and gave him water. He waved us away, and Raya took me into the kitchen to show me where everything was.

"He is okay. Thanks for defending me, anyway. It was brave of you. Usually he is the most cordial person, one of the 'blue blood people.' A French governess and all kinds of fancy tutors brought him up. That was before the Red Revolution. We, whose grandparents regrettably contrived that revolution, wouldn't know of such upbringing."

Raya went on explaining that Alexey Nikolaevitch had been a high-ranking officer in the Czar's army. When the Revolution came, he and his wife took a train to Brussels to wait for the Soviet regime to end. Waited and waited, never growing roots. His wife died many years ago. He worked at some factory during those years; now they were paying him a pension, enough not to starve.

"In recent years he started using us, the close-to-free service, because he can't do much on his own. It's a shame—one beef cutlet a week, that's all the meat this man can afford."

I became a once-a-week maid to the old Czar's officer.

I knew the Czar himself and those around him were practicing anti-Semites. They were the ones who put up the walls around barren villages, forcing Jews to live there. The bloody pogroms were of their making. Was my employer among those?

Alexey Nikolaevitch recalled Russia the way he knew and loved it—the snow-white bride who waited for her exiled groom. His Russian language carried genteel words I never heard. Those were words in exile too. The names for fanciful foods that Russian soil stopped producing, elegant dances, and courteous manners disowned by the crude workers who didn't see a need in them.

Sharing the episodes of my life with Alexey Nikolaevitch, I repeated the words of the Soviet song we would sing as children:

"My widespread beloved country where equality is the most beautiful of all words..."

Indeed, those were beautiful words, representing ideas we held dear since our birth. As we grew up, the empty words were all that remained of that equality.

Old Alexey Nikolaevitch, wearing a threadbare three-piece suit, washed-out shirt, and a tie, sat in his well-broken-in chair and listened.

Dusting and sweeping, cooking and washing, I told him stories of my real motherland, the young and brave state of Israel I fell in love with after emigrating there from the Soviet Union. The old man was an attentive audience. If he had any misgivings about the subject of Judaism or Jews, he didn't voice them.

***

On my workday mornings, I took Gil to a Jewish kindergarten, where the little children of the Russian refugees were provided with free care alongside the Belgium children.

"Mom, I don't want to go. Please let me come to your work," Gil wailed, unbuttoning his coat and throwing it on the ground. "I won't play with those children. I don't even know what they are saying. They don't speak Russian or Hebrew. I told you so, but you never listen."

"Gil, I don't have a choice. I explained it to you. We need the money." I squatted in front of my son, buttoning his coat back up.

"So, don't buy me the wooden dog I asked for and you'll have more money," he continued feebly.

It was the same in Israel in any daycare or at the babysitters. Gil stayed close to the door, clutching his bag with a clothing change, not sharing in the games of other children, not drawing pictures, or building blocks. He waited for me to pick him up.

My darling baby. He was still a baby, living a life he couldn't fathom.

"Okay, only today, but promise you won't resist the next time."

I couldn't imagine he would be happy sitting still for four or five hours, waiting for me to clean Alexey Nikolaevitch's house.

My child surprised me. He talked with the old man, drew some pictures to give him as a gift, and looked at the yellowish photographs with undivided attention.

When I had to go shopping for the weekly groceries, Gil stayed with Alexey. "His name is Alexey Nikolaevitch," I whispered to no avail to my child, who didn't grow up with the Russian custom of using the patronymics as the show of respect. Upon my return, both the old and the young avoided looking at me.

"Did something happen?" I asked, not knowing to whom to direct my question.

"I wanted *kaki* and uncle Alexey took me to the toilet, but didn't know how to wipe me. He said he never had a chance to do it. So I explained and he did it." My little guy emphatically illustrated with the corresponding movements of his hand.

***

"Oh, hi there. I'm Eva. You are Lilli Kaplan. There, behind the pot with a dead tree, is adorable Gil who, I was told, is the smartest of all smarts. What else? Yes, I know you are looking for a dirt-cheap place to live in and I could help."

I wasn't much surprised when coming to a Russian hotel on a free afternoon I was greeted by a girl with a dark pageboy haircut and dancing eyes. I had heard of her, of course. Eva was likable at once. The community of Russian Jews was cozy with everyone knowing everything about everyone else. She was only seventeen, knew some French and a lot of English, and was never too lazy or busy to assist with translation or any other help.

"Ha ha. Let's see what I know about you," I said. "I know you set your eyes on Nathan, and I approve. I have some juicy details, but you are too young to hear them. You live in the building where there is something strange going on, but who cares—if the rent is cheap, we want it."

When I finished my diatribe, we both were laughing, sitting on the frayed chintz of the old hotel's sofa.

There was an available apartment in the building where Eva lived. The landlady was, we learned first-hand later, the weirdest creature. Eva talked to her and left a message for me at the hotel. I packed again and we moved again.

I found more household jobs and worked most days. Unfortunately, Sergey couldn't find anything to replace the duke's villa after it was finished. The man's pride was at stake. I knew the idea of his wife working while he stayed at home bothered him. He didn't talk to me, and stayed under the covers when Gil and I left in the mornings.

***

My son and I walked slowly. In between the bird and dog poop all around the sidewalks, it was essential to look under your feet. I clutched little Gil's hand, not trusting him to step carefully. Seemed the pigeons from all over the world had announced their annual convention—there were literally millions of them around.

“Mama, pee-pee please.” My son couldn’t wait; he stamped his feet in urgency.

Who knew where was the nearest bathroom? Okay, my child was three. Not such a big deal.

“All right, come here behind that tree.”

I heard loud voices behind us.

“Let’s zip it,” I commanded, and not waiting for Gil to do it fast enough, swiftly straightened his pants and coat.

Two middle-aged women were waving their arms and screeching, pointing at the trickle Gil had just produced. Both were holding tiny poodles, dogs’ leashes color-coordinated to their own outfits. I felt a heat of shame changing my face into a ripe tomato, though the irony of avoiding dog shit all over town struck a nerve.

Oh God … what did we get ourselves into and why? I hated it here. There was no place for people, only birds and dogs. Neither spoke French and shit all over the place. Still, no one yelled at them.

I needed to sit down and write a letter to someone who loved me. It was my salvation.

Dear Sonia, my beautiful, dearest friend,

I love you dearly. All of you whom I met and befriended in Israel became my rock, my steadfast pole to hold on to. Doesn’t matter that I knew you for only a short period of time. You remember how much I protested against moving away. Sergey didn’t want to leave there either, but sided with his parents nevertheless. I can’t help feeling that all is his fault. We don’t discuss our situation, just go through the motions of living. Anyway, when I’m at my lowest, he usually stops talking to me, anticipating my anger. I can’t write to my papa about our present life, he’ll be heartbroken. And something else happened. I became a thief. Stole some sheets and towels from the hotel. I also keep opening containers to sample food in the supermarket before I buy it. I'm terrified to get caught, but I don't know what's written on the label and Sergey eats only certain foods. You know his ways. Yesterday, I walked into a vegetable market to buy a few items. On the way out, an armed security-man stopped me. I peed in my pants. I didn't know what he was saying, till he pointed at my overstuffed pocketbook. He wanted me to open it. I didn't take anything from that store, but my worn and dirty house-slippers were inside. I take them to be comfortable when I clean people's houses. I said: "No French." He grabbed me by the arm and called for additional forces. Sonia, my dearest friend, I stood there with my stupid bag open widely for everyone to see my shame. My face was wet, my pants were wet, and my hands were wet. Why didn't you do something to stop me from leaving Israel? It's unfair to blame you, but why didn't you?

CHAPTER 14

Brussels, Belgium

1975

Some people from our community in Brussels were getting desperate. The kind of work we could obtain without working permits was in short supply. America was choosy—interviews at the American consulate didn't always conclude in visas. We knew Russian Jews who didn't want to chance the refusal from the United States officials and arranged meetings with the Argentinean, Brazilian, and South African consuls.

"You know what happened to Igor and a couple other of Nathan's friends," Eva relayed to me when both of us relaxed away from everyone on the top of our building's staircase. "They filled out applications at the South African Embassy and a representative told them, hardly glancing at their applications: 'You're way overqualified for us. We've enough specialists in the fields of your expertise.'

"Right, they've plenty of their own Jews. They're not interested in acquiring someone else's."

"Eva, why do guys even want to go there? Would they be welcomed there or killed on arrival? Would they have friends or families or people there who look like them or speak the same language or think the same thoughts? What do they know about South Africa besides the fact that some very rich Jews live there? In Israel, we had a neighbor who came from South Africa. Their laws don't allow taking money out of the country. Over there, she had household help to take care of her family. In Israel, she had only herself to do it all. A really pitiful creature. She had six or seven kids under age twelve. Most days she stayed in the bathtub, soaking, adding cold water when the weather was hot, adding hot water when outside was drizzling and cold. The neighbors took turns feeding her brood."

Why were we so anxious to share someone else's culture? We did it for generations and centuries, were thrown out of every country but a few, and learned zilch. Why didn't we feel lucky that there was a home of our own and live there the best we knew and could?

The crew Sergey was part of finished building the baron's house outside Brussels. Towards the end, the men didn't want the money, didn't want to see or hear about the villa. They were miserable and dirty and hungry. Sergey vomited for a week after the baron brought them a bucket of questionably fresh oysters for dinner.

After that job, there wasn't much else for a while.

One night, we were asleep in our new apartment that Eva had negotiated for us, when we heard a knock.

"Is there someone at the door?" I asked Sergey, not opening my eyes.

"I'll check." He pulled a pair of pants on and looked at his watch. "It's two in the morning."

A slight tapping came from our third-floor window. Sergey looked down.

"It's Long Alex throwing pebbles at our window. He's waving for me to come down," Sergey whispered, not wanting to disturb little Gil, sleeping not two steps away from us on a love seat.

Alex, a tall skinny fellow, nicknamed "Long," worked with Sergey on the infamous Polish villa. He was a professional violinist who, while in Brussels, rarely found musician's work.

I went back to sleep and Sergey stepped out the door. The story that followed I learned in the morning.

He closed the squeaky door of our room slowly, then walked two flights of steps down in total darkness. Unexpectedly, he felt some presence on the staircase in front of him. Frightened, Sergey asked in Russian, "Who is there?" Instead of an answer, a hysterical laugh followed. The bright beam of a flashlight blinded Sergey for an instant, but also fished out our villainous landlady. The she-devil was in her usual state of drunken stupor. She didn't know and didn't care about the time. Her excitement at finding an audience was limitless.

Sergey didn't move or speak, not that the woman cared. She talked and waved her hands and flirted, making eyes at Sergey from under her fashionable wig. It was perched on the left side of her head, revealing her hair colored into different shades, giving her a two-headed look. The double head had only one face. But what a face!

Her two days' worth of makeup was thick and smudged, like she'd rubbed it up against a painter's palette.

Sergey, not finding any other choice, grabbed madam by the hand holding the flashlight and twisted it, forcing light to sting her eyes. She wailed and let him through.

"What took you so long?"

Alex wore an outlandish outfit of long torn shorts and his concert tux top under a heavy parka. Stepping from one foot to another, he looked ready to throttle Sergey.

"Don't ask—I won't be able to explain what happened," Sergey answered.

"There's work available. If we are there at five in the morning, we have a chance."

"Do we have to kill someone or what? Only yesterday, I told Lilli that stateless contract-killers probably aren't as hopelessly unemployed as we are."

Alex wasn't in a joking mood.

"You're a funny guy, but I'd like to catch some sleep, if you'd only shut up and thank me later. See you at *Sarma* supermarket in a couple of hours."

All that I also learned later from my husband, who was glad another black-market job had become available. Now he'd have a place to go to and earn some bread money. Before Sergey left, he laughed, saying to me that to his relief he didn't have a second encounter with the madam, who probably fell asleep agains someone's door.

At five in the morning, Sergey and Alex weren't the first in line. There were other homeless and jobless immigrants, speaking various languages if they were with companions, or standing quietly if they were by themselves. The job sounded witless, according to the only one French-understanding person in that crowd. Not one of them refused it.

The supermarket chain *Sarma* was ready to open a new store, but the contractor wanted to vacuum more money out of the owners. He hired speechless foreigners to show up in large numbers. They were given brooms and told to start sweeping the floors. In an hour, all the sweepers were locked in an empty room and ordered to stay quiet. Then they were let out and told to go and sweep again. Then back to the room.

The idea was to show that work-force was needed for many more hours before the project would be finished. The contractor's pockets spread wide, so he didn't mind sharing some of the unlawful gains with the illegals he hired.

***

> *Dear Mom and Dad,* wrote Sergey to his parents in Israel, *You, along with us, were granted an interview with an American Consular representative. You have to be here in three weeks. We're waiting for you eagerly.*

We walked the streets of Brussels again, trying to find an affordable, furnished apartment for Sergey's parents. Now we knew the city and the areas where such rentals were possible. Still, nothing came up.

"Eva, darling," I appealed to my younger friend, when we met at our usual spot on the staircase leading to the roof, "there is nothing, nothing available in any of the regular places. I can't walk anymore. My shoes are dying on me. Sergey is ready to weep, which is something he's never done. Would you ask among your younger crowd? Maybe someone heard of an impending apartment emptying?"

"If I would be in your place, he could weep all he wants. His parents—his job. After everything you told me about them, I don't understand you, Lilli. I don't. Why you do it? Let them come and walk their feet off. They forced you out of the place you loved. They are willful tyrants who are used to ordering their son around. And you, you're just a free attachment to him. They order him, he orders you—and you look for an apartment. I would never be like that."

"Eva, you are young, unmarried, and know nothing. The only choice I see is to bring them to our place and continue looking."

"How do you imagine doing it?" Eva asked. "That I want to see. I myself am a graduate of the Soviet communal living and thought no amount of people in the tiniest room could surprise me, but how the five of you would fit in that minuscule closet of a room…"

Our one-room apartment was tiny and bleak. The window looked onto a wall of another building, with only a narrow courtyard in between. The constant darkness brought a musty smell to every piece of clothing we owned, not that we paid any attention to "a little rancidity."

Before we moved in, we learned from Eva who lived one floor above the vacant apartment, that madam Dupree, the building owner, spied on her tenants, hoping to limit their washing, cooking, and any other activities that cost her additional expense.

We took showers at lightning speed when she went to buy her liquor. When drunken madam locked herself in the building's only washroom, we rushed to our cooking plates to prepare meals. On the way from the bathroom, she banged her well-known fist against every door from where she smelled cooking vapor.

We washed our clothes, hanging it out to dry on the line outside the window. Our landlady stood in the courtyard screaming French curses we started to understand.

She insisted that we, the insipid immigrants, would burn down her house, so any kind of heating in the house was banned.

The day of Sergey's parents' arrival, we went to the airport to meet them. Had it been only a couple of months since the *three of us* arrived in Brussels? It seemed like a year to me.

When we flew in, a day before Christmas, little Gil with a fever above 102° and was listless and quiet. Now he was talking and laughing, eager to see his grandparents.

The Sabena plane arrived on time. We waited at the gate. "There! There!" yelped Gil and before we could react, he ran inside the incoming crowd and disappeared.

"Gil!"

I pushed my way through the human mass, but the little boy in a dark blue jacket, homemade denim pants, and white shirt was nowhere to be seen. I ran to the right but saw Sergey running there and turned to the left.

"Gil!" I tried to yell, but fright tightened my vocal cords. "Gil!" I mouthed wildly, again and again.

"Mom, I found them, I did!"

My darling child stood in front of me in between his grandparents, holding their hands. His brown eyes gleamed with pride, the small face too electrified to be chided. My tears took over.

Terrified and out-of-breath Sergey caught up with us. On seeing our baby alive and in one piece, he hugged and kissed him, swallowing <u>his</u> tears.

Sergey's parents were dressed in their best. You could see an old-fashioned tendency of showing all you've got when coming to a new place—the woolen suits, the fine shirts, shiny leather shoes, even some expensive jewelry.

In order to bring his parents from the airport, Sergey borrowed a little Reno from one of the guys. The car didn't have working brakes and all four doors were held in place with pieces of rope.

On the way to our apartment, my in-laws seemed enchanted by the beautiful city, nonchalant and calm about their future.

After the initial greetings, I didn't say much to them. My thoughts remained not voiced for someone else to hear, but very loud in my head:

You insisted we leave Israel, where we belong. You wouldn't rest till your son agreed with your decision and left me without a choice but to follow. You are the reason for our miserable living and our unknown future. Stay here and admire all you want. Just let me out.

From some perverse sense of satisfaction, I waited for their reaction to the "grand" lodgings they would have to share with us.

Sergey was embarrassed for not preparing an adequate living space for his parents. He tried to cover it up with an easy chat. After a few topics of conversation were used up, he made the announcement,

"Mom, Dad, you'll have to live with us for a few days until we find an apartment for you. We looked around but nothing yet was available in our price range. The room we are renting is not large. Actually it's rather small, but it'll have to work for now."

We walked upstairs and entered the room, bringing their suitcases in. The five of us didn't have enough floor-space to stand there. Sergey continued talking without giving his parents a chance to react to what they saw.

"The main problem is … the landlady is a horror. She'd better not see you at all. We all will end up on the street if she spies you. If we're not at home, don't even use the bathroom. She's that bad."

The sleeping arrangements were decided beforehand. Mother Kaplan would sleep on the bed with Sergey and me—on Sergey's side:

my condition. His father should take Gil's love seat, leaving the two chairs tied together for our child.

Sergey didn't meet my eye. Or maybe I didn't try to find his eye. The only person joyful from the adventure was Gil.

I didn't sleep. I felt overwhelming sympathy towards my husband. In his way of thinking, his parents had done everything possible for him in every situation. Now he couldn't ensure even a minimum of comfort for them.

My back towards him, I softly touched his hand resting on my waist. His hand immediately covered mine in a sign of thanks. And then, slowly, he caressed my shoulder and breast under the nightgown. I felt his warm lips on my neck. The room breathed deep and tired sleep.

Sergey needed me at this moment more than ever. I felt the hardness of his intentions and wanted to explain the impossibility of them but was apprehensive to stir or whisper or change the position of my limbs.

The next morning we walked outside, looking for an apartment again.

"Sergey," I said, "your mother could've heard you last night."

"What do you want me to say? She's a grownup."

"Besides the obvious embarrassment, after last night I could be pregnant."

"So we'll have a second gorgeous and smart child. Didn't Raya predict you'd leave this place as pregnant as she and so many of the other girls?"

"Sergey, you treat it as a joke. I'm the one to carry the child and to be sick and all. You forget things too easily. I stayed in bed with Gil almost throughout the entire pregnancy. But I had Papa David to cater to me."

"Are we fighting already? I cannot believe how fast you jump to conclusions. Maybe you are not pregnant and maybe this pregnancy would be an easy one. Don't assume the worst scenario yet."

***

That morning, I reached Alexey's house later than usual.

"Hello, Alexey Nikolaevitch. Were you waiting for a long time?" I knew how anxiously he stayed in his armchair, anticipating our talks. "I'm sorry. It's just that my in-laws flew in yesterday and we tried to find them an apartment."

I spoke while picking up a few items that had fallen from his feeble hands. What would he do for help when all of us left Brussels?

"Did your wife sew?" I asked him, pointing to the compact Singer machine I dusted every week.

"Oh, yes. She was a beautiful dressmaker. She didn't do it for anyone else, of course. But her dresses were famous for their elegance. Do you know how to sew?"

I remembered Raya's description of our employer as a "blue blood." Even if his wife did take sewing orders to help with the money, he'd never admit to it.

"I certainly do. I've sewn for other people as well as for myself."

I continued dusting, a thought entering my mind.

"Alexey Nikolaevitch, would you mind lending me this machine? I could make some money with it. I'm sure there are women-immigrants who need affordable clothes."

A sudden huffy expression in the old man's eyes changed his usual friendliness. I had offended him somehow. A weak person had been transformed into a lion in front of me. He straightened up and shed years. He looked young and brave and powerful.

"I never…"

But he didn't finish, and in a matter of seconds turned back into an old White-Russian officer dying alone in a foreign country.

"I'm sorry. I never let anyone touch her things. Does it make sense? She was a kind soul, my Lyubushka. She'd be happy if you could use her machine. Don't mind an old *durak.* But before you leave for America … please bring it back."

The very next day I got a few sewing orders. The women carried fabrics in their suitcases and they wanted new clothes. Our small room shrank even more with the arrival of a sewing machine, fabrics, notions, and women trying on their dresses.

I wasn't a very experienced dressmaker. I tried to imagine Mama next to me, giving me instructions. Regrettably, only one episode of our combined efforts came to mind.

I was seven and wanted to help her. Mama had just finished the dress for a customer who was due to pick it up in a half-hour. As she was busy with something in the kitchen, she asked me to pull out white basting threads seen throughout the dark fabric. I was not a novice at that task, working first slowly, using scissors carefully, and then I got careless, wanting to finish my work faster.

"Yikes!" I yelped. With the last movement of my hand, I cut material instead of a thread. Mama was by my side at once.

"Did you cut yourself? No? Good, out of my sight. Don't come near me."

She worked for the next hour. Whatever she did saved the dress. I was ashamed for a long time.

My in-laws tried to help. They read books to Gil and took him for walks. Still, I imagined their boredom in the prison-like atmosphere of our room.

When I took sewing orders, we started to sew together. My father-in-law sat by me and operated the machine's hand-wheel. On my "Now," he spun till I said, "Stop." My mother-in-law hemmed the dresses by the window.

My next new job came like the very first one in Brussels from the Jewish Family Service. An orthodox family with three little girls needed a cleaning woman. The girls' mother worked as a teacher in a neighborhood school and had to leave the house early in order to drop her kids at their schools.

The first morning I arrived to clean the apartment I felt my heart pumping wildly. It was probably from the brisk walk. I sat down to rest.

After fifteen or twenty minutes, I dragged myself off the living room chair and into the kitchen. The second I looked at the mess left from the family's breakfast, I ran to the bathroom and threw up.

Got you! I knew it. Got me! There was no doubt in my mind regarding my current situation. I was pregnant.

CHAPTER 15

Brussels, Belgium

1975

The building where we found a room for Sergey's parents had another vacant one for us. Both apartments were on the third floor, and the only bathroom on the first. The landlord didn't live in the building, a definite improvement after dealing with our previous landlady.

That morning, my pregnant self woke up with persisting nausea, which wouldn't be a big deal if not for the three deep flights of steps down to the communal bathroom. There was no way I could stagger down all that distance to throw up. Didn't I know the pitfalls of pregnancy? I should've bought a plastic pail to retch in. And then what—carry it down to empty?

I reached for a robe and stepped to the table, where a coveted slice of lemon waited for my morning nausea. As I sucked on its magic sourness, a red spot on the sheets caught my attention. Here I go again, bleeding. The second time this month.

No reason to panic. I had the same experience during my pregnancy with Gil and he was fine.

Yes, he is, but then I stayed in bed almost the entire duration of my pregnancy with my papa catering to my every need.

Last week I had gone to a doctor, who donated his services to the needy Jews here in Brussels, for a consultation.

"Mrs. Kaplan, could you stay off your feet and not work?" he asked, slowly digging for forgotten Hebrew words to communicate with me.

"Of course not, Doctor. I'm happy for any job that finds me. And my jobs are not exactly a desk-and-chair type."

This morning, I was glad to be by myself. Sergey found a loading job at the street market for a few days. Gil was next door at his grandparents. I tiptoed by their door and took the stairs down to the street.

Early mornings, all Brussels storeowners washed the sidewalks in front of their businesses, pushing the bristled brushes and soapsuds through the streets, trying to free them from the dogs' and pigeons' messes. Too bad they didn't try to scrub the mountains of bird shit from their awesome gothic architecture.

The waste on the streets accumulated faster than brushes could reach it, because the dog walkers with their pets were out and about too.

I reached the tiny park where five streets interlocked into a square. It became my perfect letter-writing place. I sat on one of the three benches under one of the five maples, this spot literally at the crossroads—quite appropriate in my case.

Shalom my dearest Sonia,

I'm pregnant. Isn't it wonderful?! Don't you think it's a most glorious omen? I want this child desperately. It's like I'm drowning in the bottomless river and this baby became a branch sticking far out from a tree on the shore. He appeared in order to save me. Does it make sense?

Sergey is glad about the second child but doesn't dwell on it. I suggested not sharing our baby news with his parents and for reasons of his own he didn't argue with me.

My mother-in-law rules all of us. On her last morning drop-in, she spied some toys and clothes thrown on the floor in our room and refused to step over the threshold. From the hall she wailed that her son never lived in such a mess. Then she discovered some stains on Gil's t-shirt and refused to take him for a walk because of it. But at least they read books to him in their room. You know Gil and his books.

Stupid me—I related the confrontation with his mother to Sergey. He shrugged. "Not such a big deal. Pick up a few things and stop complaining." When we first got married, he cautioned me, "Don't make me choose sides. A man has only one mother." Does it mean if I'm not careful around her he would leave me any place any time and that's it?

Sonia, I couldn't share the news about the baby with Sergey's parents. This baby belongs inside of my heart. I don't want them inside of my heart; it doesn't feel right. Am I making sense?

I felt less lonely after sharing my concerns with a friend. I slapped a stamp on my letter to Israel, dropped it into a mailbox, and started back towards our house.

"Oh, my God. Oh…" The intense pain pushed me down, right there in the middle of the street. Even sitting, I doubled from a jolt in my right side. Couldn't budge or shift, or even get air into my lungs—any motion felt excruciatingly impossible.

"No, no, I can't miscarry—here on the street or any other place," I whispered to myself.

Passersby started to gather.

"No French," I responded.

"Do you speak English?" one younger man asked.

"Just some."

"What is wrong? Do you want us to call an ambulance?"

Try explaining to him that my tourist visa expired already and what if I lost consciousness…

I remembered enough English words to refuse: "No, no ambulance, no hospital, please."

The moment the pain let me be, I appealed, using mostly my hands for clarifications: "Would you, please, move me to the side, from under everyone's feet."

The strangers sat me down by the building's wall. Spasms of pain gripped me on and off, holding me prisoner on a sidewalk for a while longer. Slowly, I walked home.

At last upstairs in our room I faced Sergey, who, still angry and unresponsive from the previous day's argument, had just walked in.

"You bring a doctor here and now! Do it!" I said.

He heard the resolve in my voice and saw agony in my eyes and ran out to the Jewish Family Service to request a doctor for an emergency home visit.

I crawled down the three flights of steps to use the bathroom, then blacked-out.

"Lilli, the doctor is here…" Sergey's voice arrived through the fog. They found me on the floor between the bathtub and the toilet. Gil sat next to me, holding my hand. I peered at my husband. He cried openly. My husband cried! He and the doctor carried me up to the third floor.

I didn't miscarry. I had a urinary infection. The doctor spoke passable English and I knew the word "baby." Pointing to my midriff, I showed three fingers, and said "baby."

The doctor smiled and said, "The infection will clear up with an antibiotic. These pills are safe. Take it. No harm to the baby."

In the evening, Sergey took Gil back to his parents. My whole body ached from exhaustion. I was dozing when my husband's voice spoke: "Let's talk. I'd like to explain some things." Sad words, no defiance, no life in them.

He didn't turn on the lights. In the duskiness, I couldn't see his features clearly.

"I never planned to tell you my parents' story. It's their past and it should've stayed private, but I don't see how to otherwise ask some compassion from you towards them."

Sergey lit up a cigarette and sat in the opposite corner, away from me, facing some unseen dot in the sun-bleached blue-flowered wallpaper.

"My father was a big-time Communist who was born into a family of a blacksmith in a Jewish village in the Ukraine, one of six children. He didn't have an education. Bolsheviks didn't ask for the diplomas. They gave you a gun and permission to shoot on their behalf. In the years after the revolution, a lot of Jews were in. They were smart, decisive, and often ruthless. They didn't have anything to lose. They hugged the idea of everyone's equality to their heart. They hungered for equality, having not been equal ever before."

Sergey's words were rolling out, hanging inside of his cigarette smoke, held up by their intensity. My eyes adjusted to the darkness. I stared at the smoke.

"It was a drunk time for those who were on the inside. My father was an insider. He had a chauffeur. He carried a gun and a card to buy from a store for the privileged. His young wife was envied. She felt deserving of that envy. Originally, when introduced into the Kaplan family, she wasn't accepted as an adequate match by his siblings. She fought for a place in the family and the victory was sweet, indeed."

At this moment of his tale, the thought came to me that I was the incidental recipient of her being angry at not being accepted into the original Kaplan family. I probably uttered something then because Sergey stopped talking, but then continued.

"In 1939, the Communist party sent my father to be their representative in the western part of the Ukraine. It was a territory the Soviets got as part of Stalin's agreement with Hitler. Those two were friends at the time. The natives didn't want to belong to the Soviet Union. They fought, but couldn't stand against the tanks of *tovaritch* Stalin, and lost."

Those were the facts of the bloody Soviet history very few citizens braved to discuss.

Sergey lit another cigarette.

"My father did what the particular situation required of him. Thus he and his family remained in favor. The chauffeur with the car and the caviar on the dinner table remained."

I listened and Sergey told me that when World War II started, in 1941, Sergey's father was one of the very first political officers to be sent to the front. His mother was evacuated deep into Siberia with the rest of the family.

Sergey went on: "Father was through the worst fights and won medals for his heroism, until in 1942, a German bullet was shot into his head.

The doctors decided it was safer to leave the bullet inside of his skull instead of operating. That's when he lost eyesight in one eye and the hearing on the same side. Even today he still suffers from headaches at any odd time."

I lowered my head, envisioning the man in the next room, who at this very moment was reading a fairy tale to my son.

"After the hospital, he was allowed to go convalesce with his wife in Siberia, and that's when I was conceived and born nine months later. My father returned to the front, a soldier again, tired, wounded, but still a soldier, following his orders. Walked on foot into Germany in 1945, and from one political assignment to the other. He didn't see me until I turned three. He came home a Soviet hero, not only for me, but for the country, too, at the time."

Layer upon layer, Sergey was unwrapping his father's poignant and intense history, which till now had been carefully preserved inside of his son's heart, freed at last to present to me. I recognized a gift when I received one.

The next layer was torture: "The problems started later. Dragged into the KGB, he was grilled about the 1939 events: 'What are you doing?' my outraged father demanded. 'I did what you told me to do. I abided explicit instructions.'

'That's not what we were told by the eyewitnesses. You overstepped your superiors. You acted in haste, and we had to smooth a number of feathers. You'd do better to confess.'

He didn't respond. Loyal to the party, to the Soviet country, and yet he knew it didn't count with the rats that tried to save their own skin. The insider—he knew the rules.

"The court was swift. The judgment—'the enemy of the state'—usually brought death."

Sergey coughed, adjusting his suddenly raspy throat, determined to carry on with his story. Could it be still worse?

"Mom sold everything: the furniture, the dishes, our clothes. The payments into the deep pockets of those who counted saved my father's life—ten years of 'hard labor' was slightly better than immediate death.

"The authorities decided our apartment was too large for the two of us and moved us into some neighbor's corner. Mom found a job. She'd hoped that even though Father's siblings didn't want to know her before, they would come around. But no, not a chance. His brothers and sisters lived their lives like nothing out of the ordinary had happened. Maybe they were scared. Many others were. There were millions of people sent to the labor camps in those years. So many lives destroyed. The people whom it didn't touch—didn't see it, didn't know.

"First, my father was a part of that merciless killing machine and then he was its prisoner. And nevertheless, he was a soldier, a war hero."

Every syllable Sergey uttered was a torment. And yet he wasn't done; there were more secrets to come. What wouldn't I give for that drink of vodka for both of us.

After a breather, he went on: "At age thirteen I transferred to a night school and went to work at a blacksmith shop, helping, learning the skill. Mom and I, we were really tight, doing everything together, like a family should. The letters from the camps were scarce. He was alive. How much alive we didn't know, and his letters didn't say.

"I was fifteen when my father returned; he walked in, and I didn't know him: dark man, swarthy even, hair almost gone, teeth too, loose clothing, nothing like his old photographs.

"He didn't come alone, though. He arrived with a five-year-old boy. 'Here,' my father said, 'is my son.' The boy looked like him. Like my father on the pictures, like my father I expected to return to us. It was weird."

That was a shocker! That was a secret he saved for later! I stood up. What were the appropriate words in this case? "Weird" wasn't the least of it! I groped for the little lamp near the bed. Even with a light on, I couldn't see Sergey's eyes. He didn't want me to see them. His skin had lost its color; his lips, his freckles, even his eyebrows, appropriated the same beige tone.

His hand shook; he was struggling with the lighter to start his fifth or sixth cigarette. I walked over and lit two. I needed one as well.

Sergey still continued: "My father told about the woman he met there, and how she'd saved him, and so on. Mom cried and didn't listen. 'Take him away from me,' she said. 'She saved you for herself and her bastard, not for me, not for our son. Do you have any understanding of how we lived through the years? Maybe you think *your* family helped? They probably knew about your whore right along. Of course she was a whore. To sleep with a married man, to have a child with him, she'd have to be a whore.' Mom opened the door and told Father to leave with the boy."

"She threw them out? You can't be right?" I exclaimed. Sergey didn't react.

"Many things my mom said were true. I couldn't imagine my father sleeping with that other woman and fathering a child. I felt sorry for the boy who looked so familiar. The boy never said anything. He just sat there in the corner and eventually fell asleep. Skinny boy he was, in a tight coat with short sleeves from someone even skinnier. Maybe the clothes were his, but from when he was younger.

"Father left that night. Took the boy with him. Returned alone a few days later. I didn't want to hate my father. I didn't know him at all. I was so mixed up. That is the story."

My husband expected me to bear sympathy to the two people he loved and this I couldn't do. I ached for him, the boy of thirteen, and the one of thirty-two. My tears showed up in solidarity.

A few more words left to be spoken:

"Mom doesn't talk to father's family. Father doesn't know what to say to Mom's relatives. After the camps, his health wasn't any good, though he worked till the emigration." For the second time this day my husband's eyes were wet.

"What happened to the boy?" I asked. "Where is your brother now?"

"My brother? That is an interesting part. He is in Israel. Father never told us, but he kept in touch. The boy lived with some childless relatives of Father's. When it first became possible, they left for Israel, much earlier than we made the same choice. He's a graduate of a military academy—an officer in the army. He came one day to my parents and introduced himself."

Sergey Kaplan didn't choose sides—since the age of fifteen he'd grieved for all of them: the innocent youngster with the familiar face, his father who found comfort in someone's arms, and mostly his mother who was his own anchor throughout his life.

We lived in Brussels for ten months. In September of 1975 United States consul in Belgium handed us American visas. We were ready to go and start a new life in New York City. I had a free day and one Belgium post stamp remained. I wanted to talk to Josef. That was long overdue. I addressed the envelope to Papa.

Hi, Josef,

When I was leaving Kiev, you told me not to correspond with you, because you were afraid of authorities reading your mail. So, I am sending it to Papa hoping that you would have an occasion to visit him.

Papa wrote you lost your job because of me. Sorry. What else could I say? You chose to remain there and you paid for it. If we hadn't immigrated and had stayed in Kiev, you would still have your job and my family would be miserable forever. Don't expect me to beg you for forgiveness. One sorry is all you get.

Anyway, it wasn't me leaving you. You were the one to walk away from me. Not on the day I left the country. Not on my wedding day. You were leaving me, slowly, long before that. Maybe because you couldn't live in Kiev? Maybe because your life was so hard? But was it my fault?

Maybe when Mama died. I know we weren't quibbling at the time. On some levels we became closer then, but something was amiss.

You were my protector since I remember myself. But as weeks, months, years were exiting, more and more I felt vulnerable in a way I couldn't understand and didn't know the reason. You were there and you weren't there at the same time. I stopped being aware of you being nearby; felt uncovered, if you know what I mean.

Is it feasible that you, too, felt defenseless after her death? You—big, strong, blue-eyed and blond person couldn't possibly feel unsafe, but maybe I'm mistaken.

You were Mama's golden idol: gorgeous, smart, talented, and also you were by her side during the war—I couldn't top any of it. Never envied you. You were too high above for any logical envy. You deserved her love.

She told me about those years, when at age five or six you walked through the woods to get to school and wrote your homework on newspapers' borders—the only paper you could find. Her little hero!

I was but a plain "nice" girl.

As a child, I'd think what havoc I should create to prove I wasn't "nice." Then I misbehaved, and you were the one to beat me up. Never complained—knew I deserved the punishments.

I wanted Mama to love me with the same abandonment, to wake up and start thinking of me at once; to talk about me too in those endless food lines, showing my photo and not yours from time to time.

I'm carrying on with nonsense, needing this word flood. Maybe by touching the past I can understand the emptiness in my present.

Did she say to you—Don't dream—dreams don't come true? Or was it reserved for me, the girl? Did she say—I can't teach you cycling—I'm too tired? Of course she didn't—she wasn't tired when you were a young boy.

Did you know she beat me once real hard? I was six. We went to a sea resort. Her cousin (don't remember her name) went along, taking her twins for my company. The two heartless bastards were cheating on me in every game. I cried the entire time. Mama was probably tired of me by the second day.

She said, "You were never good at games. Face it."

They were cheating the whole time.

One night I changed into my nightgown, and the pair started with their usual taunting: 'Lilli is a skeleton…' Remember how skinny I was? Something twisted inside—I started shrieking, on and on and on. People from the surrounding villages were running toward my screams.

I got the beating of my life—the only way Mama could stop me from screaming.

Nothing to do with you. I just coincidentally remembered the beating.

Once you beat me for a real reason.

I was maybe nine. Mama and I spent a month in that rented shack near the river. I detested the dark room and the stench of an outhouse and the crowd of pubescent girls dressing up from early morning with no place to show off.

You came to visit us.

Mama, does Lilli behave herself?" you asked and she said, "She's too young and doesn't understand I need help. Don't worry, she'll grow up and recognize these things. She's still a child."

I did understand, refusing to be nice. What a moron I was! Mama needed my assistance. I was aware of her being ill. All her surgeries during the years. They always cut something out of her. Did they do a biopsy at the time to check if something was cancerous? Who knows? Those doctors were puffed up from self-importance ... remember them? The colon-specialist who arrived without an instrument to check for polyps in her colon ... oh, God! You had to go outside and get a cab to take him back home to pick it up. Mama laughed hysterically, if you could believe it.

Anyway ... I was remembering that ugly little room by the river, when you came to visit us. You got mad at me for not helping Mama. You tried to catch me in order to punish. Mama said, "Don't do that, Josef." Then I walked up to you and got my beating.

After that incident, you went to sleep, because you traveled for hours and were exhausted. I stood nearby and waved the flies away. There were nasty big greenish flies in the country.

I loved you then and always.

Mama often explained to our father: Lilli is a good girl and don't worry for her. He insisted I was a weak female, and males would take advantage. Also, he said, Lilli has too many non-Jewish friends. Whom would she marry? She would remain an old maid. That was my death sentence. I hated those discussions. I tried not to listen, but it wasn't possible in our hole of an apartment with only that sickly-yellow curtain between the two rooms.

I didn't yet say anything about your lying. Just another one of the cute things you did. The dumb little sister believed you. Every damned fib. Do you remember any?

You saved your poor wife from dying of venereal disease. You went to prostitutes to pay her back for all the grief, yet your honor prevented you from actually sleeping with them. These are just the tidbits coming to mind.

Mama believed I couldn't keep secrets. But I did it, kept all your little confidences safe, making myself sick, worrying to slip and expose them somehow. I loved Natasha, and didn't wish any pain on her. I was twelve, thirteen maybe, at the time. And all of it, every droplet was a lie. Don't ask me how I know it. I do. Now, I do know, not then.

There were times in my life when my need for you was overwhelming: badly, absolutely, incredibly, desperately. There were things happening that I still can't utter. Those were not child's play events. No ... can't speak of it as yet. Maybe next time, if there would be a next time. For now, I would like to know what did I do to you personally to deserve your back turning towards me?

Before I sign off, I want to ask you something. A very long time ago, Papa said something about you not being his child? Did I dream that up? I seem to remember him saying it. But it didn't make sense at the time and it still doesn't.

Lilli, always your sister, but not so little anymore.

CHAPTER 16

Sheepshead Bay Projects, Brooklyn New York, USA

1976-1977

A Queens' machine shop hired Sergey as a supervisor. Most of the workers he supervised were themselves non-English-speaking immigrants, the rest born-in-USA high school dropouts who conversed in street slang. Sergey knew machines. He showed workers how to work them. His limited vocabulary didn't get in the way.

His starting salary barely covered the rent on our Brooklyn Ocean Avenue apartment plus the daily expenses. Since the head-of-household found employment, NYANA didn't help us anymore with rent money.

"Lilli, I met a guy I knew from NYANA, and he told me there is a low- to middle-income housing project not far from here in Brooklyn, and the rent depends on your income. With our income, we'll pay close to nothing. Let's sign up for it."

We did, and soon a family freed a two-bedroom apartment in one of the project's buildings. Our name was next on the list.

All the buildings in the project looked exactly the same: spotted by rain with yellowish chipped walls. At night, when tenants lowered their identical off-white plastic shades, the houses looked eyeless, blind. The metal mesh fence in between buildings added to the institutionalized appearance. In spite of all that, the endless ocean of green lawns in front and back of those buildings prevented the place from appearing gloomy.

Our small apartment was on the third floor: a living room with an off-the-kitchen corner for dining, and two bedrooms off the corridor, seemed extravagant to us. Sergey and I carried over our things one-by-one, like the old legless mattresses, Benny's crib, and a folding kitchen table. The clothes and the pots and the dishes fit into our patched, rickety Chevy that Sergey had bought recently to drive to work.

On every trip out the door some new person approached us to say hello. The neighbors seemed nice. I would be able to make friends here. In our previous Brooklyn place, I didn't have a chance to become acquainted with anyone.

In front of every project's building, green benches were chained to the ground. There, at any time in any kind of weather, the tenants sat, women mostly.

"Oh, show us your baby." The old and the young, with shopping carts or with baby carriages, they stopped me passing by with my children.

Gladly I obliged, especially because Benny, now a year old, adored the attention. He laughed raucously, showing dimples in his fat cheeks. "How cute, look at him laughing." The praises were offered by all. For me, they were still voices not yet attached to the faces and names.

Little Ben wasn't able to sit still for more than a few minutes. The moment I turned my head away, he climbed out from his stroller and was on the run.

"Mom, I'll get him." Gil ran to catch resisting and hollering Benny, pulling him back by the collar of his shirt.

"Wow, this is a big boy, mommy's helper. How old are you?" The women's chorus switched their attention to Gil. My older son didn't like the questioning strangers; his velvety eyes searched mine, begging to leave.

As days and then weeks progressed, I didn't get beyond the constant, "How you doing?" thrown at me from the benches. Their smiles were wide, though the expressions on the faces displayed boredom. Why did they ask? They didn't care. Weren't they tired sitting long days on these straight-backed benches? Didn't they have anything better to do?

My sons enjoyed playing in the grass, acquiring friends, together with them building huts out of the branches, or just running in circles pretending to be birds. I stayed on the bench, watching them.

"How nice to see you relaxing," a short, middle-aged woman from the bench across the walk remarked. Great—here was the one who wanted to talk.

"I enjoy looking at my children when they play," I answered loud so she would hear from where she sat. I didn't know if whatever I said was grammatically correct and if the woman understood my accent. In answer to my voiceless question, she walked over.

"The housing project is perfect for the family like yours," she said in a conspiring whisper. "You don't have to work ever. You take care of your family. You always would have time to relax."

What was she saying—not to work? How a woman would ever get any respect if she didn't work? How could a family get ahead on one salary? I planned to start working the moment Benny would start school. Slowly I picked my words, wishing to explain my point of view, hoping she would get it through the layers of my accent and poor vocabulary.

"Every person should work. Every person has a duty to develop herself and enrich the world."

The woman stood up, mumbled something and left while I was in the middle of the sentence. What did I say? Maybe I mixed up words? Didn't matter. Let her announce to the whole project that the new woman with a Russian accent was crazy. If all of them were of the same opinion, I didn't care to know them.

As a little girl I envied my girlfriends whose mothers worked. When the teacher asked what their mother was doing, they had a profession to report: a teacher, a doctor, an engineer. What did I say? Mumbled something, ashamed of Mom, who stayed at home.

No way. A stay-at-home mom was not a role I wanted. Life devoted to taking care of the children, cooking, and cleaning, felt confined and irrelevant. Food discussions gagged me; the secrets of spotless cleaning brought on a wish to smash things instead of cleaning them. Was there any other option open for me? I chewed on this question, not seeing any way out. Small children. No profession. No language. On every wall in every room I perceived big-stenciled words: YOU DON'T HAVE A CHOICE!

I made a pact with myself: I give it one year. In one year I'll find a nursery or babysitter for Benny and see about getting a job.

Our life looked better than ever: healthy children, nice apartment, income to cover our modest expenses. Sergey already decided that his first job would be a stepping-stone for the next, better one. He returned from work with complaints about his boss, but every Friday proudly brought home a paycheck. Both boys missed their dad during the days, waiting for him anxiously. When I tried to convince little Benny to "go potty," he would cross his chubby legs, saying, "Pee-pee with Papa."

Armed with our first VISA card, we ordered living-room carpeting in shades of brown, beige, and gold. While we waited for the carpet to be installed, I fashioned frilly curtains from the remnants of sheer ivory lacy fabric.

A few couples we met at the NYANA and became friendly with brought us a house-warming gift—a floor-size ceramic vase I filled with tree branches. The books we stored with our friends when we left Israel arrived; Sergey built sturdy shelves to store them. A small black-and-white TV set stood on top of its box, which I covered with wood-patterned contact paper. The room looked cozy and inviting. We loved it and our guests praised it.

In the six years since we married, it was the very first time I was able to use my own taste to decorate the place we lived in. I enjoyed my handiwork.

Slowly, as Sergey's salary would allow, the furniture appeared. We became adept at finding inexpensive, modern-looking, serviceable pieces: the brown leather living room set, the plastic and vinyl dining room set, the bright yellow children's room furniture.

Only our bedroom remained empty. Bedroom sets displayed in the local stores were either unaffordable or ugly. The two of us continued sleeping on the donated legless mattresses.

Once, leafing through a *1001 Decorating Ideas* magazine, I spotted white Formica furniture "do-it-yourself" for a hundred dollars. They would send a precut set and then we would put pieces together. I was sure Sergey could do it. I jumped from the sofa, dancing a little jig with Benny on my shoulders, waiting for Sergey to come home.

"Sergey, look. You think you could? Look how beautiful it is. Just look. Only a hundred dollars."

Please like it, please do—I begged silently. The bed, the headbox bedding storage, and the desk were exactly the furniture we needed. Sergey seemed pleased with my find, eager to build something beautiful that wouldn't cost us a fortune.

Before long, the arguments around that furniture building enterprise became pretty loud.

"You wanted this furniture more than anyone, so stop carrying on about every little nick," my husband admonished me, when he had to size piece of Formica that was too big.

"It's not so little." I pointed to a gaping cut through our dining table. "Look, you slashed it with your saw. We aren't going to buy a new table that soon."

"I work at my job and then at home. Isn't it enough for you? I don't have one moment of free time. I don't need your lectures."

I knew what was coming next. I knew his next words only too well. I'd asked for it.

"I'll leave this second. If this is what it takes to shut you up—I will. Is this what you want me to do?"

It was easy for him. He had his parents to go to. I would be left with the kids, like so many of the others in this housing project. His words reached me through a tearing noise inside of my skull.

"Sergey, let's talk. I agree it's my fault. I shouldn't have said it. You do work hard."

He didn't respond, didn't look at me. He stopped building the furniture. For a week. The boards and the Formica and the tools remained in the middle of the apartment. Sergey slept alone on the living room coach and didn't join us at the dining table. I knew he didn't eat out—he came home at the usual time. Only in the evenings, when I took the children outside for a walk, some food inside the refrigerator vanished. As many times before, he starved himself to punish me. It worked. These tearing sounds in my head were ongoing. I woke up with them, went to sleep accompanied by them. It terrified me. Maybe I was slowly dying.

No, it was the tension. I hoped.

"Mama, I like it. Sticks and nails around," Benny declared.

“You are a stupid baby, it’s dangerous and messy. I hate when Papa doesn’t talk to us.” Gil was aware when our family dynamics were disturbed. How would the children react if their father left us?

“Sergey, let’s talk, please. I know it’s my fault,” I tried every day.

Saturday morning, wordlessly he picked up his tools and continued with the furniture making. I thought it was safe to talk to him when he breathed out: “Has nothing to do with you. The money is already spent for the materials. So I’ll finish what I started.”

The noise in my head brought a horrific headache on. But the peace in the household was restored. The same day, Sergey came to the dinner table and ate but spoke to the boys exclusively. Gil kept glancing his troubled eyes from his father to me. Benny was thrilled with his father’s attention. I was worried for nothing. He was not going to leave!

I cleaned the sawdust that covered every surface of the small apartment. I gave the excuses to the neighbors complaining about the annoying electric saw noise. When one of them complained to the housing office, and we received an admonishing letter. I didn’t trouble Sergey with it.

The furniture finished and the mood in the apartment festive, we took the old mattresses to the sidewalk curb. Friends came over with a bottle of something *Manischewitz* and we toasted the results of Sergey’s hard work.

* * *

Gil started kindergarten in the neighborhood’s public school. The first day I walked him over, bringing Ben along. To my surprise, every other five-year old came accompanied by the set of parents, two sets of grandparents, and siblings.

I felt like an orphan, hoping Gil didn’t think so. The teacher called on each child and he or she stood up and their relatives cheered. “Gil Kaplan,” she read. My son didn’t react. “Here,” I said and pointed at him, but couldn't applaud with Benny in my arms and I was too shy to make loud noises like the other parents did.

Our routine was established. Most mornings I fed and dressed both children, took Gil to school, and then pushing Benny's stroller in front of me, hoping he wouldn't climb out, walked to the supermarket.

While picking the needed products, I didn't always notice what Benny's hands caught on the way.

"Benny, I can't believe it. Did you do it again? Ate the entire container of cottage cheese, again. When did you even grab it that I didn't notice?" The foxy face smeared white looked at me innocently, his both hands covered with cottage cheese, an empty plastic box next to him in the stroller. "People will think we're barbarians, stealing and eating with our fingers."

Next time it was a package of "Hebrew National" bologna. "I'm sorry," I said to the cashier, "I'll pay for it. Here is a wrapping. My son ate the sausage." She made a face, entering the price in the register and throwing the empty packaging into the wastebasket with her two fingers. It could be funny.

At least Benny wasn't hungry after the grocery shopping and we stayed outside. I sat on one of the benches while he played nearby. No one tried talking to me anymore. I listened attentively to the neighbors chatting between themselves, learning more English and becoming familiar with the local life.

I understood that tenants had to report any financial changes to the housing authorities, because the rent calculation depended on family income. Now I knew what that short woman had tried to educate me about months ago.

The women entertaining each other on these benches didn't work. Some had many babies in their arms; some took care of cash businesses for their husbands. No one discussed working opportunities, only weather and food recipes.

Their hopes were to save money while paying low rent. Mine—to learn English, work, be respected by those in my family and maybe by others.

How could I move towards my goal if I was busy all day with the children and the housework? The voice inside nudged me on. During the day it seemed easier to shut it off like a lamp.

Nothing helped to fight my nightmares: in them I'm striding somewhere dressed in a business suit. Gaping holes are opening in front of me. "I'm going to work and I'm in a rush," I whimper out to no one in particular. "Don't go, stop walking," someone behind me orders. I see a crowd of my Kiev neighbors screaming in Russian: "Why did you leave us? Were you tired of hard life? Do you have it easy now? Answer us!"

I hesitate, not knowing what to say and wake up.

Trying to rid my head from the tension, while Benny napped, I wrote comforting letters:

> *Papa, we are good. Gil likes his school a lot. He thrives on learning. For the first time in his life he is glad to leave me and be with others. Remember, he never wanted to do it before?*
>
> *Sonia, my darling friend, how are all of you in Israel? Please write to me, I miss you terribly. We are surviving.*

***

I turned thirty. I was old! It was cold and gloomy November. One morning I opened my eyes and faced the emptiness of my days with renewed clarity. What to do? What could I do? I'd always sewed. Mama taught me when I was little, and in high school I took sewing as a required specialty, and then sewed for myself and my friends. In Israel I tried my hand at altering ladies' clothing, though didn't earn enough to continue.

That's what I'm going to do, I thought. I started sewing. The remnants of different fabrics at the specialty store cost very little. Throughout that dreary winter, all four of us obtained an impressive wardrobe of my making. Every shirt, pair of pants, or dress came out beautifully.

One day after work, Sergey walked in, smiling mischievously.

"Lilli," he called, "I brought you something. See if you can use it." He held a large cardboard box with leftover drapery fabrics. "I pass a decorating store every day on the way home. Today a guy came out and left that box at the curb and, don't know why, I glanced inside. Saw all those neat fabrics. Look."

My next project found me. In a short while, the shoe-holders, the letter-pockets, and the cute pocketbooks to give away as gifts depleted the box of its contents. The box of garbage-found *shmatas* evolved into senseless pockets seemed to satisfy me…After the last scrap was gone, I was at a loss again. Why am I that way? Why not happy with the reality? My reality should be enough. I shopped, cooked, cleaned, washed our clothes, and tried to keep peace in my family.

But that's what my mama did throughout her life and I swore I was not going to be her. She polished floors, cooked elaborate dishes, ironed my pinafores, and placated my papa. Did she enjoy any of it? She died before turning fifty-six.

Another six months passed. One summer morning I left Ben with a neighbor, who agreed to babysit, and traveled to downtown Manhattan.

Before leaving my house, I checked myself in a mirror, always in a rush to get out of the shower, out of the house, to be ready with dinner ... I wondered how I looked for someone else to judge me: a slim woman, dressed in a straight, knee-long, denim skirt, and a white short-sleeved buttoned shirt. She looked like a stranger to me. Her dark hair cut in a short no-nonsense style; her wide eyes the color of dark amber staring with hope—pleading? The woman looked fine, young enough to work, old enough to be responsible.

For days I practiced what I'd say: "I need a job. Please help me. I could sew. I could obtain any skill on a job. I know I could."

From the days when Sergey looked for a first job, I remembered the agency "Project Cope," a combined effort between the city of New York and the Jewish Family Service. Even the name of the person who helped him got filed in my mind—"Mr. Feinman."

In the offices of "Project Cope" I recited the prepared speech with my accented, slightly trembling voice.

Mr. Feinman, tall, stooped, wearing a dark skullcap, took his counselor's duty seriously.

"Do you want factory work? What do you want with that dead-end job with a minimum pay? You need both: language and profession, not skill, not factory work. You are too young and educated for that. Describe what you did in Russia?"

My achy head! It was spinning from his good intentions. If I described my total career as an operator of an adding machine, any effort to sound dignified would be ruined.

"Please, I don't want to go to school. I hate school. I'm not good at studying."

He didn't listen.

"There are exams for a bookkeeping course going on as we speak. We'll check your mathematical knowledge, English, and logic—nothing too difficult for a college-educated woman. You'll be sorry if you don't try school first before settling for a working trade."

I wanted to interrupt his words about a college with a smirk. Yeah, I did write "college" on my application. College … you should've been at that college. Maybe meet my dear brother, Josef, who was instrumental in my getting into that college. Two-and-a-half-year junior college built specially for the radio-plant's workers. Some of those workers had never been to high school. Josef and Papa wanted me to get a college diploma. My brother shared a bottle of vodka with its director … I was admitted.

I knew Feinman's words were sensible; he wanted to help. He didn't know the distaste I harbored for the word "bookkeeping," since my mama used to suggest it was a good profession for a girl.

> *You dolt, how old are you? You aren't a child rebelling against her mother, who by the way isn't even alive to hear your protests.*

The English exam was the most complicated. I tried to remember my high school foreign language class, but we didn't study the big words. Our teachers were satisfied with the basic ones. The household terms I picked up from my neighbors in the project didn't help either. The guessing and supposing was silly. I stopped in the middle of the test and failed of course.

A week later, someone in the agency administration checked my file before discarding it. They decided to give me another chance and called me in for an informal interview. Ben stayed with a babysitter once again.

At the school's office, an old man wearing *Hassidic* clothes asked me a few simple questions, then said to write down: "I love my husband and children" and "I am a good person."

"You passed my test and are accepted to a six-month bookkeeping course. *Mazal Tov*," he said. Was he crazy?

"But I have a baby at home. I need to find a nursery for him." My face flushed, my tongue glued inside my bitter mouth. I still tried to stop events from happening.

The man smiled. Did he see through my fears and uncertainties?

"Your son is three, right?" he asked, while jotting a note to the Brooklyn orthodox nursery school, where they accepted three-year-olds.

Benny was two-and-a-half, but I thought it was wrong to disappoint a nice person. I nodded. Maybe they knew better what was good for me? Sergey knew better; my parents knew better. Even my brother, Josef, when he cared, knew better.

***

My first Sunday after the week at school, I ran back and forth through the apartment, trying to do all the household duties at once while mentally reviewing the teacher's home assignments.

"Mama, come here," Gil called impatiently from the living room.

His voice reached me in the kitchen. I didn't have a moment to spare for child's games. Gil was a clever boy and would have to solve whatever problems by himself.

"Mom, listen to me. I talk and talk and you don't listen." The voice of my first-born turned to exasperation.

"So I'm a bad mother. What else is new? Go and talk to your father," I hollered from the kitchen where I cooked for the three days ahead and read my English schoolbook propped on the windowsill. "I can't cook and study and listen to you at the same time."

"I tried talking to Papa already. He sent me to you. He is on the bed reading the newspapers about jobs, and he is mad and won't listen. He just yelled that if he wouldn't find a better job, we would be poor forever."

I set the big soup-pot filled with water on the stove, wiped my hands, noticing some food stains on my yellow cotton T-shirt. The hard kitchen-work was displayed on my clothes.

"Mama…" At this point, Gil walked into the kitchen and tugged at my brown shorts, making sure I listened. I smiled as I glanced at his darling face, a pale oval framed by long black curls—a perfect picture of a face. Then, quickly rearranged my expression into a serious mode, I folded my arms in front of my chest.

"Talk fast, but don't ask me to leave the kitchen while I cook."

His words started spilling out rapidly: "There is this girl in my class, Nancy. Her hair is blond and soft and wavy, and I invited her to our house. I'm cleaning and cleaning, but Benny is a pig and throws everything back. I already cleaned five times." The tears in his voice sounded close to the top.

I marched into the living room hiding a smile that kept on appearing. A girl? He was only six-and-a-half, our Gil. The chairs stood in the wrong places. The books from the lowest shelf were out and around, and papers were spread all over the carpet, covering everything, including Ben, who sat in the middle of it all.

"Benny didn't move these chairs," I assumed in a shrill voice, not finding a logical explanation for the mess in the house and getting angry.

"I moved the chairs because I wanted to vacuum under them, but he started messing with the newspapers."

Benny's round, pink face peeking from under the *Sunday Times* looked devilishly angelic.

Now I had to clean, too. First I picked up the little nemesis, and then the books and the newspapers. "Here, sit in the armchair or I'll smack you good."

Benny started to cry. "Pee…" he announced all of a sudden through his tears, getting attention away from his misdeeds.

"You aren't a little baby anymore, for God's sake. Just go to the bathroom."

Ben disappeared behind the bathroom door, away from the expected punishment. There were no tears anymore, shiny black eyes darting from his brother to me, the dimpled smile of a fox covering all bases.

Peace and neatness were restored in the apartment. Gil set up a chair in front of the living room window and patiently waited for the blond Nancy, till it became dark and he couldn't see anymore. He didn't say anything and afterwards sniveled just a tiny bit. I felt his pain, but a strength too when facing his very first love-disappointment.

He'll be upset for a while, hopefully not for long, I told myself. On Monday, Gil returned from school and told the fat Mrs. Kovalski—she babysat both boys after school while she took care of her two German shepherds—that he had to wash up and go outside to wait for a friend. She waited with him, holding her dogs on their leashes from some distance, as he instructed. The little blond girl, accompanied probably by her mother, appeared soon. Alone, she went over to Gil and they spoke for a while and then shook hands. The girl left, going back to her waiting mother.

"Congratulations," I remarked of his date, learning about it from the babysitter. "Nancy is a smart girl. She changed her mind about seeing you."

"Nancy didn't come. I asked Vikki. She is blond too."

***

I was a student and I was doing well. Hooray! I couldn't believe my luck. No more headaches, and I wasn't tired from all the work. I felt great. I actually used my brain, and surprisingly, I still had a brain to use.

There were fifteen women in our study group, all of them Russian immigrants. Mostly younger than I, still unmarried and childless, they complained about the heavy load of homework, preferring to go out to parties. The few older women, the tired baggage of their old life on their shoulders, listened to the lectures warily, not hoping to find jobs after investing months of study.

Faina sat next to me in our English class. It was impossible not to notice her. Big-breasted and broad shouldered, she walked in wearing the old-fashion hairdo of a Russian schoolteacher. Her waist-long, heavy black hair was braided and pinned around her head like a halo. Looking pointedly at Faina, one of the youngest girls whistled comically, giving the others permission to smirk.

Flustered Faina turned to me and whispered, "Everything is a joke at their age. I've spent a lifetime braiding my hair. Is it that bad?"

I tried to be impartial. "Just unusual. Today most girls give up their braids at age five. Don't mind them."

The very next day, the "new and improved" Faina with the shortest of haircuts walked in. No one spoke. Her small head above her full-bodied figure resembled a tennis-ball topping a mountain.

"Listen, Faina, I saw a wig-store on the way here. There are a lot of orthodox women around and they wear wigs. Did you know when those women get married, they actually cut their hair very short so they look ugly for other men? I don't understand how their husbands find them attractive, but that's what it is. Why don't we stop there at lunch and you select one of those long-hairdo wigs, till your own hair grows back?" She liked my suggestion and bought one plain, less-expensive wig. To our relief, the women in the group didn't comment on that development.

It seemed Faina's goals were similar to mine: she wanted to study and dreamt of getting a job. We became friendly.

"Lilli, could you and Sergey take me and my husband along whenever you go someplace on weekends. We don't have a car and stay home most of the time." Though she sounded needy and insistent, I saw no reason to refuse.

I only hoped Sergey wouldn't object to driving out of his way to pick up some strangers to take along on the family outings. "It's fine with me," he said. "Hopefully her husband is not a total jerk."

Returning from our first joint trip, which happened to be to the Museum of Natural History, Sergey proclaimed, "Her Edward is the most irritating person on the planet Earth." Faina's husband appeared drowsy. He was moving and talking uncommonly slow.

"Does he know how to think for himself? Faina speaks for him. Did you notice that?"

I did. I also spotted a sarcastic grin on Sergey's face whenever Faina answered a question directed to her spouse. Edward seemed used to her directing their family's traffic. Was Sergey the one to command our lives?

The next time our two families were together, Sergey brought along chess set. Both men enjoyed playing and our following outings went smoothly.

Gil and Benny begged us to go somewhere on a picnic. We decided to drive upstate New York to Bear Mountain. Saturday morning, I fed them and packed a picnic lunch.

"Toys…" Benny started to whine at the last moment.

"We were supposed to leave the apartment half-an-hour ago," Sergey retorted. "Lilli, why didn't you think about preparing his toys? Anyway, he doesn't need them. He always loses everything he brings outside."

My head ... the noise from inside of it overwhelms ... I have to think. Without his toys, Ben wouldn't stop crying. If I allow him to return, Sergey would construe it into a rebuke to his authority, and we'll stay home, and he'll stop talking to me for a week, at least. Why didn't I think about toys? Now the pain was splitting my head apart.

Aching head and all, I took Benny back to his room. He had too many favorites and couldn't decide. "Here, take this one and this and this one." I piled a batch of miniature cars into my bag, not leaving any time for him to do the selection.

Sergey waited and didn't remark. In no time we were outside and on the road, driving to pick up Faina and her husband. My brain was pounding. I closed my eyes, trying to relax during the long drive upstate, the familiar tearing noise on the inside drowning the children's arguments.

Later that afternoon, after we returned from the picnic and dropped off our company, we walked into our apartment when the phone rang.

"Oh, hi, Lilli." Faina sounded anxious.

"What happened?" Did something happen after we parted?

"Nothing much. We are fine," Faina continued. "Does Sergey know anything about TV antennas?"

"Sergey, Faina is on the line and she questions your competency on TV antennas," I yelled over to my husband, who was changing his clothes in the bedroom.

"What happened to their antenna?" Sergey wanted to know.

"Faina, what's with the antenna?" I related his question into the phone.

"How am I supposed to know—the damn antenna is on the roof."

I repeated the words back and forth, not giving it a thought.

"Lilli, why do you even repeat this hogwash? Try thinking before you do. Give me the phone." Sergey was by my side, eyes darting furiously. He grabbed the receiver out of my hand.

"Faina, why doesn't Edward go up on that roof and find out what's wrong?"

"Do you think he is an idiot to go up on the roof?"

Sergey slammed the phone down. "So her husband is not an idiot to go on his roof but I am? Do you believe this?"

Sergey was understandably upset and I couldn't blame him. I shouldn't have brought that couple into our life.

We didn't take too many outings after the "antenna" incident. Without the company of the other family, we mostly stayed close to home, letting our boys play on the green lawns of the housing project. Though, when they repeatedly asked us to visit the Bronx Zoo, we took them.

The day went as most of our outings did.

"Benny, stop trying to shake hands with the monkeys. They bite."

"Gil, I understand you want to stop where the big birds are, but we don't have time for everything."

"Gil, please, watch where we are going. You're going to get lost." Our older son seemed to be in a daze. He didn't pay any attention to anything any of us said or did. He carried a big zoo book and carefully checked the names of the animals we saw in the cages against the ones in the book.

"I'll work with the animals," he announced when we returned home. "I'll treat them when they are sick, and I'll pat them, and they'll fight for me and protect me when other animals jump at me."

"You, Gil, can be anything you decide to be," Sergey said meaningfully. He wanted to end the day with an important message to his impressionable young son.

I stopped unpacking our bags, forgot about my head, and listened, not daring to make a sound. How great Sergey was! I loved him even if sometimes his moodiness got to me.

He wasn't afraid to dream and to wish and to know his mind. He would teach our sons to be brave.

Was I the heavy appendage of his, afraid to think five minutes ahead, trying to place one foot in front of the other, making sure the ground was steady? I didn't know how to dream. I didn't want to wish for something that wouldn't materialize anyway. I was blessed to have such a husband.

Gil's aspirations reminded me of someone very dear to my heart, someone who lived far away.

"You know, Gil, your uncle Josef was an animal doctor in his younger years. He worked with the cows and horses and sheep." Not often did I mention my brother. My husband knew only the blunt and harsh side of Josef and I didn't blame him for not trying to understand the other gentle and kind side that I remember from my childhood. After all that was the only side that Josef divulged to Sergey.

"But I don't know him," our little boy informed me, his eyes sparkling with interest.

"And lucky for you." His father was fast with mean words, like they were right there on the tip of his tongue, waiting.

Josef wasn't an easy man to like, and he didn't bother befriending Sergey when he became his brother-in-law. The relationship between the two men didn't have a chance to form before we emigrated from Russia.

What could I say now? I had chosen my husband over my brother and forbade myself to ever review my decision. I lived with that pain. My only wish was for Sergey to understand how much Josef meant to me when I was a little girl and a youngster. He was my shield, the only one I trusted endlessly.

Well, it was like my mama always ordered: bury silly wishes before they bury you.

CHAPTER 17

Sheepshead Bay Projects, Brooklyn New York, USA.

1977-1978

"Lilli, really, why do we have to park our Dodge so far away from the house?" Sergey inquired, pushing Ben's stroller in front of him. "You keep insisting and I listen to you instead of ignoring." We were coming home from his parents' place in Brooklyn on Church Avenue.

"Because the neighbors talk. You know that. No one knows we are left penniless after the down payment on that car. Seeing a brand new car, they would think we are loaded," I explained and held tightly to Gil's hand while we were crossing the street.

"It reminds me of a similar conversation we had in Israel when I bought our very first car ever. You haven't changed. Why do you care so much about people's opinions of us? We don't steal and don't cheat on our income reports to the housing. We save on everything," Sergey said, pointing at his and my trousers made by my own hands from gray lightweight wool. Gil's striped t-shirt I bought for a dollar from a Korean store and his pants sewed by me from a denim remnant. The best-dressed guy was our Benny. I made myself proud with his cotton, white-and-blue checkered, two-part ensemble.

"I know. I know. You don't have to convince me. I'm the only mother who doesn't buy the ice cream from that damn truck that comes every day and plays cute music some days as many as five times. I refuse to pay fifty cents for a cone when there is a gallon of perfectly good ice cream in the freezer.

"You have to listen to Benny cry and see him fall flat on his tummy on the sidewalk. Though Gil doesn't beg, it kills me to see his eyes getting bigger and sadder each time that accursed truck rings its bells. By the way, do you know that pregnant woman across from us, the one with five kids?" I asked.

"Of course I know her. Her husband had a vasectomy this past week. He felt so proud of himself—he handed out cigarettes to all the guys who were out." Sergey laughed.

"I heard the whispering and the snickering going around. Good for him. So, she buys ice creams and sodas for all her kids each time the bells ring. Maybe she knows some secret on handling finances that I can't comprehend."

***

Since the day my bookkeeping classes started, I was always in a rush to jump on a bus, switch to a subway train, get to the downtown building, trying not to be late. Leaving the house, I dashed by the sitting neighbors once in the morning and later in the afternoon, nodding my general greetings into their direction.

The only person I tried to catch a glimpse of was Nellie. I became friendly with her in my previous, not so hectic existence. We had a really nice time back then, sitting by Benny's carriage and having a heart-to-heart. Now she was too busy with her newborn daughter to stay on those benches any longer. I knew I had to find a moment to drop in and see how tiny Alicia was doing.

Nellie didn't talk to other neighbors. Usually she perched on the edge of a lonely bench with her young son sitting not far but apart from her. I assumed the boy was the woman's son from the way she watched him out of the corner of her eye, while he looked in the other direction whenever she spoke to him.

The boy's skin had an unusual color, not regular creamy white, more like dull beige, almost bleached brown. You couldn't ignore his remarkably adult eyes staring at you. They were huge and defiant.

The mother was young, skinny, and pale to the extent of appearing sickly. That pair intrigued me. I wanted to know more about the woman and her child.

One morning, on the way back from taking Gil to school I walked over, pushing Benny's stroller in front of me. I spoke fast, before I lost my nerve. The limited vocabulary of an immigrant didn't allow me the flexibility with words.

"Hi, I'm Lilli and my baby's name is Ben."

"Hello, I'm Nellie," the woman answered.

From a close distance, she looked hardly older than a schoolgirl. She was pregnant, but not that far along in her pregnancy. I guessed she took her son to school earlier.

"You just moved in recently, right?" Nellie asked.

"Yes. Sorry for my English. I know a lot of words but pronounce them wrong, and people often don't understand me."

When I introduced myself that way, neighbors on the benches weren't apprehensive to correct my mistakes. That's how I learned.

Nellie smiled sadly. "Look, I'm born American, but people seldom understand me either. Though they question my actions, not my words."

Her eyes were huge like her little son's, with the same defiant expression.

I smiled at Nellie's words and sat down, curious even more.

"I watched your son the other day," I said to my new acquaintance. "He seems very young and very old at the same time. Beautiful boy."

Nellie waved her hand, dismissing my words as irrelevant. When she spoke again, she sounded harsh, affirming every word, "Did you see my husband? Let's make one thing clear before the bullshit about Michael's beauty. Answer me: did you see my husband?"

Why was she so rude all of a sudden? Did I see her husband? I didn't know. What was so special about him? Was she mad? Would she do something crazy? Maybe I'd better leave? I mumbled something, forgetting the needed words.

"I'll tell you, but you probably know it already: He is black. My husband is b-l-a-c-k, like in 'Negro' black. Michael looks like his father, though his skin is light. And he is beautiful." She finished speaking through the tears, yet with the defiance I'd already assigned to her and her son as their trademark.

"I said—he is beautiful. I guess I never met your husband. Yes, I understand your life is not…" I stumbled, looking for the right expression: "Dizzy with laughter…"

What else could I say to her? I'd better go home. I didn't want to cry about her sad life. Mine wasn't so great either.

"Maybe our children could play together, later after school. Your Michael is probably the same age as my Gil. Five, right?"

After that, we met almost daily, talking and sharing our lives' pitfalls.

I learned that Nellie and Nelson married against the wishes of both families. After a while, Nellie's sister and brother, and then the parents, reluctantly accepted Nelson. When Michael was born, he had a doting grandmother, and also an aunt and an uncle to babysit him.

Nelson's parents and his siblings blamed the whole white race for all the wrongs in their lives. They never spoke to him after the marriage. At one point, one of Nelson's brothers started visiting them, first seldom and then more and more often. Young Michael adored that uncle. He walked by his side listening to the tales of the family he knew little about. Idolizing the relatives he never met drove the little boy to rejection of his mother. She, the white woman, was at fault for the break of the families.

To me it wasn't surprising at all. In the Soviet country, families weren't black and white, they were Russian and Jewish. Same result—anger, arguments, division of families, lonely babies growing up without the benefit of loving grandparents. A divorce in a lot of cases.

One day, on the way home from the grocery shopping, I walked through the narrow asphalt passages that crisscrossed the projects' green lawns. In my left hand I carried a shopping bag filled with groceries, with my right pushing Ben's stroller, speeding to get home. Benny was impatient, wanting to run. Every time he climbed up, I stopped, pushed him down, yelled, "Sit down and stay down."

A group of young boys was throwing stones at the first floor apartment window in one of the buildings. I heard their shouts, inciting each other. One voice sounded familiar.

"Michael?" I asked, not believing my ears and eyes.

The little boy looked up and down, pressed his lips together, and dropped a rock he held into his pants pocket. He whispered to his accomplices, and they stopped their search for more ammunition.

“We don’t do nothing.” Lying didn’t come easily. He didn’t look at me, didn’t turn around to face me. “Nobody lives there. The housing people are thieves anyhow, so let them fix the window.”

I recognized the familiar defiant notes in his voice.

“Let’s go, Michael. Let’s go home. I’m sure your mother is worried looking for you.” I didn’t know if Nellie was home or one of the relatives was left in charge. “You don’t want neighbors calling the cops on you.”

“Yeah, I want them to! I’d like to go to prison. They teach you there, and you get friends there, and your friends watch over you.” Michael became animated. My heart sank. Grabbing Ben out of the stroller, I plopped there my overstuffed grocery bag instead. It was faster that way. I headed straight to Nellie’s apartment.

Nelson walked out, and after hearing my words immediately ran out. His face lost its brightness and his hands shook.

“No son of mine, no way!” I heard his angry, pained words as I boarded an elevator going up to my third floor.

Now I didn’t see much of Nellie or Michael or baby Alicia. Between the school and the housework, I was never free. I stopped at their place only once when Alicia was born. The tiny girl looked like Nellie, yet her coloring was her father’s. “Be happy, little angel, it won’t be easy,” I mouthed, and left a toy I brought.

At the end of November, cold weather reached me unexpectedly. The streets were getting darker much earlier, and my perilous mood followed that trend. I was an ancient thirty-one. Who would hire me? What was the use of that diploma I was working so hard to get?

Was it me skipping steps only two months ago, running up to our floor, impatient to wait for an elevator? Was it me laughing and hugging Gil tightly at a subway turnstile, passing together as one person? “It’s wrong. Don't you ever do it," I said to him right after, feeling like a teenage nincompoop.

I was tired, felt guilty for my ambitions. Should've been glad for what I had instead of taking all this time away from the kids. My school work didn't seem so important and I did fewer and fewer of the assignments, not expecting to find a job and use the acquired knowledge.

"Lilli, you were the most hopeful of us all," one of my classmates noticed. "For five months I watched your eyes shine. Now they've lost their luster, turned flat, look darker somehow. What is happening with you?"

Was it a dream—I'm in an abandoned airless basement. Slimy creatures with numerous extremities around me. I climb up the wall. My survival depends on getting away from the monstrous enemies. Was it my mother-in-law standing behind them, shaking her head from side to side? Did I lose my senses and don't know the difference between dreams and reality?

Once I thought that I woke up from not being able to breathe. My nose felt stuffed with the almost forgotten odor of resin glue I lived with for many years back in Russia. Then, already away from that dream, I saw my mama in her bed, wearing my last birthday gift to her—a practical cotton nightgown with tiny pink flowers, her face gray and lifeless. No, it was just another dream.

"Lilli, I can't help you—you are too far. In the worst-case scenario wear red—it'll make you feel better," she said tiredly.

"Mama," I screamed, terrified, "don't worry, there is no need for you to worry. I'm fine." Behind her stood my papa frowning crossly, saying, "You promised. You remember at the airport you promised you'll be happy."

"Leave me alone!" I hollered at the top of my lungs, only then waking up. "What do all of you want from me? I am happy!"

My scream woke up Sergey, too. "At least someone is happy. Don't see any reason for you to wake me up," he grumbled.

In my very next letter to Papa I wrote:

> *Papa, I know you don't expect many letters from me while I'm at school. But knowing you, you sit there hoping to hear from me. Yes? So, here is a quick note to let you know I'm fine. Busy, but fine. I've been having those dreams ... you and Mama there and you all worry for me, thinking me miserable and lost without you. You have to believe me: I'm fine. It's important for me that you do.*

Only one more month left until my graduation. In only thirty or so days I would be a paid office worker somewhere in Manhattan. Come on, brain, think faster. Come on, feet, move faster. We're almost there.

Walking home, in front of my house, I saw Nellie clad in her usual uniform of heavy army jacket, jeans and sweatshirt, bending over her carriage, the baby bundled warmly. I kissed Nellie on the cheek, dropped my briefcase on the asphalt, and scooped the infant out.

"Hi, darling. Hi, gorgeous. I can't resist your silky skin. You are the best sight and touch and smell for my wounds."

Unsmiling Nellie stood nearby, her cold hands inside her jeans' pockets. It seemed to me she waited for my gush to stop.

"Listen, Lilli, the local population is on your tail." Nellie didn't mince words, and I liked it about her. "They say they care about you. Not that I believe them. They discuss your going to school in order to get a job and earn money and so on."

"Yeah, okay? Was I ever secretive about my plans? They always gossip. How does it concern me?"

Nellie tried her best to explain. "Lilli, I'm your friend and I do care. The moment you get your first pay, one of them well-wishers will knock on the door of a housing office with the information. Your rent will go up faster than you can cash that first check."

I handed baby Alicia back to her.

"Nellie, what are you saying? What do you suggest I do?" I didn't intend the sharp tone, but from the tiredness and the anxiety of the last month, my patience wore off fast.

"Maybe hide those books, maybe change the direction you are going in the morning or carry some regular pocketbook instead of a briefcase. I don't know, use your common sense."

I stared at my friend. Nellie had her share of sleepless nights and frustrating days. I tried not to notice the bluish circles under her eyelashes or the ashen oval of her small face. So what? I had my own life to live and my own unbearably noisy tension in my head to fight.

"You know what, Nellie? I'm proud and thrilled that soon I'll earn my bread and butter. I see now that I don't belong in that life of yours, and I don't need your advice. And you know what else…?" I was on a roll. Nellie supplied what I needed—a real, live adversary who stood in the way of my future.

"We'll just move from here, as simple as that. Bye, Nellie. I expected more from you."

Hearing my angry voice, the little girl began to cry. That sound brought Nellie's haggard face into focus. What did I do? The mean words were nailed in and I couldn't yank them back.

Impatiently, I waited for Sergey to come home. After working for ten months as a supervisor in a machine shop, he found an engineering job on Long Island with better pay and better prospects for the future.

That new company had plans to build machinery for Russia and needed someone experienced in the Soviet industry. Sergey was exactly what they were looking for.

My adventurer husband listened to the account of my earlier conversation and said, “It’s time for us to move anyway. Not that I care about Nellie or the other bitches in the project.”

We decided to look for an apartment in Queens so Sergey would have a shorter commute to his job. The following weekend, we circled the ads from the “Apartments for Rent” section of the *NY Times*. We looked at a couple of places before we found a suitable apartment on the first floor of a beautiful building in Flushing. Its rent was almost twice what we were paying at the city housing. But so what? We believed in taking chances.

I was lucky to have a “dare-devil” for a husband. Who else would agree to move to a new apartment in a matter of weeks? Two-bedroom, two-bathroom, living room twice the size of our present one—we were moving to a palace. The polished parquet floor and a fireplace added to the unfamiliar sense of luxury. No more public telling us what to do, no more income verifications, no more traces of an immigrant boat. We’d be all on our own.

For that next rank-up relocation, we hired a moving van. The accumulated possessions of the lower-middle class Americans required careful packing and handling for the further advancement in life.

At the new apartment, I had just unpacked the boxes with the books and toys and dishes when Sergey’s boss called him in and explained that for health reasons he had to dissolve his business. He would stay open for another month to finish the few projects in progress, but that was it. He was sorry to give the bad news to a good person.

This transpired one week before my graduation.

We had almost no money left after the move and the two-months' deposit and the rent for the new apartment.

"No regrets," Sergey announced loudly, and maybe outsiders believed him.

"That's a bad break for us," I mentioned. I knew I shouldn't have.

"Any other wisdom going to come out of your mouth? Say it all at once. Or even better—shut up." The world failed Sergey. I represented this world. He stopped talking to me. In a tough situation we were each on our own, only I had two kids to care for.

While I had another week till the end of my course, I figured no office would ask me for a diploma from a six-month bookkeeping school. The search for a job started. There were some classifieds in a bookkeeping field, all asking for a specific experience: in a real estate office, accounting firm, or department store. My knowledge was strictly general and came exclusively from the teacher's blackboard in downtown Manhattan, though my resume stated extensive work in a field of bookkeeping in USSR. It was a lie, of course, but not the one any executive could verify.

"Lilli…?" I heard Sergey's mother's voice on the phone and cringed as always. What happened now?

"Maria and her family are relocating to Houston. They hate New York. They are tired of crowds and dirt and noise. She said if you are interested she'll speak with whoever is in charge in her office and maybe they'll hire you as her replacement." My mother-in-law had brought me some good news—that was a first.

Sergey's cousin Maria had graduated from a course similar to mine and worked as a bookkeeper's assistant for a large fundraising outfit for the children's charities.

I couldn't believe the lucky coincidence. I needed a job, Maria was leaving a job. Would Maria help me? The two of us weren't especially close. Didn't like each other from day one; didn't approve of each other, which was an open secret in the family. Though when they arrived in New York a short while behind us, we did help with whatever we could. Found them an apartment, explained everything unfamiliar and strange, translated instructions and letters. Why wouldn't Maria help me?

She promised, but as the days passed by I started to think that Sergey's cousin hadn't mentioned me to the management.

What if they weren't satisfied with Maria's performance? Then why chance her relative?

While waiting, I went to a few uninspiring interviews to the places on file at "Project Cope" where I went to school. At every place they smiled so sweetly and promised to call. Oh well … I knew better. They didn't plan on hiring me, waiting for better contenders. Not wasting any time, I took a train to a few employment agencies, leaving my resumes in their "in" box.

Sergey still worked, knowing that the day when his boss would say, "Sorry, but today is the day. Don't come tomorrow," was approaching. Coming home, he looked at me questionably. I reported my tries:

"Today I called three places from the ads in the newspaper and people told me the openings were filled and the ads in the newspaper came out too late. Maybe they spoke the truth or maybe didn't like my accent."

Smiling ironically, Sergey shrugged wordlessly. His silence accused me with a hidden reproach. I wanted to defend myself, so I imagined our conversation to continue, with me saying:

> "*Am I not an adult to understand the seriousness of our situation? I took a bookkeeping course in order to be an equal partner to you and earn money, so I definitely want to work. Do you have any reason not to trust me?*" I was on a roll, and apparently talking out loud.

"Mama, Dad isn't here and you're saying things to him," Gil noticed.

Sergey's silences continued progressively longer. The usual tension in my head mounted. The familiar noises of fabric being ripped on the inside of it worked overtime. The talking helped, even if it was to myself. I felt better coming up with multitudes of needless words. I was talking all the time. As time passed, I couldn't squash any of those words flying around my mouth.

CHAPTER 18

Flushing, Queens, New York, USA

1978

My call to Maria regarding her promise to help me with a job interview was the ultimate act of desperation. She wasn't home. And I didn't get a call back from the office she worked in.

I didn't think she bothered to ask them about trying me out. They probably never heard of my existence. Should I go there on my own? The feeling of hopelessness fortified me. I decided to act.

Early one December morning, one of the coldest and snowiest on record, I found myself on the Flushing subway line going towards Manhattan. I was shivering in my "presentable" lightweight maroon coat. My warmer coat was second-hand, made out of small rabbit patches. It wouldn't create a good first impression. This morning, I didn't brave wearing my black patent shoes. I wore old boots and carried my shoes in a shopping bag.

That winter's unlimited supply of white powder persisted to swallow the sidewalks and everything else around us. I thought back to my childhood love of snow. Nothing changed a person's perspective like real life. I didn't pledge undying love to my precious snow any longer.

The offices of "Pioneer" were located in Midtown on the east side between 35th and 36th Streets on Madison Avenue. The dull gray building covered an entire city block. The inside, painted in heavy gold, adorned by marble, crystal chandeliers, and seasonal December decorations stunned me. Wow! I wanted to run away the instant I opened the door and the glitter of the lobby burned my vision. Then I imagined Sergey's reaction if I returned home empty-handed and explained that the building seemed too rich for my blood.

"Let's do it. The train-money spent already," I whispered, and boarded a gilded elevator. I took it up seventeen floors and then down seventeen floors a few times until my fingers and toes defrosted. On one of the rides, I glimpsed an inconspicuous corner on the fifteenth floor behind a potted palm where I could possibly store my scruffy boots. I worked that plan out while other passengers were getting in and out the elevator.

To feel less silly, I explained the up-down trips to myself: "I am an actress playing a spy."

It was a great idea! I would continue playing a role during the entire meeting at Pioneer. That is, if the manager would agree to see me.

"I was hoping you'd have a few minutes to talk to me," I said with a smile to the office manager, after her secretary advised her that I was there. Before she had a chance to refuse, I rushed in with my presentation. "I don't know if you started a search for Maria's replacement. She described most of her duties to me and I'd like a chance to demonstrate my knowledge in all things involved."

Sitting comfortably in the beige contoured chair across from the manager, I leafed through my portfolio with the class-work, pointing at different pages.

Did she even listen? The heavy-set, middle-aged executive kept flattening the top of her outfit, which obviously had been bought when she was two sizes smaller.

"I certainly see," the woman agreed, "that you've had appropriate experience. I also understand that though the banking system in the Soviet Union worked differently, it's not a big deal to pick up the details on the way. I'm sure you're a quick study."

She didn't even rephrase my reasoning, she simply repeated all of it. She was buying my performance: the experience I didn't have, the Soviet banking system I knew nothing about. She liked me. I deserved an Oscar. So what if I was the only one applauding.

"By the way, do you have any children?" she asked towards the end of the interview. My answer was rehearsed way in advance: "Yes, I have two boys. They are in school during the day and my mother-in-law watches them afterwards."

"We'll let you know. Thanks for coming," were her last words, leaving me with hope.

Mama, your little Lilli learned to lie with an ease of a natural-born liar.

By the late morning I was back on the train #7. Wasn't I great in my role of an actress playing a role as…whatever? Only now, I was back to being Lilli Kaplan, unemployed mother of two small children. Speaking of children—I had left Ben with a babysitter for five dollars per hour. That was a lot of money. My headache took over—bam, bam—tearing, tearing—my personal music. I closed my eyes.

My station was the last one on the Flushing line, so I didn't have to fight to exit. Maybe my head would stop aching when I got outside. Taking a flight of stairs to the street, I stopped and got out a pair of gloves. *Was this a billboard for a temp agency across the street? Was it always here?* I didn't see it before. Among the jobs listed there was "bookkeeping." Who knew if that manager from Pioneer was sincere in her praises? After all, she didn't promise me that job. I crossed the street towards the sign.

The agency was all the way on the third floor. Where was the elevator? My feet were stiff from the cold and it was difficult to take all those steps up. I took one step at a time. In a few minutes I'd get my regular "we'll call you," and then I'd go pick up Benny from his babysitter. My conscience would be clear—I tried, even if Sergey doubted it as usual.

A middle-aged, properly-groomed and quietly bejeweled woman sat inside the small room. She didn't look especially happy to see another applicant.

"Hello." My greeting brought an expected recognition on her face—accent again. Are no Americans looking for jobs anymore, only the greenhorns?

Now the woman would ask, "Do you have any American experience?" That's what they all asked after hearing me speak. Their faces got that glazed smugness because they knew the answer.

I wanted to shout, *We've been living in this country for three years and my baby is only two-and-a-half years old! When did I have a chance to gain your experience?*

This one didn't say it but forgot to erase the arrogance from her face.

"Here, answer all of it. Guess, if you're not sure." She propelled a few pages of the standardized bookkeeping test across her desk. My icy hands shook and I couldn't grip the pencil, so I put my gloves back on and sat there reading the questions.

There was nothing to it. Anyway, there was no chance that harpy would find me a job.

I marked the appropriate squares throughout the pages. Without saying anything to the woman, I handed them back to her.

"Now sit somewhere and wait while I check it."

I saw her reaching inside her desk and pulling out the booklet with answers. I stopped worrying. Whatever will happen … I waited.

"One mistake." She startled me with her loud voice.

"Which one is wrong?" I was astonished by the unexpected "only one" result.

"The last one, about the bank reconciliation. You marked that you check the bank statement against the book, and the correct answer is: the book against the bank statement."

"You'll get the same result. The idea of reconciliation is to bring both to the same total. You find differences and analyze them."

"Listen, dear, I am not a bookkeeper. I don't understand any of it. The book states you're wrong, so you are wrong. By the way, are you Jewish?"

What? How dare she?

"As a matter of fact … I am Jewish." I didn't care anymore. "Do you have a problem with it? Because if you do—I don't want your job."

I felt lightheaded; my stomach begged for food, my feet were sore. I didn't need some brainless dame displaying her anti-Semitic mindset.

"Wait a second, I'm also Jewish. I was just curious, that's all. I get a lot of girls here with a Russian accent and they're all Jewish. It's really surprising that every Jewish girl in Russia worked as a bookkeeper."

The woman continued: "Don't worry, dear, you look decent enough: the clothes, the grooming. I'll refer you to a place that needs clerical help in their bookkeeping office. It's a minimum pay job, but with your heavy accent I don't see many opportunities coming. You sure your husband won't object to your working?"

I couldn't take it anymore. I grabbed the referral slip out of her hand and left.

All the way down the stairs, I was thinking of the women from my downtown bookkeeping course. Back in Russia, they worked in the different fields, all of them college educated. They were teachers and musicians and engineers. They came to America, and like me, took the only course available at the time, which happened to be bookkeeping. They were non-English speaking immigrants who needed to buy food and pay rent. If bookkeeping would provide a paycheck it was good enough for them. Did I have to explain it to that ignoramus?

How many generations was she away from a boat? Was her grandmother the one to sit at *Ellis Island* waiting for a sponsor, or did her father survive the war in Europe and come here so she could be born an American?

***

I picked up Ben and we walked not more than a block when he spied a huge heap of snow piled by the snowplows during the last night.

"Mom, Mom, I'm a snowman," my three-year-old shrieked from the top of a snow hill.

"Benny, please get out of that snow. We must go home," I appealed. It was cold to stand there without moving. My presentable coat didn't protect me against piercing wind. How could I get my little fox out of there? My hands were busy holding a briefcase with papers, one bag with my good shoes, and a second one with Benny's daily supplies: change of clothes, food containers, books, drawings.

"Benny, I'll just leave you all by yourself, and you won't find our house," I tried again.

“I would too, I would too,” he cried. “You never play with me anymore. I like snow.”

My genes at work—he liked snow. Sergey hated snow and cold and wind. What I wouldn’t give for an hour of playing with my son right there on the top, clamping some perfectly round snowballs, throwing them at each other, and laughing.

When I was only a couple of years older than Benny, I helped our building’s super to shovel snow off the sidewalks. The cold stamped my cheeks and nose while the rest of my body was covered with layers of clothes. My muscles ached from lifting the loaded shovel, but it was preferable to the heavy smells and gloomy mood at home.

“Bury silly wishes before they bury you,” Mama said. Mama was right. Now, I had to force Benny down the snow and up the street, then inside the apartment and out of his wet clothes. Then keep him away from his brother until I finished cooking dinner, which by the way, I had to start … five minutes ago.

“Benny, today you played with the babysitter. Tomorrow I’ll take you and Gil to the park. Okay?”

Did he believe me or just lose interest in arguing? Ben tumbled down the hill and even took a hold of my two available fingers. Probably got tired.

During our seven-block-walk home, Benny yelled out riddles nonstop, expecting me to laugh with him. It was easy—I looked at his dimpled face, bright with smudges of today’s menu: the red of sauced meatballs, the yellow of fruit juice, and every other color in his favorite crayon box.

Inside the apartment, I didn’t follow my little son into the room. I stood in our little foyer and listened to the silence. It didn’t last.

“You broke my book,” seven-year-old Gil yelled loudly so I would be aware of his suffering on account of his brother.

"I didn't, I just waved my hand. I'm allowed to. Ask Mom." Without looking in, I imagined the sparkling teeth on the face that seemed perpetually suntanned.

"Your hand was too close. No one is allowed to touch my books."

"Even Mom?"

"Mom doesn't touch my books."

"You are a big fat liar, Gil Kaplan. Ha! So, everyone held your books, didn't they? Ha!"

"Just shut up. You're stupid. You don't read. You're making noise all the time on purpose."

I directed my feet towards the master bedroom, not thinking of the boys' asinine argument. The words I couldn't ignore were those of my husband, even if they were only in my mind. He wasn't back from work yet, but the rooms were laden with his sarcastic voice.

"*So, another day went by and you didn't find a job*," I heard.

"*I'm not sitting idle. I'm looking!*" my brain shouted back.

"*Looking and not finding doesn't amount to much*." His irony irritated.

Shaking my head, I tried to rid it of Sergey's intonations, wanting to think of anything else.

When did I last write to Papa? He knew my time was precious and never complained, but it wasn't the lack of time but rather the heavy mood that kept me from keeping him posted of our strides.

My eyes fell upon our extensive Russian library that covered an entire wall in the living room. First we'd crated them to ship to Israel, then we left them with our friends and they sent them to America. We'd packed them a few times more to move from one apartment to the other.

"What a waste! How little we'd understood of our future. Our boys don't know how to read Russian. *We* must read English in order to know it better. Who is going to read these books?" I wondered aloud. "I sure know who is going to dust them."

I was still holding the bag with Ben's soiled clothes. *Oh, stupid me, I never changed him out of his snow-pants*. Now it was too late—everything around him would be wet and smelly.

I dropped soiled clothes from that bag into a bathroom hamper and walked into our bedroom.

Changing out of my one "interview decent" outfit, I resumed listening to the voices in my head. My Kaplan mother-in-law continued where Sergey left off:

"*I don't know, Lilli, but our neighbors' daughter found a position on the first try*."

Next, my own mama's dogmatic advice came forth through the decades and oceans: "*Lilli, bookkeeping is an appropriate profession for a girl. I was a bookkeeper for years*."

> *What do they all want from me? Am I the only one without a voice?*
>
> *Mama, please be on my side, please. Tell them how many times I hollered at you for mentioning the word 'bookkeeper.' A silly me imagined it the worst possible drag, like I knew what I was talking about. Maybe it's a drag, but I took the course and studied and was a good student and now I'm trying to find a job. I am too. The joke is on me. I'm looking for a job I detested the most. Are you proud of me, Mama? You tried so hard to prepare me for life's disappointments. Well, I was never a quick study. Are you listening, Mama? Because no one else does.*

While changing, I spied a woman in the closet mirror. She wore a pair of brown woolen pants and a worn black bra, her hair a disheveled mess and her eye make-up smeared. Was I the crazy woman in the middle of the room talking to myself?

What time is it now? I don't have dinner ready!

I ran to the kitchen not even noticing a dining chair in the way. Shit! I hit my knee! It hurt; it really hurt.

I started to slice meat and chop vegetables. My brain emptied of voices.

Gil was fed up: "Mom, tell him to leave me alone."

"I didn't do nothing. He won't give me the book I want to read," came Ben's whining loud and clear from the boys' bedroom.

"Lilli, I'm home." Sergey sounded lethargic. "Why are they screaming? Why don't you do something about it?"

I heard him, choosing not to interrupt my work. He was hungry, as all of us were.

I visualized my husband's face as he stood in the same foyer I couldn't move from a while ago. His thirty-five-year-old face looked fifty these days. The bloodshot lines of exhaustion muddled the hazel irises of his eyes; the dark creases around his mouth and nose were deep. A sprinkle of freckles on his face, instead of adding youth changed its color to splotchy dark.

Sergey didn't speak again. He waited for my response.

"What do you want me to do? They always scream, and I have to prepare dinner, don't I?" I asked, not coming out from the kitchen.

Sergey distributed punishment, not trying to pacify his sons. "Okay, the two of you come here and fast! There're two corners and there're two boys who don't know how to behave. Stay there until you know, and not a sound out of you!"

Both boys started to shout explanations and cry at the same time. With dinner being ready, I planned on serving it, then the shouting intensified and I rushed out to the living room, wiping my wet hands on the way.

"Sergey, don't do that. Just talk to them. They're but babies. I don't want them to cry all night."

"You don't want? I work and look for a job. I'm drained. I have plenty of problems and they're screeching. Maybe you can stand it but I can't. Why do you always protect them from me instead of teaching them discipline? Forget about dinner. I'll eat when I'm in the mood!"

Sergey marched to the master bedroom, slamming the door shut. When my husband was upset, he didn't talk and didn't eat.

I stood slumped in the middle of our prized living room. The shiny parquet floor, the lacy-green palms in the bright orange-yellow clay pots, even a big modern TV, bought on credit after Sergey's parents insisted we needed one, mocked me.

A few toys on the floor, the basket with unfolded laundry, one child's sneaker; a few open newspapers on the sofa waited for the turn of my hand.

The children were positioned in the corners. Gil was quiet, his face pale, his righteous little soul indignant—he felt wrongly punished. Ben, his face the color of beets from all the crying, couldn't stop whimpering. His resentment grew wings—he only wanted a book, never mind he forgot which one.

Sergey chain-smoked on the bed behind the locked door. From my vast experience I knew he couldn't let go—didn't know how. It could continue for days.

I rationalized his frustrations, but what about me? Didn't I deserve some hole to crawl into?

I was the woman of the house, the mother of the children, the wife of the husband. These titles didn't give me solace, didn't provide peace of mind. I held on to a dishtowel, my tears sliding towards it.

CHAPTER 19

Flushing, Queens New York, USA

1978-1980

A few days passed after my interview at Pioneer and no one from that office called me. Obviously, I wasn't an *Oscar* deserving actress. The *Oscar* would go to the office manager who made me believe she liked me.

I felt empty like a lemon squeezed dry. My brain stopped searching for a loophole out of the current situation. My joblessness, Sergey's moodiness, children's squabbles, money getting tighter, endless housework—it came full circle and turned off.

When the telephone rang it seemed too much effort to walk over and pick it up. But its insistent ringing got on my nerves.

"Lilli, why don't you pick up the phone? I was ready to hang up." Maria sounded annoyed. She didn't wait for my explanation or apology.

"The management will take you in my stead. I overheard they interviewed two men and both asked for a salary above three hundred dollars.

They employ me for half of that. You, surely, don't expect more. Come here tomorrow and I'll introduce you to everyone. Bye."

One hundred sixty dollars was all I asked for my salary. It was what I'd hoped for a start. It was what would enter me in the working class of America and earn the respect of my husband. No more worthless status for me. Now I had a minimum price of one hundred and sixty dollars.

The *Oscar* went to the two men for not getting my job. Let them look at the little statue while I'd be off to wash my hair and check my gray skirt for stains, getting ready for work.

I announced the good news to Sergey and the children.

"I'm glad. Your taking charge and going there for an interview worked," my husband admitted, his eyes instantly warming up.

"We're rich!" shrieked Benny.

"Not rich, you stupid baby. Dad's job is almost finished," Gil said, reminding all of us of our reality. His reaction slightly chilled my enthusiasm. Gil trusted his father's earning potential more than mine. So did I. Sergey was the one we all trusted. He was so smart when it came to politics and science and math. He was smart. Wasn't he the one to insist we leave the Soviet country?

***

In the next few days, as expected, the company where Sergey worked let go of all its employees. The first day without a job, he walked into the unemployment office only to find out he couldn't collect for the first jobless week. Dark-faced, shoulders sloped, he drove home muttering Russian and English curses.

With me, Sergey tried for the confident tone: "We'll be fine. I've been sending out enough resumes to wallpaper the entire town. Now I have American experience. I worked as a supervisor in a metal manufacturing shop at my first job, and at my second the boss trusted me to supervise the workers and design new products."

"Listen, husband of mine, don't try to convince me. I believe in you and your knowledge. You're the one dissolving into particles," I insisted. "Maybe you should take an elocution lessons to help your accent. It would be easier to secure a job you deserve."

He felt low. Maybe if his hands would be occupied with some task, his mind would stay away from problems. I knocked on the bedroom door where he went to hide from the world.

"Sergey, the wall-panels toppled over a few times during the last week. It's a miracle they didn't hurt Benny when he walked by pretending not to see them."

Since we'd moved to this apartment, the panels we'd brought from the previous apartment stood by the wall in the living room.

"I already punished him for that. Evidently not strong enough."

"Just nail them to the wall whenever you feel like it. It's the simplest solution."

Next Saturday morning, Sergey stood on the ladder, nailing the boards to the master bedroom's wall, when the phone rang.

A man on the other end, the owner of a company that had advertised for a mechanical engineer, had received Sergey's resume and wanted to meet him. The company designed quilting machines for mattresses, and thermo-protection for the space shuttles. It was located thirty minutes walking distance from where we lived.

I listened to Sergey's end of the conversation. He only asked: "What is the salary you are offering?"

He went for an interview and got the job, and even bargained for better pay.

With both of us starting work, finding a nursery for Benny became an emergency. After calling every school on the Yellow Pages list, I located only one that agreed to accept such a young child sight unseen for the full-day program.

"Benny, you remember we spoke that when I start working, you'll go to school, like Gil does? A school bus will pick you up in the mornings, and you'll go all by yourself like a grown-up, and there, in school, you'll play with kids and learn stuff and eat and nap a little. You will like it very much."

***

The day after Christmas holidays, four days before Benny turned three, I woke him up early. He let me wash and dress him; he ate his favorite "*Alpha-Bits*" cereal, and only on the cold and windy street he did wake up enough to object to the entire "going to school" enterprise.

"Benny, just try today. If you don't like it, we'll find a different school for you. Okay?"

"Okay…" he whispered, and sniveled some more, then his eyes brightened and he took the bag with his belongings out of my hands. When the yellow mini-bus arrived, Ben stepped in holding an envelope with his documents and a bag with some Pampers and a clothing change. Yes, I swore to the school director Benny was toilet-trained, but we weren't so lucky as yet.

Mama, you wanted me to be practical.

Back home with the same bus that picked him up in the morning, Benny blew kisses to the driver and the teacher's assistant, reported an abundance of great things inside the school, like toys and games, snacks and little cots to sleep on, even recited the names of his new friends.

Nevertheless, come morning Benny wailed through the wash and the dressing, chanting "I'm not going" in between a few spoonfuls of cereal that reached his mouth.

After Ben was safely inside his bus, not a moment to spare, I ran inside the apartment.

"Gil, let's go. I have to make a 7:45 subway train."

I cherished that short time with Gil on the way to school. Even in the poor weather, the two of us had fun, running soundly, trying to get away from the rain or wind. During the rainy sprints to school, I joked about my dirt-splashed pantyhose and Gil's soaked school bag, while he continued his story of the day, anxious to finish it before we parted.

He told me of the girl he liked.

"Mama, Tara's the smartest one in our class. She always raises her hand when no one knows the answer."

"You're smart, an 'A' student. Can't you give an answer?"

"I don't like to speak in front of everyone."

The imposing-looking circular school building didn't open until later. Their safety regulations didn't allow students to enter the school ahead of time. After I left him by the building, Gil waited, leaning on the wall and reading, holding a book in his gloved hands.

The image of Benny's tear-streaked sleepy face and Gil's gloved hands holding a book stayed with me throughout the day. I left my babies and ran to earn us money and self-respect, independence, and acceptance.

***

"Lilli, the phone call is for you, pick up on two." The receptionist's voice in my office caught me just coming in.

"Hello. Yes, it's me. Yes … thank you. I'll be there." My hand shook holding the phone. I hung up and glanced at my immediate boss, Sylvia, who waited for the conversation to end, drumming the pencil against her desk.

"What happened?" she asked. The way Sylvia dressed and sat and laughed and ate was big and wide and not to be missed. Bossy and loud, Sylvia was someone you noticed. Although during the few months we'd worked together, I learned to appreciate her. When you knew her better, she was warm and smart and caring.

"Look, I'm sorry, but … they called from Benny's school and said he's sick. They asked me to take him home. If you think you can't let me stay in my job because I'll have to leave sometimes, so be it, but it would be awful."

In my mind I already was jobless and penniless, living on the street with my children.

"Go, of course, go," Sylvia responded at once and added, "We understand about your Benny's special needs. You look pained every time you talk of him, when you talk of him."

Special needs? Did they think he was retarded? Now I understood the sympathetic looks on their faces. My gorgeous, quick, smart baby! Purposely, I tried not to talk about little Ben so my coworkers wouldn't guess that he was but a baby and not an older schoolboy like I had lied during my interview. Shame on me!

I didn't know where exactly in the borough of Queens Ben's school was. At the subway station I showed the street name written in my address-book to a guy in the booth. "Here, the address. What train goes there?" He glanced at it, first the way I propelled it to him and then turned it the other way around. Great, he couldn't read my handwriting.

“Take ‘N’ train, then ask people. If you’re going into the wrong direction, you could always switch trains at Queen’s Plaza.”

I should’ve looked at the map when I first signed Ben up at this place. Even when they called me, I could’ve asked their exact location. If anything happened to my Benny…

Why didn’t I think of calling Sergey? He had a car and maps of the city.

He wouldn’t go. He had responsibilities to his workplace—other people depended on him.

I remembered the definition of “a good husband” my girlfriends came up with many years ago—He who doesn’t drink, cheat, or beat you up. According to them, my husband was perfect.

From the train I took a cab that brought me to a nondescript private house surrounded by an overgrown garden, overrun by weeds. The broken gate was hanging on one hinge. A few stray cats played in the grass. That’s the school I signed up my baby for? That was where the little yellow school bus brought him after we said our goodbyes?

I asked the cabby to wait and walked inside. Listless Benny sat near the wall.

“We have a chicken pox scare,” his teacher, Mrs. Miller, informed me. “A few of the children from Ben’s group got it. It looks like he’s next in line.”

Oh God. What was I going to do? Chicken pox could take weeks.

Clutching Benny in my arms, I took the waiting cab to our pediatrician’s office, hoping the doctor would be in.

Doctor Dreifuss tried to calm me. “Relax, Ben doesn’t have chicken pox yet, just a cold. But he’ll get it if his playmates are sick. Look, children have to get their share of children’s illnesses.”

A German emigrant, bent and slight, always impeccably suited, our doctor cared about the children he treated. I often felt an urge to confide my worries in him, to question him: "Do you think if parents don't exhibit warm loving relations to each other, their children suffer?" Or "If there is a gloomy atmosphere at home where children live, could they nevertheless grow up happy?" I never did, thinking the doctor wouldn't become involved with the private lives of his patients.

On the way home from the doctor I carried subdued Benny to the subway. Additional cab fare was much too much for one day.

***

During school holidays, I brought Gil to the office of the children's charities organization where I worked. He read a book or drew, waiting for me to take him outside during my lunch-hour. I explained to him about the envelopes with donations I opened as part of my duties. I taught him to be proud of the culture where people were helping each other.

"You see that..." I showed him the check written by the shaking hand of an eighty-nine-year-old woman living in a nursing home. "She's poor, probably lonely and sick. All she could spare is one dollar. But she sends it in anyway, because somewhere far away is a child who is poorer and sicker and lonelier than her."

And then I showed something else to my son.

"Here is a check from the well-to-do person's estate. His lawyers wrote it and the amount is large. This person left the instructions before he died because he cared about those poor children too. His money would help a lot of them to eat and get treatments and even to learn."

Gil wanted to help. I let him stuff envelopes for one of our fundraisers.

One day, coming from work, I walked into our apartment and a third-grade Gil waited for me at the threshold.

"Mom, do you want to read the book I wrote? Mrs. Swift gave me an A+ for it."

"My son the author! Of course I want." I'd be late with dinner, but he was so eager, so anxious.

On the first page was a photo of Gil as a six-month-old, dressed in Russian baby clothes—a heavy flannel shirt washed to an unknown color and a clumsy diaper covering his bottom. I remembered the feeling of the crude fabric in my hands.

On the second page he gave my description of him as an infant: his eyes were big and spoke volumes, his skin pale, the features perfect, his hair black. He even mentioned the absence of eyebrows.

The third page said: *My favorite person when I was a baby—my papa and accordingly, my first word: Papa.* I completely forgot about this. I was the one to tell him about all that and then forgot. Both our babies adored Sergey.

And then:

I am happy when...

I have friends,

I have good luck,

I can play different sports,

I can climb a tall fence and

Jump in the grass,

Somebody tickles me,

My birthday comes,

I pet dogs,

I get presents,

My mom comes from work.

I joked that my firstborn owed me a bunch for the most difficult pregnancy and horrific delivery. Many times, looking into his perfect face, I thought—if this is not a payment, what is? But holding that smallish book covered in brown wallpaper, I felt wings I didn't know I owned.

I am sad when...

I am falling,

I get in trouble,

Somebody hits me,

My best books break,

I am sleepy,

I go some place far and

I am tired,

I jump and land in water,

People laugh at me,

People call me names,

I moved to a new house.

Can I protect my child from the outside world? Could I avert all of the above?

We moved from the projects to better our life, the children's as well as our own. We didn't ask the children if they wanted to move. The children depended on us to be happy.

***

"Sergey, don't you think there's something wrong with Gil's speech? Do you always understand what he's saying?" I asked Sergey. "It seems like he swallows parts of the words. Maybe it's just my Russian ears having difficulties with English comprehension."

"I did notice. He speaks faster and faster, like he's afraid I'd stop listening. As a result, I hardly know what he says. Maybe you should check with his teacher."

Gil was a quiet boy who spoke only when asked to and his answers were short and precise. His teacher didn't see any problem. I called on a school nurse and she recommended taking Gil to Queens College for a speech evaluation.

For over an hour, two Ph.D. specialists accompanied by five bored students listened to Gil speak. They drew charts and graphs, and later explained that my son was a stutterer.

They complimented the eight-year-old Gil on having an exceptionally developed brain which covered the deficiency automatically without him being aware of it, thus talking fast and word swallowing.

They mentioned specialists, who worked with such children, charging from thirty to fifty dollars for an hourly session.

"Does insurance cover the therapy?" I asked, though I knew the answer.

Seeing my distress, the stocky speech-pathologist with bespectacled motherly eyes took me inside the next room. Away from my son's inquisitive eyes, I began to sob at once. "Doctor, we don't have the money to pay for the treatments. Also, those doctors work during the day and so do we. What am I going to do?"

"Mrs. Kaplan, don't cry," the woman said. "His teachers told you it's not a problem. Right? Gil doesn't complain. Right? Maybe he'll outgrow it. It's possible. You're a good mother—it's not your fault."

Gil waited for me, sitting in the bright blue chair, reading a book about animal behavior.

"Are we going home?" he asked. "I don't like those tests. They ask a lot of silly questions and record it all in their papers. I am okay. Yes, Mom?"

"You're very much okay. Let's go home."

***

The morning train to mid-town where my office was located was crowded with rush-hour commuters. While becoming part of that crowd, I enjoyed my rare solitary time of the day. Usually, I read one of the fat engrossing novels written by authors like Belva Plain, Gloria Goldreigh, and others who favored tales of the immigrants who came before me.

The women in those stories could be my sisters and cousins. The clever penniless beauties from the old country established their happiness after stormy but confident battles with negative forces. It was conceivable in this land. The books carried hope.

I didn't think myself especially smart or beautiful, but I married a brave guy with a vision for our future. I wanted to believe that together we'd overcome all that stood in our way.

Since we got married, I'd been following Sergey's fast stride. It just happened. No advance notice, no rehearsal, go, go, go. I'd been exhausted for the longest time. Maybe I felt entitled not to rush, but to reflect and give in to my fears? But did I want to be left behind in some previous century?

What if I said to him: "I cannot run anymore, let me be." Would he leave me alone? What would I do? I don't know what I want or need besides to stop and rest? It's not a goal. And what about my babies? I gave birth to the two little souls with their entire existence ahead of them. Was it fair to stop their lives' progress because one of their parents would like to rest?

Mama, please, tell me again: Bury silly wishes before they bury you.

Our train going to Manhattan stopped in the middle of the tracks and some incomprehensible, disconnected voice presented the verdict for the next fifteen or so minutes of our commuter's life. I looked up from my book at my fellow travelers. They were different shades of different colors, different shapes and clothes, yet the different packaging didn't affect the two very distinct expressions on their faces: boredom and dread.

Some people didn't have stable jobs and established careers. They were frightened off losing their weekly paychecks. Their impatient knuckles drummed at the windows, feet stomped on the floor; clenched teeth let mutters through.

Then there were the emotionless people who didn't give a damn. They read or slept or daydreamed.

Would I be fired if the train made those emergency stops too often? Would I be forced to go through the employment agencies and interviews again?

I decided I should write a letter to Papa now that the train wasn't moving. He checked and rechecked his mailbox daily and, not finding my letters, imagined some catastrophe befallen us.

"Lilli, is it you?"

The fashionable woman in her early twenties with short black hair and enormous blue tinted eyeglasses had been sitting next to me from the very first station. She was reading a large, rather heavy book, a manual of some kind.

When the train arrived at the platform, we all were in a rush to get seats, not looking left or right, not noticing who was sitting in the neighboring seat.

"Eva? I can't believe it. Is it really you? Here we are sitting side-by-side not noticing each other. How are you? You look great. What are you doing? You coming from Flushing? Do you live there too?" It was thrilling to see my friend from our time in Belgium.

"Lilli, I didn't recognize you at the beginning. Of course—the last time I saw you—your face was all but hidden behind your pregnant stomach," Eva teased me.

"Oh, come on, it wasn't that bad. The last time you saw me on the plane to New York coming from Brussels, and I was in my sixth month only. Of course, you at that time were in kindergarten or was it elementary school? I forget which."

We picked up our old easygoing banter.

When we met, Eva was a seventeen-year-old schoolgirl. That indeed seemed baby-age to me the twenty-eight-year-old wife and mother of a three-year-old son.

Eva still laughed a tinkling easy chuckle. "So who did you carry in that huge stomach of yours: a boy, a girl, or both? Remember I was there from the first day, holding your hand."

I hugged Eva. "It's so great to see you. You must come and meet Benny, the adorable bundle of energy and mischief that drives all of us crazy, especially Gil, who is constantly looking for a quiet corner to read.

"And what is this on your finger? I don't believe it! You got married? You did! I'm afraid to ask—is it Nathan, for whom you fought like a tigress with all other eligible young ladies?"

"The one and only. I won him in the end." Eva's face didn't look that carefree and young anymore. Was she unhappy or just tired, trying to survive the mundane like the rest of us?

"Eva, do you remember our talks back in Brussels? Do you understand now why I followed Sergey against my own wishes all the way from Kiev to New York? As a married woman, would you act any different?"

Back in Brussels, sitting closely on the top of the staircase of our rooming house, we discussed the events that transpired in my married life. Eva, a fiery little thing, proclaimed, "I would never follow any man if my plans in life would differ from his."

Now she didn't voice an opinion. For the last few minutes of our ride, we sat smiling and holding hands.

With Eva's phone-number safely inside my bag, I left train #7, but not the memories of our ten-month-long Belgian "vacation." For the better part of the day, that lonely and gloomy time was all I could think about.

CHAPTER 20

Midtown, Manhattan New York, USA

1982-1983

For the last ten minutes I sat behind my desk in the office staring at the phone. My Russian accent made my English words misunderstood by many. Especially on the phone.

I hate you! You're the instrument of my torture!

Slowly, my left arm stretched for the receiver and dialed the number of the Amalgamated Bank.

"Hello, I'm Lilli Kaplan and I'm calling from Pioneer. My account number…"

"What? Who are you? I didn't understand. Repeat it, please." And so it went.

On the last statement the bank made a mistake by charging us the same fees twice. This could be corrected in two minutes, if the faceless and toneless bank clerk listened to the matter at hand instead of insisting he didn't understand me after the first word I uttered.

Many people working for the New York banks were themselves immigrants, and between my Russian mouth pronouncing English sounds and their ears born in other parts of the world, we, on both sides, often lost patience during those phone calls.

The person at the bank tried again: "Are you saying your account is overdrawn?"

I didn't see any sense in persisting.

"You, sir, are a complete nincompoop and I pray you comprehend this word." I slammed down the receiver.

"Shit, shit, shit, and I don't care if it sounds like sheet, sheet, sheet. I know what I meant," I said aloud in the emptiness of my office.

"And so do I," someone answered back. He was young, about six feet tall, with olive skin, wearing a t-shirt and jeans, looking like a typical inner-city deliveryman. And he continued, "After that discussion, I doubt you're in any mood to go out and buy yourself some new sheets."

He had chosen the wrong day and the wrong person.

"Who are you, sir? I'm not in a mood for any stupid jokes. How did you get to my office? Last I looked it was on the end of a corridor. Whatever you delivered, you could've found someone in front to sign for it."

I hurled the words at him and turned back to my papers with the unsolved issue of overpaid bank charges. To my astonishment, the guy sauntered over and sat at the chair next to my desk, taking off his baseball cap and patting down his black curly hair.

"I'm Paul Fernando. They hired me here and pointed to your office to set up my pay information. And I excuse your bad manners, this one time only."

His smile under his dark mustache dazzled with the whitest of teeth. His callused handshake introduced formidable muscle.

"They hired me to work as a printer, shipper, and all-around needed person. By the way, I'm Puerto Rican and I know you're Russian and your name is Lilli. I overheard your explanations wasted on some jerk that doesn't separate his ass from a chair all day."

The guy sounded like fun. I was sorry for jumping at him before.

"I'm Jewish, not Russian. Even if I speak Russian and lived in Russia—not even Russia, but Soviet Union, because the Americans don't know the difference, I stopped explaining after the first year. Why do you announce that you're Puerto Rican? What's so good about it?"

"I love being Latino—the food, the music, the people. There's a lot of negative publicity around us. We do come in different packaging. It's because we're not ambitious by nature, just fun-loving people."

Paul leapt from the chair and, accompanied by an invisible drum, started dancing in the middle of the room, illustrating his last statement, one hand outstretched and the other on his tummy, his eyes closed in delight.

I started to laugh.

After that first day, we talked non-stop every free moment.

"I've been plenty in trouble…" Paul wanted me to know the truth. "A wild kid, as in another-minute-they'd-call-the-cops-on-me. In the Lower East Side neighborhood, mothers watched each other's offspring from the stoops and windowsills. You misbehaved—this big woman with rough palms took you by the ear and up the stairs to your own mother. Most of us around there didn't have fathers, though women, believe me—you knew they loved you with everything they've got.

"Not all of my friends turned out alive and well. I did drugs—didn't enjoy the feeling of losing control. Got myself a girlfriend, always loved a pretty girl, then—both seventeen and expecting a child. We did the right thing, got married. Two stupid kids with the responsibility of a newborn."

I felt pity for my friend who didn't have it easy growing up.

"You know, Paul, after listening to you, I'm not going to complain about my childhood and youth. My father and mother were there for me, as were other relatives, with whom we lived in the same apartment. The drugs weren't known in the part of town where I grew up. The children stayed outside till all hours, not threatened by violence. Usually I left the courtyard where we played when the taunting became too much for me to take. How long could you listen to 'You are ugly-Jewish' or 'Your kind drinks blood from us, the regular people.'"

"Strange," Paul said, confused by my admissions, "my mom repeated through the years, 'Follow your Jewish classmates and learn from them. It's not for nothing their names are Goldbergs and Goldensteins. They know how to make money.' She respected Jewish people."

I exploded, "Add Goldblooms to your money-bags list."

I spit my maiden name at Paul and insisted, "That is pure anti-Semitism. We are people like any other. You work with Jews. How many of us are rich? You see those one-dollar donations coming from the Jewish nursing homes. Maybe the names are golden, but the senders are often poor."

Paul seemed astonished.

***

I was back in Russia, sobbing, trying to absolve my parents from smirking six-year-old mates, vowing that my mama and papa weren't sending money to support Israeli Zionists fighting against Arabs—friends of the Soviet Union.

In the yard of my childhood, all families were of similar income level, all working from payday to payday, borrowing from each other in emergencies. But the centuries-old baseless beliefs stood in front of the facts.

I knew I had to explain myself better to Paul. I wanted him to continue being my friend.

"Good morning Paul," I said, stepping into the building elevator one morning and seeing my friend there. "I want to talk to you."

His mumbled "Hello" sounded odd. His eyes didn't leave the floor. In another corner I saw a woman, her face chalky with tension, clutching her pocketbook with both hands. She looked in fright at Paul's unmistakably Latino face.

Before I came up with some mean words to splash at her, the woman left the elevator.

"What a bitch! I wish I came up with some killing words."

"Like that: 'Don't be afraid of my Puerto Rican co-worker. He's not going to steal from you.' Yes? I go through scrutiny of suspicion daily. Should I fight with each and every one of them? Did you say much to your Russian bullies? You tried to survive by not wanting to have any part of being Jewish—didn't help. I show pride in my heritage—doesn't help. They still hate us, because limited minds need to feel superior."

One morning I read of a robbery gone murder on Paul's street in Uptown Manhattan in Spanish Harlem. When I reached our office, he was sitting in the kitchenette, spreading cream cheese on his bagel.

"Why do you continue living in Harlem even though you could afford a better neighborhood?" I yelled at him, before taking my coat off. "Every other day someone is killed, hurt, robbed. If you don't care about your own life, think of your daughters."

Paul bit into his bagel and waited for my anger to expire.

"Would they accept me in that 'better,' you mean 'whiter,' neighborhood? And the main question is—do I want to be accepted by those 'better,' you mean 'whiter,' neighbors? I do think of my daughters. They'd have an entire life of people looking down at them. Let them feel equal for a while."

It was what I had wanted when I was growing up—to be equal. Why would I wish something different for Paul's daughters?

My friend noticed a change in my face. He sat deeper into the kitchen chair, raising its front legs up, a light smile touching his lips. That's what he usually did when I gave up arguing and stepped inside myself for some soul digging.

"You, Lilli, are so predictable. Once again you had an opinion but agreed with mine. Now you think yourself wrong, searching for reasons to change your mind. Man, it's bothersome inside your head. I wouldn't want to be there. I could imagine the fights your brain cells are having. The heat is unbearable."

As Paul spoke, I recognized the truth of his perception. But he wasn't through with me yet.

"Then you come to work and complain about insomnia. Of course you don't sleep night after night. How could you? You have to listen to the arguments on all sides of your skull, and there are numerous sides, I'm sure. No envy from me here. No wonder you hear those strange sounds in there, the ones you described to me as old material being ripped."

One day at lunch, we walked out to the elevator together.

"Lilli, don't you know how great you are, how admirable? Start trusting your own judgment." Paul surprised me with those words, before we parted at the building exit.

I stopped him. "What's to admire?"

"I only read in the newspapers about the prisons and the gulag they threw your people in when you wanted to leave there. You lived it. You're smart and educated, and nevertheless go through hoops just to be understood by all kinds of jerks. Nothing is easy, but you do it. When I talk to my daughters, I bring you as my example of what I wish for them to become."

"Thank you, friend." I was glad he didn't see the frightened and lonely inside of me.

***

One day, Paul asked permission to leave the office for a few hours, because his brother was in the hospital. He didn't respond to my questioning gaze.

The next morning he sat with his newspaper and cup of coffee, buttering a bagel. We had about fifteen minutes before our workday would start.

"How is your brother? And what's wrong with him? You never mentioned he was sick." I settled down by the kitchenette's table, expecting a detailed explanation.

"Oh, that? He died last night."

"What? What is with you? Are you normal? Maybe you are sick? Is it shock?" I knew how important family was for Paul.

"What do you want me to say? Anthony did it to himself. He had AIDS. I call it suicide. Am I sorry? I lost my brother when he took his first sniff and used the first needle. He never returned from that trip. I talked to him, tried to stay close, took him for his first hour of treatment, then cried for him."

Paul stood up and moved around, not finding peace. "Oh, shit! I'm sorry. I'm sorry for my mom, who has to take care of his son now. And this boy is bad! He's worse than his father was at this age. He's eleven. No one knows where his mom is. Maybe he has other grandparents someplace."

Paul's dark eyes darted right and left, up and down.

"I'm glad he died. Maybe my daughters will think twice before deciding to get high. Not that they're unaware of the death from drugs. But they also see the shiny new cars of the drug dealers. They see it every day."

Paul slumped back in his chair.

This man doesn't bend to suffering. He overcomes obstacles and gets stronger.

He believed I was strong. In truth, with every step I felt more out of place on the inside of my skin. Wasn't it weird?

Thoughts of Paul and his brother stayed with me. Paul's brother died and it was too late to change their relationship. I had a brother, too. I shouldn't wait for something to happen to him.

The very next day, I took a pen and a brand new notebook, preparing for the serious work of scrubbing my soul. Needing to be alone, I remembered the little park across the street from my office.

I wanted to believe that nature shared my feelings of loneliness and heard the surrounding trees grumbling of the late autumn cold. And why wouldn't they, standing leafless and apart from each other?

Why did I feel that alone, despite having a husband of sixteen years, two beautiful sons, friends?

CHAPTER 21

Flushing, Queens New York, USA

1984

"Gil, Benny, come here. We have to do the clothes' work," I yelled into my sons' room.

It was a Sunday in April. I reached for the old suitcase we called "summer-winter trunk." Light in the winter with shorts, t-shirts, and swimming trunks, it became backbreaking to lug down from the closet's shelf in the summer with sweaters, snow and corduroy pants, boots, hats, scarves, and mittens.

Gil, at age thirteen, could hardly fit into most of his previous year's clothes, and then Ben got to wear them.

Some pants needed patching. Those I put aside to wait for the pause in my workday. This was a chore I enjoyed, considering myself an artiste in the field—even creating a way of lengthening pants without anyone seeing the line of an old fold.

Nine-year-old Ben didn't have the patience to sit down and wait for his turn. He bounced around and tickled Gil. Giggling Gil couldn't continue with the fitting. Trying for more laughs, Benny wore his brother's shorts on his head and ran circles around the sofa where we sat. He waved his arms and made wild faces, insisting that Gil's shorts fit his head better than Gil's butt. He did look cute—mischievous eyes peeking from under the green shorts, dimpled cheeks pink. Only then Gil stopped laughing and stood up, trying to catch his brother.

"Boys, stop that! We need to finish with the clothes. There are sales around and I have to know what you need for the summer."

"Papa t-told you we s-shouldn't buy anything," Gil reminded me.

He stuttered more. The new research in the stuttering field tied worsening speech patterns to the wrong posture and breathing. The specialists didn't think that nerves or tension were to blame for the fluency problems. I didn't buy this theory.

"Chicken, you are chicken…" sang Benny. "Mom knows that we need clothes. Mom is an adult. Yes, Mommy?"

"No fighting for one day, please."

So the boys overheard Sergey's and my quarrel, and as usual Gil was scared of Sergey's outbursts, while Ben tried to act cool.

The day before, Sergey appeared more preoccupied during our dinner. After the children left the table, I wanted to talk to him about Gil's speech, but my husband went first.

"Lilli, we have to talk."

Sergey sounded serious. I moved away the plate in front of me so I could lean my elbows on the table, supporting myself.

Sergey sat on the other side of the dining table, ready for me. "With both of us working, and Benny attending public school, I'd hoped we'd save a fortune—but it didn't happen. There're no visible changes in our savings account. Any explanations?"

I was in charge of money. I shopped, I paid bills.

Sergey waited, his face darkened by the gloomy mood.

"We're four people. We eat, we grow, and we spend. I'm always careful, but I can't remember what I did with every penny, if that's what you're asking. The prices of everything went up. Stop for once in a supermarket and see for yourself. Do we have to economize on food, for God's sake?" My frustration sounded loud.

And so did his. "You're yelling. I can't talk to you. You get defensive and we don't ever reach a solution. Forget it. I'm sorry I talked to you. You won't hear my voice in the near future. Goodbye." It was back to not talking.

That was our Kaplan-style discussion. The joke had it: men deal with big important problems, like starting wars and building bridges. Women on the other hand coped with small unimportant dilemmas, like ... what to do about a son's stuttering.

***

Coming into my office, I sought Paul's friendly ear.

"One kid yells and throws things and says 'no' before he hears your question. The second doesn't talk, stays in his room, and reads books. He's blocked out every single occurrence from his earlier life. His stuttering is worse. Doctors think it's not psychological, but I don't believe them."

"Overly smart children confuse me," Paul admitted. "I'm not comfortable around your oldest, for sure. Never saw a twelve-year-old who doesn't smile, doesn't jump, doesn't kick hell."

"Oh, yeah? Gil is simply a peaceful boy. He doesn't enjoy rough games and loud sounds. What's wrong with that?"

“Nothing, if you want a sissy on your hands. What does Sergey say about all this?”

“Don’t you know? He’s a man, which includes working long hours to earn a salary, blueprinting our glorious future, and receiving deserved respect from those around him.”

“I wish to have a glorious future, too. What’s wrong with that? Lilli, what is happening with the two of you?”

Mine and Sergey’s relationship was a minefield I refused to think about. More than ever, Sergey returned home agitated after arguments with the owner of the company he worked for.

“I need my own business,” he insisted, “to be my own boss. That’s the only way for us to get somewhere. I waste hours on politely trying to prove to a jerk that, while he’s not a total idiot, he’s not competent enough. He knows it too, but we go through the routine anyway.”

I didn’t have a solution to our money problem, but as usual I was afraid to lose the relative comfort we’d reached.

“New businesses often don’t work out. My salary is two hundred dollars a week. Gross. It takes me over two weeks to make the rent money. The four of us couldn’t survive on it,” I said.

“If this is your answer, forget I’d ever spoken.”

After not talking to me for three days, grim-looking Sergey found me in the kitchen. I was preparing the next day’s dinner for the boys and me and him too—in case he’d change his mind and eat at last.

“Lilli, did you find a divorce lawyer?” he asked, his face folded in frown. At the end of a few last disagreements, Sergey had mentioned the word “divorce” before stomping out.

How would the break-up of the family help him with his plans for a better future?

He stood there in the kitchen, looking at me crossly, waiting for some response. The noises in my head responded to the harshness of my husband's voice. For a while I hadn't heard them, or perhaps got used to them through the years and stopped paying attention.

Then my brain supplied the words: "Sergey, I don't need a divorce lawyer. I told you before and I'm telling it to you again—you want a divorce—you do it. Any lawyer will explain to you that a wife with children gets everything. And what do we have, besides the household stuff? Do you think you need it more than we?"

Sergey didn't listen.

"Write down what you want from the apartment..." He continued with 'b' just because he had said 'a.' "I have an appointment with my lawyer later today," he insisted.

After his father left, Gil, wearing light blue pajamas, entered the kitchen. "Mom..." His angelic features begged to be protected from any worries. "Are the two of you g-going to d-divorce? Many p-parents in our class are d-divorced. I d-don't like it."

Benny, wearing his underpants only and standing close behind his brother, piped in: "We don't even need him. He works, and he reads his paper, and he looks for business. We don't do anything fun. Every Monday you promise we'll go places, but weekend comes—it's back to 'Dad is busy time.'"

"Kids, we'll be fine. Dad and I aren't going to divorce. This coming Saturday we'll take a train, just the three of us, and go to the city. We'll have fun." I wished to believe my brave words.

What if Sergey would indeed act on his intentions? I wouldn't ever seek money from him to support the children and me. It was humiliating. He was my family. Besides our children, he was more my family than anyone. *I don't want to be without him.*

What if I tried to vocalize the desperation eating at me? Maybe he'd feel sympathy and stop the embarrassing threats. No, it wouldn't work, he had zero patience for "psychological bologna." He would say, "Be specific."

Specific? Would a comparison to a closet overflowing with old and not needed clothes provide a clue of how I felt? A place that wasn't empty, though not usable, and devoid of light— the emptiness of a full, dark closet … was that specific enough?

"Sergey, let's talk already. For the whole week we have been passing each other like two strangers. You just nibble at the food. You'll expire from hunger."

Yet Sergey didn't respond.

Should I say: *Sergey, it's the wrong time for playing a victim? Nature can't wait. I need your input on something that concerns both of us. I need your opinion as to have or not to have another baby. Yes, Sergey, I'm pregnant. It happened in one of those short-lived intervals of peace between us. I guess no protection is a hundred percent safe.*Or should I say: Y*ou see, Sergey, I'm not sure I like the way the two children we've got are developing. Is Gil's quietness and Benny's wildness normal? What do you think? Gil doesn't laugh. Marches straight to his room and opens a book. Ben walks in and starts hysterics for one or the other reason. What about Gil's not bringing any friends home and Benny's bringing everyone, discharging them at once if they don't play by his rules? Aren't you worried sick about them? Is it fair to bring another child into our family*?

My life was work and worry, work and sleepless nights, work and nightmares, work and headaches, work and guilt for being a lousy mother and even a lousy wife. I was so tired. I couldn't have another baby, no way.

A baby? A little, soft bundle of pink warmth … maybe a girl … a twenty-four-hour-long marathon of changing, washing, feeding a new human, who would depend on me for its survival.

I was so tired.

An enormous clock inside of me ticked.

No way would I have another baby, and that was final.

I made arrangements for an abortion with my gynecologist.

The day of the procedure, Gil woke up with a fever. I called Dr. Dreifuss and asked him to see Gil later that same afternoon. He didn't have an opening, so I explained about my abortion, asking to be accommodated.

"You want to bring him at four, yet at twelve you have a surgery?" he asked dubiously. "It's none of my business, but where is Mr. Kaplan in all of this scheduling?"

Our pediatrician was more like a family member, caring for our children for years.

"Doctor, we had a disagreement. My husband is a proud and stubborn man. He cannot give an inch." I felt I owed an explanation to the old doctor. "Don't judge him too harshly, please. I didn't tell him about my pregnancy, not knowing how to introduce the subject, since he doesn't talk to me at all."

"Go and have your abortion. See if I care that you don't want to produce any more patients for me." Sensing my despair, our doctor used a lighter tone.

I walked into the Queens gynecological surgery clinic and looked around. There were couples, some younger, some older, but all in pairs. As soon as I sat, I took out a pad and a pen—my personal weapons against loneliness.

There were many women waiting their turn for surgeries that day. I had plenty of time to write my second letter to Josef, to share the story of my first abortion buried so deep in that Russian snow that I nearly forgot about it.

Hi, Josef,

It's perfect time for me to share some things I never told you.

I was nineteen. A year after Mama died. Soon after you arranged my working at the radio factory and be a college student. Everyone around was drinking as a matter-of-fact. Dutifully, I tried to teach myself to drink and not get drunk after the first glass. Whatever piss I poured into myself, cheap wine, vodka, didn't matter—I got sick, dizzy, stupid, and unbalanced. If lucky for me, I got home before splattering it out somewhere inappropriate, you saw me on my knees puking out colorful dirt in our bathroom. A few times you beat me up, deservingly, I should say. Not that it helped. Papa David's hurting eyes make me smirk.

I felt caged in between other humans and my own reflection in the mirror, and both weren't pleasing. My mirror didn't change its display of morbid Jewish eyes, wide eyebrows emphasizing the gruesome face, the dark droopy hair. What kind of boy would like this? One I wouldn't look twice at.

And then someone's wedding happened and I was raped.

Yea. Only couple of my girlfriends knew. It was winter with a lot of snow. Mountains of snow. The party was somewhere in a private dilapidated old house. From my boredom I suggested my help to the bride; she was such helpless orphan and I felt pity. Well...I even sewed her dress. Then I had a few drinks and you know that I can't drink. Wanted to pee, wanted to throw up, no toilet inside the house. Smelly outhouse in the yard. Don't remember much. Fell in the snow and that's it. Remember hands on me and pain. Sobered up fast. Understood. No one to complain, no witnesses, just stupid drunk me and a lot of snow.

I folded the letter I was writing and capped my pen. I looked at the written pages—in some places my pen tore the paper; some words were smeared by tears. For the first time I had summarized it like that—from the beginning to the end. The minor fragments came back to life from time to time for some or other reason, but not the entire thing, not ever.

It was time to face what had happened so many years ago. Even if I couldn't continue with the story for Josef's benefit, I had to for my own.

I never found out who did it and didn't care. Who asked me to behave so obnoxiously?

I became pregnant that day. Of all the bad things that could happen!

Abortions were legal and more popular than teeth extractions, yet if a woman wasn't married and tried to keep it a secret in a free Soviet system, she had to pay.

It helped to have all those girlfriends. I was lucky with this. One of them became pregnant on her wedding night and divorced the next month. There was no way she wanted to keep a baby of a man who beat her up twice in this first month. She made an appointment for an abortion in a local clinic.

We worked out the entire scenario with her doctor. I came in with my girlfriend, not registering at the desk, entered the office with her, and inside the operating room waited for her to be done first. Two for the time of one.

A doctor pocketed my money to keep her mouth shut—no big deal.

After the surgery, I walked home—an overnight bed was registered in my girlfriend's name. I walked slowly, bearing the pain. It was too cold to sit in the park on the bench. But to go home to be seen and questioned by David was intolerable.

When it got dark, I approached my house and stood by the brick wall for support. Blood surged through my stockings. My other girlfriend, who lived on the floor above, was coming from work late and brought me to her house for the night.

I bled for days. The same doctor told me that while the bleeding was extensive, there was no permanent damage to any organs. My heart didn't count.

CHAPTER 22

Flushing, Queens, New York, USA

1984-1986

"I need my own business," Sergey repeated daily. I suspected he was trying to convince me, at the same time boosting his own resolve.

"I know you do. It would become your favorite baby while I'd continue taking care of the two we gave birth to. On weekends they would want to go places and I'll repeat my worn slogan: 'Dad is busy and there is no money in the house.' Anyway, where would you get the funds for it? Our savings aren't enough."

Nevertheless, he checked the *New York Times* regularly and one day called a man about a small metal production shop that was listed for sale.

Once a thriving business, it lost the bulk of its customers since the owner's beloved wife of fifty years died, leaving him with no will to go on. Sergey filled out papers at the Small Business Administration for a loan to cover the down payment.

"Lilli, that's the American way," he proclaimed. The business became his. His face lit up. He was as excited as I was terrified.

In the following months, Sergey left the house before six every morning and returned sometimes close to midnight. I glanced at the bags under his swollen red eyes, stooped shoulders, and the pants in need of tighter belts, and didn't mention that my lousy two-hundred dollars gross a week didn't stretch nearly enough for the four of us. Yes, hopefully, this business would provide for us one day. One day, maybe, but today, taking care of the household was my responsibility.

"We agreed to let Gil go to a sleep-away camp this year," I reminded Sergey one night, after a dinner he hardly touched—too tired to be hungry.

"I know." Sergey didn't waver. "Let him go. One way or another, we'll pull it off. Borrow from credit cards. Eventually, the customers that used to buy from the previous owner will come back. My prices are low and deliveries timely. You'll see the business will pay us back."

When? I didn't actually ask him that. He couldn't predict it anyway.

Thirteen-year-old Gil was going away to a horse-ranch camp. At "Rawhide," each child took care of the horse assigned to him throughout the season. Gil read all horse books and talked about the adventures waiting for him. The camp management sent us a long list of needed items. Nightly I sat in the bedroom by my sewing machine, attaching "Gil Kaplan" labels onto all of his things. While my hands were doing their thing, my brain was on the go too.

For the phone we owed only twenty-six dollars—I didn't have time to use it and it showed. The electric was low this month, too, though the grace period for the rent was over. If I paid it in full there was nothing left for the food shopping. But C-Town accepted my personal checks, so if I shopped on Friday they would deposit the check on Monday and only maybe Tuesday would be notified that there was no money in our account. That way I'd have time to pay them from my next paycheck.

I kept accurate lists with dates and amounts and priorities. At nights, I didn't even try to sleep, because in my dreams everybody was asking for the money at once.

"Please, could you wait till the next week, please," I begged. Once I woke myself up forcefully in order not to pay a bill.

"Mom, why are you crying?" Gil whispered to me in the morning. "If you don't want me to go to that camp, I'll stay home this summer."

I couldn't believe that apparently I'd woken not only myself that night but also my exceptionally sensitive son.

I calmed his fears: "Don't worry, you're going to be a horse-rancher and everything is going to be fine."

While I was sewing the camp labels on Gil's clothes, Sergey's voice from the living room reached my ears: "I hope to get that government order I bid on. If they believe a small guy has enough resources to satisfy all their requirements, I know I could do it."

In all probability my husband spoke to me, but though I heard his words, I didn't concentrate on their meaning. My hands continued working with the labels and my brain continued its accounting task. I also remembered the dirty dinner dishes soaking in the sink. I'd leave them till tomorrow, but the city cockroaches would start liking our apartment too much.

***

I sat on the brown leather sofa in our darkened sleepy apartment wearing my long silk nightshirt and a fluffy red robe.

Every few minutes I checked the time, waiting until after midnight in New York, which would be early morning in Kiev, the morning of my papa's seventy-fifth birthday. I wanted to make sure to get him early, before he ran out to do his thousand-and-one errands.

Luckily, the next day, the twenty-fifth of December, everyone was off for the Christmas holiday, so I'd be able to sleep later.

When I was growing up back in the Soviet Union, any observance of God was strictly forbidden, yet the religious customs were handed orally within your own family from generation to generation. In my Goldbloom family we knew nothing of Christmas, though a watered down Chanukah became an annual event.

The birthdays of the Jews of my father's generation were remembered according to the proximity to many Jewish holidays. My papa was born around the days of Chanukah, so the Goldblooms celebrated his birthday and Chanukah on the same day.

All the aunts and uncles came to the Pushkin Street house. The children anxiously waited for the *Chanukah-gelt*—a small *ruble*-bills gift—this holiday's custom. Once, after wishing happy birthday to my father, one of my uncles asked me what day did they come to celebrate? I promptly reported: "The money-giving one."

After receiving the awaited annual 'donation', the children went outside to play in the snow, always plentiful that time of the year. We built castles and had snowball fights, which often ended with one of us getting knocked on the head with a hard snowball.

This year, in New York, snow was coming down steadily. With its crispy white cover, the streets at last had lost their imperfections: no more potholes, cigarette butts, or advertising leaflets on the sidewalks. When Gil and Benny were younger, I taught them all about the snow's magic powers. Together we used to watch those tiny flakes, one inside the chain of others. And if we watched keenly, sometimes they surprised us by combining forces and becoming bigger upon reaching the ground.

I hadn't seen my father face-to-face for thirteen years. His last photograph showed an older, skinnier man. It was good for his health to lose some weight, but the sunken cheeks worried me.

I set his photograph on the coffee table in front of me by the phone so when I talked to him I could see his face. The warm, velvety eyes staring from the glossy photograph didn't change. We had the same eyes. Looking like him used to upset me to no end when I was a silly little girl, thinking that eventually I too would grow a similar bald, prominent head framed by the whisper of grey hair.

How many years did I waste on hating my father? So he wasn't perfect. Was I perfect? I left him there all by himself instead of persuading, or even forcing him to go along.

Papa David backed Sergey and me all the way. When we decided to leave the USSR, Sergey was fired in punishment at once. I had just given birth to Gil and wasn't working at the time. If not for Papa, where would we be?

He bought food for us and took Gil in his carriage for long walks. He even cooked for us when I was tired taking care of a newborn. He also trudged doggedly through the government offices, helping us with all kinds of required documents needed for emigrating.

"Do you realize we could imprison you for helping the traitors of the Soviet motherland?" a bureaucrat asked him in one of the offices. "Your daughter is leaving. We consider her and her husband enemies, traitors. But you're staying with us. Think about it."

His life didn't worry him.

"I'm an old man," he replied. "I'm staying so not to be a burden to them. I know my odds. Believe me, that's why I'm helping them to change theirs."

I checked the time again—not quite yet. I adjusted the pillow behind my back and straightened my cramped limbs. On one side of the apartment I heard the soft whistles coming from Benny's stuffed nose and Gil's dreamy mumbles; on the other Sergey's rugged, almost thirty years' worth of nicotine-poisoned breathing. They were my New York family. And now, let's see—twelve o'clock and fifteen minutes—time to call my family in Kiev.

The words: "Happy birthday, Papa!" formed inside of my mouth, ready to jump forth. I punched in the many digits of an overseas connection.

On the very first ring, the receiver was picked up, my call was expected, but the voice wasn't Papa's.

"Josef? Is it you?" I couldn't believe my ears. My brother sounded eerily clear, like he stood next to me. "What happened? Is it Papa?"

"Lilli, he told me you were going to call on his birthday. He's in the hospital."

No 'Hello,' no 'How are you,' no 'Glad to hear your voice'—that was my one and only brother speaking.

"Josef, you scared me to death. He's sick, but he's not dead or something, right?"

"Lilli, his leg has to be amputated. It's his only salvation. He has gangrene and it spread high above his knee. Do you remember Mama used to swaddle his legs with shawls? His circulation has been poor since the war. But with the diabetes and all…"

"Oh my God. Oh, please. I can't even go and see him. Your stinking country wouldn't allow it. Maybe through the Red Cross … I could try … but it would take ages. I'm nobody to be sympathetic to."

"Stop carrying on! I waited for you to call, not drive me crazy. Just listen."

My tears subsided because Josef ordered them to quit. He was in charge, like always.

He continued: "He knew you'd call on his birthday. He is child-like now—waits for you to tell him to go ahead with the surgery. Keeps saying, 'What if Lilli would be allowed to come and visit one day, and here I'm without a leg.'"

I lost it. I forgot about my boys and Sergey sleeping. I wailed like old women do at the cemeteries.

"Josef," I sobbed, "don't let him die. I need him."

"Don't be an imbecile. I won't let him die. Though I can't believe I'm in charge of his life now. After all the years that he wouldn't accept me as his son. Anyway…"

"Don't talk rubbish. He's our father. Just don't let him die. Josef, how would I know how is he doing? Your hospitals don't even have phones for the patients' use. I'll call this home number all the time. Hopefully I'll catch you. Give him my love. I don't need his leg. I need him."

Papa, don't die. Wait for me, please. You didn't see the boys' latest photographs—they came out really good. I think both of them look like you. I'm sure they do. I love you. Did I tell you how much I love and value you? Do you believe me, Papa?

Memories of him helping, taking care of me, and later newborn Gil, blanketed me.

"Doctor, I'm Lilli Kaplan's father. She complains of pain in here." David pointed at the spot above his waistline. That was when I was first pregnant with Gil and cranky, refusing to go out and see a doctor. My papa went instead of me to the clinic. Maybe they laughed at him. He wouldn't notice.

He used to carry newborn Gil's carriage up to the third floor. The iron carriage imported from East Germany weighed a ton. But he didn't want to take the sleeping baby out of the carriage and wake him up. My papa wore the carriage on his neck, his outstretched arms supporting it in front of him, his satisfied grin shining onto the tiny face. That was some sight.

I was in second grade when my appendix burst. The experience was engraved in my mind—never mind the crude scar through my belly.

I tried to listen to my teacher while the pains in my stomach were getting worse. Zoya took me to the nurse's room and the school called my parents.

"Don't worry," they assured me, "everything will be fine."

I was in and out of sleep for most of the time from the medications, but lucid enough when we got to the hospital and a matron drew me a bath before emergency surgery. One sympathetic doctor whispered into my papa's ear that the hospital had a chickenpox epidemic. My papa was furious and forced his way inside the room.

"I'm taking her away. How dare you all!"

He didn't wait for the nurses to return my clothes. He wrapped me in his and Mama's coats and hurried, running to the next hospital. I felt secure in my father's arms while he carried me. I felt his body sharing my pain and easing it too.

Now he was in the hospital. And it was no child's illness. Thank God for Josef!

"Josef, don't let him die," I whispered again.

Many times a day I tried to check on Papa's condition. No one answered the phone. Josef called five days later.

I started whimpering on hearing his hushed: "Hi, little sister."

My father complied with his doctor's orders. He knew it wouldn't help anyway. It was his body, not the doctor's. He felt the infection spreading throughout. But he'd do it, if Lilli said so. He'd let them amputate his leg.

"I didn't expect you of all people to take care of me," he acknowledged to Josef towards the end. Their relations always were strained. The spreading infection needed more medications. The tired heart couldn't take any more of the assault. It stopped.

***

The snow hadn't let up since before Christmas. Why did I always feel safety in its whiteness and softness? How did the feeling come about? It was exactly the opposite— everything bad happened to me while it was snowing. Mama died when it snowed; I was raped with all that snow under and around me. Now Papa was gone and the damn powder didn't cease. It hunted me through the continents and years; it planned to bury me under its weight.

I called one of my co-workers to cry about not having a father anymore. The next day my office called, suggesting I should stay home for the customary seven days of Jewish mourning. To do what—watch the accursed snow? I refused.

My sons didn't ask many questions. The grandfather on the other side of the ocean remained a stranger.

Sergey's philosophy on death was known: "I'm sorry, Lilli, but we all will die."

I wanted to talk about my papa but didn't know anyone who would listen. The not-shared, not-voiced pain tormented me endlessly. The guilt woke up with vehemence: if I had been nicer to him before, if I had forced him to immigrate with us, if I had supported him throughout … too late for all of the above.

CHAPTER 23

Long Island Suburb New York, USA

1992

May - November

The day came—one of the happiest in our life. Gil, the little baby out of Kiev, the small boy of our wandering years, was graduating Phi Beta Kappa from prestigious Cornell University. He would go on for his masters and doctorate program in molecular biology at Berkley University in California.

We invited Sergey's parents along for Gil's graduation. Festively dressed, they occupied a second seat in our roomy Voyager. Benny sat up front, changing radio stations, and didn't say a word through the five-hour trip. I had the third row all to myself.

"Let the Jew in your belly die," a woman in the Kiev street had damned him. She'd rushed to be the first in line for some household item and came into contact with my nine-month pregnant belly.

“Put your baby on the grass. Don’t clutch him so tightly. He’s a Jew going to live in the Jewish State,” the woman in our Vienna transit camp, on the way to Israel, had said in flawless Russian, sounding like a song in an exotic tongue. “You better start teaching him to be fearless.”

“Mom, I want pee-pee.” His little feet stomped the ground, his little body not able to fight the urge any longer. I let him do it behind the tree when the two Belgian women with their poodles protested in disdain. They thought we were savages. I hugged my three-year-old, crying in sorrow.

“I want to work with animals.” He was four and five and six. “You could do anything you want to do,” Sergey assured him. “No limits of any kind. You can do everything.”

“M-m-mom, you argued … w-w-with Dad again. Is h-h-he g-g-going to d-d-divorce us? I a-am afraid.” He was eight and ten and twelve.

“How come you don’t have any memories of your childhood? Was everything so bleak that you blocked it out completely?” I insisted when he came home during his college break. “Mom, don’t worry. I have a great life thanks to you and Dad,” my beautiful, adult son assured me.

The memories lulled me to sleep.

My dreams followed my memories. With my eyes closed I saw my mama and I explained to her all about Gil’s honorable diploma. “He’s like Josef liking sciences, but because we’re Americans he’ll live wherever he wants, Mama.”

Then I appeared alongside Sergey and our children and a few close friends inside an unfamiliar Manhattan apartment. There were many spacious rooms inside. We were examining each one, admiring the paintings and statues, though in one room Sergey didn’t appreciate the color of the sofa and insisted it to be exchanged for another. Did this grandiosity belong to us?

In that dream, one of my friends announced that the greeting parade was about to start and we walked to yet another room. The various groups were taking part, marching with the bands and placards representing their organizations. My family and friends stayed up on the platform welcoming the procession. Unexpectedly, my papa walked in with one of the groups. He wore the blue uniform of a laborer. His face, younger than ever, was ashen. I rushed to him.

"Papa, I'm so glad to see you. Enough of that independence business, come with me. You belong with the family."

He didn't respond, didn't move, staring emotionlessly at my surroundings.

"Papa…" I tried again. "Now we're able to afford things. We bought that apartment and it represents an achievement in life. The people came to congratulate us. We could help you with anything your heart desires."

Does he believe me? He stared and stared; I couldn't take his lifeless stare anymore and woke up.

Did I dream about that Manhattan apartment because recently we bought a house on Long Island? My papa didn't live long enough to have a convincing proof of us going up in life.

When Sergey started talking about the house, I refused to participate.

"You want the house, go and find one," I replied. "Let me know when we're going to move and I'll start packing."

At work, Paul Fernando listened to my grumble in disbelief.

"There's something wrong with you, girl. Any woman would kill to have a husband who wants to buy a house and could afford it. And don't give me all this shit about being tired. A house is what the American dream is all about. So you work hard for a little longer and then you hire help. See what I mean? It's all easy when there's money in the bank."

"Paul, you're right, I know money is necessary. I believe to live in a house is better than in an apartment. And it's not the work I'm afraid of.

It's my mental state, which is in turmoil. I feel like an intruder. The farther we go up in that life, the more of an intruder I am."

"Lilli, please, do me a tiny favor—don't fight Sergey on the house. I need a friend with a house in a suburb. Would you mind a bunch of Puerto Ricans descending at you for the weekend?"

"Ha-ha. Only to accommodate you I'll try to enjoy my new suburban status. You deserve it, if only for listening to my complaints."

***

"Benny, do you have a minute?"

I tried to choose a moment when my seventeen-year-old son would be willing to talk to me. Our conversations didn't last for more than five words. I planned and rehearsed those five words for hours, still not finding the appropriate ones.

Ben, with headphones covering his ears on the way from the bathroom to the kitchen, listened to music loud enough for me to hear it.

Feebly, I spoke anyway.

"I was your age once and had to go through the confusion of being seventeen. Talk to me, you'll see for yourself," I begged.

He heard me. "Don't make me puke. You lived in the dark ages. You were forbidden everything, including shitting without permission of your Communist leaders. You left there and now you're trying their methods on me. Forget it."

For a kid who didn't read, he'd obtained an extensive historical knowledge. From the TV, I bet.

I went to my bedroom to cry.

What if he used drugs? Who were his friends? When he brought them and I happened to be at home, he ushered them away. It spelled trouble.

No. No. No. All of this was only his pretense at bravery. He was as scared of growing up as I was at his age. I shrugged off the depressing thoughts. I was still scared. But he wasn't me—he is an American kid. I have to have hope. What else could I do?

"Sergey, there's a parent-teacher meeting tonight."

I mentioned the upcoming event a week ago and Sergey nodded his half-agreeing response, and tonight, watching him sluggishly eat his supper, almost forcing his mouth to open for each bite of food, I wasn't sure he'd go.

"I'm dead-tired. The problems at the shop didn't stop the whole day. Can't they have those meetings on Saturdays?"

I didn't respond. When he just started his business and worked twelve-hour day as a laborer, salesman, engineer, and everything in between, he still went to meetings with Gil's teachers. Of course, nothing but praise had been distributed there. Now he had an entire staff and a capable supervisor and the secretaries to tend the office, so he isn't even as tired as those years before.

"Do you think I like to listen to Ben's teachers' complaints? Nevertheless, I don't want them to think we're not involved in our son's life and don't care." Sergey agreed and together we walked to school.

Wanting to look better than I felt, I wrapped a black African scarf with golden lions painted on it around my shoulders. Sergey didn't change out of his usual grease-stained worker's uniform he wore all day.

Benny stayed at home, locked in his room, his thoughts, hopes, and intentions hidden inside the smart-alecky mind under fashionably half-shaven head and clothes twice the needed size.

It seemed like a merry good time for the parents of other children. They met old friends from the neighborhood, catching up on the news, sharing jokes, boasting their sons' and daughters' successes.

We didn't know the other parents. We'd bought the house in the suburbs recently and both worked full time. And what would we boast about?

And then the conversations with his teachers. "Your son comes late for every physics class. Instead of just doing his work, he invents arguing contests in order to stand out and be noticed."

"Ben has the ability to write English essays, though I have to take his word for it. He tries my endurance by doing the wrong work for every one of my assignments."

"I loved your boy for the first half of this year. I told you so at our last meeting. He started as the most promising student in my audio-visual class. But the picnic is over. He doesn't show up for it anymore."

We left the school without saying a word to each other. Could I, please, run away somewhere, please? What was going to become of Ben? *Why am I even thinking of his future? Sergey will kill him now, tonight and blame me. It's always the mother's fault.* I glanced at Sergey. The unshaved face, the dark circles under the eyes, and the eyes … they blazed with an expression of utter madness. *He'll kill his son tonight. He will.*

"Ben, come here!" Sergey exhaled in an ear-splitting blast the second we stepped inside the house.

Nothing moved in the upstairs bedroom.

"Be a man, you son-of-a-bitch! I'll punish you—you won't sit on your ass till you're one hundred."

"Sergey, it doesn't help. You tried punishments." I didn't expect my husband to listen to my words. I was only trying to postpone whatever was coming.

"Of course you protect him. You did it before and you do it now. You're the reason for this situation. Did you know my first job was at a blacksmith shop? I was thirteen. Yes, thirteen. I supported my mother and did my homework too."

"You don't really want him to support us. That's why you work so hard. Don't you?"

"If I'd wait for him to support us—we'd starve, living on the street."

Sergey didn't sit down through the entire exchange. His head turned towards Ben's bedroom again and he roared again: "You loser, you moron, come here and listen to me. Don't wait for me to come get you."

The door from Ben's room swung open with mighty power. The wall cracked from the force of the doorknob. Ben stood on the little balcony above our living room, staring down at his much-shorter father.

He was close to six feet tall, still childishly lanky, lips quivering with pity for himself but mostly with the impotence of a child. His face with its first grownup stubble, usually a healthy pink, now lifeless.

"Kill me. I'm not afraid. I don't give a damn. I hate you anyway!"

"Please, both of you stop it. You'll be sorry for anything you do or say. You're foolishly stubborn, the two of you."

No one listened to me. My mutterings were no more than sounds of a half-crushed bee or the dry yellow leaves in the backyard. They were defending their suffering manhood and nothing, but nothing, was more valid.

Like the slow motion of an old film, which you watch again though you know every little moment of it, I observed Sergey step two feet back to the dining table and pick up an open ketchup bottle. I noticed him grabbing the bottle upside-down by its neck and raised my hands to stop him; opened my mouth to advise him of the bottle being open—no words emerged. The first red drops of ketchup appeared on the table. The stunt continued with the bottle flying through the air, aimed towards Ben's head.

The blood-like drops followed its path. There was bright light all around me. Who was screaming inside of my head? My feet refused to hold the heaviness of me. *I have to sit down*. Our red oriental rug was heavenly soft. My African scarf was very beautiful, with those golden lions all over it.

I had a perfect viewing point—the middle of the living room. Ben's clothes appropriated bloody drops. The wall above the balcony did, too.

That's nice. Red is my favorite color. Now we'll have beautiful red background for our life.

The first slam of the outside door sounded all over the neighborhood.

The second one came a moment later.

Mama, why don't you help Josef? There's blood all over. There's so much blood but so quiet ... why is no one screaming? Everyone left me. Vasilisa did too. I'm afraid to be by myself. Where am I? I'm hurting. Is it my blood everywhere? Am I dying? Mama, help me.

"What happened?" I asked, but no one was around to hear me. I looked around and saw the ketchup drops all over. "Ben? Where is Benny? Sergey? Are you home?" I was lying on the floor, wrapped in the African scarf with the golden lions painted on it.

I have to clean up all that ketchup. The wall was ruined; the rug could be cleaned … maybe. Where was the cat? *I don't have a cat. Am I mad? Did they let my cat out? The food is still on the table—it'll go rancid and I'll have to cook again*. Where was the cat?

CHAPTER 24

Long Island Suburb New York, USA

1992-1993

I saw the inside of my skull like an ex-ray machine. And what I saw were safety pins of different sizes: tiny, small, medium-sized, really big ones. They were needed to hold together that material inside of it that was rustling while coming apart.

A safety pin is a lazy person's tool, Mama warned. As usual, I didn't listen to my mama and was paying dearly for that now. The noise in my head wouldn't let me sleep through the night. And when I did sleep, I didn't dream. Even the dreams ran away, disturbed by the racket.

Going to work on the LIRR train, I couldn't read. I stared at my fellow passengers. Why didn't I ever notice how unattractive and sloppy most of them looked?

Like this young woman—she is short and wears a mid-calf length skirt, which makes her look dumpy. Am I lucky or what to have had my mama as a teacher! And look at this one with the longest thread following her all the way to the exit. It hangs from the lining of her coat. I bet, first it was just a smidgen and she ignored it, and it got caught in some crack somewhere and was pulled longer, and now it's gigantic. Yeah, nobody had my mama to explain the importance of checking yourself in the mirror before leaving home.

Maybe I could help those innocents? Have a small scissor with me and cut the hanging threads before the public becomes aware, before the disaster occurs.

And do it on a subway train rather than on my Long Island Rail Road one. City people are in a bigger rush and don't have time to take care of themselves. That's the plan! Not to forget to dress into something real pretty and look presentable, so they would see at once that I'm no threat and appreciate my good deeds on their behalf.

The satisfactory decision brought me a sense of calm. The very next morning, I dressed in my favorite fire-red coat with an elbow-length cape of the same material and its skirt swirling low around my ankles. I brought it from a Paris trip and wore it but two times. And of course, all the accessories that went along with it.

On the platform and later, inside the LIRR train, passengers were noticing my outfit and it made me glad. Mama, thank you a million for teaching me fashion.

When my train arrived in the city, instead of going straight to work, I strolled over to the 34th Street subway station and boarded train "D". Straphangers here were not staring at my clothes. As I predicted, they were in a greater rush to get to their destinations.

Ah, here she comes, the woman I came to save. She is dressed in a drab, plaid coat on top of a two-piece, brownish dress with a long woolen appendage of a thread reaching all the way to the ground. Poor thing!

One red-gloved hand holding on to a pole, I opened my beautiful red leather purse. A silver manicure scissor shined at me from inside. I took it out carefully, watchful of not cutting my silky gloves, and approached the one I chose.

"Sorry to disturb you. Possibly you're unaware that you've this long thread hanging from your skirt. My mama always told me, 'Lilli, a hanging thread could unravel an entire outfit and you'll stand naked in public.' You don't want it to happen, of course?"

Saying that, I bent swiftly and snipped the disgusting thread an undetermined shade of brown. *Should I advise this woman that brown wasn't her color?*

"Get away from me! You're crazy! Somebody call the police! This woman in red is crazy! She has a knife in her hand!"

What is she saying? My God, am I really mad? Why did I do it? I better get off this train fast before I am arrested. What was I thinking?

Scurrying away from the few hesitant hands trying to grab me, I switched trains a few times, first not even looking at the destination, later realizing that it was a work day and I was a working person. Somewhere in between trains, I lost one red glove, broke the heel of my red boot, and then noticed the scissors still clutched tightly by my frozen fingers. *That's all I needed to be caught. Where was a trash can?*

Trying to catch my breath, I walked into the offices of Pioneer and dropped into my chair.

"So what is all this about?" Of course Paul noticed my disheveled appearance. "You look like a third grader after he stole a piece of candy from a neighborhood grocer and was speeding away in case someone noticed. So?"

For the last five years Paul had been in remission from liver cancer. He underwent surgery and subsequent treatments. The doctors guessed that his stamina, sense of humor, and easy acceptance of whatever life dished out kept him alive and free of the sickness for the moment.

"Don't you start being all sappy around me," Paul warned everyone in the office when his diagnosis became known. "Keep in mind I'm a Latino male, all muscle and music. My sickness is between me and my doctors."

Since, Paul mentioned his illness once—after the loss of his facial hair. "I don't look Puerto-Rican anymore," he noted.

"Paul, I could've been arrested today, on the train."

He whistled. "I wasn't entirely wrong after all. What would they arrest you for? Throwing a speck of dust on the street? Did you explain to them that usually you recycle it?"

"Paul, I'm not joking," I whimpered and sniveled. "It's like I held on to myself with all the strength I owned and cannot do it anymore. I went mad. Lost a grip on normality."

"You seem okay now. Shaken, hair out of place, eyes red, but mad … no, not more than usual." He wanted to make it easier for me.

"I need a therapist, probably medication too. Paul, it was awful. Like in a dream—you understand your actions perfectly and you don't see anything wrong with what you're doing."

"For God's sake, what were you doing?"

"Cutting threads from a stranger's coat on a train. With my manicure scissors. Talking to this person, giving advice as to what to wear. Thanking my mom for teaching me that. It seemed utmost important. Paul, I didn't just happen to have my scissors with me. I brought them for the specific reason of helping women to look better. How will I explain it to Sergey?

Should I not confess? He hates therapists. Poor guy doesn't deserve a crazy wife by his side. Worked hard all his life, pulled and pushed me along. He deserves better."

"Sergey loves you. In his weird way. You know my opinion of your hard-knuckle Russian macho-man characters out of the Siberian taiga—you taught me that word. And now, girl, start working before they fire you and you won't be able to afford a shrink."

***

Susan Cohen was the therapist I found and liked from day one. Slightly older than I, probably in her early fifties, elegant in a soft woolen slacks and white crispy shirt, kind smile lighting her eyes before following down to her lips. She knew how to listen. Even if it was part of her training, I still appreciated it.

I started from: "If I'll tell you that there is a fabric inside of my skull and it's shredding, would you call an ambulance and pack me in a straitjacket?"

"No way. I would like to hear all about that fabric. I'm having fun already. Why would I hand you to someone else? By the way, if you *needed* a straitjacket, you wouldn't know it. Understood?

"There is a reason why you came up with this most refreshing allegory—the shredding fabric inside of your head. Do you know the reason? When did it start?"

"Here we go. You want to hear all about my childhood? You would love it. Let me tell you about the life of a little Jewish girl in the city of Kiev, USSR. Are you ready?"

The glass-enclosed room smelled like wildflowers, probably some potpourri invisible to the patients. Two palms by the light green wall added the feel of being close to nature. Susan settled in her oversized, corduroy, brown armchair, glass of water by her side, a notebook and pen in her hand. She was ready and so was I.

We continued through the long winter months. I went twice a week. After work, from the train station where my car was parked, I drove to her little house in the next town, found a cup of freshly brewed tea on the end table by the sofa where I sat and the words spilled out.

One of those days, after I made myself comfortable, Susan suddenly asked: "Lilli, do you love Sergey?"

I grinned. "When coming home from work, I approach our house and see his car in the driveway, I'm so happy, so happy. Don't know why—we'll start arguing the moment I step in. Love him? Of course I love him!"

CHAPTER 25

Long Island Suburb New York, USA

1994-1995

After our father's death, communication between Josef and me flowed. Left motherless and fatherless, we went back to being siblings.

In 1991, the Soviet Union died, which was inconceivable, but the fact nevertheless. For me personally, its demise didn't bring any obvious benefits beyond being able to talk to Josef on occasions when their phone lines were fixed. Now, without the censure, we both wrote frequently, wanting to squeeze the years of detached existence into many short and long missives.

> *Josef,* I wrote, *don't you think we judged Papa too harshly? Were Mama's sicknesses and subsequent death really his fault? Since I'm a wife, I know that marriage is demanding and nonstop work, and sometimes no work is enough if the two people are unsuited for each other.*

My brother wouldn't have any of it: *"This subject had been closed with her casket lid. Never reopen it, never."*

I responded:

Wrong or right, think of how troublesome their life was. And here comes a son with a big mouth and a stubborn streak, fighting for his independence in the world where a person had to shit surrounded by a crowd.

I myself have one of those darling combatants. Everyone loves him but no one is willing to take him home with them.

In his following mail, Josef raged on:

David didn't give a damn about me. I was a thorn in his heel since day one. My carrying his father's name didn't help. If I had been like, 'Yes, Papa; you're right, Papa,' maybe I'd have been tolerated, but he was a jerk and didn't deserve me agreeing with him.

Yes, Josef, yes, I remember the times—Papa would say "black," and you'd jump in with "white." Why did I expect you to change?

Josef's huge slanting words on the pages brought on the memory of the funny poems written in the same handwriting when he was fifteen. Holding me, aged five, on his lap, my finger pointing at words on the page, he read them to me.

Then when I was seven and eight and ten, rushing home from school, anticipating finding mail from my brother, the university student. *Don't you worry, my little sister, I'm fine,* insisted his beloved slanted lettering.

So you had difficulties with Papa. On other hand, Mama loved you more, you big moron. I laughed at my old, silly sentiment. *Mama and Papa are dead. No refunds or exchanges are feasible.*

If you persist complaining about Papa, I will counter-complain about Mama preferring you to me at any given day. I never doubted your deserving it though. She told me how during the war when the two of you lived in Siberia, at age five you walked to school through the dark woods. Then, coming back, you charged to her side and stayed close, watching her at work. How could I compare?

He wrote: *My little sister, be glad you didn't have to live through those years. People were dying. I still shudder thinking of the day when a neighbor ran in and shouted: "Your old man froze to death on a sidewalk." That was Mama's dad, our grandfather; you were named after him. I was scared Mama would die, too. That's why I tried to watch her when possible. My elephant memory can't release any of it.*

One of Josef's letters confused me greatly. It said:

My dear little sister, you suffered so much. I blame myself for not paying more attention to you after Mama died. I was wrapped up in myself for years to come. I'm enraged and would kill the bastard who did it to you. Can't believe it happened right under my nose, and I didn't even know about it.

This was a belated response to my letter written in the waiting room of the New York abortion clinic. I shouldn't have opened up about the rape. It should've stayed buried in the bottomless Russian snow. I didn't expect a response, only unloaded my pent-up anger.

Lilli, my little sister, Josef wrote hesitantly, not like his forceful and brazen self, *could I come visit you, please? Would Sergey be against it? Are an invitation and a ticket very expensive? It's one ticket only. Natasha would have to stay put like the insurance against my not-returning.*

Since the Soviet Union disintegrated, the trips to and from former Soviet republics became possible. Not effortless, but feasible at last.

I mentioned the request to Sergey.

"Lilli, he is your brother. Invite him. Don't expect me to explode with joy. Back then, he didn't give me a moment of his time or attention or anything else. How do you want me to react?"

"Would you feel neglected?" I asked.

"And jealous, too," he emphasized.

I called Josef. "It's okay. I'll arrange all of it. I'd love to see you. Benny is at school in New York City, so you'll be able to meet him. He rents a studio in the city, but comes here often, mostly to see his high-school friends. Gil lives at Berkeley. It's far from us, in California. He is doing his graduate work at university there. Maybe he'll fly over. I'm so waiting for you to see both of your nephews."

I sent an invitation through the Ukrainian Consulate, paid their fees, bought a round-trip ticket, and signed an affidavit promising to take care of my brother's medical bills, if such occurred.

The early October day was as pretty as a mixed bouquet: cool air and hot red-gold leaves on the trees as far as you could see. We drove to JFK airport to pick up Josef.

After long separations, the scenes around the terminal, where the Air Ukraine landed, were bursting with excitement. Many more brothers and sisters; mothers and children were whispering and screaming Russian words, forgetting prepared formal welcomes and wilted flowers in their sweaty palms.

We were a middle-aged Lilli and Josef. We looked different but we were us. Both emotional, we cried and hugged, and cried some more and cried again. We forgot about Sergey and a few of the Goldbloom relatives who'd immigrated to New York in the last years and who'd come to greet Josef.

It all came back to me: the arms of my protector, the face that loomed validating a life worth living—I forgot how sweet it felt.

In the car on the way home, Josef stared at the other people seated in their cars stuck in traffic—while I studied my sibling. Dressed in a brown woolen suit, surely the best one he owned, he was still burly and imposing, but something was amiss. What was it?

We drove him to our suburban house out on Long Island and showed him around. Josef didn't say much. He walked around a few times, thoughtfully touching walls, appliances, windows.

"Is he considering making us an offer?" Sergey whispered sarcastically.

Later, Josef unpacked and gave us gifts from Natasha. Handmade gloves and sweaters, socks and slippers appeared from the bottomless cardboard suitcase tied with belts. Natasha was a marvel with golden hands.

"Guys," Josef said, "I would like to say some things that took me a lifetime to understand. Please, be patient."

I glanced at my husband. Sergey didn't look especially interested, but the smirk disappeared.

Josef continued: "I'm sorry for every damn occasion I was stupid, blind, and obnoxious. This covers all the years of my life. I prepared different words to say, and then changed my mind while in the car on the road to your house.

"I worked up ways to appear sorry for many of my previous words and actions and still save my honor, which seemed important. Now I say sorry for that too."

I continued watching Sergey. He didn't hide his satisfaction. After a while, he stood up and poured us all a drink.

"*L'chaim*," Sergey said, and we said, "*L'chaim*."

That same evening, Josef expressed a wish to leave Ukraine and immigrate to the United States. He didn't plan these words and he didn't plan these wishes.

"I watched the Americans at the airport. I watched them sitting in the cars on the highway. They're just people. You…" He pointed at Sergey and me, "are just people. You're settled in your skin. You're affirmed in your life. You don't strive to live better in order to point out our Russian misery. I don't know how to explain it any better.

"We, over there, got used to being inferior and despaired while pretending it was not so. We fix the look on our faces, which is distaste and distrust towards everyone else. We refuse to learn anything that didn't come from us.

"I've worked since I was fifteen. I changed professions and jobs, trying to prove that I'm of value. I'm close to sixty. I'm not interested anymore with impressing anyone. With any of my acquired skills I could make a modest living here in your country and enjoy life. Would you help me to come live here permanently?"

I took time off work. We talked sitting in a car, walking on the street, standing in the middle of my kitchen, or curling on the futon he slept on in the basement. No scraps of paper could replace the beloved voice insisting to know the ins and outs of my existence.

"Josef, recently I went mad…"

"Yeah? Not very original. I could count numerous occasions when you were that way. I'll fly over witnesses to testify if you wish."

"Josef, it happened. I took Mama's old silver scissors to cut strangers' threads on the train. Remember how Mama used to explain about hanging threads could unravel your clothes and you'll be naked?"

"Why would she talk to me about threads? Those were girl's issues: threads, skirts, dresses. Did you really do it?"

"I wanted Mama's approval. That's all. I went to a psychologist after what happened. She said this was about Mama's approval. Wanting to be a good girl for Mama's sake."

Josef's face became ashen. He grabbed me, squashing the air out of my lungs. I didn't protest. My brother's arms around me—wasn't that the idea?

When explaining all things American to my off-the-boat brother, I watched his face for the familiar childish smile to appear and grow into a resounding man's hoot of joy. Josef was bliss to be with. The two of us went everywhere together. He noticed the traffic lights.

"Your government doesn't want you dead." He forced me to stop at the corner and count the seconds when on both sides a red light remained.

He remarked on the length of the New York subway, carrying millions of people to their destinations.

"Ours is made out of marble to show off," he reminded me.

"Show and tell. Right?"

Josef seemed confused. "What do you mean?"

"When the kids were in elementary school, teachers gave them assignments to bring something interesting to class, something they all could discuss. That's your Soviet metro. Foreigners come, see, talk about. They don't know it may cost fifty percent of the national capital with the rest going to the military. And nothing left for the people to stay alive."

After showing him all the usual touristy stuff, I arranged a special trip for my brother. Only the two of us were invited, only the two of us knew it was the best trip yet.

I drove Josef to a Home Depot. He walked in like into any other place I brought him to, except inside it was no ordinary place for my dearest brother.

He touched screws and patted tiles. He hugged hammers and blew dust off pliers. He bent to place a fallen lock back on the shelf. The expression on his face played symphonies. I knew him well.

Thanks, whispered his eyes.

For years I'd watched Josef make all these items by hand. There was always something else missing when he was building his house, and he was always building his house. If he couldn't make a tool from scratch, he stole it from the plant where he worked. No one thought of it as stealing. Weren't we all the proud owners of everything in the socialist country of workers?

That was one of Josef's good days. I learned that he had many not-so-good days. Now I knew what I'd noticed in my brother's appearance on the way from the airport. He was battling a serious illness. His blood pressure would skyrocket and drop down in a matter of minutes. He devised his own treatment: jump into the cold ocean if it was near, take an icy shower if it was available, or walk barefoot on the dewy grass early in the morning.

"Look at me," he boasted. "No sickness could catch me!"

He also took to raiding our bar. I hoped Sergey wouldn't notice and proclaim Josef an alcoholic. Probably he was—the bottles were emptying rapidly.

I felt helpless—baby sister who didn't know how to help her big brother. I didn't tell him that if he were to become hospitalized our savings would be wiped out and it wouldn't be enough.

We took him to meet our friends. Sergey pulled me into the corner.

"Lilli, he embarrasses us. Who else laughs so loud that people run from every room to stare?"

"He's fun. He's not like anyone else and it doesn't mean it's embarrassing."

The next time we were at our cousin's birthday party at a restaurant, Josef had a few straight vodkas and then danced all by himself in the middle of the floor with abandon. I joined him so his drunkenness would be less obvious.

"I'm overwhelmingly happy, Lilli darling. The food is scrumptious. The faces are dear to me…" I held him tight, then glanced at Sergey and knew it was time to leave.

"Lilli, my little sister, Sergey doesn't like me. He still doesn't like me. He is snippy with you all the time. I overheard him even growl at you. It's all my fault. What can I do to earn his approval?"

"Sergey is a very private person. He's also a shy person. He gets upset when people notice us, and since your arrival we became visible. If I'd ask you to tone down your laugh or dance movements, or maybe I'll go for the moon and ask you to drink less in and out of the house, would you try? Oh, Josef, never mind, just be the way you are. You're almost sixty and never were any different. Why am I asking you to do something you're not able to? You do drink way too much. I love you, my dearest brother."

I enjoyed Josef, but what would happen when he immigrated here and would often be in Sergey's view?

My two-week vacation ended. After being home with Josef, I returned to the office. My coworkers exclaimed over my high color and high mood. I didn't know what prevailed: my joy at being with my brother or worry about his health. I also didn't discuss what if he needed hospitalization? Was I selfish?

We drove Josef to Brooklyn to stay with our cousins. He borrowed an old bicycle and rode through neighborhoods, wanting to see as much of America as possible. No one explained to him that Brooklyn wasn't exactly "Main Town, USA."

I called him daily.

"Josef, for my sake, watch where you're going. You don't know the dangerous areas. There're streets where knife-carrying thugs protect their territory. And what if you get lost? You don't speak a word of English to ask a question."

Josef's return ticket was for December 10. His two months in America were concluding. I helped him pack. He needed an additional suitcase—I couldn't resist his delight at every little item and bought him enough clothes to start a men's clothing store.

We were sitting at the airport. Sergey said his goodbye earlier and left us alone. Even while giggling, I couldn't stop crying.

Josef declared, "To fly over the oceans to another continent and find one person who knows how you feel when you feel it and why you feel that way was a remarkable experience."

"To write a breezy letter about one's rape, to shell out money for the ticket from Kiev to New York and back, to sign your life away in case the ticket-holder gets sick, was worth it," I swore.

The plane left the gate and I still didn't move. Sergey lent me his shoulder and I continued whimpering, leaning into my husband.

After Josef's return home, we spoke a few times. He'd already started taking an English course and tried to sell life-accumulated treasures. Natasha, as expected, refused to accompany him. Josef believed she would give in eventually. He became a man driven by a goal. At almost sixty, he didn't have time to waste.

For our usual Christmas vacation, we booked a trip to Hawaii. Gil took time off from his studies and we met him there, arriving from California. Benny, the university student, back for a winter recess, refused our company, preferring to stay home partying with his friends. I suspected one or two of his old school girlfriends being a reason for his home-stay as well.

On January the fifth our plane arrived safely back at JFK airport. The flight was uneventful. Our luggage arrived relatively fast. A car service waited as prearranged. The snow was knee-high, but we were in too good a mood to be bothered by it.

"It's good to come home when everything is going so smoothly," Sergey decided. "Remember when we came back and Benny tried to launder the carpets because they were stained at the party he gave?"

"Wait, we're not there yet."

I wanted to enjoy and cherish the last moments of our vacation, knowing how busy Sergey's usual after-vacation schedule was. He would wake up earlier and start his day with a cup of coffee, forgetting to eat till much later. Let him laugh a little longer.

Though he had learned how to relax too. I would never believe it was possible—he'd changed so much, my husband did. I liked to compare his "now" and "before" pictures and a different man stared at me from those. I wouldn't be able to describe the changes to those who didn't see them. The phrase: "Older age looked good on him" would certainly apply.

We laughed all the way home.

Benny, wearing his old high school sweats, exposing a just-acquired tattoo of a snake on his arm, waited for our arrival. *A snake…?* I wanted my younger son to hear my opinion about such art but thought better to do it later. We kissed, said hello, and he ran back to his old room, away from my lecture.

"Dad, come here for a second. I have to show you something," he yelled out. At last they were friends.

When Sergey came back down, his face was grayish, his wrinkles cut deeper, tan waned, and his eyes didn't meet mine.

"What?" I sat on the edge of the couch, patting its luxurious soft leather.

"Lilli, please, sit down," Sergey said, and I started to laugh, loudly and stupidly. I didn't want to stop. I knew when quiet would fell something horrible and irrecoverable would be said.

Sergey waited and I stopped laughing.

"Lilli, I'm sorry I have to tell you this … Josef has died."

I didn't sit on the couch any longer. The words pulled me onto the floor. The words held me imprisoned, not letting me move or inhale air into my lungs.

"He's gone? He promised to come back! How dare he! He lied again! I knew it—he always was a liar!" I went on, terrifyingly long and senseless.

"Lilli, he was sick. You knew that."

“Don’t talk to me! You wished it on him! You didn’t hide your loathing of him! Don’t try to play innocent with me!” I didn’t care what was said. And then I didn’t speak.

“Mom, may I sit with you?”

Ben walked into my darkened bedroom. Wasn’t he supposed to be back at school? His eyes were puffy. Was he crying?

“Mom, if I tell you I absolutely fell in love with your brother when he visited, it wouldn’t be an exaggeration. I bet you didn’t notice I used to return home nights when he stayed with you.

“When we were just babies, you used to tell us how much you loved your older brother. You were talking mostly to Gil because he was older and loved animals and nature, all those kinds of things, like uncle Josef did too. The way you were saying it … with relish, those stories sounded like the fairy tales about a giant who protected a little girl, you. Also, he always was in trouble with the adults, like me. I liked him a lot. It settled in my head. I didn’t expect to ever meet him. But when I did, I wanted to really get to know him.”

I studied my beautiful son in disbelief. So kind and smart. When did he become an adult? I had missed his transformation.

“Josef didn’t speak English. You retained but five Russian words. How would you…?”

“Not five words, come on … Mom, we spoke. You would be surprised. He was patient with me, explaining things. He wrote poems when he was just a boy. You never mentioned it. Maybe my writing abilities came from him. Also, he was some stud in his day, you know…

“We were doing a little bit of drinking in our basement, at night. He showed me some odd ways to drink vodka. I knew you wouldn’t be happy about it, but he told me you were doing some of it in your youth too. I hoped you wouldn't be too mad. I wasn't driving after."

"Benny, my brother was never known for his sense of good judgment. I would be raging mad if I had him here to be mad at."

"He was a joyful human being, enthusiastic about everything. I have the feeling he died the same way he lived—on the go and without regrets."

"That's what I'm crying about—his joy. He anticipated returning here with legal status and going to work and being with us. He never even met Gil. It seemed overly complicated taking him on a plane to California. I expected they'll meet next time…"

My tears were out again.

Josef died on December 31—Benny's birthday. Benny was like Josef in so many ways. Even his elephant memory: he remembered when I told them Josef stories and he was three at the time. Was my younger son born to replace my brother in this world?

I want my brother alive.

I dialed Natasha, who refused to talk to me.

"If he didn't go to you to your America, he'd still be with me." She believed so with all her heart. "He was too sick to saunter around the globe. But not for his beloved sister."

Every lunch break I went out from my office and bought sweets. Candies soothed the palate, and a bit of soul too. I stuffed myself up to ten additional pounds. Old clothes didn't fit. To go and buy some new outfits wasn't on my present agenda. When passing by the large hall mirror and seeing my bloated image wearing the sweatpants and oversized t-shirt, I resolved to turn to the other direction the next time and not look into the mirror.

"Lilli, talk to me," begged Paul. "Do you need my help? I know you loved Josef. He was ill. It's not your fault."

While I contemplated my response, Paul went to the hospital for chemotherapy treatment. His cancer had returned and stubbornly wouldn't give up. The guy was trying to survive terminal cancer and he wanted me to talk about trying to survive my brother's death. Was it fair?

Susan, the psychologist, could probably suggest some trick-of-the-trade … the thought of driving to her house, talking, remembering … all bothersome. I preferred to sleep all day, confiscating hours from reasoning. I didn't have any vacation time left, but work wasn't on my mind.

At Pioneer we had a new office manager, hired by the board of directors to find ways to cut costs. I asked her for an unscheduled vacation. She heard of my situation, even sent me a condolence card.

She acted properly official, "I'd appreciate your formal request."

"Refused," she then wrote across my memo, using a red pen for emphasis.

I felt not annoyance, rather a release from an additional burden. I used her red pen to write my resignation.

CHAPTER 26

Long Island Suburb New York, USA

1995

"Mom, Dad, come and sit with me on this one, please."

Benny lived in New York City, studying film at NYU, working at the SoHo restaurant, clubbing, and doing everything else Manhattan allowed its young, brave, and money-less.

He breathed in and out of our house whenever one of his old high school friends called about a party. A quick "How are you?" a glimpse of his tanned, dimpled face, shoulder-long dark hair, a layered outfit of washed-out t-shirts and jeans, was accompanied by a kiss for me and a hug for his father. Then a disappearing rear of a dusty red Mitsubishi with more mileage than we wanted to think about.

We paid for the SoHo studio, where he disconnected lights and painted walls black for inspiration, hoping he still could function with a tiny flicker of light coming from only the candle. He obviously did, because a number of finished movie scripts arrived in our mailbox for safekeeping.

If not writing, Benny didn't sit still for long; he even ate while moving around. This particular Saturday afternoon he circled the living room, got a soda from the refrigerator, took the stairs to his old room for some poster he forgot to remove previously, and then dove into the basement to use a chin-bar, declaring: "Boy, am I strong!"

"Nothing bad, don't start thinking crazy," he warned, when Sergey and I settled with cups of coffee in our hands. "I have an announcement. It's something awesome. It's something I've waited my entire life for."

He said nothing bad, though my heart drummed buckets of blood in and out. Yes, life was good. He was healthy. He sounded happy…

"There is this guy who comes to the restaurant every afternoon and sits at the bar. Orders soup, glass of wine and a slice of bread and he talks to me. You know, I'm a bartender—good they never figured out I'm nineteen as yet—everyone spills their guts to me. He's a painter, a successful one, not a bullshit one. I went to his showing. Each painting cost like ten thousand and they fly from there. A nice guy, not a showoff or something.

"I let him read my screenplay *The Good Money*. About bank robbers. Some of them are good, some mean bastards. All die at the end during that robbery. The guy, this painter, his name is Stephan, says, 'Let me talk to my partner. We were thinking of investing in a movie production if the right material comes along. I like what you wrote a lot.'

"Mom, Dad, they are willing to put money into my script. I would direct it, as well. Ben Kaplan, aged twenty—writer and director. This is for the Oscar acceptance speech. How do you like that?"

"Benny, it's very exciting. Unbelievably exciting. We are thrilled for you. Don't spook the Oscars, though. Wait a while."

Sergey and I were jumping up and down, kissing him, kissing each other.

"What about school? Are you dropping out? You still have a way to go. We wanted you to pick up more credits so you could graduate earlier.

You said you weren't in a rush. Wait a second. Did they tell you how much money they'll put in? Do you have a budget? Would they be responsible for distribution?"

Sergey the businessman was asking relevant questions while I sat back, trying to adjust to my baby Ben being in the business of making agreements with the money people and then directing a film. It was too scary to absorb.

"What if they give you the money but you are not able to make the film? Do they know you never did anything like that before?" My doubts woke up. Sergey and Ben started to guffaw.

"Lilli…"

"Mom…"

I guess they knew me well enough not to be surprised.

"That's why I kept it from you. I didn't want to say anything before it came closer to being real. The prep work is going on for a while now. I already found a producer. He did a few local productions. Strictly small stuff, but we have to be a low budget. That is the agreement, a hundred thou or around it. The ads are out for the actors and camera person and sound guys and grips, some others. They all know each other, so if one is hired, he'll bring most of them along. Stephan is in on every step. He wants to stay during auditions, too.

"That's what I want to ask you. Not to bug me about school. I'm taking time off. I spoke with the school. They are encouraging. That's what they want from their film students—go, find projects, get experience. Also, I cannot possibly continue working at the bar, so I'll need more pocket money."

In the next two weeks Ben called nightly to give us daily reports. Their absolute minimum total for the budget came to one hundred and fifty thousand. The actors were hired at scale pay. Kids, dying to be on the movie set, even for free, were coming in droves for extras and assistant production jobs.

Stephan stayed during auditions. Stayed in the background, dutifully recording hirings. The contracts were signed. In a week, the money from the investors' account was supposed to be wired to a newly incorporated "Never at a Loss for Words" film company, its president Ben Kaplan.

"Dad, they bailed out," Benny called on the afternoon of the expected day. "There was this clause in the contract about a termination option during the first week after signing. The lawyer explained it was there for both sides' protection. Like I would've cancelled…"

His voice cracked.

Sergey heard his tears and called me to pick up the second receiver.

"Stephan said he voted for me and the other guy didn't. He said it made more sense to start with a known writer-director and gamble on the next project than with the unknown. For now they just invested their money into some … shit."

How dare they! Poor baby. What now? What is he going to do? The actors were hired. The DP, an old drunk with tons of filming experience, postponed a different project in lieu of Ben's, which he liked better.

At home, standing in between huge pots filled with exotic plants, looking at our prized pedestals with works of good sculptors and the equally interesting paintings on the walls, we gripped the receivers to our ears, both with tears in our eyes. Our son needed us. We weren't prepared to give up.

"Benny, we'll raise the money," Sergey said quietly, awaiting my reaction.

"Yes, we'll do it," I yelled into the phone. "We'll be your investors. Investors with love."

"You sure? Do you have such money? Oh, thank you so much. You are the best. I love you. I love you, Mom, Dad."

We borrowed against our life insurance policies. We signed a second mortgage on the house. In the next few days, Sergey was constantly on the phone, raising funds for our son's movie. I took a train to the city to meet his crew, to check the numbers in a budget. My bookkeeping experience did me good. To restrain the budget, some scenes were prepared to be shot in our house. One morning, the group of about twenty drove in, scattering through the lawns, to the delight of our neighbors, who seeing movie cameras expected to meet known actors.

"Mom, don't tell anyone my age. I look older anyway. Don't tell them anything at all. They think I did do a few flicks before. Okay?"

Ben was seen at all places at the same time. Mostly he hoped that every hired person knew what he or she was doing. I listened to his "Action" and "Cut" and hoped for the best.

Needing to share the excitement, I called Sonia a few times in Israel. She chuckled at my description of "a much older with plenty of movie-producing experience" Benny.

"Are you okay, Lilli? You sound marvelous," she said, wanting to make sure. My previous call to her came during the Susan-the-shrink time.

My answer was honest: "I'm great, darling."

I buzzed my old Brussels' friend Eva, busy now with three little children and a CPA business on top of it.

“When Benny is all famous, you better tell him I knew him before he was born. The way he sounds, this child is some son-of-a-gun.” Eva laughed. She remembered my hopes for a second child bringing me joy and serenity.

Some nights after the grueling shooting, the entire crew stayed over to catch the early morning sun. They all played a game of soccer on our lawn and then settled to sleep on the floors everywhere. Together we ate catered chicken and lasagna from the large aluminum trays delivered daily, snacking on junk from their craft services. Proudly, I accepted respect reserved for a director's mother.

The girls were keeling over from their handsome director, darting angry stares against the ones who seemed to succeed with him. “What does he like?” I was asked. “Does he have a girlfriend?” That was a popular question. I smiled sweetly, keeping true to the orders not to open any “state” secrets.

For the main scene, which was a bank robbery in progress, the location scouts discovered the old building in Manhattan on 14th Street and Union Square. Previously it housed a bank, and now empty, provided a space for numerous films' location.

That was the most important and difficult scene with many extras, special effects—which couldn't be duplicated and were supposed to be perfect on the first try—shootings, and blood flying and settling in puddles.

I walked in the building while the scene was getting set. The huge cavernous building was quiet, eerily quiet, not the normal quiet when forty-some people were present. All forty or such stood around the floor, all facing the door I walked in through. All were staring up. What were they looking at? I turned around.

There, very close to the ceiling, on the stoop above the entrance, stood my twenty-year-old Benny. I tried not to remember his age. I tried not to remember his first-time-director status. His six-foot frame in a torn, dingy t-shirt, worn inside-out seemed out of a Hercules legend. His hand on the wall-clock little hand adjusting the time according to his script was steady. His exotic face looked collected and thoughtful. He knew what he was doing.

I gave birth to him. I stood holding his hand waiting for a little school bus to pick him up and take him to nursery school.

"You wanted to go to school like Gil does," I told Ben, not three years old at the time. He wasn't that sure anymore, a little afraid, but the adventurous soul took over. He took the bag with the clothes change out of my hand and stepped in. He wasn't toilet-trained and I waited for him to grow up. He had.

The film was in the can, the money paid out. Ben went to Los Angeles trying to find a buyer.

***

Gill made his doctor of science. He was twenty-five. We were bursting with pride. There probably wasn't a person in this universe who didn't hear about it. He liked the Bay Area and planned to stay there. He told us that after four years in cold Ithaca he never wanted to see snow again.

The laboratory that hired him was doing cancer research and that's what he wanted to do. Sergey told child-Gil he will do with his life whatever he wants; no one will stop him. There is no unattainable dream.

CHAPTER 27

Long Island Suburb, New York, USA Kiev, Ukraine

June 1996

"Sergey, I'm going to Kiev."

"Go."

For weeks I toyed with clarifying explanations in case he would object. Why did I think he wouldn't understand?

The hardest was saying goodbye to Paul Fernando. I called the office and told that I wanted to meet him.

His cancer wouldn't let him be. The devil wanted my friend. The devil seemed in a rush. Ten years was enough, the devil said.

That was his eleventh year in the fight; Paul got weak and thin. He tightened his belt and turned the cuffs of his pants up so they wouldn't sweep the floor. He could hardly walk and couldn't ship packages and couldn't work the printing press.

One grim day, Paul brought himself a replacement.

"Everyone, meet my nephew Ernest. I'll teach him as much as I've time for and you'll show him the rest."

"Paul, I'm going." We stood looking at each other for a long while. That was goodbye forever. Paul couldn't wait for me to come back.

"Lilli, call on my girls from time to time, just to keep an eye on them."

"Find someone livelier with more energy."

"You'll do fine. I trust you more than you trust yourself."

I called Natasha again.

"I'll be happy to see you, Lilli. Sorry for my rudeness the last time you called."

Kiev, the city of my birth, seemed a stranger. I didn't recognize the sights. Streets looked worn out. Cars parked diagonally all over the sidewalks. In my youth there were very few cars and no need for parking spaces. Cafes and restaurants had replaced the ground-floor apartments, and music blared from all of them. Elders, wearing suits, ties, and many honorably-earned war medals, were turning over garbage receptacles looking for food.

Probably there were some city views worth admiring, though they didn't jump out at me. I didn't feel like a tourist interested in attractions. Twenty-five years had passed since the soldiers with "uniformed" dogs in tow—or was it vice versa?—made sure we boarded a plane.

A taxi took me from Kiev to Natasha's suburb. Their old house looked like a child's Play-Doh construction. I remembered Josef building and rebuilding it, adding rooms and storage areas and greenhouses. He dreamed about it and talked about it and loved it like a dear woman. I hated that house with its constant needs then, and I hated it even more now. At least before it wasn't that ugly, because I didn't know any better.

My brother's life ended before he finished adding all the structures he envisioned.

Was it all worth it in the end? Looking at our comfortable American home, did Josef think he wasted his life?

Natasha took me to the cemetery. The town where most of the population was Russian and Ukrainian Orthodox had only one cemetery; a cross topped every grave. There were but a few Jews in that and neighboring towns.

Was my Jewish brother buried under a cross? Josef didn't live like a Jew. But who in that forsaken place ever had?

When in New York, Josef happened to be in a section of Brooklyn called Borough Park, where the Hassidic Jews prevailed. Standing there, he watched the unusual-looking people in wonderment. Who were they? Then, like an animal recognizes his same kind when far away from the familiar forest, he grabbed the nearest bearded black-hatted man.

"I'm *Yid*," he proclaimed in a mixture of English and Yiddish. The frightened man wanted to run but changed his mind and hugged Josef instead. That man accepted my brother for his own. For days Josef boasted off his triumph.

I didn't say any of this to my sister-in-law. Natasha was the wife with the right to bury her husband any way she saw fit.

I noticed the grave from afar. There was no cross, but instead Josef's recent photograph on the stone. He seemed to smirk at us. In death, like in life, he was an "in your face person." The low white fence separated

Josef's plot from the surrounding ones. On the inside of it, a few fresh bouquets rested against the monument. The smell of newly-picked flowers sweetened the air.

"They're not from your garden?" I asked, sitting next to Natasha on the white bench inside the fence.

"Women bring flowers. Your brother was liked around here for, let's say, his different talents. Does it surprise you?"

"Nothing surprises me about my brother. But don't you want to throw it all into the garbage?"

"I loved Josef since I was a silly college student, even before we graduated. Then we met again and got married. We argued, we fought, we loved. We were human. He enjoyed women, I take it … slept with some. They miss him now. If he were alive I'd tear his hair out. He's not alive. Flowers are pretty. I didn't tell you this on the phone, Lilli. He did die from a stroke, though he wasn't home at the time. A woman called to ask me to come pick him up. Was I enraged? Mostly worried."

I slept in Josef's bed. He had his separate bed. It was comfortable. I slept well. Even my mother-in-law, the main character of many of my nightmares, didn't visit. Maybe she was too far away.

Natasha asked a friend to drive us to our parents' cemeteries in Kiev. Through the drive, I sat clutching my mouth, trying not to puke my guts out. My Americanized soft-living persona forgot the usual ride in the sweat-smelling, no-air-conditioned, no-open-windows car on unpaved country roads.

Mama and Papa were buried an hour away from each other, at two different cemeteries. Josef had decided they didn't belong together.

First we arrived at Mama's cemetery. When she died, Josef and Papa argued about the monument. Josef didn't care what Papa wanted.

He turned his back to all his suggestions and proceeded to do what in his opinion was right by Gita.

Now the inscription was seen clearly on the pink granite:

GITA GORSKY

1910 – 1966

FROM GRIEVING FAMILY

Mama would have appreciated how well Josef's handiwork had held up. I sat on the ground by the monument surrounded by the tiny forget-me-nots. I didn't need to hold back my tears.

"Mama," I murmured. "Our Josef died … he was sick. I live in America now. He came for a visit. We had a great time together.

"Mama, you would love my boys, Gil and Benny. They are beautiful and kind and honest, so talented, so smart. Benny likes to fib some, like Josef did. What could you do? Actually, it turns out in his favor—he is a writer, writes for the movies. Recently made one. Imagine that? I taught both boys to cook and iron and sew buttons on. I wanted them to know how to do things. You would enjoy them.

"I know you can't hear me. I'm not crazy, Mama. Though, once, I almost was … for real. Not anymore. Sometimes, it's still difficult to just … live, you know, not to think about what was before.

"Mama, don't worry. I'm okay."

Natasha waited in the car, giving me privacy. Then I saw her coming over.

"Lilli, let's go. We still have David's cemetery to visit. Remember?"

My father's grave wasn't familiar. Of course I hadn't seen it. The stone was dark and impressive. Josef wanted to inscribe only one word—"Manager." He told me all David ever wanted was to be a boss. Thankfully, my brother changed his mind. The gold lettering with the name and the years was there:

DAVID GOLDBLOOM

1910 - 1985

FROM GRIEVING FAMILY

The letters and the numbers had lost some of its brightness.

My feet on their own account started to stomp and my fists on their own account started to strike the stone.

"How could you, David? What was inside of your heart when you couldn't find one pleasant word to say to the nicest of all people, when she lived and breathed and wanted to laugh and be happy? Only when she was dying were you kissing her and holding her hand and caring.

"Papa, I'm sorry. Those words burned in me for the longest time. You turned out to be the best father to me, the best anyone could wish for. You confused me with your goodness and selflessness. I loved you dearly when I wanted to hate you.

"Then, you go and die."

Natasha stood close to me.

"You know, Natasha, I wish he knew how much I loved him. When I was growing up, through my stupidity, I never realized how good a father he was. At least to me. Did Josef ever mention David's words about Josef not being his son? I asked him in my letter. He didn't answer and I let it go. The notion was too bizarre to pursue."

"Lilli, we'll talk later. Let's go home."

On the way back, neither the car's smell nor the road bumps bothered me. Coming home, Natasha placed a slim blue envelope in my hands.

"Lilli, I hate doing this to you. Yet, it's not my place to be a keeper of your family secrets. Please, take it for what this is—ancient history."

The yellowish page was titled:

MARRIAGE CERTIFICATE

THE MARRIAGE CERTIFICATE OF GITA GORSKY AND DAVID GOLDBLOOM, dated … FEBRUARY OF 1937.

It couldn't be. It was all wrong, Josef was born in June of 1937. Mama was five months pregnant when they married? She told me they knew each other for four months before they married.

Gita was pregnant when she married David. She was pregnant when she met David. Josef wasn't David's son.

"When did Josef find out?"

"After your mama died. He was looking for some papers. You weren't home at the time. He confronted David. They had it out, but what could it change? He stopped coming to your house for a while. I don't know if you remember the time. He didn't want to see David. At the time he couldn't think that you were there and you were his little sister. But this, Lilli, never ever changed. He always adored you."

I understood so much from what she said.

"After Mama died, everything changed. I didn't feel his love anymore and didn't know why he stopped loving me. I blamed myself for years. I didn't know where to turn—not to Josef, for sure. He became a different person, unrecognizable. One moment he would talk to me, give orders, laugh, and the next act like I didn't exist…"

"You were a young girl, needing love. Your brother couldn't give it to you—he was full of hatred. Whom could he hate—mother whom he worshiped? Or father with whom he couldn't find common language since forever, and who nevertheless brought him up? He hated himself.

"You remember Josef's old dog Pushok? Neighbors complained that he barked too loud. Josef took him to the forest and shot him. I didn't sleep after that for many nights—that shotgun had more bullets in it—I could be next."

"Everything that wasn't considered a 'norm' was kept a secret. So much suffering and for what? Who benefited from not knowing the truth? I can't get over it, Natasha. Did David ever say who Josef's father was, what happened to him?"

"Yes. Gita was first married to the man in the beginning of the thirties. He was a doctor, a known cardiologist. Someone from Stalin's inner circle became deadly sick and was brought to him to be treated but died before he could be helped, or maybe he couldn't be helped. In a matter of a few days the court decreed the doctor a murderer, a Jew who killed on purpose. The executioners didn't linger."

"Oh God! Those were the horrible times we all read about years later. Men and women were disappearing. The courts were swift and deadly. So her husband was killed and she was pregnant! Could you imagine how terrified our mama was, how ashamed, confused? David must have seemed like a savior to her. I always wondered … they were so different. She told me 'He was a gentleman and he was persistent.' That's why they married so fast. Poor, poor Mama … wretched life…"

Secrets, more secrets…

I burned with fever, couldn't move. Vomited all the food Natasha had cooked for me with such love and skill and was fighting diarrhea as well.

She prepared some home remedy and held my head while I drank it. She stayed by my—Josef's—bed and changed the wet towel on my forehead.

"Lilli, I understand it's too much to digest. Though, look at it differently. It explains things, questions you had, even the ones you didn't know you had. Don't be like Josef. He internalized everything. David wasn't his father. True. The man brought him up since day one. He *was* his father. He wasn't a good father. But was Josef an angel? No, we both know he was a pain to live with.

"Lilli, we are the leftovers. Let's toast their lives the way we know how and you tell me all about wonderful life in your America."

***

I told her about Sergey wanting to travel more and see the world; about my kids, how interesting Gil's molecular biologist work was with the genes and the proteins, which I understood nothing about. And of course, Benny's movie, his energy to do a million things at once, and unexpected patience with each and every script he worked on, perfecting it.

I didn't dare to go into my personal almost-disaster, cutting threads in the subway. Natasha had enough sorrows on her plate. The country she lived in had stopped building Communism, wrecked Socialism, and now wasn't sure what to do next. The people went hungry because their government didn't have money to pay its workers. Many would never recuperate from the Chernobyl catastrophe. The warning signs were there, though no one talked about it anymore.

Natasha was too resourceful to be needy. She sewed and grew vegetables, then exchanged the products of her labor with someone else's. She treated her own ills with the old home remedies and believed they helped, even if I was dubious.

***

I returned home to the States. The lightness in my head felt liberating. No more guilt to get over, no more search for perfection. I felt like a little girl, without experiences and problems. I wanted to dance and smile and laugh because the heaviness was gone.

Mama, Papa, Josef—they all loved me. I was the only one left. It would be a waste not to be alive and sane.

If I did do things that were wrong, so be it.

If Mama would know about my latest adventure in the NY subway on her behalf, she would shake her head and say: "Lilli, don't do me any favors. Though you do look pretty in red. So wear it and go dancing. Threads cutting … are you crazy?"

Josef, my dearest sinner, I'm trying to remember some clever remark of yours worth repeating to my heirs.

"Don't wear green underwear—a man would run from it as fast as he could." Also "Don't walk under a tree after it's stopped raining. Water drips from the leaves after a rain." At least this one may be helpful. What else? How come I can't remember any other stuff? Maybe it wasn't that important.

Why do I need it anyway? What was it I wanted to do? I don't know, but I was in no rush.

I have many years ahead of me, many years of many days of many hours. I am in charge of my life.

Thanks to my sons for bringing me into 21st century and to their father for making my life possible

Thanks to my writing teachers who encouraged me to write and told me I have a STORY and a VOICE to tell it

Thanks to my writing buddies, who believed in my work more than I did (Long Island NY ladies, wherever you are.)

And my friends at Mira Costa writing workshop - I am indebted to you forever